Praise for *Deadly* .

"This is the first book in the Kinncaid Brothers series and let me say it's fantastic. Ms. Clark writes with passion and gives life to her characters on many levels. These pages are filled with suspense, murder, and mayhem as well as love and humor. I recommend this book and can't wait to . . . read the next chapter in the Kinncaid family. Enjoy!"

— *Fallen Angel Reviews*: Five Angels: Recommended Read

"I won't give away the rest of the story but I will say it gives the reader not just romance but a great who-done-it, and with an assortment of suspects it will be interesting when the beast is revealed to you. I really feel this book deserves the rating I gave it, if there were ten hearts I would have given it that. Ms. Clark has given this reviewer a novel that has kept me engrossed until the end, and for that I thank her."

— *Coffee Time Romance*

"From author Jaycee Clark comes a fast-paced romantic suspense that will keep readers on the edge of their seats. *Deadly Shadows* is a well-written, riveting tale filled with fascinating characters and an engaging storyline. . . . Jaycee Clark pens an in-depth and captivating story with *Deadly Shadows*. I highly recommend this tale to all readers."

— Sinclair Reid, *Romance Reviews Today*

"Ms. Clark has written a spine-tingling tension-filled story with characters that the reader comes to care about. . . . There are enough twists and turns in the story to keep the reader guessing to the end. *Deadly Shadows* will make you shiver and leave all the lights on in the house. The best news is that there will be another Kinncaid brother starring in his own story. . . ."

— Jenni, *A Romance Review*

Books by Jaycee Clark

Angel Eyes
Firebird
Talons (coauthored with Shannon Stacey, Mandy Roth, Michelle
    Pillow, and Sydney Somers)
Black Aura
Ghost Cats (coauthored with Mandy Roth and Michelle Pillow)
Ghost Cats: Revenge
The Dream
Deadly Shadows
Deadly Ties
Deadly Obsession
Deadly Games
Phoenix Rising II (coauthored with Donna Grant and Mandy Roth)
Ghost Cats 2 (coauthored with Mandy Roth and Michelle Pillow)

Deadly Shadows

Jaycee Clark

BEYOND THE PAGE
Publishing

Beyond the Page Books
are published by
Beyond the Page Publishing
www.beyondthepagepub.com

First digital edition copyright © 2004 by Jamie Houdyshell
First print edition copyright © 2004 by Jaycee Clark
Material excerpted from *Deadly Ties* copyright © 2004 by Jaycee Clark
Second digital edition copyright © 2011 by Jaycee Clark
Beyond the Page print edition copyright © 2012 by Jaycee Clark
Cover design and illustration by Dar Albert, Wicked Smart Designs

ISBN: 978-1-937349-37-0

Acknowledgments

I have to thank the readers for loving the Kinncaid family as much as I do, for wanting their stories still. So here they are, to all my readers.

I'd also like to thank Andie Ruggera of the Mt. Crested Butte Police Department for patiently answering all my questions when this book first came out. Any mistakes are completely mine.

I have to thank my family for all the holidays to the Elk Mountains in Colorado — where the idea of this book and the Kinncaid family was born.

This one is for my kids

Prologue

He wiped his bloody hands on the soaked crimson cloth. A soft sigh escaped as his rage ebbed into a calming storm. The monster no longer roared within him. It was content — for now.

Death filled his senses, bringing with it the promise of peace. He looked out over the night-blackened mountains, towards the glittering heavens.

Why? Why must they be so evil? So selfish! Jezebels, the lot of them.

Hadn't he been taught that?

Yes. Yes, of course he had. It was his turn now to teach others. They needed to learn the valuable lesson that vows were important, a covenant. The holy sacrament must be kept, not taunted. Not tempted. Never defiled.

Punishment. That is what was needed — punishment and discipline. But, no one must ever know, he shook his head, quite certain of that. No, others would not understand.

The howl of a wolf pulled him from his musings. Thoughts echoed the rage, stirred the monster. No, the monster must sleep, must rest. Had to.

Again he looked down. The moonlight played over her lax features, her red hair dull in the pale light.

She looked so innocent, so perfect.

But it was a lie! A lie! Their purity and fake sweetness hid the whore lurking inside.

Then they smiled. Smiled!

He never looked the other way after that. Someone had to stand for the faithful and true, the honest, Law-abiding men. He would, for it was his destiny. He would be the Avenger, the Punisher, the Righteous.

The sluts must pay for their sins and he was seeing to it they were. He gave them back their salvation.

Slowly, he drew in a deep cleansing breath, heavy with the smell of spring. The snows were melting, muddying the air with earthy fragrances.

He should hurry. No one was likely to come along the road at night, but it could happen, campers or hikers. Unlikely, but possible. He looked over into the ravine. The darkness swallowed up the space just beyond him, hiding the bottom, the lush undergrowth, the jagged rocks. Dark clouds skittered over the sliver of moon.

No one would ever know. With one last swipe of the bloody knife on the cloth, he stuffed the dirty rag into her jeans and pushed her over the edge

1

with the toe of his boot. No one would ever find her, and if they did, it would be much too late.

When silence settled around him once more, he turned to leave and felt the euphoria begin to wane. The tension and excitement of the beast unfurled as he drove away from the evil behind him. Berlioz played on the stereo, chimes and strings almost discordant as they swirled together, creating his favorite symphony. A smile pulled at the corner of his mouth. He was happy and restful now that the monster had been sated.

Chapter One

Aiden Kinncaid pulled his Jeep up in front of the dark house. Apparently, no one was home. Great. Just great. His entire day had been from hell, why should it suddenly change now at nine p.m.? Sighing, he rubbed the back of his neck and wished he'd taken something earlier for his headache. With an inward groan, he put the Jeep in gear and pulled into the far slot of the three-car garage set off several yards from the house. An older red Jeep was parked in the space beside him. Maybe someone was home after all.

He opened the door, grabbed his overnight bag and briefcase, and climbed out of the vehicle. Cold June air, carrying the smell of pine, whipped down off the Colorado Rockies. Aiden stood and stared at the giant log and stone house. Every window was dark, even though the other Jeep sat in the garage.

He should have stayed at the hotel.

Shuffling his bags to one hand, he dug in his pocket for the key his friend had given him, in case the owner wasn't home, and walked up the front steps.

Even though he was overseeing the opening of one of his family's hotels in this resort town, he didn't want to stay there. He liked to keep his staff on their toes, never knowing when he'd show up. And by staying someplace else, he could leave the office at the office so to speak.

Because of his quirk, he often rented houses in places such as this. If it were a large metropolitan area, he'd probably stay at another hotel, check out the competition. But, as it was, there had been little time to look around. Quinlan, his brother, was supposed to have handled this problem, but somehow Aiden had ended up seeing to it. He'd contacted Tim to find out where he could stay, or a place he could rent. And Tim said he'd set him up. His friend had come through in a matter of hours. Aiden had the rental as long as he needed it.

One small catch.

The owner of the house lived here also. Though as he understood it, the woman would stay above the garage in the mother-in-law suite while she rented the house out. He looked back over his shoulder to the darkened cottage above the garage. Apparently, the owner wasn't there either.

The deep porch was dark, no outer light shone down in welcome. Owners needed to brush up on their hospitality, he thought. Guests should always feel welcome.

As he unlocked the door, he wondered why the alarm didn't sound. Tim had given him the code, but it looked like he wouldn't need it. The thing wasn't even on. The light pad was off and not a sound registered. No shrill sirens sounded. Nothing. As the door shut softly behind him he wondered who the hell would build a home like this, go to the trouble to install an alarm system and then not even bother to turn it on.

Maybe she was a retired lady, one who forgot things easily, and decided to stay here in this lovely climate instead of transplanting to Florida or Arizona or some such place. And why did he even care? Aiden shook his head.

Sighing, he set his bags down on the hardwood floor. "Hello? Ms. Black?" No reason to give the little lady a heart attack in case she went to bed early or something.

Silence blanketed the house.

"Guess it's just me." Aiden flipped the nearest switch and the room flooded with soft light. The entryway was large and airy, giant logs speared up from the floor level straight through to the ceiling. No second story here. The décor went with the terrain, ranch, mountain motifs, Southwest blends of colors and textures.

He roamed the downstairs, noting the refrigerator in the top-of-the-line kitchen needed stocking as it only contained some yogurt and juice. The bare shelves screamed for objects. With a glass of water in hand, he took some aspirin and finished checking out the rooms downstairs. The kitchen, dining room and living room all basically ran into the other, one great room. A cluttered office near the back of the house gave testament that someone at least lived here amongst the shelves and stacks of books, and papers scattered all over the place. If the rest of the house didn't look so neat and tidy he'd think someone had broken in and tossed the place. It was so disorganized he wondered how anyone could find a single thing in the mess. Though the computer sitting on the corner was dust free.

Upstairs the hallway split off into more bedrooms and bathrooms. Nice and roomy. The master suite was enough to make him smile. A large, four-poster, king-size bed sat in the middle of the room. Made of heavy, blond logs, it demanded center attention. A red and blue quilt covered it. He saw clothes, black lingerie—he raised one brow—trailed out of one dresser drawer and the closet stood open, jeans and shirts hanging haphazardly and piling on the floor amidst jumbled shoes. Did little old ladies wear black lingerie? Why hadn't he asked Tim more about his landlord?

He sighed. Though he'd love to stay in here, it seemed the owner had yet to clean up. Fine, he'd take a guest room for tonight. As of now, he didn't really care. And to be fair, he was here a day early. Tim Kerrin, his friend, assured Aiden his early arrival would not be a problem.

Aiden hoped to hell the guy was right. That was all he needed, to have no place to stay. Not that he couldn't find another. Money opened locked doors, but he would rather not have to go through the trouble.

He chose the last room down the long hallway. Yawning, he tossed his overnight bag on the bed and sat down wishing the aspirin would kick in.

Today was bad enough as it was. There hadn't been room for his jet at the local Crested Butte airstrip, so he'd had to land at the nearest town, Gunnison, thirty minutes away and drive up here. The contractors at the hotel were behind schedule, but he'd be damned if The Highland Hotel wouldn't open on time. The painters pulled their contract. Aiden smiled. He'd see about that. By the time the Kinncaid lawyers got through with them, the company would be history. He wasn't Kinncaid Enterprises' CEO for just PR. Now he had to find a contractor to come in and fix all the screw-ups. If they had to work twenty-four-seven, the damn hotel was opening on the scheduled date.

He pinched the bridge of his nose and wished his headache and the whole damn day to hell.

* * * *

Jesslyn Black looked at the clock on the dashboard. After midnight. On the off chance Maddy would still be at The Copper Dime, she turned off Gothic Road onto Elk Avenue — picturesque with its neo-Victorian buildings — and drove up to the alley entrance of the bar and grill.

The Copper Dime was a steak and beer place, dubbed simply The Dime by locals. Ski and summer tourist seasons were their busiest times. Jesslyn was the minor owner of the establishment. Madelyn Brooks's SUV was parked outside the back door, along with Timothy Kerrin's — the major owner.

Jesslyn cut the engine of her pickup and climbed out of the four-wheel-drive rig. Climbed being the operative word for her. At five-foot-three, she used the running boards on the side for more than just show. Tim told her they were, in her case, stepladders.

Shaking off the wayward thoughts, she rolled her neck and stretched, wishing the drive from Denver wasn't so damn long. Warm air, full of liquor, grilled burgers and the faint whiff of coffee, hit her face as she pulled the back door open.

"Lucy! I'm home!" she called.

A bottle crashed to the floor. "Son of a bitch." Tim stood up from behind the bar. "You're paying for that."

"I didn't drop it," she told him. "What was it?"

"Half a bottle of our best Scotch. And, I wouldn't have dropped it if not for you." He glared at her as he grabbed the mop from the corner and started to clean up the mess.

Jesslyn leaned against the old scarred bar and crossed her booted feet. His gray eyes narrowed on her.

"You have fun at your meeting?" he asked.

She shrugged. "I guess so. I needed it. Authors must meet with their editors. Though the drive I could have lived without."

"You could have flown to New York."

"Oh yeah. You know how much I just love New York." She shuddered at the thought of all those people crammed in one place, shuffling through the streets. One on top of the other. Like little ants. "Denver seemed convenient for the both of us."

He huffed out a breath. "Well, now that your little vacation is over, you can get back to pulling your weight around here."

"Ah, and here I thought you really missed me." She stood on her toes and ruffled his salt-and-pepper hair. "When are you going to dye that? You want to look old or what?"

He cocked a brow at her. Tim Kerrin was in his late thirties, about five-eleven, with a wiry frame, narrow face and sharp gray eyes. He'd owned The Dime for almost ten years and took her on as a partner three years ago.

"I haven't heard the ladies complaining."

Jesslyn snorted. "What ladies?"

"And you last dated when?" he tossed back.

"The ass you set me up with."

"Who? I bet you don't even remember his name."

Shit. Leo? Lloyd? "It started with an 'L.'"

He shook his head. "Lyle. His name was Lyle."

She snapped her fingers. "There you go. Lyle. And he was an ass and a bore and your matchmaking skills suck. Please spare me your next attempt."

"It wasn't that bad."

"No, it was worse." She snagged a pretzel out of the wooden bowl on the bar. "I'm going to talk to Maddy."

She was at the swinging door leading into the kitchen when he added, "Glad you're back."

The door swished open and a familiar sight greeted her. Maddy, The Dime's chef, was rubbing herbs into a huge slab of roast.

"Hey," she said, walking over and grabbing a beer out of the fridge. "What's for dinner?"

Maddy didn't answer. Normally, the smiling redhead had a comeback for anything, but she didn't so much as look up.

Jesslyn frowned as she unscrewed the cap. "Everything okay?"

Maddy sighed. "Fine."

"Uh-huh. And I'm Suzy-Sunshine." Jesslyn hopped up on the counter and waited.

Maddy wrapped the meat in foil and put it in the refrigerator. Water gushed from the sink, filling the silence as Maddy washed her hands.

Jesslyn studied her friend. A china doll face, full lips complete with dimples, and bright blue eyes added to her fiery red hair. What she wouldn't give to have boobs like Maddy. Tall, athletic and built for a man's fantasies, Madelyn Brooks made women envious, men salivate, and did not have a clue to her charms. But now her straight red brows were pulled into a frown.

"Maddy? What's wrong?"

Maddy opened her mouth but the thump on the swinging door cut her off.

Tim stuck his head in. "Let's go home, ladies."

"I've got some stuff to wrap up here," Maddy said, "then I'll lock up and head that way."

His eyes narrowed as he studied Maddy. Jesslyn knew that look. Tim appeared autocratic and cynical, but she knew he was a softy under it all. He'd given her a job when she needed interaction with people. Now they were more partners than boss and employee.

"Everything okay?" he asked.

"Fine," both she and Maddy answered.

"Uh-huh. Well, I'm outta here. I've had enough for one day. Bar fights with college kids," he muttered with a glance at the clock.

"What?" Jesslyn asked, taking a swallow of her beer, the salty taste cool on her tongue.

"Oh," Maddy said, "he's still pissed about the college kids who started a fight tonight."

"Flying chairs do not sit well with the family at the next table trying to eat their burgers and chicken strips," Tim grumbled.

Jesslyn could only imagine. Swallowing past the chuckle, she said, "How bad was it?"

"Busted table, busted chair and I threw them out and called Garrison."

"And did our local Chief Tight Ass ride to the rescue?" she asked.

He only glared at her. "Your sympathy is too much."

"Look at the bright side," she told him. "It could always be worse. Could have burned the place down or something."

His smile was razor thin. "Your optimistic attitude is so refreshing and only reinforced with that cheery motto."

Maddy snorted. "Optimism and Jesslyn are not words that belong in the same vocabulary."

"True," Tim added.

"What is this? Pick on Jesslyn day?"

"You've been gone." He looked again at the clock. "And I've got to be going."

"Hot date?" she asked.

"Will you lock up?" He pulled on his coat.

"Who is she?" Maddy added.

"Night, ladies," he waved.

"We'll find out," Jesslyn said.

"Night, ladies." The door swung shut.

"We will!" she yelled.

The muted thump of the back door echoed in the quiet bar.

"Okay, spill it," she told Maddy.

Maddy was gathering her stuff up. "Nothing new, just problems with Kirk."

Kirk the Jerk.

"Maddy, why don't you ditch the guy? You could do so much better." Kirk Roberts was not worth a woman's time. He'd tried to make a pass at Jesslyn during the Octoberfest last year. It hadn't been the last. The man had an ego problem and apparently lacked simple rudimentary listening skills. "No" seemed to be beyond his comprehension. Jesslyn hadn't told Maddy because she didn't want to hurt her friend. "He may be the president of Crested Butte Bank, but he doesn't deserve you. He's a womanizing prick and only wants you to complete his 'perfect' picture with the two kids he already has." She took a drink, knowing this was old ground. Then asked, "Why do you think he has such a problem with you working here? It's beneath him, tarnishes that ideal image he's created."

Maddy held up a hand.

"Sorry," Jesslyn said. "I'll keep my opinions to myself."

"Like I said, it's nothing new." Her sigh was heavy.

There was something else. "So if it's not Kirk, then what?"

Maddy looked at her. "I got another bundle of lilies for my birthday."

"Oh." For several weeks, Maddy had received lilies from someone. "Still no card?"

"No, just the stupid things on my doorstep again."

At first they had laughed about it. A secret admirer. But now?

"Did you tell anyone?"

Maddy nodded. "Yeah, I told Kirk to stop sending them because I don't like lilies and it was starting to creep me out." She shrugged. "That's when we started fighting again. He thinks I'm seeing someone else and it just got blown all out of shape."

Fine for him to boink his secretary at the teller bar and try for any other woman, but not for Maddy to get flowers. Figures. Jesslyn took another swallow of beer hoping this would really be the end of Maddy and Kirk's on-again-off-again relationship. "Well, I don't know what to tell you."

"What? No, 'dump the dick'? Forget the creep? You're better off without him?"

She couldn't hold in the grin. "As I said, you know *my* opinions where Kirk's concerned. Want to come to my place and trash guys? I'll make brownies."

Maddy smiled. "No thanks. I'm going home and soaking in the bathtub and don't plan to get up till noon tomorrow."

Jesslyn hopped off the counter, poured the rest of her beer down the sink and threw the bottle in the glass bin. Together they walked out and locked up. The June night air was cold against her arms and she rubbed them, turning to Maddy.

"You call me if you get any more of those flowers." She reached over and gave her friend a hug.

"I will. Promise. Something about the whole thing is just creepy."

* * * *

He watched them as they stood beneath the alley light. Both women by their vehicles. He wondered what they were talking about. Friends.

After tonight there would only be one. He'd watched them through the window as they'd talked about something that seemed serious. The way they both frowned.

Frown. Smile. Smile. Frown. It was too late — she'd already smiled at him.

The shadows hid him from prying eyes, darkness closed in around him.

He breathed deep and caught her faint scent on the breeze, perfume that always surrounded her. Spices and herbs, like a potion concocted by a witch.

A witch, a whore. Both were the same as far as he was concerned. Red hair glinted in the dim lights from down the street.

A cool breeze blew up the alley, chilling him.

He watched as they hugged. Waited as one got in her vehicle, the engine rumbling to life in the quiet night.

She turned and he could have sworn she looked straight at him. He gripped the knife, the handle smooth in his palm.

Time. Right this moment was not the time. He knew where she was going. He would wait.

Hurrying through the shadows, he slid through the darkness, scurrying back to his own vehicle. Starting it, he pulled out and down the street. Perfect.

Only minutes later, he cut the lights. Quietly, so as not to awaken anyone, he shut the door. Hurry. He had to hurry.

His shoes rustled through the underbrush of the woods. The sharp smell of pine tickled his nose.

At the edge of the clearing, he realized he was gasping. Deep breaths. Deep breaths. It would all be over soon.

Where had she gone? Her car wasn't here.

Headlights curved along the ground just in front of him.

A smile creased his face as his heart began to pound. Sighing, he tucked the knife down by his thigh.

Her car door clicked open and he hurried forward.

Gravel crunched beneath his shoes.

Her head turned towards him.

"Hello? Who's there?"

"It's just me."

* * * *

Jesslyn slammed on the brakes as a cyclist zoomed across her turnoff. Something in the backseat slid into the floor. Shit. She'd had her blinker on. Had the idiot just not paid attention? It was dark as pitch tonight. She could have mowed him down. Glancing back, she saw it was Maddy's birthday present that had fallen into the floor.

She'd forget her own head if it weren't attached. For about a second she thought about waiting until the next day, but decided the stupid gift might cheer her friend. She'd gotten Maddy a singing marmot at a specialty shop in Denver. It was like the mechanical flowers with shades that burst into annoying songs whenever someone walked by. Maddy collected little figurines of the mountainous creatures so when Jesslyn saw this, she knew Maddy would like it. The furry marmot was dressed in a hot pink Speedo and sang "Hunka, Hunka Burning Love."

Jesslyn laughed. Yeah, Maddy would get a kick out of it. Looking both ways, she did a U-turn in the middle of the road. She headed back down the hill and then pulled off onto the dirt road leading to the small community of Meridian, with its properties scattered along the edge and slopes of Meridian Lake. It was only five minutes from either the historical town of Crested Butte nestled in the valley or Mount Crested Butte Resort sprawling across the mountainside.

Her cell phone shrilled, scaring her. God, her nerves. Who the hell was calling her after midnight? She flipped it open. "Hello?"

"I should give you a ticket for that traffic violation."

Ah, Tinks. "But why waste your valuable time?" she asked, turning on her blinker and driving down Maddy's road.

Jesslyn smiled. T.J. Stephens was the only female police officer on the small local force and the other friend in their trio. With short dark hair and ice blue eyes, her friend was a no-nonsense, kick-ass woman with a gun. The image was totally ruined by T.J.'s fairy-like build and Minnie Mouse voice. Just for annoyance, Jesslyn called her Tinks. She'd actually lived to tell about it.

"Where are you going? I thought you were still in Denver?" Tinks asked.

"I was. Headed back early. I'm now—hang on." She down-shifted, her engine grumbling, and turned into Maddy's drive. "I'm at Maddy's. We just left The Dime and I forgot to give her her birthday present."

"Well, better late than never."

She reached into the back floorboard and grabbed the gift sack. As Jesslyn got out of her pickup, she noticed Maddy's car door was still open, light splashing along the ground, the repeating ping echoing in the night. "Hey, did she tell you about getting more lilies?"

"No."

"Well, she did." Maddy's purse was lying on the ground. Jesslyn stopped.

Goosebumps pricked her skin. "I think you might want to come over here," she said into the phone, swallowing.

"Why?"

"I don't know, something's not right."

Jesslyn hurried forward, something urging her on. "Maddy!"

No answer.

"Jesslyn?" T.J. asked through the phone.

She rounded the corner of the house, at the back deck. Her foot slipped on something and she looked down. A dark puddle of liquid gleamed in the moonlight.

Some noise made her look up. The shadows shifted and a man ran at her. He knocked her aside, something slapping her in the face. As she slammed against the side of the house, the present slid from her hand.

"Hey!" she yelled after him.

His footsteps crunched across the gravel. She caught a blur of black clothing and a glint of something in his hand as he darted across the lawn and the beam of her headlights. He stopped, looked back at her. For one instant something dark reached across the space between them and iced through her veins. Then he grabbed up Maddy's purse and scurried away. The edge of the forest swallowed him.

"Jesslyn!" T.J. was yelling.

Jesslyn realized she'd dropped her phone. She grabbed it up. "Yeah, I'm here. Some guy in black just tried to mow me down. Maddy!" she hollered.

Again no answer.

"Stay on the phone with me," T.J. said.

Jesslyn could hear the spit and static of the police radio in the background. That was when she noticed the smell.

Sweet.

Lilies.

It filled her nose and her foot crunched a bloom.

Lilies.

Maddy!

Jesslyn hurried up the steps of the deck. "Maddy!"

A hand lay pale in the moonlight.

Oh, God. No.

She dropped to her knees, slid in liquid. She reached a hand out. "Maddy?"

Jesslyn touched Maddy's chest. When she jerked her hand back, she saw it was wet and sticky.

Blood.

No. Oh, no. "Maddy."

Sirens wailed across the lake.

Think. Think. CPR. CPR. Oh, God.

Carefully, she leaned over to see if Maddy was breathing. Her chest didn't move. No air came from her open mouth. Jesslyn's hand shook as she tried to find a pulse.

There was no beat, no breath, no life.

Please. No. Not again. God, not again. She couldn't lose someone else.

"Maddy. Maddy!" She pulled her friend's head onto her lap and rocked.

The coppery scent of blood filled her nose, laced with the sweet smell of lilies.

Funeral flowers. Murder.

It was the perfume of death.

Chapter Two

Dignity and death were not synonymous. At least that she could see. Or maybe it was just violent death, but dead was dead and it hardly mattered.

Jesslyn didn't move. Someone had thrown a blanket on her. She sat in the yard, in one of Maddy's iron chairs, and watched as if in a dream.

Bright lights illuminated the scene. Yellow tape marked off the perimeter of the yard, Maddy's car, and the deck. A camera flash momentarily shifted the scene, as if someone blinked and things should have changed.

But they didn't.

Red and blue lights rotated and flashed in the night from the police vehicles. People milled and shuffled about. Each was probably doing something important, but her mind couldn't compute what it was. Neighbors stood behind the tape in the front yard. She could see them from here, in their robes, coats, gowns and pajamas. Couldn't they bother to at least get dressed before they came to gawk?

A shiver danced through her yet again. Jesslyn raised her hand, intent to bite at a nail, but stopped. Blood. There was still blood on her hands. Maddy's blood.

She closed her eyes, fisted her hands and fought for control.

"Ms. Black."

She turned and looked at the Chief of Police, Derrick Garrison. "Garrison."

"I think we're through here. Did you think of anything else to tell us?"

They'd gone over everything time and time again. It was almost three in the morning. Not that she cared.

"Through here?" she asked. Nothing would ever be through here. Death didn't make things *through*. It just cut them off. Left them dangling and shattered lives. She ought to know after burying her husband and children. Death was never *through*.

Garrison was young, in his thirties, she'd guess. Brown hair, brown eyes, and almost six feet tall. Or maybe he just seemed that way to her. At her stature everyone was tall. He might be handsome if one went for the seriously somber type.

He squatted down in front of her, his nylon jacket with *Chief* on the back rustled. She looked over his shoulder and saw a man unfurl a long, black vinyl bag. Another strobe of a camera flash echoed across the darkness. One man unzipped the black bag and it ripped across the night, straight through her heart.

Jesslyn swallowed and looked to the trees. Was he out there now?

"I'll have someone drive you home," Garrison was saying.

She licked her lips. "I can drive myself."

He shook his head. "I'm sure you can, but you won't." There was the flat yet edged voice she was used to from him. He stood. "I'll come by in the morning to see if you remember anything else. You'll be surprised what sometimes surfaces after some sleep."

Jesslyn shuddered. "Oh yeah, sleep is most definitely at the very top of my list." She couldn't think of anything worse.

For a moment he said nothing, then, "You need me to call anyone?"

Someone else had asked her that earlier, though she didn't remember whom or when exactly. Everything blurred together.

"Who?" she asked. "Maddy and T.J. are the only real friends I have here. Maddy's . . ." Dead. "T.J. looks like she's going to be busy for a while."

He looked over to where T.J. Stephens stood at the edge of the house talking to a man with *Coroner* on the back of his coat. Garrison rubbed a hand over the back of his neck. "Yeah, knowing Stephens, she probably will. Maybe you can talk her into staying the night at your place. You were both close to Maddy."

Jesslyn doubted she could talk T.J. into leaving this scene. "Did you find a magic wand lying around here somewhere? Tinks does what she wants to do."

His mouth twisted in a frowning smile.

The man was being nice even though they hadn't always gotten along. She'd used Garrison as a source of research for one of her books and knew he thought of her as the flighty writer. The man was not shy in stating his true feelings about a person. But tonight, he gave her his undivided attention. And his concern, though she knew it was warranted, seemed to make the evening more surreal. He wasn't acting right. Nothing was right.

Jesslyn shook her head and looked away from his hard, whisky-colored eyes.

She wanted to be alone. In her house. Where she could turn on the alarm system and not see police, crime scenes, and blood.

"Will you at least ask her to stay with you?" he asked.

What had they been talking about? Oh, yeah, Tinks.

"Sure. Won't mean she will. As I said, she'll do what she wants to."

"Yeah, she does. Same as you. You going to be okay? I can call Tim, if you want."

Tim. She shook her head no. "I'll be fine. I just need to get out of here."

For a moment he said nothing. "I'll talk to Stephens, I'd rather she stay the night with you. You've seen this guy."

"I didn't see enough of him."

"But he saw you and I'd rather not have to come to your house in the middle of the night under similar circumstances."

A shudder danced down her spine.

Garrison continued. "Knowing Stephens, she'll be hardheaded. Think I'm taking her out of the loop or something," he mumbled more to himself than to her, his voice softer than she normally heard. He cleared his throat. "In any case, someone is staying at your place tonight."

"You make it sound like I'm in the middle of nowhere. And I don't really like people around."

Garrison leveled a look at her, his eyes flat. "Madelyn Brooks was hardly isolated. And until I know for certain this was not just a mugging gone wrong, you'll put up with people around."

The man had a point.

Jesslyn stood. "Whatever. I don't care right now. I just want to go home."

Again she looked out to the trees and wondered why, wondered who, and wondered if she could have stopped it if only she'd gotten here sooner.

* * * *

17

He watched the goings-on with a sense of giddiness. Tonight had been entirely too close. The roped-off section of the driveway and front yard kept the curious at bay.

And wasn't human nature an interesting thing? He looked at all the people standing in their pajamas, coats thrown over gowns and robes, slippers and tennis shoes, galoshes.

Was it any reason they were called sirens? The noises the emergency vehicles made? Like the women of old, they called forth the curious to stand, to look, to wonder in awe.

And he, he *had caused it all.*

He took a deep breath. The chilled night air stung his nose with pine and the stronger fumes of diesel and exhaust from the emergency vehicles. He breathed deeper and on the breeze he smelled them. The lilies. Harlot's flowers.

A movement caught his attention and he turned. She stood from the lawn chair and nodded. So lost, so alone, so broken.

Why? Why had she come tonight of all nights? He frowned. That one almost ruined it all. He'd pulled the harlot behind the house to finish the ceremony, to leave her with his mark, his salvation. Then he'd planned to pull her deeper into the woods behind her house and bury her. Never to be seen again. Like the others, she wasn't meant to be found.

He'd barely finished when the other woman had driven up.

He sighed, shoved his hands in his pockets and watched as the law enforcement personnel tried to shield the public from the gruesome scene. Two men lifted the body.

Death was a strange thing. Everything realigned in death, everything changed. Her body, that she had flaunted, was now no more than a shell. They put her in the bag and he shifted, moved to the side so he could watch them zip up the bag.

"It's just horrible. Just horrible. Things like this don't happen here," a little old lady said.

Oh, my dear, but they do. Oh they do.

He nodded, serious in his agreement with the elderly woman. Inside he smiled, fingered the bracelet in his pocket. The one he'd jerked off her. He had to keep something.

Didn't he?

*He blinked, wondered for the barest moment if he'd done the right thing.
If he'd followed the right signs, understood the calling correctly.*

A door shutting jerked him back and things fell back into focus.

Of course he was right. He was always right.

*He watched as the other woman was led to a police vehicle, a blue
blanket around her shoulders, brown staining her hands, the knees of her
khaki pants.*

*He hadn't meant to hurt her, not that one, but in the end she'd be better
off. The harlot had no place near that one.*

That one was not a harlot. She was . . .

Alone.

Why had she come tonight?

*No answer readily came, but he knew one would. Good or bad, he would
understand if there had been a reason for her to be here, to almost see him.
And when he had the answer he would know what to do.*

* * * *

Jesslyn rode shotgun in the police SUV. She watched as the
darkened landscape blurred outside, the headlights dancing on the
wildflowers and tall vegetation on the side of the road. Sergeant
Merrick didn't say a word and for that she was thankful. The radio
splattered and spit as she was used to it doing when she'd ridden
with T.J. But tonight she didn't try to decipher what they were
saying, didn't care to.

She clutched the blanket tight in her fist and shut her mind to the
reality around her.

Headlights cut through the night and glared off the side mirror.
T.J. followed in Jesslyn's pickup. Merrick turned onto the highway
and a mile later turned onto the Moonridge Estates' drive. He pulled
up behind a large pine tree in front of her house. Everything was
dark. The house, the porch, the garage set out behind the trees.
Maybe she should put some motion-detection lights in.

"I should check the place out," he said.

As they shut their doors, her pickup rumbled up behind them
and T.J. cut the engine, climbed out and tossed the keys to Jesslyn.
She missed and they landed at her feet.

"Sorry," T.J. said.

Jesslyn shrugged, bent down and picked them up. They all walked up the porch steps, their shoes thumping on the wood. The dark was heavy, the moon long since having set. On a sigh, she put her key in and unlocked the door.

That was good. At least the door was locked. Like the guy would use her front door.

She reached in and flipped on the light switch before anyone could stop her. T.J. glared at her and Merrick huffed. He was young, yet reminded her of Barney Fife. Maybe it was the eyes. She wasn't sure. Jesslyn watched as he unclipped his gun and wondered if he'd ever fired it. What if she had a cat or a dog and the animal scared him? Would the jumpy man shoot it?

* * * *

Aiden awoke. One minute he was asleep, the next he was wide awake.

What woke him?

He listened. There. A thump.

Great. Just his luck. The house with the non-used alarm would get broken into the night he decided to stay there.

On a curse, he looked at the nightstand and realized there was no phone. And his was downstairs inside his briefcase.

Hell.

It wasn't as if he even had a weapon. Though the iron, artwork lamp appeared heavy. He reached out and lifted it. Yeah, that would work.

Wishing now he'd stayed at the hotel, he pulled on his dark pants. Quickly, Aiden jerked the plug free and hefted the lamp, wrapping the cord around its thin base.

A lamp. A damn lamp. Didn't even have a phone in this room.

Maybe he could make it to the master bedroom. Surely there was a phone in there. Though with his luck, the owner had some phone quirk and there wouldn't be one. He'd rather call the cops who dealt with this than put some burglar in a coma and then get sued by the grieving family. Life in America. Only here would alarms be installed and not used.

If he met his absent landlord, he had a thing or two to discuss with her.

He eased the door open and slid into the hall. The master suite was only a couple doors down the hall. He just needed to get to that room.

* * * *

Jesslyn rubbed her forehead and watched as Barney checked downstairs.

Glancing at T.J., she said, "I'm going upstairs and I'd rather Merrick not check out my room." She looked at her hands, saw they trembled and fisted them. "I *have* to take a shower."

T.J.'s ice-blue eyes filled with tears and she nodded. For a moment, they just stared at each other, then T.J. slung an arm around her shoulders and they started up the steps. Neither said a word. And Jesslyn wasn't about to start thinking about things now. On the landing, she passed the light switch, thumped it on and turned to go into her room.

Shadows moved in front of the window.

Fear trickled through her.

A man stood holding something in one hand and a lamp in the other.

She was shoved to the side and heard T.J. yell. "Police! Drop it! Drop it now! Put the weapon down!"

Jesslyn realized her friend had drawn her gun and aimed it as steady as you please at the intruder. Maybe she should get one.

"Merrick!" T.J. shouted, back over her shoulder. "I said, drop it, you sonofabitch!"

Lights from the hallway cast a long line into the room. She reached over and flicked on the lights in the room.

The man held a phone in one hand and a lamp in the other.

He was clearly shocked, his dark blue eyes wide. "Don't shoot."

Jesslyn stayed back against the wall. How had he gotten in? And why didn't he have a shirt on? Or shoes for that matter?

"Put the weapon down!" T.J. yelled again.

Merrick sidled into the room, his gun drawn.

The man put the lamp on the bed, kept his hands palms out, though her cordless was still in the other.

Something was very wrong with this picture.

"Now put the phone down," Merrick ordered.

The dark-haired stranger shook his head and dropped the phone onto the bed.

"Kneel on the floor with your hands behind your head," T.J. said, moving closer, her gun still aimed on him.

Aiden looked at the tiny woman with the gun. She appeared no more than twelve, but the gun looked real enough.

Definitely should have stayed at the hotel.

As he eased down onto his knees, he said, "I think there's been some mistake."

Slowly, so as not to startle the police officers, he placed his hands on his head.

The two moved in and cold metal clinked as they cuffed his right wrist. They lowered it and he looked at the woman standing straight against the wall, pale and frowning.

His other arm was jerked down and the cuffs clicked into place.

"You are making a mistake," he tried again.

"Uh-huh," the fairy-like policewoman said. The guy cop hauled him to his feet. The hardwood floors were cold.

"Shoeless, shirtless criminals. What next?" the woman against the wall asked.

Everyone stopped.

He looked at her and their eyes met. Something in him focused, sharpened as he studied her. She stood straight, clutching a blue blanket around her short frame. Or maybe she just seemed short. And why did he even give a damn? Her eyes were dark, almost black in her colorless face. Light brown brows, the color of her hair, furrowed as she frowned.

Could this be his landlord, or come to think of it, would that be land*lady*?

"Ms. Black?" he asked.

"Shut up," Fairycop snapped.

The woman against the wall shook her head. She wasn't Ms. Black? Then who the hell was she? And what in the hell were all these people doing here?

At least he'd managed to call nine-one-one before the melee burst into the room. Sirens wailed from outside. And the radios the cops carried sputtered.

Aiden closed his eyes and waited to wake up. This had to be some bizarre dream brought on by stress. It had better damn well be.

"Come on," the man said. Everyone filed out of the room and down the stairs.

Another cop came in the front door, a dark nylon jacket embossed with *Chief*.

"Did you call for backup?" the woman cop asked the other one.

"No, thought you did."

Aiden said, "I did."

The new "backup" also had the word *Chief* on his ball cap. He looked past Aiden to the woman wrapped in the blanket.

"You okay, Ms. Black?" he asked her.

Ms. Black? Aiden whipped back around and glared at the owner. Ms. Black? It was the owner and she'd done nothing to help him? Anger, held in check, pumped hot and fast through him.

The woman nodded and looked to him. Their eyes met and again everything stopped. Then she blinked and everything moved.

"Yes, I'm okay, Chief."

The chief turned whisky-colored eyes on him. Aiden didn't move, didn't blink, but returned the stare, noticing he was a few inches taller than the man. "Would you mind telling your officers to take these cuffs off? Or am I under arrest? And if I am, I'd dearly love to know why."

The fox eyes narrowed on him. "Not till I have some answers."

Aiden turned back to Ms. Black. "You going to help me out here?"

Confusion flared on her face as her eyes narrowed. She shook her head. "Why the hell would I do that? I want to know what you're doing here as much as everyone else."

The woman had a twang as wide as Texas. Then her words registered. She had no idea what he was doing here?

Aiden sighed and swallowed his anger. He really did not need this. He looked at the chief. "And your questions would be . . ."

"Who are you and what are you doing here?" Chief asked.

"Aiden Kinncaid, owner of the new Highland Hotel and I was attempting to sleep before I was awoken and realized someone was in the house. Then I, being the good citizen that I am, called the magic number to bring the boys in blue running. Is it my lucky night or do you arrest everyone that calls nine-one-one?"

"Who did you say again?"

"Kinncaid." He turned back to Ms. Black and gave her a look he knew sent board members running, opponents scurrying, and enemies hiding. "Aiden Kinncaid." Silence hung in the air. Her expression didn't change. Didn't she have a clue as to whom she rented her own damn house to? "CEO of Kinncaid Enterprises, we're reopening the old Sharlaton." He faced the Chief.

"Oh my God," a woman drawled. "Oh, my God." A small strangled laugh rumbled out of her.

"Figure it out yet, blondie?" he asked her.

Her eyes widened.

Timothy Kerrin strode through the front door and into the melee. "What the hell's going on?"

Thank God.

"Timothy, I love this town of yours. This house, the *owner*," he added with a narrowed look at Ms. Black. "Truly, I do," he quipped, not caring if the sarcasm was rude or not. "I'm arrested, in case you can't see. Though they've yet to tell me why." He turned and showed his friend the cuffs. "Mind telling your local law enforcement what exactly it is I'm doing here."

Tim frowned, looked from him to Ms. Black to the cops. "Uh— uhmm . . ."

"I'm so sorry. I'm sorry," Ms. Black said, though somewhat vaguely.

"For?" the chief asked.

"He's renting the house."

"What?" three cops asked.

"He's my renter. I think." She looked from him to Tim, a question in her eyes.

"You think?" the little female cop asked.

"Yeah, I think that was the renter's name." She shook her head as if trying to figure something out.

"Yes, he's the renter," Timothy said, coming into the living area where everyone was. "He came in a day early and I gave him your spare key you leave with me," he apparently explained to Ms. Black.

She chuckled, a low husky sound that whispered at him, but it caught on what sounded like a sob. Again she shook her head before meeting his gaze. Her gaze was direct and unapologetic regardless of her words. "This might be really funny any other night. Oh, God. I am really sorry for all this." She waved a hand at the group and shrugged.

Aiden noticed there were brown stains and smudges on her fingers. He waited patiently, then cleared his throat. "If you'll be so damned kind as to remove the cuffs, I can get my wallet with my I.D." The words were bit out, but he'd really had enough for one night.

The chief nodded and Aiden felt the cuffs loosen. Feeling a twitch in his jaw, he didn't say another word. Instead, he took the stairs two at a time and came back with his wallet, pulling his shirt on. He handed it over to the chief.

The cop raised his eyes and handed the I.D. back to Aiden. "Vacationing?"

Aiden smiled, and he knew it held no amusement. "In a manner of speaking."

The chief closed his eyes and shook his head. When he opened them again, he said, "Merrick, Stephens, outside, now."

Aiden noticed the woman, Stephens, went to Ms. Black and gave her a hug, whispering something in her ear. Ms. Black nodded and the blankness shifted from her eyes. Pain, hot and raw, shone in the depths.

The chief held his hand out. "I'm Garrison. Sorry for the inconvenience, Mr. Kinncaid. It's been a bad night here and we're looking for a man."

Well that narrowed things down. Aiden looked at the offered hand for a couple of seconds before shaking it.

"I take it that man's not me?" He shoved his wallet and hands in his pockets, watching as the other officers filed out the door. Tim walked over to Ms. Black and wrapped her in a hug. The woman laid her head on Tim's chest for a moment, then pushed him away. How close of friends were these two anyway?

"Don't really know. Where were you about midnight?"

The question jerked his attention back to the man in front of him. "Here asleep. Why?"

Garrison's eyes narrowed. Then Ms. Black spoke. "It wasn't him."

The men turned to her. She pointed at Aiden. "He's too . . . too tall."

"You're sure?" Garrison asked.

Ms. Black nodded. "Yes. And Mr. Kinncaid's not even wearing shoes."

Garrison gave him one last look then said to Tim, "You staying tonight, Kerrin?"

Tim nodded. "Yeah, I'll be here."

What the hell was going on?

Garrison nodded. "There'll be someone outside, just to keep an eye out. Probably Sergeant Merrick, or maybe I can talk Stephens into staying. Ms. Black, I'll be back by in the morning."

Aiden crossed his arms over his chest. Ms. Black looked like a strong wind could blow her over. She needed some rest from the looks of things, not that he should care, given the night's events.

"I'll call first," Garrison added to Ms. Black. The chief walked out, closing the door behind him.

No one spoke as they listened to the footsteps on the front porch, and a car driving away.

Aiden rubbed his hands over his face. God, what a night.

"Mr. Kinncaid?"

He turned to Ms. Black.

"I really am sorry. I'm—I'm—" She huffed out a breath. "Don't worry about the first week's rent."

He waved a hand. "I don't want to talk about this now." He studied her. "I want to know what the hell is going on."

One brow rose. "Well, excuse me."

"Do you always rent to people without getting their names?"

"No, I made an exception with you." She rubbed her forehead and he noticed again how pale she seemed.

"Should you sit down or something? You don't look so good."

A ghost of a smile flitted at one corner of her mouth. "Figures. Good-looking. But the compliments and arrogance are such a hinder." She took a deep breath and blew it out.

Aiden cocked a brow and crossed his arms. "I really should try implementing your welcoming technique at my hotels. Alarm guest, arrest guest, and insult guest. Do you have many return renters?"

Her expression didn't change. Then a thin, condescending smile lifted the corners of her mouth. "It's a special technique only reserved for certain visitors."

Aiden stared at her and continued to stare. Her eyes narrowed and she walked up to him and poked a finger in his chest, tilting her head back to look at him. "Look, I said I was sorry. I can't help what happened tonight, so get the stick out of your ass and go back to bed or something 'cause I'm really, *really*," her voice cracked, "not in the mood to placate you."

"This is your home. Why couldn't you help it?"

Raw pain shifted in her eyes. This close he saw they weren't really black, just a deep brown, like dark, sinfully rich chocolates.

Aiden shook off the thoughts. *Stick up his ass?*

"It's a long story," she whispered, stepping back, paler than she had been, if that were possible.

"I think you really should sit down," he said, reaching out in case she fainted.

She looked at his hand, started to take it, but then dropped her hand back to her side, looking at him with an arched brow. "Afraid I'll fall prostrate at your feet? You would have an ego."

What was with her? Something about her wasn't adding up. The paleness, the pain in her eyes contradicted the edged words and attitude.

Tim shook his head. "Like two damn cats," he mumbled. Then louder, "Aiden's right, honey. You should sit down." He led her towards the kitchen, but she shrugged him off.

"I'm fine, dammit," the last word wavered in the air. "I am."

No one spoke. Aiden leaned on the newel post.

"Jesslyn," Tim said softly, reaching again for her.

She jerked away, the blanket falling from her shoulders to land on the floor.

Palms out, she shook her hands. "You two catch up or whatever guys do. Bond, build a fire, get drunk. I don't care. I've got to take a shower. I've got to get this off. I have to take a shower."

Her khaki pants were rusted from the thighs down. It looked like blood. Dried, caked blood.

Aiden straightened. "What happened? Are you okay?" He took two steps towards her and halted at the raw emotion in her eyes.

"Oh yeah, I'm just peachy." She smiled, thin and humorless. Then she shook her head and said in a softer voice, "It's not mine." Again she shook her head. "It's not mine."

He watched her fist her hands at her sides, swallow. She looked to Tim. "The Jameson is in the living room in the armoire." She motioned towards Aiden. "Or whatever his poison is. I'll be back. I need some coffee."

He moved aside as she walked past him and up the stairwell.

Aiden watched her go, then turned and asked Tim, "What is going on? I feel like I just woke up in the Twilight Zone."

Tim shook his head. "Sorry about what happened earlier. I forgot to tell her about you being here and all. My mind was on alcohol limits and fights. She came back from Denver early." Tim huffed out a breath, looking up the stairs. "Wished she hadn't."

"Why?"

Tim stared at nothing, shoved his hands into his pockets, then met Aiden's gaze. A muscle bunched in his jaw. "She found her friend murdered."

Chapter Three

Hot water beat down on her. Jesslyn sat on the tiled floor, her head on her knees. The thunder of water against her scalp shoved everything else out of her mind.

It had to.

Heat wrapped its steamy arms around her and still she was cold. Cold down to her very soul. Her body was tired, her heart was tired, and she didn't have the courage right now to face what happened tonight and what it meant. She hated death. It stole happiness, ripped out souls, shattered worlds, and in the end faded memories. Being a widow and childless for the last three years, she should be used to it, but she wasn't.

Jesslyn rubbed her hands over her face, mixing her tears with water. Crying helped nothing, only gave her a headache. She knew that. She had no idea how long she'd been in here, but it had been a while. On a sigh, she stood up, surprised at how unsteady her legs were. Maybe she'd give herself a heat stroke, pass out and hit her head on something. Then she could just be in oblivion for a while.

Though the idea held a degree of merit, she wasn't about to throw herself on the floor in hopes it might work.

She stepped out and wrapped herself in her silk robe. As she tied the towel around her head, a knock at the door startled her.

God, her nerves. She'd love a cigarette, but she'd quit. Hell, she'd even take a Xanax if she had any.

"What?" she asked.

"You okay?"

T.J.

Sure. I love images of death and murder in my mind, goes great for research.

"Fine."

"We're out here in your room."

"We?"

"Yeah," T.J. continued. "Tim, that renter Kinncaid guy, and me. Hurry up."

Kinncaid. That thought stopped her. They were all in her room. Tim, T.J., and Kinncaid.

"Why?" she asked, straightening.

Silence. She could picture T.J. tapping her foot. Finally she said, "We just wanted to make sure you were okay. Hurry up and get dressed, there's tea and coffee downstairs."

Now that she was out of the shower, the faint rumble of their voices filtered through her door.

She picked up her comb and pulled it through her wet hair.

Kinncaid. Now there was a man, arrogant though he was. Black hair swept carelessly off his forehead, dark cobalt eyes, strong jaw shadowed with dark stubble. He was tall, a couple of inches over six feet if she were guessing. When she'd poked her finger in his chest, she'd had to crane her neck back just to glare at him. Her finger had also been at her eye level. The man probably went for the no-end-legs-size-C-cup-willowy-frame-model-face type.

Jesslyn stared at herself in the mirror. None of the above fit her in the least. In high school she'd finally given up on long legs when she hadn't grown in two years. Her face was long, wider across her cheeks, almost an oval. The deep widow's peak made it more an odd-shaped heart. Her eyes were normal, as far as she could tell, and she'd always thought her mouth was too small. As she shed her robe and put on the camisole and panties, she looked back in the mirror. Size C? Maybe with toilet paper and in her wildest fantasies. There was a reason the bra termed *The Miracle* was Victoria's greatest secret.

Okay, everyone was in her room. Her clothes were on the bed. On a sigh, she jerked the robe back on and loosely belted it.

As she walked to the door, she caught herself looking in the mirror again.

Why?

She decided not to even answer that one. But, at least the musings kept her from thinking darker thoughts. Denial was a wonderful thing. Denial could keep her together for just a little bit longer.

The cold air from her bedroom swept across her as she opened the door.

T.J. leaned against her dresser and Tim and Kinncaid were both lying across her bed. Kinncaid propped up on his elbow, Tim lifted his head.

"'Bout damn time," Tim muttered.

She halted, staring at Kinncaid.

A man reclining on her bed. A very handsome man. In her room. On her bed. He straightened from his leonine pose, lean and powerful.

This is where she was supposed to say something witty. Something blasé. Something. Anything?

His blue eyes bore into her and a friction of awareness tingled along her spine.

She licked her lips and blinked, tearing her gaze away from Kinncaid and over to Tim, who studied her with a smirk on his face. Time for flippant. "Oh my!" She strived for her best Scarlett O'Hara voice. "Look, T.J., two strapping men in my room. On the bed. Let's tie them up and have our way with them. I've always fantasized about an orgy."

Kinncaid arched one black brow, the blue in his eyes shifting. Though in the low light she could be wrong. Slowly, he rose from her bed. Her libido, which she thought was probably nonexistent, whispered along her nerves. Great damn time for it to awaken, she thought. It must be all that dark stubble peppering his lean jaw.

"Your humor, as usual, is beyond me," Tim mumbled.

T.J. chuckled.

Jesslyn jerked her eyes off Kinncaid and faced Tim. "I know, like most things, it generally is. And it's either pop stupid ass jokes or I have a breakdown. Take your pick."

Tim shook his head. And motioned to Kinncaid. "Aiden Kinncaid, meet Jesslyn Black. I don't think we ever got around to actual introductions before."

Aiden.

It fit him. As stupid as that sounded, the name fit.

He crossed the space between them and held his hand out. Jesslyn stared at it, momentarily wondering what in the world she was supposed to do. The entire night was surreal.

Shoving the memories away, she focused on his hand. Long fingered, dark hair dusting the back, it reminded her of an artist's hand. No rings and a strong sinewy wrist. She reached out and grasped it, and shock danced up her spine from the simple contact. His hand was warm, nothing more, but the light touch of his palm on hers, his fingers closing around hers made her want to jerk her hand back.

"Hello, nice to meet you," he said.

His voice reminded her of the promise of a storm, a rumble, softened by the patter of rain. Why hadn't she noticed that before?

"Hi," she answered. "Nice to meet me? I take it you're over your snit then?" She licked her lips, and gently tugged until he released her hand.

"Snits? I don't get in snits." He cleared his throat. "I'm sorry about earlier, snapping at you and all."

"Did that hurt?"

His brow furrowed. "Did what hurt?"

"The apology?"

He moved his jaw out then back in. "Not as much as I thought it might. Are you always like this?"

"Like what?"

"Contrary, edgy?"

Tim laughed. "I'd use bitchy."

She ignored both Tim and T.J., who laughed as they walked out of the room. Aiden's eyes were fascinating. All that blue surrounded by thick black lashes. She took a deep breath and smelled a faint trace of his spicy cologne. She licked her lips again. Did the man taste as good as he smelled? "Probably."

"Probably what?"

You probably taste good? Shaking off the wayward thoughts she remembered what they were talking about. "Yes, I have an attitude problem, or so some think. Why?"

"Just wondering."

Silence settled between them. She was in panties and a camisole. *Naked* flashed in her mind. It didn't matter that she had a robe on. "As fascinating as this is, would you please leave? I need to get dressed."

For a moment, he didn't move, just watched her. "Guess so since Tim and the woman with the gun walked out of your planned orgy, and I'm not really into sharing anyway."

She bet he wasn't, but quirked a brow, saw the amusement, the challenge in his eyes. "Well, as to that, I don't know that you qualify into sharing or otherwise."

"Depends," he said, as his gaze raked over her, from her head to her bare toes, and with every inch of his look, her blood hummed, "on what I'm sharing. And why wouldn't I qualify?"

Was she really having this conversation at—she glanced at the clock by her bed—half past four in the morning with a virtual stranger?

"I'm waiting." He had a voice that could coax angels to sin.

"You're not my type." She planted a hand on her hip and pointed towards the door. "If you don't mind, I need to get dressed."

"Dressed?" He frowned. "Aren't you going to bed?"

And he wanted to know why? "No."

He shook his head, and turned and walked from the room. At the doorway, he turned. "You want the door open or shut?"

"I'm about to change and don't care to do a striptease in front of you. Shut."

A grin, lightning fast and just as lethal, flashed, showing her his straight white teeth and a dimple in his right cheek. "Aww, but I have my own fantasies."

He shut the door. For a full minute, Jesslyn stared at it, at a loss as to how she was supposed to process that remark. Probably the way he processed hers earlier.

Then a knock thumped.

"What?" she snapped.

"I was wondering where my apology was."

She could hear the amusement in his voice.

"I already apologized." Jesslyn walked to the door and swung it open. He had a hand against the door frame, his dark blue button down pulled and stretched with his upraised arm.

"Yeah, but I was the one arrested. It was *not* a good experience."

"You're whining and you were hardly arrested. Snitting again."

"Men don't snit."

She just stared at him.

He crossed his arms. "Have you ever been accosted by the police, felt like you were going to be on *Cops*?"

"Have a problem with cuffs?"

His eyes narrowed fractionally. "Depends."

"Your ego is entirely too large."

That dimple winked in his right cheek. "That's usually not what the women refer to."

He stood there. She started to shut the door.

"If you do, I'll just knock again."

"Fine. I'm sorry your pride was bruised."

His chuckle was rough, yet soft, reminding her of crushed velvet. "Did that hurt?"

Ass. "More than you know."

She shut the door in his face, but still heard his laughter as he walked down the hall. At her bed, she realized she was smiling.

Not what the women usually refer to? She'd bet not. Confusion slithered through her and she looked at the door, wondering what his point had really been. At least he'd gotten her mind off Maddy for a moment. Guilt shifted through her even as images, blurred and hazy, sharpened to bloody points.

God, Maddy.

Jesslyn swallowed and closed her eyes, willing the truth, the darkness away.

She couldn't deal with this right now. Not right now.

Coffee. She'd just get some coffee and go write. At least in the worlds she created, she could control what happened, leaving nothing to shock or soul-shredding pain.

* * * *

Aiden walked down the hall, his smile sliding away. That was one complex woman. Her smart-ass attitude seemed like a front. He had no idea how he knew that, but he did. He got the same feeling as he did when a floundering company he took an interest in tried to convince him they were fine, that there were no problems. One of his brothers called it his bullshit detector.

Then again, maybe he was wrong about Black. Sleep deprivation was a terrible thing.

In the kitchen, Tim poured mugs of coffee. He turned as Aiden entered. "Have fun?"

Though his friend smiled, there was an edge to it.

"You have a problem with that?" he asked.

Tim had assured him earlier that he and Jesslyn were just friends, but who knew.

Those gray eyes Aiden knew so well leveled at him. "Don't screw around with Jesslyn."

"Last time I checked, we were both adults."

Tim grumbled something. "She's not Brice."

"Thank God."

"That's not what I meant. Jesslyn has teeth and a bite-my-ass attitude, but she's really . . ." Tim frowned and rubbed his fingers down each side of his mustache. "She's not . . . Hell."

"You hurt her at all, even think about it and I'll shoot you," said a voice from the doorway.

The female cop. He looked from her serious expression to her gun. No doubt she'd do exactly as she said.

"What do you two think I am, some pervert?" Aiden asked.

"I told you, she's a widow," Tim repeated.

"Yeah." Tim had told him earlier how the woman had lost her husband and kids in an auto accident some three years before. Damn, the idea was unimaginable to him.

"She's not your average type to just jump in and have fun and then say, *c'est la vie.*"

The female cop snorted.

Aiden studied his friend. "You're serious."

"Yes, damn it. I don't want to see her get hurt."

"Such faith is humbling." Aiden strode to the counter, grabbing up his mug. Why he was drinking coffee at almost five in the morning was beyond him. Guess he didn't want any sleep.

"All I'm saying is be careful with her. She doesn't look it, but she's fragile."

"She would kick your ass for saying that," T.J. said, coming closer to them and holding her hand out for a mug. Tim handed her one. "But I have to agree with you."

Aiden thought about what they said, inclining his head towards Tim. They were wrong though. There wasn't anything fragile about Jesslyn Black. There was strength in her that practically shouted out. It was in her stance, ready to fight off the world. Yet, there was softness in her. Not fragility, but something under all that rough exterior. Though the exterior hadn't looked rough. He smiled into his coffee.

And why did he really care anyway? He was renting the house for a few weeks, not looking for a relationship. That was the very last thing he needed, or wanted.

The other two moved to the table and sat down.

Her dark eyes flashed in his mind, hurt layered under exasperation and a gleam in her eye as she'd snapped at him upstairs.

Complex.

Feet thumped down the stairs. Ms. Black stood in the doorway, stopping for a minute before she came towards him.

Aiden leaned against the counter in her way. He should move. Call it perverse curiosity, but he didn't.

She halted and looked up at him. He could still smell her fruity, floral scent that had teased his senses earlier. Shampoo? Soap? Lotion? Who knew? But it made his mouth water.

He'd just been too long without a woman. That had to be it. And tonight hadn't helped one damn bit.

"Would you move?" she asked.

Aiden reached back and grabbed a mug, handing it out to her. "I've always said polite manners have been overrated."

She snatched it out of his hand and turned, leaning against the counter adjacent to him.

Didn't want to get too close apparently.

"Is this decaf?" he asked Tim.

Jesslyn chuckled, low and throaty. "There isn't a grain of decaf in the house. What's the point?"

"I would have fixed it, but as she said, there wasn't any," Tim said. Then his friend leveled a cold steely gaze on her. "You should be in bed or something."

T.J. snorted.

"You know me better than that." She took a sip of the coffee and winced.

He watched as she set the mug down and poured sugar in the black brew.

"Need some syrup?" he asked.

"I like it sweet, thank you very much."

Apparently.

This time when she sipped it, she closed her eyes on a sigh. "There is nothing like a good cup of coffee."

Aiden could argue that point with her, but for some reason, he had the sneaking suspicion in the end he'd lose.

"So how long have you two known each other?" she asked them, pointing to him and Tim.

"Since college," Tim answered.

"Huh."

Aiden watched her over the rim of his cup. She had on some sort of tight black pants—leggings, weren't they?—with a large black fleece shirt. And little, sexy, black oval wired glasses.

Black liked black. It seemed too pat, too cliché.

"You should get some rest, Jess," Tim said.

She shrugged. "So should you. And you," she added to her friend. "But I won't, so there's no point in trying to talk me into it." She moved away from the counter. "I'm going to write. Y'all make yourselves at home."

"You and that damn computer," Tim muttered.

"Denial," T.J. added.

"Yeah, well, at least I can control it," she added quietly and left the room.

What the hell was that all about?

Aiden thought maybe he'd go get some sleep. But instead, he sat at the table with Tim and T.J. "Is she always like this, or is it just tonight with everything?"

Tim had told him about how the woman had found her friend murdered and had a run-in with the guy. The thought floored Aiden.

"Jesslyn?" Tim asked. "Yeah, she was when she first moved here. Then, I don't know, it got better."

The other woman shook her head. "No, we all just got used to her prickly nature."

Tim shrugged. "She works and writes, that's about all I know. Jesslyn is just Jesslyn."

"Oh," a voice said from the doorway. They all turned. "I forgot, I'll stock the fridge later today if you'll leave a list of what you like. And I'll get all my stuff moved to the cottage so you can move into the master suite," Jesslyn said, her eyes on him.

Move into the bedroom? His gut tightened and he had no idea why. Okay, he did, but he'd just as well ignore it. She had *stay back* plastered all over her. Aiden watched her, leaning in the doorway, her wet hair slicked back from her long, heart-shaped face, her complexion smooth and unadorned. Except for those little glasses. Who would have known he'd find glasses sexy?

"What?" he asked, clearing his throat.

She cocked a brow and frowned. He wondered how she did that. "Move out to the cottage. That's how I do things. All rooms except the back office are free to roam. Damage is charged to the renter and —"

"I know, I read the damn contract," he said.

"Then what are you asking?"

"Do you think it wise to move out there now?"

"Why?" Her fingers thrummed on the door frame.

"Well, considering what's happened and all, I didn't think the police wanted you alone?"

"I'm not alone. You're here in the house, and Barney will be out in the driveway."

"Barney?"

She waved her hand as if swatting a fly. "Barney Fife."

T.J. clarified, "Merrick. The cop outside."

Jesslyn sighed, telling him it was pointless to explain. "Never mind."

The more he thought about it, the more he didn't like the idea of her out over the garage all alone. "I don't think it's a good idea."

"And you have a say because . . ."

"He's right," T.J. added.

Who the hell knew why he wanted a say.

"Thank you." He saluted the policewoman with his mug. "As the person renting this place, it would be a tad awkward if something were to happen to you because you were up there and I was in here with the alarm system. Which reminds me." Aiden stared at her hard. "Did you bother to turn it on?"

She waved her hand. "It's broken, or glitchy or something."

"Damn it, Jess," T.J. said, turning to glare at her friend. "You said you'd get it fixed."

"I'll have someone come out and look at it," Aiden said.

"It's *my* house," she told him, narrowing her eyes.

"So?"

She shook her head. "Are you always like this?"

He smiled. "Like what?"

"Nosy? Pushy? Arrogant?"

"Yes. Always."

"How annoying." She turned and walked away.

Tim chuckled. "You two. What happened to your fabled charm? Used to be all you had to do was smile at them and they fell at your feet."

"I think it was more the name they were after." Like Brice had been.

"She burned you really good, didn't she? You ever gonna tell me why you really called off the wedding two months before the big event?" Tim asked, sipping his coffee.

"I realized she wasn't the woman I wanted to spend the rest of my life with." Among other things.

"Well, my friend, few are. They're like spiders, draw us in, wrap us up, and suck us dry."

Aiden chuckled. "Another wonderful experience for you too, huh?"

"Don't ask."

"I won't."

"So back to you and Jesslyn," Tim persisted.

"Men," T.J. mumbled, shoving her chair back and leaving the room.

Chapter Four

Jesslyn refilled her coffee cup, the quiet of the house settling around her. For the last hour she'd typed on her latest manuscript. Her heroine was currently being kidnapped and the hero was pissed because she hadn't stayed where he'd told her to. Not a lot of work, but at least it was something she could do.

Something to keep her busy, her mind occupied.

A place to hide.

Stop shrinking yourself.

At least I don't have to pay some quack to do it.

Grabbing a throw off the pine Southwest ladder against the wall, she opened the front door and quietly closed it.

"Oh," she said, setting her mug on the wooden railing of her porch and tossing her throw into the rocker.

The Hewetts walked up her driveway. When she'd first moved here, David and Sally Hewett, owners of one of the local coffee shops, The Mountain Bean, had hired her. She'd gotten to know them both. The Hewetts were one of those couples who looked alike. Both were of the same medium height, both lean, and both fair-colored and complected.

"Please, tell me you brought me some real coffee," she said, stepping off the steps.

Sally hurried forwards and engulfed her in a hug, sniffling. "I'm so sorry, Jess. So sorry." Sally patted her back and pulled away.

Jesslyn only nodded.

"Are you okay?" David asked, handing her a large paper cup with a slanted white lid.

She opened it and sniffed. Ah. She could smell the espresso. Nectar of the gods.

"You will be in my will." Closing her eyes, she took a tentative sip. Perfect.

"We know it's early," Sally said, "but we thought we'd stop by on the off chance you'd be up."

Jesslyn gave her a small smile. "You know me and how much I generally sleep. After last night, I did not care to 'get some rest' as so many advised."

"You have company?" David asked, looking at the cop car and man behind the wheel.

Jesslyn nodded. "Yeah, my renter for one, Tim and T.J."

"Well, if I'd known that, I would have brought more coffee," Sally offered.

"Thanks."

"We'll leave you alone," Sally said, her blond bob swinging as she latched onto David. "We're heading to the shop. If you need anything, Jess, anything at all, you give us a call."

Jesslyn nodded, awkwardly returned both their hugs and watched as they drove off.

Sighing, she took another drink of the strong brew and walked back to her deep-set porch. It wasn't even dawn yet. She sat, drew her knees to her chest, wrapping the blanket around her. The rocker creaked. Cold morning air, crisp with the fragrance of pine, mixed with the perfume of wildflowers.

The sky lightened as the sun awoke behind the mountain. It was after six and her system was starting to slack, but she didn't dare go to sleep. Therein lay the way to madness.

Nightmares and blood.

No thank you.

The door behind her opened and Jesslyn turned.

T.J., her cheeks flushed, her dark hair spiked, shoved her shirt into her pants.

Jesslyn thought for about two seconds. T.J. had been coming around The Dime a lot lately. She hadn't thought much of it, but now . . .

"Tinks, did you leave Peter Pan asleep or make him fly?"

"Peter Pan?"

"Tim."

A grin flitted around the corner of T.J.'s mouth. She reached over and snatched up Jesslyn's forgotten mug off the railing, gulping the coffee down.

"Oh, we flew," she muttered. "We flew."

Jesslyn chuckled. "Yeah, that fairy dust does it every time, huh? Did you make him wish on stars?"

T.J. shook her head. "Hell, he made me see them."

"Oh, do tell."

She checked her watch. "I can't. I don't know what the hell I was thinking." She handed the mug back to Jesslyn. "I wasn't thinking, that was it."

"Who said something to me about denial earlier?"

T.J. ignored the remark.

"You running out?" Jesslyn tsked.

"I'm going to the station, I think." T.J. leaned over and gave her hug. "Give me a call later, and for God's sake, keep a lookout."

"Yeah, you too."

At the steps, T.J. turned. "You're too damn pale. Go not-think with Kinncaid. That man is one a woman could just lap up in one gulp. He looks like he could put some color in your cheeks. On second thought, don't gulp, you should definitely savor. Slowly."

Jesslyn ignored her and rocked, watching as T.J. left. The coffee was good, but her stomach was starting to hurt. She shifted in the rocker.

Again the door behind her opened and Jesslyn turned. Aiden Kinncaid.

A day's worth of stubble shadowed his jaw line. It had only been an hour since she'd seen him, but he'd showered, his hair was still wet. Instead of dress pants and a button down, he wore jeans and a dark blue Henley, a plaid shirt thrown on over it.

"Didn't go back to bed?" she asked. His cologne wafted on the air and she licked her lips. *Lap him up?*

"Didn't see the point." His voice was still as deep and calm as she remembered. "You?"

"Nope."

He stood in the door, a mug in hand, and stared at her.

"What?"

For a moment he didn't say anything, then he stepped out onto the porch with her, sitting in the other rocker.

"I apologized for jumping all over you earlier about the cop thing," he said.

"Yeah? I remember. Taking it back now?"

He didn't smile, his face impassive. "I'm sorry about your friend. Are you okay?" he asked gently.

Jesslyn quickly looked out over the mountains. Of all the things she thought he'd say, that hadn't been it. Dawn was approaching, the mountains coming slowly to life. Life. "'And our hearts . . . like muffled drums, are beating marches to the grave.' Longfellow, I believe." She took a deep breath.

"You two were close?" he asked, jerking her gaze back to him.

"Longfellow?" He didn't so much as grin. She took a deep breath. "Maddy. Yeah, in a way we were. Not childhood best friends, but we were close. Talked. She was," she stopped. How to explain when she was only herself beginning to understand? His eyes held her stare. Out here, they were the color of the darkened sky in the west as the sun slowly rose in the east.

"She was what?" he prodded, his voice soothing.

What happened to the smart-ass he'd been earlier? Where did this guy come from?

"If you don't want to talk about this, that's fine. Sorry, don't mean to pry," he mumbled, taking a drink of his coffee.

His eyes never left hers and Jesslyn found herself talking.

"Maddy was this spunky, no-nonsense woman that pulled me back."

"From?"

Smiling, she tried for flippant. "The Pit of Despair." Jesslyn shrugged, the chilled morning air teasing her hair. "She—Maddy, T.J. and I had some great girl nights. She was a good friend. I wish I had been a better one to her." Jesslyn shivered, remembering the blood, the stench of the flowers and the man. The man with the knife.

"Are you cold? I can grab you another blanket."

She shook her head. "No, but thanks."

Jesslyn took another long drink of her coffee, and as the black acid hit her stomach, she held her breath, waiting for the pain to abate. So she was stupid, what else was new?

"Well, for what it's worth, I am sorry about your friend."

"Yeah, I am too. Thanks."

Silence stretched between them. She could hear the cars whirring by on the highway, people traveling up and down the mountain.

"This must be hard for you all things considered," he said, quietly.

"Ah, Timothy has been talking again."

43

She heard the scratch of his fingers on his stubble, like sandpaper. For some odd reason she wondered what it would be like to kiss him. Jesslyn looked at him.

She needed sleep.

"Actually, he was warning me off you."

She blinked. That didn't sound like Tim. "Really?"

"You sound surprised."

"I am. Normally, he's trying to set me up and get me to move on with life." She really didn't want to get into the past tonight. Maddy. Jerrod. Hannah. Holden. Too many deaths, too much pain. Shoving the thoughts aside, she took another deep breath of mountain air and tried to identify the smells. It was a trick she'd learned when she'd first moved here. It relaxed her. Sometimes.

"I'm sorry too about your family." He shook his head, frowning.

"You didn't know them." Realizing that was rude, she added, "But thanks."

"I can't imagine," he muttered.

No one could. The pain she'd gone through after the accident had taken her entire family. Her husband, her children. "I'd never wish for you to."

"Yeah, well, sometimes we find out anyway, don't we?" His voice hardened.

"Who did you lose?" she asked.

He opened his mouth, looked at her, then shook his head. "I'm sorry. Damn, I seem to say that a lot to you. I didn't mean to bring all this up."

She took another drink of the lukewarm coffee. Pain twisted her stomach, harder to ignore than the ones she'd had earlier. Maybe she should go in and get something to eat, but food didn't sound appealing. An antacid would be good.

"I know," she muttered, at his remark. "Death is one of those sticky subjects people tend to avoid."

He made some noise in the back of his throat. She had no idea what it meant, let alone what to say back to this man sitting on her front porch with her at dawn.

Life was strange.

She really should have eaten something. Nausea swirled through the pain in her stomach. The espresso was already hitting her system, she could feel it skitter along her limbs.

Aiden was silent, pulling her gaze back to him. His eyes were so intense as he studied her. Jesslyn tried to think of everything she'd said, but her tired brain wouldn't cooperate. "Sorry. I'm probably not making any sense. I'm tired."

"You could always go to sleep."

"Not a chance." She vehemently shook her head. "Soon as I do, especially in this state, the dreams will come." And she had enough to deal with right now besides worrying about nightmares.

"Normally women like dreams of me," he said lightly. His lips spread into a grin and that dimple winked at her from his cheek. Jesslyn took a deep breath.

Big mistake, his cologne filled her nose and mouth.

If nothing else, the man made her smile. "It's probably the only place they get satisfied."

His eyes widened and he shifted as if ready to pounce. "Care to test that theory?"

What the hell was with her when she talked to this guy?

Care to test that theory? The thought warranted some consideration, but . . . well . . .

"It would be sad to see your ego deflated." She knew she was talking too much, but it seems she wasn't exactly normal around Aiden. The early morning light played with his face, casting it in shadows, highlighting the planes and angles. Eyes, such a rich blue, stared back at her. His hair was a little long for her image of a CEO, but that was okay. The black stubble peppering his strong jaw gave him a sexy early morning look. God, what a face. She saw he was tired, not like her. She didn't think this had anything to do with emotions. Or maybe it did.

Aiden watched her study him, the way her dark eyes narrowed, the way she pulled her bottom lip in. His gut twitched and his body responded to her. *Care to test that theory?* What the hell was he thinking? "Like what you see?" he asked.

"Thank God," she muttered, a smile edging her mouth.

"What?"

"I'd begun to wonder where you'd gone. The charmer threw me there for a while."

"Where I'd gone?"

"The smart-ass."

"Normally I'm the charmer. You didn't answer my question," he said softly.

"What question?"

"Like what you see?"

She only smiled at him. "Haven't decided yet."

The woman had a way of keeping him on his toes. It was a new experience. "You keep telling yourself that."

The crunch of gravel turned her attention to the drive that led into the estates from the highway.

"Well, shit."

Her expletive made Aiden raise his brows. "Problem?"

"Only if you consider lowlife bugs problems."

Aiden watched as the silver Lexus coupe pulled to a stop in front of her house.

At least the police were attempting to do their jobs. He took a sip of his unsweetened coffee and wondered briefly if Barney—and she was right, the guy looked like Barney Fife—would arrest this new guy. And who the hell was this new guy?

Out of the corner of his eye, he saw Jesslyn stiffen ever so slightly, the pull of her brows, the way her hands tightened around her coffee cup. Then she closed her eyes and clenched her jaw.

"You okay?" he asked.

She only shook her head, looking at him. "I'm fine."

The edge of her mouth was tight, her knuckles almost white. Shallow breaths.

"Are you hurt?" he asked, starting to rise.

On a deeper breath she shook her head. "I'm fine."

The voice of the new man and the policeman carried on the wind across the yard. After another second, he turned his attention from her to the two men.

"I can't let you see her," the cop tried.

"Who the hell are you? Her damn bodyguard?" The man was dressed in a rumpled suit and his blond hair stood in spikes as though he'd run his fingers through it.

Appearance was important, Aiden had always believed it. First impressions had an adage for a reason. And on appearance alone, this man would not win any points.

"It's all right, Merrick. Let him say what he wants and then he can leave," Jesslyn spoke beside him.

The man stalked up the sidewalk and stopped at the bottom step. "Do you have *any* idea where I spent all damn night?" the man asked through his teeth.

Jesslyn took a sip of coffee.

Silence stretched.

Was this an old lover? A pissed ex-boyfriend? The man was definitely upset.

"I'm shaking with anticipation," she drawled, her twang more pronounced. "Please, don't leave us in suspense. Though, I'll warn you, if you came to gloat about your latest screw, I don't care."

"You're such a bitch, Jesslyn," the guy said.

Aiden shifted, the rocker creaked.

"Another guard dog?" the guy asked, his lip curling derisively.

"If you like." Jesslyn didn't move.

"What I'd *like* is to know why in the hell you couldn't bother to pick up a fucking phone and call me last night." He stepped up the first step.

Her stare was dark and razor sharp. Aiden would bet lesser men backed down at that stare. The man stepped back down into the yard.

Jesslyn uncurled out of the rocker and stood, the blanket falling off her shoulders. "Honestly?"

"Are you anything else?" the man asked.

"Aiden?" she asked.

"Yeah?" He stood.

"Would you excuse us please?"

"What? Don't want to introduce me?" the man asked.

She shrugged. "Aiden Kinncaid, CEO of something important, meet Kirk the Jerk Roberts, the *estimable* president of one of the local banks." She turned back to him and Aiden saw the anger and humor dance in her eyes. "Personally, I use the other bank just so I don't have to deal with Kirk. I'd do the same if I were you."

"Why you . . ."

"Now, Kirk," she admonished, "don't whine. It's annoying."

A muscle bunched in Kirk's jaw, a vein pounded in his forehead. Aiden eased a bit closer to Jesslyn, who stepped to the edge of the porch.

"I didn't call you because I didn't think about it."

Aiden could hear the man grinding his teeth from here.

Kirk balled his hands into fists. "More like you didn't want to. If not for you, Maddy would have married me."

"And divorced you the first time she caught you fucking your newest secretary." Jesslyn set her cup on the railing with an ominous thunk. It toppled and fell off the railing. "Well, hell, there went a perfectly good cup of coffee," she said, looking at her cup on the ground. She gazed back at Kirk the Jerk. "Why don't you go home, Kirk? What the hell are you doing at my place at this time of morning anyway?"

"I loved her!" he yelled.

"No," Jesslyn's voice held no mercy. "You didn't love her. You used her to complete your ideal picture. And if you wonder where I got that, remember what *you* told me back in October."

Kirk's eyes raked Jesslyn up and down. Aiden lounged against the railing.

"They think I killed her," Kirk bit out. "I spent all night at the goddamn police station being questioned!"

For one long moment no one said a word, no one moved.

"Do you have any idea how this looks?" Kirk asked, raking a hand through his hair.

Jesslyn straightened as though jolted. "Excuse me?" She stepped down two steps, getting closer to the angry man.

Aiden didn't really care for the move.

"How it looks? You are such a lowlife, sorry-assed son of a bitch. Who gives a shit how it looks? Maddy is dead! Dead! Somebody used her chest as a goddamn pincushion and you're worried how it looks?"

Kirk pointed a finger at her. "Don't take that tone with me."

"No," she grabbed his finger and twisted. "You don't come to my house and take crap shots at me. I really don't give a damn how you spent your precious night." She let go of his finger and Aiden watched as the man's eyes darkened. "Where were you, Kirk, when you heard? Did the cops find you at home with the kids?" She shook her head. "Nope, my guess is that they found you somewhere else."

"That's none of your damn business."

"You're right, it's not. But whatever you and Maddy had or didn't have, she did care about your kids and they cared about her. Have you once thought about how the hell this is going to affect them?"

At Kirk's confused look, Jesslyn continued, "Nope, that would be too much to hope for in your case."

"You keep my kids out of this."

Jesslyn held up a hand. "Kirk, go home."

"I can't. They're searching my house as we speak."

Jesslyn tilted her head. "Really?"

Merrick stood at the edge of the yard yawing, but still watching the spectacle on the front porch.

Before Aiden turned back, he saw the blur of movement. Kirk reached out and grabbed Jesslyn's arm, jerking her close. "What the hell did you tell them?"

Jesslyn looked at his hand on her arm then back at Kirk.

Aiden stepped forward. "Let her go."

Neither of them paid him a bit of attention.

"What do you think I told them? Let me go, Kirk. Now."

Again a muscle bunched in his jaw. Aiden saw his fingers tighten, but before he reached them, Jesslyn fisted her hand, reared back and sucker-punched him right in the nose.

Kirk let her go.

Aiden stopped, impressed as she backed up one step and said, "I told you to let go of my arm."

"You bitch."

"Leave," Aiden said, stepping down beside her, and easing in front of her. Lot of good it did now.

Bloodshot eyes glared at Jesslyn then at him before zeroing in on Jesslyn again. "You broke my nose."

"Aren't you the smart one," she muttered.

Merrick puffed up beside them. "Come on," the policeman said. "Mr. Roberts, you really shouldn't be here."

"No," Aiden said, "he shouldn't."

Kirk held his nose with one hand, blood dripping from his palm, while he dug something out of his pocket. He pressed it against his nose. "Ja godda pay fer dis."

Aiden stepped down the last step and still looked down on the — what had Jesslyn called him? Oh yeah — sorry-assed son of a bitch. Woman had a way with words.

"Careful what you say, Roberts."

"Who the fuck are you to care?"

Aiden only smiled, and he knew it held no amusement. "You don't want to find out."

Fear shifted in the other man's eyes. Good.

Merrick grabbed Kirk's arm, but the rumpled banker jerked it free and stormed off to his Lexus. Gravel and dust spit into the air as he spun away from the house.

Jesslyn sighed. "Well, that was sure fun. Wonder what's next on the day's agenda."

Aiden watched the car swerve onto the highway, barely missing another car. He looked to Merrick. "Wasn't that a traffic violation?"

Merrick smiled. A siren chirped, once, twice, and then an SUV with CBPD followed down the hill.

"Yep," Merrick said, "and now he gets to deal with the other one."

"Other one?"

"Stephens. Don't know which is worse. Black in a bad mood or Stephens. Would rather not deal with either one of them if I could help it."

No, Aiden would guess not. He turned around and saw Jesslyn gather her dumped cup, a mug and blanket up. The door squeaked as she opened it and stalked through it. He watched as she paused at the threshold, her hand fisted to her stomach.

Aiden raked his hand through his hair. Nothing like the Rockies. Was it always like this? Working vacation his ass. If this was any indication of what the next several weeks were going to be like, he'd need a real vacation after this.

He followed Jesslyn inside. Water ran in the kitchen. She turned from the sink and looked at him, her dark eyes shifting from anger to hurt to confusion. "Sorry about that."

Aiden shook his head and stood beside her at the sink. He reached out and took her hand, pushed the sleeve up. No bruise showed. Thank God. He really didn't care for brute force against anyone. But in her case, with Mr. Roberts, he'd make an exception all the way around. He turned her wrist one way, then the other, his fingers grazing along her arm, the soft inside skin of her wrist. He traced one blue vein from the inside of her elbow to the pad of her thumb. Her breathing quickened.

Aiden looked up at her, saw the shock in her eyes glazing over the anger. "You're no damsel in distress. Remind me to never really piss you off."

Her half grin warmed him and he let go of her hand as she eased it away. "I'd need a step stool to deck you." Then her face contorted and she leaned forwards, holding her breath, her other hand pressed to her stomach.

"Jesslyn?" Her shoulder felt small beneath his hand. "What's wrong?"

She took a deep breath and slowly straightened. "Nothing." She blew her breath out.

He bent his knees to look her in the eye. "Don't give me that. What?"

"Arrogant, pushy and bossy too."

"Fine CEO qualities. Since I'm renting the place, I'd like to know if I'm about to catch a stomach virus. Now what's wrong?"

She was pale. "I'm fine, really. Though the idea of giving you a stomach bug has merit."

Again she fisted a hand against her stomach and bit down.

"Uh-huh. Tell me."

"It's nothing." She tried to pull away, but he didn't take his hand off her shoulder. "Fine," she huffed. "Sometimes when I get really stressed out, my stomach hurts."

Hurt looked as though it were an understatement.

"Do you have an ulcer?" he demanded.

"Depends who you ask," she sassed with one of her half grins.

"I'm asking you."

"Then, no, I don't."

His eyes narrowed. "When was the last time you ate?"

All he'd seen her put into her system was coffee.

She rolled her eyes to the ceiling as though she'd decipher the answer from there. Finally, she shrugged. "Sometime yesterday? Yeah, a muffin yesterday before my meeting. But it wasn't very good and—"

"A muffin?" He looked outside, checked his watch. There were perks to owning hotels. It was almost seven and his staff had better be running the hotel properly. "You need food."

"Yeah, I know. Whatever is in those pills I took earlier for my headache, it's trashing my stomach."

"And the stress isn't helping. Nor is the coffee." He sighed and straightened. "Where are your shoes?"

"Shoes?"

"You do have some?"

"Yeah, and amazingly I even manage to get them on my feet upon occasion."

He stared at her.

"They're in the closet over there."

"Get them on. We're going to breakfast."

She arched a brow. "I'm not hungry."

"Ulcers are nothing to mess around with."

"Figures. You would worry about everything too. No wonder you CEO types are known to burn out. And I don't have an ulcer."

"Your shoes." He crossed his arms.

Her jaw jutted out. "I'm fine."

"Your shoes."

She threw up her hands. "God, you're like a damn bulldozer." Jesslyn marched to the corner closet, sat on the tiled floor and mumbled to herself as she put on a pair of tennis shoes.

Aiden shook his head and wondered what perversity in him liked trading barbs with her.

Whatever it was, he didn't care. The woman needed food and he was going to feed her.

Chapter Five

He paced. No answers had come to him in the night. But the police couldn't find anything, at least he didn't think so.

Crimes were not as easily committed as they once were, even with all the precautions he'd taken.

Perhaps the last one had been a mistake. Someone might put it with one of the others. Though why they should, he couldn't guess. The possibility though lingered and he didn't like that.

They might link one other to last night's victim, but the others . . . The others were all long forgotten.

Well, he never hunted here. Went out of his way to find those that would hardly be missed.

Last night had just gone all wrong.

The question that plagued him was why?

To prove he'd made a mistake?

Or something else?

A horn blared out on the street and he startled. The smells of the early morning here wafted on the air. Pine and exhaust mixing faintly with coffee and baked goods.

He sniffed, rubbed his hand down his leg. He needed to think, some quiet to figure out what he was supposed to do about everything. The idea of going after Ms. Black did not exactly appeal to him. Not unless it was supposed to.

The problem was knowing if it was supposed to or not. She was innocent. Not like the others. He knew that.

But still . . .

He shrugged and hoped the answers would come to him soon.

* * * *

Jesslyn mopped her last bite of waffle through the lake of syrup on her plate and popped it in her mouth. She leaned back and sighed.

Aiden, his plate pushed to the side, stacked his hands on top of each other and watched her. "Better?"

It would be churlish to lie. "Yes," she admitted on a grin.

"Food does wonders."

She shrugged. They'd come to his new hotel. The old Sharlaton, a massive log and stone complex, four stories tall, set in the middle of the resort community. For some reason she'd expected to see people remodeling.

He'd laughed and asked what she expected in the foyer. Paint cans and scaffolding? Okay, so she had. And though she couldn't see the paint and lumber, the traces of it still lingered in the air.

The overall décor was what seemed to predominate all these mountain resorts. Heavy unfinished wooden furniture. Ranch motives mixed with a Southwest flavor. Seemed normal to her. Lots of stone and wood. "Nice place you have here," she said. "Did I already tell you that?"

"Not in so many words." He took a sip of coffee.

She looked at her tea, very weak tea too. "You are cruel."

"Next time you can have coffee if you don't run yourself to the ground." The lines around his mouth tightened.

"Are you always like this with people you rent a place from?"

The man gave a new meaning to the word dominating. He all but sucked every extra space out of an area and he didn't even move.

"I told you, I'm fine."

His head tilted, the early morning sunlight shining through the skylight glinted off his black hair. "So you did."

"I've eaten. Lots of carbs, bready stuff. Today's dietitians would cringe. Can I have some coffee now?" Truthfully she was craving orange juice, but knew better. Coffee, her stomach could probably handle, but not O.J.

"No."

She looked at his left hand, noticed again it was unadorned. "You're not married, are you?"

"No."

"I can see why."

Though he grinned, it was cold and did not reach his eyes. "Can you? I doubt that."

The serious CEO was back.

Jesslyn leaned up and propped her elbows on the table, her hands under her chin. "I hear a story."

"And you've a story yourself."

So she did.

"Why do you like to write?" he asked. "You do write, don't you? Tim mentioned it."

Jesslyn chuckled. "Yes, I write."

"What do you write?"

"Books."

Those breathtakingly blue eyes narrowed and she inwardly sighed.

"What kind of books?"

"Mayhem and danger. Girl finds herself in bad situation, sometimes saves herself and sometimes hero saves her, sometimes she saves hero. They, of course, live happily ever after, but that's a must in romance."

His gaze roamed over her face and she felt it like a caress. "Romance, eh?"

"Yep."

"You don't seem the romance writing type."

She sat back. "What the hell is that supposed to mean?"

"I don't know." He shrugged. "I think it's your attitude that ruins the image of some author dreaming up happy endings."

"What a stereotypical thing to say."

He grinned. "Who was it that remarked on CEOs and burnouts?" For a moment neither said a word. Then he asked, "How long have you been writing? Do you enjoy it?"

"Very much." At least he was polite enough not to crack any stupid ass jokes about romance or be derisive about what she did. Taking a deep breath, she continued, "And I've written for years. Been published for about five."

"What did your husband think of it?" he asked.

It was a question she'd gotten used to, others had asked it. But instead of answering him, she asked one of her own. "What would you say or do if your wife wanted to write about — what did you call it? — dreamy happy endings?"

He thought for a moment, propping his chin in his hand. "I don't know. If she was really serious about it, tell her to go for it."

His answered surprised her. "Really?"

"Of course. Everyone should do what they want to. If they don't, it only leads to resentment and hard feelings."

True. "Jerrod, my late husband, encouraged me." Even if he hadn't always completely understood. "He was my biggest supporter."

Aiden slowly shook his head. "You loved him."

"Well, one would hope." She didn't understand his comment. "Yes, I loved him, very much. He was my husband."

Somewhere in the back of her mind she thought this should be a strange conversation to be having with this man, but for some reason it wasn't. Aiden Kinncaid was surprisingly easy to talk to, even though she never really knew what he'd say.

"Tim said you had children?"

She could talk about Jerrod, but the children . . . Jesslyn looked at the tabletop. "Yes. Two." Pain whispered around her heart. Not the claw shredding pain it once had been, but still sharp enough to hurt. She swallowed.

"Can I ask you a personal question?" he asked.

She smiled. "What is it you've been doing?"

His brows furrowed. "Never mind."

Jesslyn waited. "It's okay. It was three years ago. Sometimes it still hurts. Lots of times it still hurts. Not so much what was, like it was before, but what can never be." She ran her finger in a circle on the tabletop and shrugged. "However, life is life and it goes on."

"What happened?" He shifted as though uncomfortable. "If you don't mind my asking."

"Was that the personal question?"

He shook his head.

"No? Well, as to what happened, a drunk driver ran a red light. And just like that, everything was . . . was ripped to shreds."

"I'm sorry." He reached across the space and covered her hand with his. "It's not easy losing children."

The words were whispered and she'd heard them before, from well-meaning friends and family. But his held that note, that dark acceptance of what could not be changed. Only people who had been there knew. "Ah," she said. "The person you lost."

His eyes looked over her shoulder. Jesslyn didn't turn around to see what it was. He took a deep breath. "Yeah. Though most wouldn't think so." Aiden shrugged. "I'm a bit antiquated, so I've been told."

Jesslyn sat silent and unmoving, not even to pull her hand out from under his.

"I was engaged, to an incredibly self-centered model, would have been married for several months by now."

"What happened?"

"I found out two months before the wedding she'd had an abortion." His forehead wrinkled on his frown. "I know this is a new millennium and whatnot, women's rights, freedoms of choices."

But not for him.

He shook his head. "I can't believe I told you that. Sorry." Aiden made to pull his hand away, but Jesslyn turned hers over and grasped his warm palm.

"I'm sorry," she said for lack of anything better.

"Why?"

"Because while I know what I'm missing, you never even got the chance." Pain shifted raw and angry in his eyes at her words.

They sat there in the early morning light streaming through the skylights, the bustle of activity in the empty dining room around them, staring at each other.

Jesslyn smiled again. "So how's the weather?"

His smile warmed her insides. "Did we just bond or something?"

"God, that's a scary thought."

"Tell me about it." He waved his hand. "Sorry for bringing all that up. I'm not sure why I did."

Jesslyn shook her head. "Don't worry about it."

"Can I ask another question?" He shifted and put his elbows up on the table.

"Of course you can, doesn't mean you'll get an answer."

His eyes roamed over her face. "You're very prickly."

She shrugged. "I know."

He opened his mouth then shut it again. Standing, he offered her his hand. "Come on, I'll take you home so you can rest."

She didn't move. "Maybe I'm not ready to leave yet." The coffee smelled really good.

Aiden sat back down.

"I want to ask some questions," she said. "You got to ply me, now I want to ply you."

A grin flickered near the edge of his mouth. "What do you want to ply?"

She ignored him.

"What do you want to know?"

What did she want to know? "Are you always like this?"

"Like what?"

"Controlling, overbearing and just come in and take over. Rearrange things to your liking?"

He steepled his fingers and studied her. "Is that how you see me?"

Lowering her voice she mimicked. "An ulcer is nothing to mess around with. Shoes. Shoes. Shoes."

He chuckled, a low deep rumble that tossed her insides. "Guess you do."

"I bet you're the firstborn."

He nodded.

"Do you have a quirk?" Something to make him a bit more approachable.

"Do you?" he asked.

She grinned at him. "Hell, honey, I've got lots of quirks."

"Such as?"

"Colors."

He frowned. "How are colors quirks?"

"Cause sometimes I think in colors."

He shook his head. "How does one think in colors?"

She shrugged. "You know, like you see a person and think: They're yellow. Or a song seems blue, or maybe pink."

Aiden leaned back up on the table, his gaze intent. "I've never heard that. You seriously think in colors?"

She pursed her lips, watched as his eyes dropped to her mouth and quickly tucked them between her teeth. "Yeah. Okay, so I'm weird. It's like listening to Beethoven and thinking of his Fifth with lots of reds and sharp blacks, purples."

"You like Beethoven?"

"Yeah."

"What about his *Moonlight Sonata*?"

"Blues and grays, swirling and melding."

He chuckled. "You're right. That's weird, but I like it. What other music do you like?"

"All kinds of music. You?" She took another sip of the tepid tea.

"Beethoven's good. I like jazz, old World War Two songs, Celtic."

"Celtic, huh? Never say so with a name like Aiden Kinncaid." So they had something else in common. Music tastes.

"One-half Irish, one-half Scot."

"There was no hope for you."

He smiled. "None."

He stood again and offered her his hand. This time she let him help her stand and didn't take her hand from his as they walked out the hotel.

"So you think of music and people in terms of color? What color am I?"

"Blue," she answered immediately.

He grinned, a glint in his eye before he covered them with shades as they stepped out into the bright morning. "But is it just blue? Or are there different shades?"

"Like your eyes."

He halted.

Oh God, she had *not* just commented on his damn eyes.

"My eyes?"

Hell. "Uh, yeah, that blue color. Yeah." Intense. The man was an intense cobalt blue. They stood on the pavement, halfway to his Jeep. She scrambled for something else to say. "Tim is navy, all somber and serious most of the time. And T.J., she's pale green or blue, like winter ice." Jesslyn shrugged. "I know it's weird. It's just how I think of things."

Aiden shook his head and helped her into his Jeep.

As he slid in, he said, "No, I don't think it's really *that* weird so much as interesting."

The drive back to the house only took about five minutes. He walked her in, nodding to the replacement cop—whose name she couldn't remember—and proceeded to check the rooms.

She stood in the kitchen and decided to wait to crank the coffeepot until after Aiden left. Tim's be-careful-I'll-talk-to-you-later note lay on the countertop. Immediately the idea of her two friends together popped unbidden in her mind. *Nope, not gonna go there.*

Aiden stood in the doorway, still in his mountain wear but now he had a briefcase.

"Off to work?" she asked.

He looked from her to the counter behind. "No coffee."

"Who are you? My doctor?" Okay so she'd *thought* it.

His gaze, cobalt and hot as lightning, ran over her again. "Depends." He walked closer. "I always liked playing doctor."

"Ooohhhh." She tossed the pencil at him. "Go to work. Get out of my house."

"I'm renting it. Have a signed contract to prove it." He stopped in front of her.

"You're impossible and I'm trying to think here and you're making it hard."

His dimple peeked at her. "That's nice to know."

The man reminded her of a panther. He set the briefcase on the center island on one side of her, reaching across, trapping her between him and the counter behind her.

"Don't move your stuff," he said, his voice quiet.

She licked her lip, looking up at him. "I was going to run to the store and get some food."

"You're changing the subject." He leaned in ever so slightly and her blood heated. "You don't need to be out there alone in the cottage."

She couldn't think with him this close. And *why* was he this close?

"I-um-I don't think . . ." She licked her lips

"Good." He lowered his mouth to hers. A breath away his eyes met hers and he smiled. "Don't think."

A spark lit deep within her as his lips, soft yet firm, met hers. Jesslyn didn't move, couldn't move. Aiden didn't touch her other than with his lips on hers. Before it started the kiss ended.

He smiled. She liked that single dimple in his right cheek.

"I'm glad to see you don't always bite," he whispered.

Bite? Jesslyn blinked, shook her head as he stepped back, though still kept his arms on either side of her.

"Depends," she whispered.

This close she watched his eyes darken. Fascinating.

"Don't move to the cottage." His voice whispered over her.

Jesslyn was surprised to realize she almost answered, "Okay."
But she didn't.

She put her hands on his chest and pushed back. "Are you a vegetarian?" she asked. "If you are, I think I'll buy steaks."

Looking up, Jesslyn barely caught his frown.

"What? Vegetarian? No."

"Good. I'm going to get to the store before it gets too busy, then I'll come back here and crash."

He grabbed up his briefcase. "Take the nap first. You look like hell."

"Compliments, compliments. My heart's all aflutter." Jesslyn rolled her eyes and managed to keep from walking him to the damn door.

She waited until she heard the click of the front door and then looked out the window and watched as he backed his Jeep down the drive before driving away.

What was with her?

A panther. She chuckled out loud. And what a sleek, smooth panther too.

Silence settled around her, heavy and almost oppressive. Jesslyn looked around the kitchen, out into the living room. Nothing had changed. What was different?

Deciding not to think about that, she headed upstairs. Maybe she would take a nap first.

* * * *

Beethoven blared in her ears as her fingers flew over the keys. Here Jesslyn could keep pain at bay. Here she was in charge and there were few surprises. Well, the muse often took off on a tangent, but it usually turned out to be a good thing. And here, Death didn't creep his cold fingers over her life.

Jesslyn's headache and nerves made it impossible to eat lunch. She'd taken a couple of ibuprofen after Aiden left, but as yet they did nothing. She could probably take something else soon, but she wasn't going to worry about that now. She was busy. The hero and heroine were dodging bullets. She didn't have time for aspirin or water or anything else.

This was her world.

The banging finally registered. Someone was beating the hell out of her door. Dammit. Jerking her headphones off, Beethoven's thundering symphony quieted. There was a reason for having headphones, to drown out noise.

Heading down the hallway, she mumbled and cursed whoever would dare to interrupt her. It better be damn good.

The banging continued.

"I'm coming!" she yelled. "For God's sake." She yanked the door open to see Tim and Aiden standing on her threshold. She was tired and bitchy, but she still noticed the foil packages in Tim's hands, the bags of groceries in Aiden's. The charred scent of grilled meat drifted on the air. Jesslyn stepped back to let them in.

"It's about damn time," Tim all but snarled.

Excuse her. "Well, I'm sorry, dear, but I was busy writing. Aiden has a key, why the hell didn't he open the door?"

Aiden said, "In case you can't see, my hands are full."

"Lord forbid you set something down." Turning back to Tim she asked, "What are you doing here?" Tim frowned as he crossed her threshold and Aiden grinned his one-dimpled grin that made her heart skip.

"We came to make sure you eat." Tim brushed past her and into the kitchen.

She caught his you-know-better look as he looked into her near empty fridge. Well, not quite empty. There were eggs and juice. Maybe some salad stuff. And yogurt. There was a carton of yogurt. So she hadn't made it to the store like she said. Aiden owned a hotel, he had a place to eat.

"Glad to see I took it upon myself to go shopping," Aiden said pleasantly, setting the bags on the countertop.

Jesslyn watched as he unloaded the bags, then stopped and looked at her.

"What?" she asked.

"You could help."

"I could." She swung the front door shut and walked to the kitchen area. "I figure they're your groceries, you can put them up."

Tim cleared his throat. "Children, children. Jesslyn, could we get some plates?"

Looks like there was going to be some company tonight. She should have moved her stuff to the cottage above the garage. At least the chief hadn't stayed long when he stopped by earlier that morning.

In the kitchen she grabbed some plates and glasses. Tim asked her to tell him everything Garrison and she talked about. Jesslyn sighed and shut the cabinet door. So much for writing. Tim meant well. Setting the table, she complied, filling Tim in on what she knew, keeping to herself the emotions she wasn't ready to face. Aiden meticulously placed things in the refrigerator. She set down the last glass and watched him. He even arranged the vegetables in the veggie drawer. Hell, she'd always just tossed everything in there.

And why did she care how the man arranged his food?

Jesslyn shook her head. She'd make some tea, concentrate on the mundane. While the water boiled, she asked Tim yet again, "What are you doing here?"

His arms crossed over his chest and he studied her for longer than she cared to be scrutinized. Finally, he shrugged. "Sue me. I was worried about you. Being the heartless man most think I am, I called up Aiden and talked him into steaks. Figured you hadn't eaten."

Aiden straightened and shut the refrigerator door, walking around the island.

She couldn't help but grin at Tim. "Yeah, you're just a coldhearted jerk, aren't you?"

"So I've been told."

Another knock at her door. What the hell was this? Club Jesslyn?

"Care if I get it?" Aiden asked from his lounge by the table.

"Why should I? You're renting the place, have a signed contract and everything. Having dinner parties and whatnot." He only leveled a look at her. "No, I don't care." The water started to boil. She turned, moved the kettle, dumped the tea in, and closed the lid to let it steep.

Jesslyn tried to tell herself it was the thought that counted, but it was hard when you found out your friends obviously thought you were weak and frail. Did they expect her to be on the brink of a breakdown or something?

"Oh. Hi, didn't know you'd be here, but I guess so," T.J. said, her voice coming from the front door. "You are renting the place."

"Hi, Tinks. You remember Aiden."

T.J. stepped into the house. "Hard to forget," she said a little lower than necessary.

Jesslyn rolled her eyes.

"T.J." Jesslyn smiled. "I think you need to join us for dinner."

T.J. stopped, her black brows arching over her snow blue eyes that looked from Jesslyn into the kitchen. "Oh."

Color surged up her friend's face.

Jesslyn turned and looked at Tim. How the hell did she forget that? Leaning close, she whispered, "Think fairy dust."

T.J. shoved her out of the way and stalked into the kitchen.

"Do you always abrade other people?" Aiden asked her, shutting the door.

"It's a gift."

He grinned, slow and easy. "Can't wait to see what other talents you can boast of."

On a frustrated mumble, she turned and followed Tinks into the kitchen.

Aiden didn't follow. She heard his feet thump up the stairs. Tim looked at T.J. "Maybe, between the two of us, we can talk Jesslyn here into your plan of drowning her sorrows and fucking her brains out."

She could only stare at Tim. "What?"

Tim shrugged.

T.J. grabbed stuff out of the refrigerator. Straightening with lettuce, tomatoes, and other various greens in her arms she winked and said, "You know, fairy dust, color in your cheeks. Lust."

"I will never understand women's analogies," Tim muttered.

Fairy dust? Lust? Her and Aiden Kinncaid? "T.J., have you been drinking?"

The vegetables plopped and rolled on the counter as she dropped them and grabbed a bowl from the cabinet. "No. I told you this morning. Tim and I both think you need this."

"Need what?"

Tim waggled a steak knife at her. "Not what, who."

She could only stare from one to the other.

"Well, the sparks between you two are obvious," Tim continued. "They were this morning. And he asked about you when I talked to him both times today."

Jesslyn threw up her hands. "Well, hell, Tim, will you pass him a note for me after the pep rally? What is this? High school?"

Her friends thought she should go for her renter?

T.J. tilted her head. "She's avoiding the point."

"Why is that?" Tim asked.

Damn him, he was right. She watched as he uncorked a bottle of wine, thinking how she did feel something around Aiden, but lust after him? Sleep with him?

Feet thumped back down the stairs.

Tim filled one wineglass with deep red liquid and handed it to her. "Here, Aiden's probably thirsty."

T.J. nodded and leaned on the counter beside Tim. "Indeed, I bet so. I was just thinking the same thing." Both of them were grinning at her, the dare in their eyes. Tim poured another glass and handed it to her.

Fine. She grabbed both glasses, sloshing wine up near the rim. Taking a deep breath, she turned and almost bumped into Aiden.

He stopped, looked at the glass, to the still-probably-grinning-fools behind her, and back to her. A small smile played at the corner of his mouth as his dimple winked at her.

"Thank you." He reached out. The moment his fingers touched hers on the glass, she almost let go. Shock. How had she forgotten what his simple touch could do to her? Jump starting her system with a bolt of — something — clear down to her toes. God, those long, lithe fingers of his. His touch was still warm. Artist's hands, she'd forgotten his hands. Masculine with their long palms, the backs were speckled with dark hair and ended with tapered fingers.

Her eyes flew up to meet his. Licking her lips, she gently pulled her hand from under his, letting go of the glass. "You're welcome."

She set her glass aside.

"You don't like wine?" he asked, his voice low.

"No, I've got a headache and if I drink, especially wine, it'll only get worse."

"Did you take anything?" he asked before he took a drink.

"Jesslyn, where the hell are your knives?" Tim asked from the kitchen, jerking her back.

Idiot. She was an idiot around this man. Why? A writer and she couldn't even remember what the hell he'd asked her, let alone answer the damn question. It was those blue eyes. Though blue was definitely inadequate. And the hands, yeah, he had great hands. And, well, hell — *let's be honest* — the whole damn package.

Smiling at him, she turned and went to the kitchen.

Everyone helped get dinner on the table. T.J. and Tim bickered about something. Dinner went smoothly. Everyone talked of movies and music likes, things to do here in the summer.

They all veered away from one topic. Maddy.

Chapter Six

Halfway through the meal, T.J.—curse her hide—blurted out. "You know, Aiden. I'm glad you're staying here. Jesslyn could use a man around the house."

Jesslyn choked on the one bite she'd managed to force herself to eat.

Aiden's fork paused halfway to his mouth. "Excuse me?"

"Well," T.J. expounded. "I was thinking you'd be a good watch dog, so to speak."

Jesslyn saw his blue eyes cut to her, and part of her wished she could crawl under the table.

"Really? And dare I ask as to why you would think that?" He laid his fork down and pushed his plate to the side.

Tim apparently decided he needed to throw his two cents in. "Well, T.J.'s right. Jesslyn spends too much time walled up here alone and what with what happened and all, it's nice to know there's someone here to look after her."

"Am I even at the table?" she asked.

Everyone ignored her.

Aiden looked from the other two, back to her, picked up his wine and said, "I have a feeling she might see things differently."

"Finally the voice of reason," she muttered.

A moment stretched between them before T.J. stood up, coughing. "I need to get going. I'll clean off the table since you were hardly thinking I'd show up to eat."

"I'll help you," Tim offered.

They both split with hands full of dishes. Jesslyn stood and started to help clear the table.

When everything was tidied, and the men were in the living room, T.J. walked to her. "I know this isn't the time, but I thought of something after I left this morning."

The knot she hadn't gotten rid of all day rolled in her stomach. "What?"

"Maddy was an orphan. She had no family, no one."

"She had us!" Jesslyn interrupted. The men looked up from the living room.

T.J. sighed. "I know that. But as far as arrangements and whatnot." She looked away, then back at Jesslyn.

Arrangements. Of course. "Oh." Jesslyn huffed. "I'm sorry, Tinks. I just—sorry."

"It's okay. I wanted to see what you thought about it. Not that we can do anything anytime soon."

No, they wouldn't be, would they? She had done enough research for her novels to know some forensic pathologist would be finding any and every detail that might help them to find out who had killed Maddy. Once the autopsy was completed and finalized, the findings agreed upon, her body would be released.

Killed Maddy. God, the words hit her again.

"Look, just think about it. I'll talk to Tim and see what he thinks." T.J. gave her a hug. "Thanks for dinner, though you didn't eat but a couple bites."

"You going to be okay going home alone?"

T.J. jerked a shoulder. "Why wouldn't I be? I've got my baby right here to keep me safe." She patted the gun strapped to her waist.

A grin caught Jesslyn by surprise. "If you get lonely, I've got a spare room." She walked T.J. to the door.

"Wait up," Tim said. "I'll walk you out." At the door he stopped. "You didn't eat."

No, she hadn't eaten.

Aiden had noticed too. Three entire bites did not count in his opinion.

Tim looked at him yet again. Aiden knew Tim had watched him watch Jess all evening, but he didn't care. He wondered if anything was really going on between Tim and Jesslyn. He was pretty certain there wasn't. His friend seemed more interested in the female officer.

Tim leaned down, kissed her on the cheek and said, "I'm going back to The Dime. You take care. And take something for your damn headache. I'll call you in the morning." Tim turned to him with a granite stare that spoke volumes on protectiveness.

"Night," Aiden said.

"Go." She shoved Tim through the door, closing it behind him and leaning against it. A pent-up sigh released as her shoulders fell. She looked tired as hell. He should probably let her get to bed, or go write or whatever she wanted to do. He had papers to go over.

A glance at the clock showed him how late it was getting. He too had a headache. Another one. Awkward silence blanketed the air between him and Jesslyn. Rubbing his neck, he caught her watching him.

"Headache?" she asked.

"Yeah, again."

"For you, it's probably the altitude. Lowlanders."

How did she make that sound like an insult?

She turned and walked back to the kitchen. "Come on, I'll give you something."

Following her, he asked, "Will it put me in the hospital?"

"Unfortunately, I'm fresh out of arsenic."

* * * *

Aiden pulled up in front of the house later that week.

For the last several days, he and Jesslyn had coexisted. She was usually walking out of the kitchen with a mug of coffee or glass of juice when he was heading to eat. Or maybe he was leaving for work while she was just getting out of bed. Sometimes he'd watch her jog down the lane, or make the loop around the estates. Once he'd even seen her go out to jog at night. But when he'd voiced an opinion on that, she said T.J. was coming to run with her. Still . . .

The whole situation was like a roommate, but not. He still didn't know what in the hell had possessed him to kiss her that morning several days ago, but since then, that simple kiss had plagued his mind, keeping him up at nights, pulling his attention away from work. For just a moment there, the edges around her had softened and something had shifted in her eyes other than hurt, or anger.

And she acted as nonchalant and uninterested as could be. He thrummed his fingers on the console. Well, perhaps not uninterested, he'd caught her studying him, but if he asked, she only said it was nothing and walked out of the room. Or made some blithe, smart-ass remark. And why did he even care? It wasn't like he wanted, needed, or was even remotely looking for any kind of . . . of . . . anything.

Aiden got out of the Jeep and noticed the cop car was still outside. He waved and walked up the porch steps. Music blared from inside, some chick mood song.

He inserted the key but noticed the door was unlocked. Did the woman have no damn care for her safety?

He pushed it open, shut it, and walked to the kitchen. Leaning against the doorjamb, quiet, not moving, he was treated to the sight of Jesslyn shaking around the kitchen, singing some chick song about bitches and mothers. The artist belted the song out from hidden speakers. Aiden shook his head, and simply stood unnoticed until Jesslyn, using a wooden spoon covered in white goo as a microphone, turned wailing out a note, and opened her eyes.

She jumped a foot and glared at him.

Aiden had never heard anyone just cut a note off, but she managed to. Right in the middle of it.

Raising her brows she stammered, "It a . . ." She looked mortified. "Gets the juices flowing and the blood pumping."

Aiden laughed. "Really? I'll have to try that sometime."

Jesslyn chuckled and walked towards him. He loved her laugh and wished she did it more. Her laugh was throaty and real.

"That I'd like to see." She smacked him on the chin with the spatula.

"Did I mention how fascinated I am by that drawl of yours?" he asked as he wiped the goo off and licked his fingers. Icing. He sniffed and realized he smelled cakes.

Her tongue darted out to lick her bottom lip. "I don't think so."

He sucked the last of the icing from his finger and noticed her eyes were locked on his mouth. What was she thinking?

"Yep, it's sexy as hell." Aiden brushed past her, aware of sliding his arm across her chest. A jolt went through him. Definitely sexy as hell. "You're baking? Would never think of you as the June Cleaver type." Cupcakes mushroomed across the counter.

"Surprises abound."

Cupcakes. Aiden turned to her. Her tongue licked something off the spoon as her eyes twinkled wickedly. Slowly, she ran her tongue up the side of the spoon, then twirled her tongue, catching the built-up icing. "Yeah, I like cupcakes. They seem happy." She looked at the clock. "You CEOs get great hours, huh?"

He shook off the image her licking the icing conjured. "Coming from someone who can claim to work in pajamas all day or night, that sounds shallow. Actually," he started, "I had an idea."

The music slid away as she punched a remote. "I bet that hurt."

This woman would never be boring. "Anyway, I realized how little I know about the local sights and thought maybe you'd like to play tour guide this afternoon."

"Tour guide?" She picked up a mug and swallowed.

Aiden narrowed his gaze at her. "What are you drinking?"

She tossed the rest back. "Nothing now."

Coffee.

* * * *

Jesslyn held the handlebars of her Polaris four-wheeler as they flew down Gothic Road, dust billowing behind them.

"You ought to let me drive," Aiden said in her ear.

Typical, typical male. Even if he was an incredibly handsome one. What he did to a pair of jeans was absolutely sinful. They molded him and taunted her.

She ignored him and only shook her head. They'd loaded her four-wheeler in the back of her truck and drove out of town to where the pavement ended. Parking there, in the little off-road lot, she'd unloaded her Polaris telling him to simply enjoy the view and to hold on.

And he was, holding on. His arms were around her, one hand resting—or in her opinion, burning—on her thigh. She tried, quite unsuccessfully, to ignore the way he rode against her backside.

The scenery, she'd think about the scenery.

Aspen trees grew tall on both sides of the dirt road, and profusions of pink and blue mallow flowers dotted the roadside. Miner's lanterns, their creamy pale green blooms spearing up, and various other flowers too numerous to name, added to the lush growth. Far below, nestled in the dark green valley, a silver slither of water wound its way like a metallic snake.

The late day was clear, or nearly so. Her nylon jacket snapped against the wind as she increased their speed.

Aiden's hand on her thigh tightened.

"Is it always like this up here?" he yelled in her ear, pointing around with his other hand.

She nodded. They passed signs posted, hiking trails and campgrounds with names like Rustler's Gulch, Judd Falls, Washington Gulch. She had always wondered who made up the names and why the places were named that.

She should probably warn him. Turning her head to the side, she yelled back at him, "Hope you're not afraid of heights."

"No, why?" Then, he exclaimed, "What the hell!"

The arm around her waist tightened, and the one on her thigh vised. Jesslyn couldn't help but grin at his obvious startlement. On one side a dark cliff of rocks, wet and glistening from the water runoff, sliced up into the sky. The black and wet road—if it could be called such—made nervous sluicing sounds as the tires crawled over it. There was only room for one normal sized vehicle, and Jesslyn hoped they would not meet another car. Their other side dropped off into a snow-massed canyon. She could hear the East River rushing against the rocks below. Cold air blew down the canyon and blasted them in the face. They kept climbing, even as Aiden's hands gripped her even tighter. She chanced a quick smiling look back at him.

"Watch the road," he all but barked.

She laughed.

Finally, there was land on both sides as she made a descent on a road off to the left. There before them was a lake, hidden and nestled in the folds of the mountains. Pine trees speared up around it on the far side, part of it was surrounded by a precipitous rocky face. They bumped along until coming to a stop on the far side of the water by the pines. The beach was black, like the road they'd just survived.

Jesslyn cut the engine and Aiden's sigh of relief blew warm against her ear.

Turning slightly in his arms, her right leg sliding against his, she looked back and up at him. "You did trust me not to run us off into oblivion didn't you?" He had yet to loosen his hold on her. "I wasn't about to kill us or anything," she added at his skeptic look. Poor choice of wording, she thought.

Kill . . . Maddy . . .

"What?" he asked, perceptive as always.

"Nothing. Nothing." *What am I doing here*?

Jesslyn tried for a smile, tried to hide the emotions that suddenly roared to life within her. Maddy. She didn't want to think about

Maddy right now. No, not right now. Not later. She'd managed to cram the emotions away for almost a week, but they were building like a volcano. Thankfully her eyes were hidden behind a cheap pair of shades.

She started to wiggle out of his hold, but he didn't let go. Instead, one hand locked on her neck as he jerked her to him and kissed her hard. There had been no prelude to the kiss, no coaxing of lips, no whispered words. Just him.

For a moment, she sat stunned. But as his mouth plundered hers, something deep within her awoke. His tongue fenced with her, teased her lips, before darting inside to claim. Reaching up, she grabbed the side of his head, letting her fingers run through the thick mass of black hair. Their tongues parried and forayed. Aiden filled her thoughts. His hand loosened, fingers trailed down the side of her neck, his thumb grazing across her throat, then up to graze along her jaw line and something shimmered inside her. The kiss gentled, going from a screaming, heavy metal song to a calm, sweet, piano adagio. He tilted his head and deepened the contact. Shivers danced down her spine to swirl through her nerves. His teeth nipped at her lips before he skimmed them with his tongue. A sigh shuddered out of her.

Just as abruptly as it began, he pulled back from the kiss. His eyes looked down at her for a moment. Jesslyn licked her lips, blinking. Then, he only said, "You have a nice ass."

He hopped off her four-wheeler and walked away.

Chapter Seven

Jesslyn blinked. What? A nice ass?

She grinned. Guess he'd know since his groin had been nestled against her ass for the last fifteen miles. Laughing, she climbed off the all-terrain vehicle and followed Aiden to the water's edge.

He could kiss good, she'd give him that. Jesslyn absently wondered what he couldn't do good. All right, better than good, not that she'd ever let him know that.

Thoughts jumbled in her mind. A flash of a dream she'd had days ago, like smoke, too illusive to hold on to chilled her, but she shrugged it off. The wind blew through the trees, carrying the scent of winter still lingering in the air and a crisp aroma of pine, the smell of wet ground.

Striving for her best airline attendant voice, she said, "As your nice-assed tour guide, I feel I should tell you this is — drum roll please — Emerald Lake." She looked out over the placid water, still and calm, mirror flawless. "The color is a deep green edged in blue, as you can see. It has always reminded me of the Irish Sea, a color forever lost between blue and green." She waved a hand to the peaks surrounding them. "This time of year, the mountains still have snow banks on them." Thin narrow ribbons fought the heat and battled not to melt. Stretches of white played with the sunlight through breaks in the trees.

"Thank you for that informative lesson. Serene place. Quiet beauty. Not bad, Jessie girl, not bad."

Jessie girl? Why had he called her that? She wasn't about to ask him, but a little thrill shot through her at the sound of it. Which was absolutely stupid.

"Come on, there's something else you should see." She held out her hand towards him, and Aiden let her lead him where she wanted.

They walked along the shore and over logs that stretched over wetlands. Their shoes were silent on the ground until a wet spot sucked at them. Jesslyn tried not to notice how her hand tingled where he touched it, or how her insides felt like a million butterflies flitting about. God, she sounded like one of her damn heroines. It took a lot not to jerk her hand back, but then that would be really telling, wouldn't it? And she'd have to deal with that smirk of his. In short time, they'd hiked to the top of the knoll and stood in a clearing.

A giant fallen tree crossed the clearing, and was as tall as her waist. She climbed on top and balanced like a dancer, walked the length of the log, until it jutted out over the small cliff, hanging in the air, its old branches like deformed skeletal fingers. Then, she turned around and walked back towards Aiden.

As if he had all the time in the world, he slowly walked towards the log. For some reason it felt like a lion stalking the zebra. His eyes didn't leave her as he gracefully climbed upon the log and sat, one arm draped over a knee.

Aiden Kinncaid was entirely too sexy for her peace of mind.

And that kiss. She licked her lips and could still taste that spicy flavor of aftershave. God, she was pathetic.

Aiden started to tell her the spot was beautiful, but he didn't. A small smile played at the corner of her mouth. He didn't think he'd ever seen that particular expression on her face before.

"What are you thinking about?" Would she share her thoughts? He hoped so.

"Wouldn't you like to know?"

"Come on, Jessie girl." Jessie girl? What had possessed him to start calling her that? Aiden had no idea, but when it popped out of his mouth earlier, he'd caught the faint look of pleasant surprise and irritation on her face. Jessie girl. It fit her.

Aiden patted the smooth wood beside him. For moment she didn't move, then she took two steps and grasped the hand he held out to her, sitting beside him.

"I'm glad you talked me into showing you around."

Straightening, he leaned close enough to smell that light airy perfume she wore. "Yes, my persuasive powers even impress me sometimes."

She snorted.

He remembered the kiss that morning nearly a week ago, calm and innocent. The one earlier, pure complete hunger. Both made him want more.

She sighed and nibbled on her lower lip as he leaned even closer, only a touch from her. Aiden knew he made her nervous. He could see her pulse pounding near her collarbone. He wondered if that spot just there tasted as sweet as it looked. His gaze was drawn to her mouth, noticed she still held her lip between her teeth. Against her mouth, he whispered, "Let me do that."

He closed the remaining distance and kissed her, teasing her lips first with his own, skimmed them with his tongue. Then, he gently pulled her bottom lip between his own teeth. He heard her sharp intake of breath.

Neither of them touched, except for their lips. The seductive kiss was killing him. He wanted more and thought Jessie might too when she leaned into him and deepened the kiss. Their tongues danced, mingled, melded. Her teeth nipped his tongue and he grinned, running his tongue along the roof of her mouth.

Slowly, she pulled back and frowned at him. Had he expected a frown? Aiden didn't think so, but it wasn't surprising to him either. Lord, the woman could kiss. She tasted sweet as honey and seductive as a dark sultry night. Didn't she know what she did to him? That for whatever reason this wasn't some simple flirtation for him? And why should she? Had he told her? Told her hell, he'd only been with her for not even a week. It hardly mattered that this damn woman had all but haunted him since he'd met her.

They stared at each other.

"I don't know what this is, but it feels okay," she whispered with a confused look on her face, her forehead crinkled on a frown.

"Okay? Is that all? Well, hell, I'll have to do that again." He closed the distance again. This time his hands came up to frame her face. The soft silkiness of her hair tickled his fingers. He tasted again.

He traced her mouth with his tongue until she opened for him and he dove in, holding her still for his kiss. Her arm came up and wound around his neck, her other on his thigh as she leaned into him. The kiss went on and on. Her breath mixed with his and his with hers. He caught her moan in his mouth. Her hand squeezed his thigh and his breath stopped. Slowly her hand rose and rested on his chest. *No more than kissing*, she might as well have said.

He touched his lips to her chin, trailed a kiss down the side of her neck, and traced her ear with his finger.

Finally, she pulled back, resting her forehead against his. "Damn."

Aiden smiled. "Damn works for me."

"It would for you." She made to get off the log, but he grabbed her arm.

"Jessie."

She turned to him.

He took a deep breath. "I haven't been out on a date since I called off the wedding."

"Which was when?"

"Almost a year ago."

This time she pulled completely back and looked really shocked. "Oh."

He loved the way the sunshine teased the highlights of her hair, how her brows rose or furrowed above the rims of her shades.

Shaking her head, Jessie hopped off the log and started down the hill. "Come on, there's one more spot I'd like to show you and we may have to hike a ways."

Didn't want to get into a serious discussion, did she? Figured.

Jessie led the way down the steep trail. She wasn't paying attention and slipped, almost tumbled headfirst down the rest of the way, but flaying her arms, managed to catch her balance.

"Be careful!" Aiden snapped. Was she trying to break her damn neck?

Turning, she grinned at him. "Calm down. Lord, you're nervous. I understand. I bet it's from being with a model for so long, huh? Don't worry, none of my appendages are singularly or collectively insured. Unfortunately, my medical insurance and life insurance didn't see any need in insuring my arms, the short legs they gave me an estimate on, but . . ." She shrugged.

He glared at her and pointed his finger. "When we get down you're going to pay for that." Raising her brow she pertly asked, "Promise?"

Then the nit-wit quickly scampered and slid down the rest of the way and took off hopping through the dense vegetation. Aiden stood watching on the hillside.

When he reached the four-wheeler, she had it revved and ready to go.

Smiling wickedly, she told him to hang on. Spitting dirt and gravel into the air, the tires spun and in a time shorter than he would've liked, they were back on the otherwise nonexistent road. This time, they continued on past the lake.

Aiden enjoyed the breathtaking scenery, and not just the mountains.

* * * *

They finished washing the dishes in silence. They'd come back here to the house, after their sightseeing venture, and cooked pasta with tossed veggies.

"I hate washing dishes," Jesslyn mumbled.

"Yes, but since we've already done it, we won't have to worry about this later."

She shrugged. "I wouldn't have *worried* about it anyway."

He chuckled.

Jesslyn looked out into the night, thinking of earlier when reality crashed in. Chief Garrison had arrived, rather upset that she'd been out all afternoon. The guilt slid back into place.

But the break from everything had been nice while it had lasted, even if she felt like a shitty friend for enjoying herself, and not thinking more of Maddy. But if she did, if she allowed one moment of grief, it would swallow her. She knew that. Garrison had said nothing new about the case, but Chief had always been the closed-mouthed type.

Tonight, The Dime was still closed. She and Tim didn't even talk about it, just knew it was the thing to do. Then again, until they found another chef, it was the only thing to do.

Another headache throbbed behind her eyes. Jesslyn hung the towel over the back of the kitchen chair and walked into the living room, flopping down on the couch.

Aiden sat beside her. She was getting used to him being around and it had only been a week, not even really. What the hell did that say about her? Desperate? Dumb?

"You okay?" His arm slid along the back of the couch and his fingers flexed on her tightened neck muscles.

She tried to shrug him off. "Yeah. I guess so. I'm used to . . ." She trailed off as he settled his fingers on the back of her neck, massaging. A low hum slipped from between her lips. She sighed. "Your fingers are hypnotic."

He chuckled, thinking of all the things he could say on that one. Aiden resettled himself, leaning back against the mound of pillows with his legs stretched out, propped on the low fat coffee table.

"Here. I'll rub the tension out of your neck, maybe it'll help."

Jesslyn looked at him, her gaze running over him. "Yeah, and what am I supposed to rub in return?"

He only smiled.

She pulled her bottom lip between her teeth. Her eyes dropping to his mouth then back up to meet his gaze. "Your eyes are so blue. This close I can see dark midnight lines dance with blue as pale as glacier ice. Fascinating," she whispered, closing the rest of the distance.

"You like my eyes?"

She grinned. "I'm a writer. I just notice things."

Aiden pulled back and kissed the tip of her straight nose. Surprise, pain and passion melded in her eyes. He pulled her down so that her head rested on his chest, and started to massage her neck.

"Not to sound trite, but darling, not tonight. I have a headache."

He caught the smile in her voice.

"Too bad," he answered in a light, off-handed manner. "Don't know what you're missing." He found a particularly tight spot and deeply kneaded it.

"So you say. Ahh. That feels sooooo good," she drawled in her sexy little Texas twang.

A low chuckle escaped him. "That's what women always say to me."

She lifted her head, gave him a raised brow. "Before or after?"

Smiling wickedly, he pushed her head back around and asked, "Care to find out?"

Jesslyn, apparently, chose not to answer him. Aiden reached up and took the band off the bottom of her braid, running his fingers through her hair. It was as soft as he imagined it would be.

"You have a lot of hair." Her autumn mass was lush and thick, and danced along her shoulder blades.

"Yeah, and it's a pain in the ass. If I cut it, I wouldn't have nearly as many headaches."

He was busy thinking what a shame it'd be to cut all that glorious hair.

Pushing her back down, he answered, "You need to relax. You're tense."

"There's a news flash."

"Remarks like that will not get your shoulders rubbed."

Jesslyn asked in feigned fascination, "You do shoulders too?"

Aiden narrowed his eyes at her reflected ones, "Care to see what else?"

"Nope."

"Are you always so testy?"

She merely shrugged. "And here I was beginning to think you were such a sharp individual. Have I been any other way?"

Soft flutes from a Celtic CD floated on the air. The silence between them stretched as he worked the tight muscles in her shoulders and neck.

"You know, I might like you after all."

Frowning he said, "I thought you already liked me."

"Haven't decided yet."

He tried to rub away her tension and worry. His hands moved to a spot in between her shoulder blades, where she obviously put all her worries.

"Do you ever relax?" he wondered, and found the tension, hard as rocks by her backbone.

"Upon occasion," she said.

"And those occasions would be?" Her hair tickled the backs of his hands.

"Wouldn't you like to know."

Yeah, actually he would. Instead, he kept quiet. After a bit, he asked. "You have any other family?"

"A dad. He's in Idaho overseeing a housing job on a military base. And a brother. He's a lawyer back in Texas."

"Mom?" He wanted to know more about her.

Her back shifted on a deep breath. "Mom passed away right before Christmas."

"Damn, I'm sorry."

"What about you?" she asked.

"Four brothers."

"Four? Good Lord, your poor mom."

His hands rubbed down her backbone and she shivered. "Yeah, well, Mom's a retired pediatrician."

"I bet you're the oldest."

He smiled. "Why?"

"It's the only thing a CEO like you would be."

She was right. "Yeah, and then there's Ian, he's incognito. Gavin and Brayden are twins. Gavin's the ob-gyn we tease went into that business to find a wife. Brayden is the brooding antiquities dealer and last is Quinlan, who helps me out with the hotels the most."

"Doing what?" she asked, her voice more relaxed.

"Well, it's a family business. My granddad got into real estate, Dad talked him into hotels. Later it was resorts. And Quin and I came up with the Luxurious line hotels. We cater to the high-end client. Buy old castles, plantations, estates and turn them into basically high-dollar B&Bs with every comfort money can buy."

"Did you write the brochure too?"

Aiden laughed. "Not impressed."

"I'm more impressed with your mom."

He was too.

"So what about your dad?"

"Dad, Jock, is retired from the hotel business. Especially after his heart attack." She shifted slightly, tried to sit up, but Aiden pushed her back down. "Be still."

"Your dad, he's okay?" she asked, her words cautious.

Aiden frowned. "Dad? Yeah, he's fine now. Gave us all a scare. Why?"

"Mom. Heart attack." His hands paused at her surprising remark, then resumed working her tensed muscles. "Your dad was lucky," she added.

Aiden had been scared to death when he'd heard of his father's attack. On the long flight, he'd been fighting anger at the fresh knowledge of the useless loss of his unknown child, then arrived to find a sick father. His mother thought he took it all too hard. His dad had been fine, even if his child hadn't. Looking back, it had been one of the more difficult times of his life. And here was a woman who had lost both family and friend.

"I'm sorry about your mom. Damn, Jessie, where do you put it all?" He hadn't meant to ask that.

Silence descended but was broken when she sassed back, "My shoulders."

He sensed, more than knew, she didn't want to talk about it anymore.

Aiden continued to rub her shoulders and neck. Little by little, she eased. His hands gentled when he realized her breathing had evened out, and he thought she was asleep. Should he get up? She was half sprawled on top of him. Her hair was soft as silk in his fingers.

He should probably get up and let her sleep, but what if it woke her? She needed her rest. Besides, he didn't want to let her go just yet. He liked her right where she was.

He should get up and go.

On the back of the couch was a quilt. Reaching back, he grabbed the patchwork blanket. As easily as he could, he unfolded it and covered them both. He toed off his shoes, worried that the slight thud as they hit the floor would wake the woman asleep on top of him.

Aiden settled her more comfortably with him and then stared at the wood vaulted ceiling. He didn't know what pulled him and Jesslyn together, but he didn't care either. The aching notes of a pennywhistle played some Celtic song on the CD as he thought of what he would do tomorrow. Her scent surrounded him, that floral-citrus aroma Aiden assumed was her shampoo, the clean scent of soap, and something else. Inhaling deeply, he smiled. Sleep crept up on him even as he was planning to rearrange his schedule to include her.

* * * *

Jesslyn vaguely remembered the feel of something being thrown over her, of being shifted, but the engulfing warmth, exhaustion and two over-the-counter migraine pills pulled her towards the blessed oblivion of sleep.

And in sleep she drifted . . .

"Mommy. Mommy," an impatient little voice said.

She knew it was Hannah's, she'd recognize her daughter's voice anywhere. Jesslyn tried to find the little girl, but it was useless. There was fog, so thick she cut it with her hand.

The silence deafened. Almost. She heard the faint lap of water, the small trickling as it fell over stones. But she could make out nothing. The cold gray hand enveloped her. It smothered. She trailed her fingers out in front of her as if through water, leaving slashes in the fog that elusively joined back.

"Hannah? Where are you? Mommy can't see you." Try as she might, she couldn't make out a single thing. Jesslyn futilely tried again to push the swirling, smoked wall away, but she couldn't. It was like being in the middle of a cloud. A dark threatening storm cloud.

A giggle. Then just a whisper behind her.

In some part of her mind, Jesslyn knew this dream was different than the others. Something was wrong. The light was supposed to be sunny and crisp — spring air. The world around her was heavy, dark, impenetrable.

"Hannah?" She caught the tremor in her own voice. She had to find her daughter, but couldn't see the little girl. Jesslyn could feel her, the sweet innocence of a child.

There was something else in the fog. Something threatening. She sensed it. The hair tickled on her arms.

Danger.

"Hannah!"

"Mommy, be careful. He sees you."

Jesslyn spun around in the fog, though it was useless, only causing the cursed mists to swirl about her, like skeletal fingers toying with her, pulling at her hair.

"Hannah, where's your father?" They were usually all together.

A soft sigh.

"Daddy couldn't come. We weren't supposed to come yet. Daddy says to say to you 'it's about time.'"

What did that mean?

"Time for what?" If only she could see.

Another little giggle. "I asked that."

A moment of silence. "For you to laugh," came the answer in a child's wise voice.

Then, thunder rumbled in the distance heralding a vicious storm. The air changed, the charge crackling the breath she took, even as the fog began to lift.

"*Be careful, Mommy.*"

Goose bumps rose on her arms at her daughter's warning.

"*Hannah! Wait. Wait.*" *Jesslyn reached out towards the sound of her daughter's voice, but only grasped the tingling mists.*

"*Be strong. I have to go. He's close. Don't look at him. Don't smile, Mommy. Don't smile.*"

"*Who?*" *The storm, closer now, engulfed, drenching her.*

The mists parted, rose quickly as though someone snatched a veil from her eyes. There was a lake, churning, swirling. Waves battered at the shore. The wind howled around her, picked at her long strands of hair, pushed her towards the edge of the troubled water.

Lightning flashed and thunder crackled, ripping the world around her apart.

She could hear voices crying on the wind. Moaning, pleading, but she couldn't make out the words. She looked down at the choppy water. It calmed to a mirror surface. Her reflection stared back at her.

Jesslyn jerked. Her face rose out of the lake, dripping wet with water, running with blood. A scream ripped from her throat. Echoed in the trembling air around her. On and on it went.

"Shhhh. Jesslyn, come on. Wake up. It's a dream, wake up." A deep voice whispered in her ear. "It's okay. You're safe."

Safe. Aiden.

His voice calmed her fears. She breathed a deep sigh. A woodsy scent laced with spice filled her senses, relaxed her. The beat of a heart against hers drove the nightmare away.

* * * *

He'd waited and waited. The night gave him what he needed.

Silently, he crept through the forest, the way easily known to him. He went back.

At the edge of the trees he watched as the moonlight shifted across the lawns and he remembered the way it happened that night—the way she'd struggled.

Softly, the breeze ruffled the aspens high above his head. He hummed his favorite symphony, the discordant notes soothing him.

What was he to do? He'd prayed for answers, meditated, and nothing had come so far.

Even when he'd seen her today, he knew she didn't know who he was.

She'd only stopped for a cup of coffee. If he'd turned and left sooner, he would have missed her. He'd studied her, liked how her hair was braided, noted she was pale and tired and that the guard was still with her. She'd stopped at several places in town, the longest at the store.

She probably didn't see anything.

If she did, he wouldn't be standing here tonight.

But what if she remembered something? Some little detail he'd overlooked.

He was almost afraid. Yet, the giddy feel of exposure was surprising.

Everyone was so shocked. Why?

He'd rid the town of a Jezebel.

And it had been so simple, so easy. He'd known her schedule, watched her jog every morning through the woods, knew when she went to work, when she left. He knew what her dimpled smile looked like. He knew what it felt like to watch the life fade from her.

The breeze quaked the leaves above him again. It was quiet.

His pulse pounded at the memory of her struggle. The monster stirred at the sweet thought. How she tried to fight him, but it only took a moment to restrain her. One quick stab and it was over. The blood flowed, and a sacrifice was made. Four wounds. Four points. Forgiveness for folly. But he hadn't gotten them all done.

The other had come first . . .

He shuddered as the beast awakened. No, not yet. Not yet. He could control it.

He could. He had to. It was too soon. He could have avenged sooner, but now he'd have to wait. Another too soon would not be wise. Though if he were meant to kill again quickly, he would.

Maybe this was a new test, a harder test, in the face of adversity.

The community's cry for justice was almost a surprise. The outrage and sorrow. He'd done them a favor! Saved them from her. He sighed, shaking his head. They simply didn't understand, and never would. He knew that, so he shouldn't be surprised.

He hummed and wondered who would be sent to him next?

Or if she'd already been sent to him.

The problem with the possible one was that she didn't look like the rest, didn't act like them.

He looked to the other darkened houses.

If they only knew. A little closer and they would find so much more. Much, much more. The monster yawned. Last night's blood wasn't the first to spill, and it wouldn't be the last.

Chapter Eight

Jesslyn sighed and leaned back in the office chair. God, what a night. The Copper Dime was once again open. Well, closed now. They'd opened two days before, after finding someone to come in and cook until a permanent chef could be found.

Dishes clanged and rattled from the kitchen, crashing undoubtedly to the floor. Wonder how many they'd have to replace?

All things considered, the night, and the one before, had gone really well. She and Tim had called Connie, a stand-in chef, to help out.

But Connie wasn't Maddy. No one was Maddy, even if they followed her recipes.

The police talked to her some more. Chief Tight Ass was as closemouthed as always when she'd asked her own questions. Jesslyn knew T.J. and the chief were fishing for something, looking for something besides the obvious. She just wondered what the hell it was.

Yesterday the guard outside her house had been pulled and Garrison explained Maddy's death as a burglary gone bad. Maddy must have arrived home and interrupted the guy.

Even though he pulled her sit-outside-and-tag-along babysitter, the chief had warned her to be careful, to keep an eye out, and call him if anything else came up.

And she overheard T.J. mention Lotten. Lotten. Where had she heard that name before? Turning to the computer, she shook off the thought as another clang echoed from the kitchen.

Aiden had come in for a little while earlier. She'd missed him the last couple of days. Work often sucked. She'd have rather spent the days with him. But, he was trying to get his hotel up to standards as quickly as possible. She was over halfway done with her latest manuscript. Between the two of them, they hardly said more than hi in the hall or in the kitchen. Okay, maybe they exchanged more than hi. But, she'd still have rather spent the time with Aiden. They'd had so much fun the other day.

Grinning, she propped her hand in her chin. When was the last time she'd just had fun? Apparently long enough, she couldn't remember. He made her smile, made her laugh, made her want to strangle him half the time. They talked about everything and anything and nothing at all.

Connections. It was all about connections, and she felt more connected to Aiden than she had to anyone in a very long time.

The lake, the sun, the mountains. The kiss. God, could the man kiss. Her blood hummed.

And he knew how to give a great back rub.

What in the hell was with her? This was a guy. Just a guy.

And Everest is just a mountain.

With a muffled groan, she buried her face in her hands and smothered a laugh. She was out of her mind. What was she doing? No enlightenment suddenly dawned, but it felt—right. It felt good. Yeah, definitely good. At least, as long as she didn't start to analyze things too closely. Which she usually did sooner or later.

"Hmmm. Either you're pretending to scream at me over the numbers or I'm being egotistical again."

Jerking guiltily, she looked up at Tim and frowned. "The latter, I assure you."

Please don't let me blush. I've got a reputation to uphold here. No, I won't blush, I won't.

She was blushing. Jesslyn Black blushing?

Tim studied her face, noted she had circles under her eyes, yet she looked relaxed, and had seemed almost lighter the last few days. And what was with the blush? He didn't want to think about that.

"You okay?"

"Tim, I'm fine, really." She stopped.

"What?" he asked. There was something else.

"Nothing, never mind."

He came off the doorjamb and walked into the room, sitting in the chair. "What, Jesslyn?"

It was his serious, no-nonsense tone that got her to comply, or at least he liked to think so. She picked up a pencil and tapped it as she asked him, "You've known Aiden for a while, haven't you?"

Great, just what I need, two friends involved, plying me with questions. Tread carefully. "Since college."

"Is he . . . Does he . . . That is . . ." She sighed.

"Spit it out. I've never known you at a loss for words." This might be worse, or better, he amended, than he'd initially thought.

She took a deep breath and hurried through, "Does he do casual? I mean, is Aiden one of those rich men who finds someone to have fun with, no matter where they are? No, that's not exactly what I mean. I know he isn't that shallow. I just don't *know*. I mean, not since Jerrod . . . Arrrggg!" Jesslyn stopped again.

Tim wanted to smile. She was so rattled and that was so unlike Jesslyn Black, the ever-composed and shielded woman he knew.

"I don't know what I should feel. Am I just diving in without looking for the rocks, or am I missing a great swim because I'm too busy standing on the shore?" Her brows drew into a frown.

Tim started to answer her, but she trudged on.

"I like Aiden, Tim. I really do. I know it sounds absolutely crazy. We've spent a few days doing stuff together. Some guy I met about a week ago. Then, bam! I haven't felt more—I don't know—something." She waved her hand in the air. "Whatever it is, I haven't felt it in a really long time. He makes me laugh at nothing and I think about the next time I'll see him, even knowing he'll say something that will irritate me. I'm just nuts." Her sigh moaned out as she shook her head. "Maybe your long-standing advice is right."

"What advice?"

"I just need to screw somebody and then I wouldn't be so—so—whatever, with Aiden. That's probably what it is. Just lust. So I'll sleep with him, and life will get back to normal."

Timothy Kerrin tried, he really did, but he could no more stop the smile that spread across his face than the laugh that rusted out.

"Poor Jess. What to do. Whatever it is between you two, and whatever happens in the end, I think you needed this. Welcome back to the land of the living."

* * * *

Jesslyn bolted upright in bed, a scream trapped in her throat. Alone in her bed, she rocked. Oh God, that one was bad. Fog and mists, Hannah's warning in her ears even as she ran. She hated fleeing dreams. Jesslyn drew her knees up and laid her cheek on them and reached for her glasses. Air. She needed some air. Flinging the covers back, she all but tore out of bed and through the balcony door. The night chilled her, pricking her exposed skin. Jesslyn gripped the wooden railing, leaning onto her arms.

The cold predawn air chilled her exposed skin. Taking one last deep breath, she sat, like she'd learned in her class. On another deep breath, she tried to let go of the tensions.

Yoga was supposed to help her relax, help her maintain herself in the here and now.

Sometimes it worked.

Right now it wasn't.

On a sigh, she stood and tried to shake off the remnants of the dream. At least she hadn't screamed out. Or if she had, Aiden hadn't heard her.

Inside, she leaned back against the doors. Deep breath. Deep breath.

It's okay. No one lurked in the shadows here.

Idiot.

Jesslyn looked at the clock. Almost four. Great. Three whole hours of sleep. There was no way she was chancing sleep again tonight. She simply could not deal with another nightmare.

Hell. She grabbed a clean towel and decided on a shower. The hot steam warmed her, washed away the chill the dream shadowed over her, and made her wish, just for a moment, that she were with Aiden. Half an hour later, Jesslyn emerged dressed in another pair of leggings and a big shirt. She made her way down the stairs to the kitchen and turned on the coffeemaker. While the black brew sputtered and gurgled its way into the carafe, she clicked on the tube to a news channel airing live off the East Coast. Forget this. She'd go write, lose herself and her mind in the world she created.

An hour later, she shoved the keyboard away. Tripe. It was all tripe. Her fingers pinched the bridge of her nose. A glance out the window promised the dawn was coming. The sky edged the darkened mountain in pale, almost white yellow. Rolling her neck, she tried to relieve some of the tension.

On a curse, she picked up her cold coffee and downed the rest of it. Nerves skittered under her skin, made her edgy. What was wrong with her? The damn dream.

She paced her office, tried to settle her emotions. Finally, she gave it up. It was after five. One thought kept comforting her, that of a tall, raven-haired man with startling blue eyes.

No, it was too early to go beating on his door. She'd handled dreams before by herself and she would again. Besides, what would she say if he did answer the door? *I had a bad dream. Can I sleep with you?*

She could all but hear his response to *that*.

Jesslyn heaved a sigh. Forget stewing around in here. She needed to get out. She'd run every morning till Maddy died without a cop watching her. Some maniac was not going to change her life. The guy was here before and she'd jogged safely in blissful ignorance.

Here before . . .

That was it!

She stood rooted to the spot. Lotten. Lotten. A woman last spring died on the mountain. A tourist here skiing. Everyone thought it was a mugging gone bad. She'd been stabbed. And the police were connecting the two. Otherwise, why would T.J. mention the name? Damn. It was too early to go to the library. Sitting back down at the computer, she pulled up the local papers from that time.

There. Elaine Lotten, twenty-eight. She was from Kansas. What color of hair did she have? And why did that matter?

An image from her dream flashed unbidden in her mind. A lake, a storm. Blood. Chills raced over her.

She'd play stupid, go by the police station and talk to T.J. about something she remembered. She knew T.J. well enough to see if she lied to her, and considering what happened to Maddy, Jesslyn didn't think that was likely. Coincidence? No, she didn't think so.

Now her nerves were pumping with too much contained energy. Jogging. She was going jogging. It was undoubtedly irresponsible, but she didn't care. Besides, there were people already out and about walking, running, and cycling. There always were. People here took their workouts seriously. And since the trail was right beside the highway for the most, and on open land the rest, it wasn't like anyone could hide behind a bush and jump her.

Jesslyn ran upstairs and dressed. She simply had to get out. A few quick strokes with a brush, swept her hair up into a ponytail. On hands and knees, Jesslyn dug through the bottom of her closet till she found her tennis shoes. Sitting on the floor, she pulled out a pair of white socks from her bottom dresser drawer, put them on, then jerked on the shoes and tied them off.

Where was her MP3? The drawer of the nightstand yielded what she looked for. Now, if only she could find a good playlist. Something loud, fast, and metallic. No soothing tunes this morning. She wanted nerves to scream through the headphones as they did through her. After scrolling for a bit, she found what she needed. "Serious Running Tunes," she'd titled it. There were several artists on this playlist, metal bands from the 1980s. Poison, Def Leppard, Bon Jovi and loads of others.

Downstairs, she found her fanny pack and dropped her phone, wallet and keys in it. Once it was secured, she clipped the MP3 to it, adjusted the headphones and cranked the volume. Jesslyn stretched against the table, then bounded outside.

* * * *

Aiden watched from his bedroom window as Jesslyn jogged down the driveway, seeing which way she went. Her ponytail swung from side to side as she pumped along. And what the hell was she wearing? Skintight spandex shorts, a sports bra and some sort of little jacket.

He'd been up for several hours already. He'd sat up with his windows open, working on his laptop until he heard Jesslyn's pickup below in the driveway last night. Finally, he'd been able to shut down and go to sleep. Then, something had jerked him awake. He lay there listening and heard her out on her balcony.

What the hell was she doing? Jogging alone? The woman needed a damn keeper.

He hated to jog. Aiden knew he brought his shorts and tennis shoes along. He'd used them on the treadmill at the hotel gym.

A few minutes later, he was puffing along the asphalt. There she was. For a little thing, she had a good pace. She was almost at the end of the lane that led out onto the highway. Sighing, he started after her and realized she must do this often. Keeping an eye to see which way she turned at the stop sign.

The air was very thin up here. God, how in the hell did the woman do this morning after morning? Hadn't she heard the medical reports that running was bad for the knees? His lungs hurt, the chilled morning air burned as he gulped it. And he sounded like a chain smoker trying out a new membership to a health club.

At the highway, she turned right. When he got there, he realized there was a wide jogging trail several yards off the highway. Cars passed them, vehicles with bikes racked on the back, or the front, or the roof, heading to God knew where. Who in their right mind would spend the morning trying to ride a bike *up* a mountain? Hell, he couldn't even jog *down* the damn road. And it wasn't even *dawn*.

He caught up with her after a while, but he stayed a couple of paces behind her. He didn't want to frighten her. They plodded along, and he, thankfully, slowed his stride to match hers. Maybe he'd conquer breathing again before she noticed him.

Up ahead, he saw the park set amidst the bustle of early morning traffic. Jesslyn veered off the road, running down the sidewalk. At the slide, she turned around, probably to start back, but she looked up and saw him.

Her brow rose in question. Idiot woman! She'd never even known he was behind her.

Chapter Nine

Jesslyn froze, her hand fisting on her hip as she tried to catch her breath. What the hell was he doing here?

Her gaze traveled from his face with its narrow-eyed expression down his corded throat to the sweat-soaked collar of his T-shirt. He used the bottom of the gray shirt to wipe his face and she caught a glimpse of the molded muscles beneath. Black nylon shorts gave way to the length of his long muscular legs. When her gaze rose to his, she saw his expression hadn't changed. Reaching down, she clicked off her MP3, killing Bon Jovi's voice in her ears. She hung the headphones around her neck.

"Mornings here are great, aren't they?" she asked as she turned around and walked over to a water hydrant.

Cold water gushed over her cupped palms from the faucet she opened. The drink was wonderful and she splashed some on her face. Gesturing to the water, she stepped back while Aiden too drank straight from the gushing stream of liquid, the muscles in his throat working. Something inside her shifted and hummed at the sight.

Had to give the guy credit. He ran pretty well for someone not used to this altitude. In fact, she was impressed he hadn't keeled over yet.

The crisp air cleared her head of ghosts, focused it on the important things. Like the fact that she was alive. Alive and breathing and wanting to see Aiden.

He straightened, shutting off the water before he planted his fists on his hips. Still, a word hadn't passed his lips.

"I didn't know you jogged," she tried, lunging and stretching. "Generally, I like to jog alone." Though running with him would be nice too. She could watch him.

His scowl darkened.

"What?" she asked, straightening. "Didn't you have your coffee?"

He took two steps to her, never saying a word, his eyes not straying from hers. Jesslyn couldn't read the look in them. Pissed was her guess, but why?

His hands locked on her shoulders. What the hell?

Aiden jerked her to him, kissing her hard. Jesslyn was so shocked she just stood there. Blinking, she put her hands on his arms. The contact must have done something because he broke the kiss with a curse.

"What in the hell do you think you're doing?" he asked.

Okay. If she knew what he was talking about, she might be able to answer the question. Licking her lips she started to answer, but he cut her off.

"You're out here jogging. Pretty as you damn well please."

His hands were still on her shoulders.

"Thank you?" she tried. He thought she was pretty.

Rolling his eyes, he stalked away from her.

What *was* his problem?

"Care to share what's bothering you?" she ventured, climbing atop one of the picnic tables. She sat on the end, letting her legs hang off and swing to and fro as she stretched her arms up and leaned one way and then the other.

She saw his shoulders fall, then he turned around, and walked to her. "You shouldn't be out here alone, Jessie."

Looking around at the activity of people, many of them families, or women with strollers, she nodded. "Hmm. Yes, I always thought this was a dangerous place. A children's park."

"Damn it! This isn't a joke." His eyes showed all his emotion, they were blue flames. Yet his face looked calm, his voice soft. However, she connected with this man enough to know he controlled his anger. Well, most of the time. He'd been close to losing it earlier when he kissed her. Wonder if she could get him to seriously lose control? There was a thought.

"I never said it was." For the life of her, she couldn't see why he was so upset. And he was upset, calm facade or no.

"It might have something to do with the fact—in case you've forgotten, and I assure you I haven't—that a woman was found stabbed to death. Forgive me if I have a slight problem with the fact you want to carelessly traipse around the mountain with a madman, who knows you saw him, on the loose."

Traipse around? Where the hell did he get that? Forgotten? Maddy? Anger roared through her, but she tamped it down.

Aiden saw her eyes flash.

"Forgotten?" she strangled out. "I assure you I have not, nor will I ever forget. And as far as traipsing around—what do you think? I'm the little woman? I can't take care of myself?" She sounded incensed. Anger surged color into her cheeks. She sat at the end of the table glaring up at him.

God, the woman was a piece of work. Why was it every time he was worried about her, she got riled? And riled, she was damn tempting.

"That has nothing to do with it," he calmly reasoned.

"Oh it has everything to do with it. It's beside the fact dozens of other people were out jogging and biking, and I've been running here just about every day for the last three years. Without you here to protect me. I can handle my own." Her hands propped on her hips. "But that never matters to men like you."

"Men like me? What the hell does that mean?"

She waved her hand in an agitated effect. "Never mind."

"Oh no, you're not. What?" He crossed his arms over his chest. Aiden couldn't wait to hear her next comment.

Her ebony eyes burned at him in righteous indignation. "Men who control. Men who want everything their way or no way. Men who can't stand the fact that—that women don't always need a knight riding to the rescue. It screws with that innate sense of protectiveness or hunter instinct or what-the-hell-ever."

He slowly started towards her, his steps measured and exact.

She shifted as if to get down and snarled, "And as to having forgotten about Maddy . . . Go to hell."

When he stood in front of her, Aiden wedged himself between her legs so she couldn't kick him, punch him maybe, but at least his manhood was protected.

"You're right." He saw that remark shocked her when her eyebrows rose above those sinfully dark eyes.

"You're absolutely right. But it's hard for me to see a small woman, like you, and think of her at the mercy of some murderer. Now, don't get pissed, you are small. I like you. I like you a lot, and I don't want to hear from Tim that some crazy-ass decided he took a liking to you or decided you're a threat and used your chest as a damn pincushion. I tend to look out for people I care about, just as I know you do. And I apologize for the 'forgotten' remark. That was stupid of me."

"Still . . ." she trailed off. A moment passed, then another. The silence stretched. She bit her lip and he wanted to tug on it again himself. When she did that small little thing all he could think about was kissing her senseless.

"I'm sorry for flying off at you like that."

"What? I couldn't quite hear that?" he cupped his ear.

"I'm not saying you're right. I mean you are to be concerned, but you don't control me. Next time, simply be nice, and refrain from low shots."

Be nice? All he could do was stare at her. "I was nice. You're the one who—"

"No." She shook her head. "You sounded nice, but you looked mean. And I don't do mean," she calmly pointed out.

The woman was illogical. "You don't do mean? Is this Jesslyn Black we're talking about? That eats nails for breakfast and breaks the noses of lowlife sons of—"

"That was different."

"Didn't your mother teach you it was rude to interrupt?"

"My mother taught me any number of things and was probably disappointed I didn't take them all to heart. In any event, I am sorry I jumped all over you, but I don't do well with—"

He kissed her. He could no more stop himself than he could his next breath. If he didn't kiss her right then he didn't know what he would do. She still tasted the same—smooth and sexy, sweet and tangy. Aiden cupped the back of her head in his hands, his thumbs brushing the sides of her jaw. *So soft,* was all he could think, even as he deepened the kiss. Their tongues dueled in a battle of control. Deeper and deeper still, the kiss plunged.

He caught her moan in his mouth as her cold hands came up to steady herself on his chest. "You taste so good," he whispered.

"You don't taste bad yourself," Jessie murmured, nipping his bottom lip with her teeth.

He pulled back from her and offered her his hand. She took it and he pulled her off the table. "We're walking back."

"Yeah, altitude's a bitch, isn't it?"

Aiden kept walking, ignoring her jab. He linked her fingers with his as he asked her about the houses up here.

He glanced at her, noting again the smudges under her eyes, the tired expression. "Are you okay? Sleeping all right?" She licked her lips, but he kept on. "You got in kind of late. And, well, it's early."

Her eyes looked out over the mountain. Aiden stopped and turned her to face him. Bending his knees so that he was on eye level with her, he asked, "Jessie, what's wrong?"

She looked at him and for the barest of seconds, he thought she might actually open up. Her eyes locked to his and he saw pain, confusion, and fear in their depths.

It's all in her eyes. If one knew where to look, one could unlock her secrets. Aiden wanted her to trust him. She opened her mouth as if to say something, but quickly shook her head. He could all but see her pulling away from him. Damn it.

With no warning, she grabbed his head, pulling him down for a kiss. Her tongue demanded entrance and he let her have it. Just as quickly as it began, the kiss ended.

Aiden looked at her, trying to figure out what the hell was going on inside her mind. Leaning over, he gently kissed her on the forehead and re-linked their hands. His eyes traveled the length of her again and his blood rushed through his veins. Did she want to drive him mad?

The tight black shorts left absolutely nothing to the imagination. The zipper of her jacket was only held together at the bottom, allowing him an expansive view of her creamy stomach, the bottom of her sports bra grazing just beneath her breasts. Aiden's gut clenched.

Thoughts of her had intruded into his world for the last few days. Or rather, she more than intruded, she plagued him. He knew what Jessie kissed like, how she tasted sweet and sultry, as sexy as that drawl of hers. Her smell haunted him, that light airy fragrance mixed with her fruity shampoo, and his mind seemed lost on what it would be like to sleep with her.

He really needed to think about something else.

They walked on in silence for several minutes, having gained the walking path. Other cyclists, walkers and joggers made the traffic heavier than it had been earlier.

"Lots of people out," he said, breaking the silence between them.

"Hmm. I seem to remember someone mentioning that." She shrugged. "The Fourth tourists."

Again they settled into quiet. The lane to the estates seemed to take forever to reach. Almost to their door, he asked, "What are you doing tonight?"

"Why?"

An idea had been playing on his mind. Every time he was with her, when he wasn't. He had a blast with Jessie, but so far, it had been she taking him places. Aiden wanted to do something for her, wanted more time with her.

"What kinds of food do you like?" he fished.

"Every kind, just about. Chicken, steaks, seafood. Love Italian, if it's fixed right. Spicy Mexican. Just not Chinese. Never can eat it." She turned to look at him. He caught the movement out of the corner of his eye. Her voice held a note of suspicion. "Again, why?"

"I want to take you out."

He wanted to take her out? Jesslyn thought.

"As in on a date?" she asked.

One ebony brow winged upward. "You have a problem with that?"

She smiled. "No."

"Seven work for you?" His eyes ran over her again, darkening in their blue.

Want stirred in her. "That's fine."

They were at the house. A date. They were going on a date. A date. Oh God. Jesslyn started up the steps, but turned to ask him something.

Aiden grabbed her in a kiss before she could so much as utter her question, whatever it had been.

"You need to work on a slower technique," she mumbled.

"Later." His hands were everywhere. "What in the hell do you have on?" he mumbled against her lips, lifting her. Jesslyn wrapped her legs around his waist, her arms around his neck.

They fumbled their way up the steps and to the door. "Sports stuff." She licked his neck, tasted the salty tang of him.

"It's sexy."

Jesslyn laughed. "Sexy, huh?"

He kissed her, numbing her mind of everything but him. Pulling back, he looked at her, his eyes narrowing. He shut the door with a kick, turned and plastered her against the back of it.

God, his hands — they molded her bottom, kneading, caressing.

Jesslyn moaned, leaning her head back against the door as Aiden's mouth trailed a path down her neck, his teeth scraping lightly along her pulse. She tightened her legs around his back, gasped when one of his hands squeezed her hipbone, traveling up under her jacket to touch the bare skin of her stomach. A fire ignited somewhere inside her. A fire she thought was only ashes, long dead. But passion, like the phoenix, soared through her.

Turning, he walked with ease into the kitchen and sat her on the counter. She could feel the hardened ridge of him between them. With his nylon shorts and her skintight spandex, there was very little between them.

His hands explored, devoured, branded. Her skin felt on fire where he touched along her stomach, causing her abs to tighten. Her jacket was quickly tossed aside, as was his shirt.

And his chest.

Chiseled and sculpted, his muscles begged to be touched. A dark swatch of hair spread across his torso, down to a thin trail that disappeared at the waistband of his shorts.

She grabbed a handful and pulled him to her. At his hiss, she kissed his chest, licked up to the hollow of his neck, where his pulse beat furiously. He was salty from their jog, tasting vaguely of his expensive cologne.

He leaned down and kissed her, his mouth plundering hers, taking, and demanding more. His tongue brushed the roof of her mouth and she shivered, moaning.

"You're so hot," he mumbled into her mouth, shifting against her with his hips.

The storm swept her up and along. His hands. She loved his hands, the look of them, the feel of those strong, elegant fingers. Thumbs dove along her jaw, even as his fingers tangled in her hair.

"You drive me crazy." His eyes were as blue as September stones, intense as emotions swirled in them.

Aiden made her forget things. His mouth met hers, this time, nipping gently, coaxing and giving instead of demanding, his tongue teasing along the seam of her lips.

She could think of nothing but Aiden. Every sense was filled with him. His touch, the sight of his turbulent blue eyes, the smell of him, his cologne, that woodsy-spicy scent mixed with an essence all his own, the taste of him. Aiden overwhelmed her. His mouth moved to her jaw, her neck. His hands whispered along her rib cage, along the underside of her breast. His thumb twirled up and grazed her nipple. The moan she had been holding escaped on a sigh.

Those lithe fingers danced up her calf, up higher still to the edge of her shorts. His palm flattened out to rub her thigh. When he cupped her, pressed his fingers against her, her breath shuddered out. Aiden made her long and want. He pressed his fingers deeper, grazed one over the one spot that screamed to be touched. Her breath shuddered out and she whimpered. He pressed harder, deeper, flicked his finger again and she could feel her own heat and wetness.

That realization pulled her away from the euphoria of the kiss and she put her hands on his chest.

"Aiden."

He looked into her eyes, as though seeing into her very soul. One strong arm was wrapped around her back. His other hand slowly lifted from her, tingling where it had only been moments ago. Heat pulsed in places she'd forgotten existed. She almost pulled him back, but she didn't. She needed to stop. To think.

"I got," he licked his lips, "carried away. I apologize." His voice was deeper than normal. Low baritone notes swirling within a symphony.

She laid her fingers against his lips, and shook her head. She had to make him understand. "No. It isn't you. It isn't you at all, or it is. But only in a good way. It's me. I had to stop."

His eyes held hers and she knew how easy it was to get lost in the blue depths. Instead, she gazed at his chest. Though that wasn't any better, so she looked at his chin. "It's me. I like you. I really do. No, it's more than like." God, she sounded like a moron.

"I care for you. And that scares me." Better to just spill the truth and get it over with. She tried again, on a whisper, "The accident left me shattered in every way possible and it took me so long to find the pieces, let alone to try and put them back together. There was only Jerrod for me. Only Jerrod. I've never done casual, and quite honestly, I don't know that I could."

It was her turn to stop. Jesslyn took a deep breath. "I know it isn't fashionable to wait, but I can't just do sex. I'm not programmed that way." Though at present, her actions probably proved otherwise. "I need some time, Aiden. I'm—I'm sorry."

She felt more than saw his grin behind her fingers. Then he kissed them, flicking his tongue against her palm. She jerked her hand back.

"I understand, Jessie. I do. There's no need to apologize. There isn't anything to apologize for." He leaned over and chastely kissed her forehead, then her brows, her nose, her lips. "I had a great morning. I hope you did."

Nervous, she pulled her bottom lip between her teeth, nodded and said, "I did, yes."

"Don't go running by yourself, please."

She'd see. "I'll let you know if I'm jogging."

He stood back and pulled away. Aiden bent down, retrieving his shirt. "I'll be honest with you. I'd love to make love to you right now."

Her stomach danced, her breasts tingled.

"Right here," he continued, his voice lowing, "right now." He leaned a bit closer, narrowing his gaze on her. "I could spend the entire day in either one, or even both of our beds." Closer. "Both of us tangled and wanting." His breath whispered against her lips. "Both of us loving every single moment." For a moment he stood, staring at her lips, then his lids rose and he looked back into her eyes. He straightened. "However, I don't think that would be wise. I want you, but only if you want me as much as I do you. Thank you for being honest. I don't want you to feel pressured in any way."

Not pressured. She grinned and chuckled. Her heart was still racing. God what the man could do with simple words.

Jesslyn had expected anger and wondered why. Aiden was Aiden. Though, his words, like his hands and mouth, kept her blood surging through her veins.

"Both beds?" She slid off the counter shaking her head. "No pressure. Nope. None. Well, geez thanks for understanding."

He turned and stopped at the kitchen doorway. "Understanding is usually the easy part. It's getting you to open up that's difficult. No, don't apologize again. Let's leave it at the fact we both enjoyed what we were doing and open to the possibilities of other times like it." His dark eyes bore into hers before he walked out into the hallway.

She stood there for a minute staring into space. The entire day? In both their beds? Shaking off the thoughts, she hurried after him, watched as he walked up the stairs.

"Aiden." Not that she had a clue what she wanted to say to him.

He stopped, turning to her. "Our date. Seven o'clock?" His gaze still bore into hers.

"Seven o'clock."

She started to turn back into the kitchen, but stopped, watched as a small grin teased the corner of his mouth.

"Oh, one more thing." His voice could coax angels to sin.

"Yes?" she asked.

"I more than like you too. And I don't do casual."

* * * *

Still nothing. They knew nothing. A town this size and everyone knew everything about anything.

And nothing.

He was surprised at the disappointment that speared him. Which was ridiculous. If he were ever caught, he'd never be able to avenge again. That would be a true waste.

He hummed Berlioz as he walked in the morning air. It was rather chilly. Of course, most mornings here were.

He smiled at the man walking a dog as he passed them on the sidewalk. Flowers grew out of pots along the walkway. Early birds were out and about. Jogging, walking, cycling. Others were grabbing breakfast.

Soon, soon it would be time to hunt again. To punish and avenge.

Quietly he walked on.

He fingered the bracelet in his pocket. He'd pulled it out the night before, watching as the moonlight sharded off the glittering diamonds.

She'd been cold. Cold and heartless, he thought. Just like the stones. That's why he took it. They all deserved what they got. They should know better. Shouldn't be so immoral!

The stars had winked at him, as though they understood his secret. His fate. His destiny. His.

He patted the bracelet snaking in his pocket. The gravel crunched under his feet. The morning was alive with life and a soft wind stirred restlessly.

The innocent was what was standing between him and continuing. He didn't want to hurt her. Being in the wrong place at the wrong time was hardly a sin. But then God willed things to happen, the heavens aligned to influence things.

He sighed, still undecided about his witness. He might unfortunately have to rid himself of that worry.

He'd almost gone hunting last night, but he couldn't. Last night there hadn't been any screams, but then, there never were. Were there?

Chapter Ten

The golden champagne tasted tart on Aiden's tongue. He studied the woman across from him. What was she thinking?

"Will there be anything else, Mr. Kinncaid?" one of his waiters asked.

"No. Thank you, Noel."

He watched as she took another sip of the bubbling wine and sighed. Her fingers fidgeted on the stem of the flute. Jessie looked great in anything, as far as he was concerned. But tonight she looked — breathtaking.

Lord knew the air had all but stopped in his lungs when she'd come downstairs. Her long black dress skimmed the top of her ankles. It left her arms bare, the sleeves stopping at the shoulders in some black filmy see-through material that probably had a name, but he had no idea what it was. Whatever it was, it teased him with the veiled view of collarbone, the rise of her breasts, before it ended in the solid black material of the dress. The neckline fit tight along the column of her throat. She was more provocative in that than in a mid-thigh, skintight, body molding number. Though, come to think of it, he wouldn't mind seeing her in that either.

She'd curled her hair, pinned it up haphazardly atop her head. Tendrils fell down the back, around her face, softening the look. Did she have any idea what those wayward strands did to him? Had she left them down to purposely tease him? Knowing Jessie, probably not.

Her foot bounced back and forth, and he looked down to see the black high heel hanging from her toes. He absently wondered how much coffee she'd had today.

Stockings? His boot-wearing, jean-loving woman was wearing stockings. A grin pulled at his mouth as he set his drink on the table.

"What are you nervous about?" he asked.

Her gaze cut to him, and she uncrossed her legs, her shoe falling to the floor in the process. Aiden leaned down just as she did. Their heads knocked together as he picked up the shoe. Holding a hand to the side of her forehead, she snatched her shoe back.

"I'm not nervous."

She leaned down to slide her shoe back on, but he took it from her. Her ankle, encased in slick stockings, was smooth as he grasped it in his hand. He watched her as he held it. With one finger, he slowly drew up her instep, circled around her inside ankle bone. Her in-drawn breath had him grinning more. She pulled her lower lip in.

"Yes, you are nervous. I know you, Jessie girl. The question is why?" He saw the goose bumps on her arm. He started to say something else, but she pulled her foot away and grabbed her shoe, sliding it on.

Aiden straightened back in his chair. "You look absolutely lovely this evening. Have I told you that?"

Her eyes held his as she straightened. "Yes, but I figure a guy like you says that to all his dates."

"Nope, just the contrary ones."

"Try to soften them up?" She sipped her champagne again.

Aiden cleared his throat. "With your attitude, it's no wonder compliments are a shock."

Her look narrowed. "I bet you kept in compliment-practice with a model. A model. I'm the one after the model." She frowned. "Honestly, Aiden. You went out with a model, for God's sake. You were going to marry her. I'm certain she knew what went with what, could probably tell an Armani from a Versace at a glance. A woman who had Valentino in her wardrobe."

She was rambling. Jessie never rambled.

Aiden grinned and leaned up on his elbows. "Something against Valentino?"

"Only designer thing I have in my closet is a pair of Italian shoes that I probably bought on sale and hardly ever wear." She tapped her hand on the tabletop. She'd probably be pacing if they weren't sitting at a table. Energy in motion. He'd rather the energy be in motion *with* him or better yet, *under* him. Hell, *beside, on top of,* as long as it was *with.*

"My idea of dressing up," she continued, jerking his attention back, "is probably not yours. Dress up you say, and won't tell me where we're going. My idea of dressing up is a broomstick skirt and boots."

What the hell was a broomstick skirt? He couldn't hold it back. "Is that a skirt witches wear?"

She rolled her eyes. "Yeah, and you know what I'm about to do with my broomstick?"

Aiden tried not to laugh. "Sex toys. Now we're talking." She glowered and fell silent. He reached for her hand, lacing his fingers through hers. "You look wonderful, and no I'm not just telling you that. Quit comparing yourself to Brice. She doesn't come close to even a hair-width of what you are."

Her look softened and he caught the beginning of one of her one-sided smiles. Her sigh relaxed her shoulders. "Of course, I'm more than she is. We contrary, bitchy types usually are."

"Complex," he corrected.

"I can deal with complex." There was that grin that pulled at his gut. "Thanks for the compliment. I guess if you like it, all the time wasn't wasted then." Her head full of curls shook. "Do you have any idea how long it took me to get dressed? Lord, I feel like I'm back in high school or something. A week with you and I'm worried about clothes! I have no fashion sense."

He opened his mouth to ask what was wrong with her fashion sense, but Jessie trudged on. "And I went shopping. Shopping, for the love of God. T.J. said I needed something new. I hate shopping. I can't see what some women find so damn enjoyable about shopping for clothes."

He leaned back and simply listened to her ramble. She was nervous, whether Jessie admitted it or not. And when she was nervous she tended to chatter. She was opening up and talking without him having to pull every little thing out of her. Whatever was on her mind just seemed to come right out of her mouth. Must be the only time she let her shields down.

She might not think she had any fashion sense, but she looked damn good to him. The long silver pendant that hung nearly to her navel caused all sorts of ideas to pop into his mind. Preferably her wearing just the pendant, or maybe the hammered arm band around her upper arm. They both gave her a pagan look. Jessie's naked body dressed in nothing but those two pieces of jewelry gave him several lascivious ideas.

" . . . And it's not like this is my first date since Jerrod." Her words pulled him back from his fantasy. "I've had others. There was Tim's 'L' friend, but that's not important."

"What 'L' friend?"

One of the waiters came back and set platters of food in front of them. She waited until the person left, then waved her hand absently. "Leo, Lloyd. No! Lyonel. Lyle? Hell, I don't remember."

She was right, the man obviously wasn't important.

Aiden finished off his champagne and watched as she talked some more, the way her hands moved, the way she leaned forward to express a point.

He'd planned to fly her to Aspen tonight, but his parents called and wanted to use the jet to fly out sometime late tomorrow or the next day. So he sent it back to Maryland that morning.

This was working out wonderfully. He liked having her all to himself in his hotel. Maybe that was incredibly selfish of him, but so be it. The dining room was empty and soft music played from hidden speakers. A romantic evening for two.

At least he hoped to hell she thought the evening romantic. There was pressuring her and there was hope.

Didn't remember the other guy's name? By the time the night was over, Aiden knew there was no way in hell she'd ever forget his name. Or he hoped so anyway.

* * * *

Jesslyn admired the way Aiden talked, stressing a point by leaning forwards. Dinner flew by as they talked about dreams and hopes, his business and her writing, discovering small things about each other. Topics covered colors, people, moods, music, birthdays, any and everything.

She loved the way he was as casual, yet powerful in his suit as he was in jeans and a pullover. Aiden wore a dark suit. She knew enough to suspect it was custom made, and what the man could do to a suit conjured up all sorts of lustful ideas. The cobalt blue shirt matched the color of his eyes, and the multicolored silk tie, perfectly knotted, pulled the whole look together without making him seem too impersonal. In fact, she thought he looked damn appealing. Candlelight played over his features as they talked and laughed.

Being with Aiden was like nothing she'd ever experienced. She'd wondered where they'd go on this date. His restaurant, in his hotel again. What Aiden Kinncaid wanted, it seemed Aiden Kinncaid got.

Here he was in his element, at ease, gracefully confident. This was his world and he was the ruler. What did that make her? There was an energy that pulsed around them, an awareness. She'd done some deep thinking today after the scene on the countertop. She just hadn't told Aiden what conclusion she'd come to.

Better to just show him when they got back. She'd already rattled and prattled like a socialite. And if she tried to explain this to him . . .

Aiden sat watching her and she realized neither had said a word for some time. He had that small almost-grin on his face.

"I did some thinking today," she admitted, her chin propped in her hand.

"Did it hurt?"

She smiled. "Amazingly, not as much as I thought."

His eyes. She could get lost in those blue depths.

"What did you think about?" he asked, his voice deep.

"Lots of things." Jesslyn sighed, and turned her hand over when he reached for hers. "I decided no more."

"No more? No more what?"

She took a deep breath. "No more letting fear rule my life, no more feeling sorry for myself, and no more shutting myself in isolation."

Might as well get the rest of it out. He sat unmoving, and under that intense blue stare, she looked at the white tablecloth.

"I've thought about you all damn week. Ever since I saw you holding that stupid lamp in my bedroom." She chuckled. "You make me laugh, make me smile. Which, if you ask anyone, is not easy. You make me feel alive again." No, that was wrong. "I mean, you make me happy that I am alive, if that makes any sense."

She wanted to look up at him to see what he was thinking about all this, but she didn't have the guts to. "It's degrading knowing that I'm spending my life looking out the window at the world instead of living it. So I came up with a new motto while I was getting ready this evening. Want to hear it?"

This time she chanced a look up at him. The tenderness in his gaze stilled her heart for the barest of moments.

"What is it?"

Jesslyn licked her lips and took a deep breath. "Live a little."

Aiden's grin made his dimple peek out at her. "Live a little?"

She smiled back. "Yeah. I had what you might call an epiphany while I was getting ready, and that's the motto I came up with."

"Well, guess it's better than kick-all-ass, or something." He rubbed his thumb across the back of her hand. "What epiphany?"

She loved how he could keep enough humor in something so that she didn't get bogged down in the oil of depression. "I'm tired of being scared. Scared of wanting more, let alone going for it."

"What is it you want?" he whispered, his hand letting go of hers so that his thumb grazed her lip.

"You."

The corners of his eyes creased as Aiden narrowed his eyes, his gaze intense and weighing. Finally, on a sigh, he said, "I need to know . . ." he trailed off.

"Yes?" It wasn't like him to be at a loss for words.

"I can't compete with a ghost, Jessie. I'm me. Just me. I want you to know that." His hand holding hers again tightened and the angles of his face seemed to pull taut.

Ahhh. "Jerrod." Jesslyn shook her head. She leaned back. Where to begin? "Jerrod was everything to me." She squeezed his hand. "But, he's gone. I, better than anyone, know that. He isn't coming back. I'm here and I have a choice to pine for what was, what could have been or to live. I get to see him in dreams sometimes and that's good. It's like visiting with an old friend."

There was no humor in his eyes, no shock, no condemnation or pity. Just Aiden, his silent, understanding stare.

"I loved him very much. Part of me always will, what we had. But, life chose something different for me. I don't know what that is yet, but for the first time since I woke up in the hospital after the accident, I want to know what that plan is. I'll always wonder what might have been, on odd days. However, it doesn't change the facts. I've just tried to learn to live with it, tried not to become bitter and hard, though I guess I'm those things too."

"You're not bitter or hard." The deepness of his voice hummed along her nerves. "Rough around the edges maybe . . ."

"Rough edges, huh? If you're wondering if you have to compete with Jerrod, the answer is, no. You don't. You have to compete with me, and that's worse."

He pulled his black brows down. "What do you mean?"

This conversation was surprising in the fact it was so easy. It might not make a bit of sense to him, but it was to her. The path before her seemed so clear now. Well, maybe not clear, but for the first time in three years she could at least see a damn path.

Jesslyn nibbled on her bottom lip. How to explain? "I'm actually thinking of spending time with another man. Of being with another man. And I don't just mean—that is—it's not just sex. It's you. It's fighting, and laughing, and wondering what you're doing." Her finger absently traced a pattern on the tabletop. She stopped.

If she weren't sitting, holding Aiden's hand, she'd probably be pacing. This was so important to her, to get this said right, to make Aiden understand. Yet, she felt like she was screwing everything up. His eyes told her nothing.

"It's breakfast dates, evening meals. It's a kiss, or just a touch. I like spending time with you, like your smart-ass comments—don't know what that says about me—and when we're apart I wonder when I'll get to see you again. It's you." She leaned over and cupped his face. "You. I hope you understand that I want to move forward. I do. While I was getting ready for tonight, it hit me like a rock slide. I was spending my life missing out. And I don't want to do that anymore. You made me see that, or maybe I would have seen it on my own, but you made me realize it now." Jesslyn stopped to catch her breath, to try and gather her scattered thoughts. She couldn't read Aiden, wished she knew what he was thinking.

She shook her head. "Hell, who am I fooling? I'm scared. I want you to understand that whatever happens between us, there will be times I'll push you away. I don't mean to. It's just something I do when things are bothering me. I'm used to holing up alone. But, since you've come along, alone's become lonely."

There, she'd said it all. Hadn't she? God, what was he thinking? Silence stretched between them. Should have just kept her thoughts and ideas to herself. She sounded like some babbling desperate woman. From seconds to a minute. If he didn't say something . . .

A small smile played at the corner of his mouth, his eyes softened. "Are you telling me I need to be patient?"

Her breath whooshed out. "Since I'm an incredibly moody person, that would be a good assumption, yeah. I'll probably require more than you've got."

"More patience than I've got? Ah, Jessie." He looked at their joined hands, brushed his thumb over her palm. Back and forth. "I don't think so. I'm sorry if talking about this was difficult."

"No, it wasn't." She took in a deep breath, released it quickly, "I haven't felt this contented, this at peace in a long, *long* time. And believe you me, I have been searching. I needed to say what I did. I hope you don't mind. Does talking about Jerrod, about all this make you uncomfortable?"

Aiden shook his head. "I'd wondered if it would, but no. I wish I had met the man. He was one lucky guy." The hand holding hers squeezed.

"It was the other way around," she told him, relieved.

"I'd have to disagree."

Jesslyn leaned over and kissed his cheek, as his heart thumped against her hand resting on his chest. Her own heart felt as if a weight had been lifted.

She started to pull back, but he caught the back of her head, his fingers at the base of her skull, sending shivers down her spine. He held her there, half sitting, half standing.

His eyes this close shot little shocks of awareness through her.

"Thanks," he said, his breath hot on her mouth.

"For?"

"Talking to me." He pulled her gently closer. "I want to know every little thing about you." His mouth closed over hers and Jesslyn closed her eyes, losing herself in the moment, in the feelings his coaxing kiss evoked.

Okay, maybe she wasn't quite at *peace*. Peace was a little too passive for what she was currently feeling.

She pulled back, pecked his cheek and sat down.

Aiden motioned with his hand and in moments a platter of chocolate-covered strawberries and coffee were set in front of them.

He watched Jessie's eyes light up at the desserts.

"Can we take these back with us?" she asked.

"Ready to call it a night already?"

She only cocked a brow.

Well, he'd discovered his perverse streak the day he met her. "I want to dance first."

The music changed. Bluesy jazz came swaying out to the voice of Etta James.

Jesslyn grinned. "How did you know I like this music?"

"I know lots of things."

For a moment, they stared at each other. Then she placed her small hand in his palm, his gut tightened, and he led her out onto the small dance floor.

A love song swagged out on the air and she sighed, putting her head on his chest and wrapping her arms loosely around his waist.

"Are you enjoying yourself?" he asked. They'd talked about life changes, and favorite foods and everything in between, but he wanted to know if she really did like tonight.

Her dark chocolate eyes made him think that he'd rather have asked her to go upstairs with him.

"Need an ego boost already?" she asked.

He sighed, and wished it didn't matter that the easy talk with her was back to barbs. "Haven't had my proper amount today."

"Well," she said and grinned wickedly. "In that case, I guess it's only fair to tell you that I haven't had this much fun in a long time." Her head rested back on his chest. "Thanks."

Tonight with her was both wonderful and pure hell. He wanted to know what she thought about everything, but found a person generally more guarded than himself. Not that she was secretive or overly cautious, but he sensed that hesitancy in her, the way she often weighed a response. He couldn't figure out what it was about this small woman that beat at him like the tide against the rocks.

"Tonight is beautiful, isn't it?" she whispered.

He looked down at her, saw so much he wanted to claim as his and only said, "Yes, yes it is."

They stayed like that, she in the protective circle of his arms until the song drifted to a close. Another started and he kept her there with him as they swayed together. Their differences in height reminded him again how tiny she was. He often forgot. It must be her attitude. Her breasts brushed low on his chest and made him think of things he might want to steer clear of for now. Better not to rush things. Right now he could at least hope how the evening would end. Once they left, he'd have to face the fact that he'd promised not to pressure her. Hell.

Chapter Eleven

Jesslyn took Aiden's hand and pulled him up the steps. In his other hand was the package of strawberries and another bottle of bubbly.

The time had come.

Sink or swim.

Run or fall.

Bravery or cowardice.

Sex or not sex.

She grinned.

"What are you smiling about?" Aiden asked.

He pushed her back up against the front door. The handle bit into her back, but she really didn't care.

She swallowed the blithe remark and decided to go with honesty. Well, not really. "Just thinking what a lovely evening this has been," she finally answered him.

God his cologne, she could all but taste it. "This is stupid," she said.

In the porch light, she watched as one ebony brow arched sardonically. "What's stupid?"

Had she said that out loud? She licked her lips.

"Quit doing that," he all but growled.

"Quit what?" Smiling, she slowly licked her lips again.

He started to lean closer and Jesslyn slapped her hand on his chest, asking, "What are you doing?"

"Living a little." He started to lower his head, but she ducked under his arm and dug in her purse.

"We'll live in a minute. I'd rather do this inside," she muttered, nudging him out of the way and slipping the key into the lock.

His breath was hot on her ear and she shivered. "This?"

Thank God. The door opened and she all but stumbled inside. Real sexy.

She dropped her purse on the side table, moved out of the way as Aiden shut the door and put his armload down. With his eyes still on her, he discarded his suit jacket and tossed it over the newel post. He walked towards her and she backed into the living room. Aiden glanced at her, then behind her. Smiling, he strode past her over to the stereo, put in three CDs and punched some buttons.

Jesslyn breathed a sigh of relief. She could do this. More importantly, she *wanted* this. No. She wanted *Aiden*.

She turned around as Billie Holiday sang out about lost love. Jesslyn smiled. "You picked a good one." The CD was one of her favorites.

Aiden bent down and lit the logs in the fireplace. Jesslyn leaned against the wall and watched him as he poked at the logs, added more paper. The blue silk shirt bunched and stretched over the muscles of his back. Finally, the blaze caught and roared to life. The fire poker clattered as he sat it back into its stand.

"You want to dance?" she asked, pulling her bottom lip between her teeth as he stared at her. Then slowly he walked towards her.

"In a manner of speaking," he said, his voice deep rich velvet.

Aiden wondered if he was rushing things as another song started on the stereo.

Stopping in front of her, he wondered how to put her at ease. She stepped the last step to him and laid her head on his chest. Moments passed and he only held her, felt the rapid beat of her heart high against his stomach.

She seemed nervous and was absolutely beautiful. Aiden pulled back and watched as the firelight danced shadows across her face. Earlier when he'd first seen her on the stairs, he'd thought his idea of giving Jessie all the time she'd need might be the end of him. Her whispered words tonight were sweet and precious and humbling. He had an idea what her confession had cost her and it amazed him.

Aiden didn't know if it was the candlelight, the music, or the grace of God, but whatever the reason Jessie had let him in, had opened up to him, he was thankful. Her almond-shaped eyes watched him, black in the low light. Aiden leaned down and did what he'd wanted to all evening. He kissed her, the way he'd wanted to kiss her.

She leaned up on her toes to meet him and he was smiling at that as their lips met. Her lips were soft and warm. His arms wrapped her to him as his tongue played along her mouth. When hers opened under his teasing, the kiss deepened, turned from one of gentle restraint to heated passion. He could taste the sweet of the wine she'd been drinking earlier. Her tongue danced with his. Aiden wanted more. His hand got lost in the silk tresses of her hair, removing the pins so it fell down. He loved her hair down.

Pressed against him as she was, her soft curves taunted him. Her hands fluttered against him, ran the length of his arms. Her moan pulled his thoughts back to where they were.

He gentled the kiss before breaking it.

"I want you. But only if . . ."

Her fingers against his lips silenced him.

"Aiden. Shut up. You CEOs think too damn much. Kiss me."

He did. This time he picked her up, plundered her mouth as a sigh escaped her. Her hands clasped his head. Her cool fingers tickled along his ears, smoothed down his jaw, traced up his hairline. Blood raced through his system, heated and hurried. He broke the kiss again to see where they were going. Just his luck, he'd fall over the coffee table and break both their damn necks.

Carefully, he lowered her to the plush rug in front of the crackling fire. Jessie kissed his neck, her tongue trailing a line of heat to flick his earlobe. The rough edge of her teeth scraped the sensitive flesh. Yes, the bedroom was too far away. This was good. Great.

They ravaged each other with their mouths battling, giving, yielding to the onslaught of emotions raging through them. He ran his hands over her, the soft, silky material of her dress gliding between them. He laced his fingers with hers, pulling her hands up above her head. Laying atop her, he pressed her to the floor, but was careful to support his weight as to not crush her. Her breasts rose and fell, the filmy material lower than it had been before. He leaned down, licking the slopes of her breasts through the sheer material until it stuck to her. She sighed, whispered his name.

He caressed down the insides of her arms, noting how she shivered as his fingers grazed over the inner part of her elbows. He watched her eyes watching him as he ran his hands all the way down to cup her breasts. The bra under the material was thin, the edge of the lace peeking over the solid bust line of her dress. He could feel her nipple growing.

Smiling he watched her, as he circled his thumbs, caressed, and weighed. Her breath froze when he finally flicked, and gently pressed the distended peaks.

He ran a hand down her taut stomach. Aiden pulled her skirt up, ran his hand up her stocking calf, her hose whispering against his hand. Up higher still to the lace tops of her hose.

Garters. He paused. The woman was wearing garters. Silky stockings were sexy in and of themselves, but garters . . . He slipped one finger under the band.

He moaned into her mouth and her lips curved into a smile beneath his.

"Thought you might like those," she whispered, grasping the side of his head, plundering his mouth with a mind-numbing kiss. Her tongue battled his, her fingers pressed into the back of his skull. He wanted to cherish, to make this last, but the woman was making him forget.

Too fast. This was all going too damn fast.

But her hands were everywhere, pulling his shirt from his pants. One of her chilled fingers hooked inside the band and skimmed along his waist, smoothed along his ribs.

His gut clenched as her hand flattened and smoothed down to his groin.

"God, Jesslyn. I want to go slow."

"Slow is for later. Now."

Aiden pulled back to look down at her. "How the hell do you get this dress off?"

Her grin was wicked. "Let me show you." Quickly she stood and began to hurry.

"Stop."

She froze one arm free, the other halfway out. "Why?"

"Slow down. I want to watch you undress for me."

A slow catlike smile spread across her lips and tightened more than his gut. The music slowed and deepened, became grittier as Holiday sang about love. Jesslyn swayed to the music, smiling that come-and-get-me smile. Slowly she drew her arm up until it was free, rotated her hips. The dress slipped from her and fell in a pool at her feet.

Good Lord. The woman was wearing black. A black lacy see-through bra, garters and hose. And stiletto screw-me heels, complete with the silver pendant and arm band.

His gaze rose back up and stopped midway. He swallowed even as his blood heated even more. "You're not wearing any underwear."

Her brow cocked at him, she propped her hand on her hip, and stuck one leg out. "I'm living a little. Besides, panty lines aren't good, ya know."

Aiden reached out and ran his hand up the stockings again, up to the garters. He leaned up, ran his hand up the inside of her thigh. He felt her heat before he even touched her.

She moved away, but he jerked her back down beside him. "Living a little? More like torturing me."

And torture it was.

She was so responsive, so giving. His hands skimmed along her smooth creamy stomach. The pale skin contrasting to her undergarments.

He leaned over and kissed her stomach, flicked his tongue around her navel. She shuddered.

God he was making her crazy.

His hot wet mouth moved higher. He licked the outline of her bra, trailed his teeth along the edge of the black lace. His fingers were quick and deft, swirling around and around, until finally they touched her nipples. Jesslyn couldn't help but moan. He suckled her through the lace, the material abrading her gently, making her want more. Lying as he was, his pants were a contrast to the tops of her naked thighs, to her core.

"You surprise me, Jessie girl. As much as I do love this look, I want these off of you."

Their hands tore at clothing, tossing barriers aside. Finally, skin met skin and his groan mixed with her sigh.

Hot breath skittered against his cheek as he kissed her throat. He wanted her here and now. His fingers again teased, tormented until she was all but begging. His mouth, tongue and teeth drove her up and close to the edge, before stopping.

She grabbed him. "Stop teasing me."

His grin was wicked. She felt his hand warm and gentle, yet determined on her thigh. Higher and higher and . . .

He cupped her, she arched against him.

God, she wanted him now. Immediately. "Now, Aiden. Now."

The man sparked a fire in her, and she had no idea it would be this inferno. Consuming, scorching, demanding to be quenched.

His chest was hard and muscled beneath her hands. She ran her fingers up his neck, to trace his mouth, before she pulled him back down for a kiss. His fingers trailed from her navel to her breast. Slowly, leisurely, torturing. Aiden was driving her to the brink.

Finally, finally, he touched her. Lights dimmed and swirled behind her eyelids as his fingers began their magic. He teased and fondled, making her wet and wanting. He circled and avoided touching the one spot. The one . . .

Finally, he pressed against it, just as he pierced her with his fingers.

"Oh, God."

He found her hot and ready.

Later, later, they would go slowly. He reached over to his pants. Thank God they were right there, and pulled out a condom. Slipping it on, he turned to Jessie.

"Later I will make you beg. And in the damn bed."

Jessie wiggled next to him. "Forget the damn bed."

Her cool hand wrapped around him and he thought he'd lose it then and there.

Aiden rolled and pinned her beneath him, entering her in one swift thrust.

"Yes!" She convulsed around him, squeezing tighter and tighter.

He thrust once, twice.

Her mouth found his, his hers, and together as though a fire consumed them, they exploded.

* * * *

"Next time, we're making love in the bed," he whispered against her throat. "My way." Her pulse beat against his lips. He kissed the warm throbbing skin. "Over." He kissed up her neck. "And over." Reached her mouth and whispered against her lips. "And over."

A husky laugh caressed him. "That sounds nice."

Aiden carried her up to the master suite, lit with dozens of candles. He looked at her and grinned.

She shrugged. "T.J. wanted tonight to be special. You think I own lots of garters? I needed some damn help here."

He laughed.

Her brows rose. "Arrogance is not a virtue."

"So I've been told. What would you have done with all these if I hadn't let you have your way with me?" he asked.

"Let them gut out and try again tomorrow," she told him on a smile and throaty chuckle.

"Contrary and persistent. You're starting to sound like a CEO."

Another throaty chuckle answered him. "Persistence. You have that too? My, what qualities."

"You haven't seen my best yet." He sat her on the bed. "Now it's my way." Aiden bent down, teased her with his mouth, kissed her until they were both gasping for breath. Her hands were as busy on him as his were on her.

They both laughed and tangled again. Jessie might be small, might appear composed, but she was consuming him. Her skin, smooth and soft, so pale he could see the blue of her veins, glowed in the candlelight. This time he would go slowly, notice those small details. Her tongue darted across his, promising, teasing, then demanding.

Two could play this game. He grabbed her to him and rolled across the bed, pinning her beneath his weight. His hands skimmed up and along her ribs, ran the undersides of her breasts, trailed along the sides. She was as soft as silk beneath his fingers. Her nipples were puckered, a soft pink against the paleness of her breasts. He ran his fingers around them, circling, circling . . .

She arched against him.

Jesslyn was lost in the feelings flooding her. Aiden's chest was wide, sculpted, and tan. The dark hair spread, tapering down to a trail. She wanted to feel all of him against all of her. Touch to touch, body to body. His lips and tongue were robbing her of any thought. Those long fingers of his, strong and deft, played along the top curve of her breasts. Teasing, taunting.

She watched him as he watched her. He traced one finger, dark against her breast, around and around. Then lowered his head, the candlelight glinting off his black locks like sun on a raven's wing. His lips covered hers and Jesslyn gasped as his chest met hers. Aiden was hardened planes and angles.

As flesh met flesh, Jesslyn's hunger grew. She could feel him hard and ready against her leg. His hands were magical. Aiden kissed her throat, her neck, suckled at the hollow of her collarbone. Her fingers speared through his hair. Soft was all she could think. Then, he lowered his head to her breasts and she couldn't think at all. A moan strangled from her throat. His mouth, warm and wet, made her forget her own name, and sparked a pull deep within her. His teeth grazed the tender skin of her breast, scraping against her nipple before he suckled her hard. She gasped and arched again. He kept up the torture, then turned his attention to the other breast.

Again his tongue and teeth had her moaning.

He continued his journey. Kissing every inch of her. His mouth blazed a trail down to the very center of her. His hands spread down each thigh, squeezing, kneading. He ran his thumbs back up the soft insides of her legs. Jesslyn trembled. His thumbs grazed over her, probed. Grinning wickedly, he leaned down and whispered against her.

"Over." He spread her lips with his thumbs, and mumbled again, "And over . . ." He licked her.

She shivered. "Aiden."

"And over." His cool thumb ran the length of her womanhood just before he laved her with his warm tongue.

The contrast arced through her. When his tongue darted out and flicked against her tiny bundle of nerves, she would have leapt off the bed, but he anchored her with his hands at her hips. She tossed her head from side to side. Wanting more, wanting him to stop, dying if he did. He pulled her clitoris between his teeth just as his finger entered her.

Jesslyn screamed.

His hands and mouth sharpened every nerve ending in her body. Jesslyn couldn't think, could only feel, only accept. His fingers trailed a path of fire along their course.

"Aiden."

The way she gasped his name almost made him forget he wanted to go slowly, to savor, to cherish. He wanted to love her, watch her, taste her. Taste more of her. Salt and honey. She was the most beautiful woman he had ever seen, and she was his. He worried he might have hurt her earlier downstairs, not taking time to ease her, but she clasped his head, surging up to kiss him.

Now was all that mattered. Not yesterday, not tomorrow. Now. Here. Them. Those tiny sounds in the back of her throat fed the fire blazing through his system. His fingers still moved in her, hot and slick. She shuddered beneath him. He had never felt like this. A flame licked through his veins. A need roared through him, clawing to be appeased. Her small hand reached down and clasped him, her fingers cool around his erection.

Aiden groaned.

"Jessie, girl." He broke their kiss and she fell back against the bed. "I can't wait," he hoarsely whispered, his forehead against hers.

"God, I hope not." Her eyes were dark, clouded with passion.

He reared over her, never took his eyes off hers. "Look at me. Only me."

"Only you." Her hands cupped his face.

His hands skimmed up her rib cage, over the undersides of her arms, stretching them above her head. Their fingers linked. One thrust and he was gloved in heat. Perfection.

"Only you," she repeated as he began to move.

And he was lost. When he saw her eyes darken, felt her tighten around him, he let go and tumbled with her over the peak.

They both lay breathless. Jessie's heart pounded against his, the only sign they still lived. He must be crushing her into the mattress.

"When I know I'm alive, I'll move," he mumbled into her hair. The fruity smell assailed his senses.

She wrapped her arms around him and rubbed the back of his calves with her feet. He was surprised at his reaction to that.

"No, stay still just for a minute." Her warm soft words teased his ear.

Aiden balanced up on his elbows and looked down at her. God she was beautiful. "I'll crush you," he said, made to move.

"You weren't worried about that earlier." Her grip on him tightened

He narrowed his gaze at her. Her cheeks were no longer pale, but blushed. Those warm lips of hers were rosy and slightly swollen from his kisses. And all that glorious hair spread about around her. Aiden smiled. "No, I had other things on my mind."

"Is that what I was on?" she sassed with a cocky grin.

Aiden rolled, pulling her with him so they were still joined with her astride him. "You are now."

A slow catlike smile spread as she leaned forward. Her hair tickled across his chest, curtained around them as she leaned down and whispered against his lips, "So I am."

* * * *

Jesslyn lathered her hair, singing one of the songs from earlier in the evening. It was well after midnight, and Aiden had taken off downstairs to get them food. She was starving. She was exhausted. She was exhilarated. The hot water from the shower steamed up around her. For the first time in a long, long time, she was happy. Content. Humming, she sluiced the water and shampoo away.

She hummed a song, forgetting the words.

"What are you singing?" asked a deep voice. Jesslyn started, opened her eyes to see Aiden step in with her. Then her eyes started stinging.

"Ow. Dammit! I know we've had this discussion before." She turned around to let the water hit in her face, rubbing at her eyes.

Aiden's arms wrapped around her, his hands moving up to cradle her breasts. His teeth skimmed her ear, the side of her neck, sent shivers down her, a contrast to the heated water hitting her.

"What's that?" he murmured

"Huh?" God, she couldn't think when he was nibbling on her ear. Hell, when she was anywhere near him, let alone when he was with her, naked, heated and wet.

"What have we talked about?" he whispered. His tongue trailed the edge of her ear.

Jesslyn sighed, shuddered. Oh, yes. "You—You sneaking up on me."

"Hmm." He nuzzled her neck, his hands lathered in the bar of soap.

Jesslyn turned around to face him. Had God created a more gorgeous man? A perfectly muscled torso, washboard abs. She liked those abs. Wanted to do all sorts of things to them. Like maybe lick every perfectly outlined muscle . . .

"I was about to get out," she told him on a sigh.

"Not yet." His hair was wet, and the water ran over his perfectly sculpted body. The promise in his eyes turned her insides to liquid.

Tiles cooled her back. Water sprayed on them. Steam rose, wrapped them together. Jesslyn pulled on her bottom lip, slowly let her gaze travel from his eyes, to his toes and back up.

"No, maybe not yet," she whispered.

Aiden's eyes watched her as he set the soap aside.

Jesslyn took her eyes off his mouth and looked at his sud-lathered hands.

"What's this?" he asked, tracing a line on her lower abdomen.

She didn't need to look to see what he was pointing to. Her scar. The cesarean scar from when they'd taken Holden from her after the accident.

Taking a deep breath, she only said, "A scar."

Then she reached for his hands and took some of the suds from his onto hers.

His gaze narrowed as he studied her face, but then he shrugged and said, "I thought I'd wash your back." His slick hands moved over her, down her. "Then you could wash mine."

She never took her eyes off of his, even when his hands began their onslaught on her body. Water ran down his taut muscles in wavering rivulets. Suds lathered on her breasts, dripped off her nipples as he brought them to peaks, caressing, sliding his fingers on her.

Stretching, she found the soap, slathered her own hands, even as her breath hitched.

His eyes never left her as his hands moved downward, further, further.

Those long fingers found her, parted her, pierced her. On a sigh, she leaned back, the soap slipped from her fingers, clattered with a dull thud against the floor. She put her hands on his chest, swirled the pattern of soap into his dark hair. A low moan bounced in the echoing confines of the shower. Was it hers? His? Did it matter?

"That's not my back," she said. There was his heart-stopping smile. Her hands raced down his body, wrapped around him. She cradled him in her hands, moved her slick, lathered hands over him. Then she dropped to her knees in front of him. The water sluiced over her. She looked up at him through her lashes and leaned in, taking him in her mouth.

Aiden's breath caught, held. His cobalt eyes darkened, bore into hers.

His deep husky voice answered, "And that's not mine."

* * * *

Jesslyn stood by a fog-shrouded lake. The water lapped in the cold wind, churning and boiling. Mists rolled around her feet, tangling the ground beneath her.

"Mommy, be careful." Hannah's voice, whispered around her.

Where was her daughter? Lightning flashed a jagged streak across the blackened sky. "Hannah?"

"Mommy, be careful."

Thunder rumbled through the mountains, ricocheting and vibrating around her.

Something charged the air, tension so thick it was palpable. On the hill sat a car. Was someone in the white vehicle? Rain began to fall, blurring Jesslyn's vision.

Then she stood beside the car, looked down the hill to a Jeep by the water's edge. What was she doing up here?

A whisper of something close to her. Dark, dangerous murmurs growled in the air. A chill stole over her.

"Mommy, noooooooo." Hannah's voice faded into the moaning wind that pulled at her hair like angry claws. Jesslyn leaned down and peered into the window.

Hair, crystals and beads, cascaded in one long woven wave against the woman's left side and back. The woman wasn't moving. Nothing moved or stirred, yet Jesslyn could feel the air all but breathe around her. Waiting . . . waiting . . .

Goose bumps rose on her arms.

She should go back to the Jeep. But what if something was wrong with the woman and Jesslyn could help her? On a sigh, she opened the door. The woman still didn't move. Jesslyn tried to shake her.

The woman started to fall out of the car, and Jesslyn instinctively tried to catch her. Wet. The woman was wet. Jesslyn shoved the woman back into the seat, her head lolled to the side. Dull green eyes stared sightlessly back at her. Jesslyn stumbled, a cry locked in her throat.

Lightning flashed. The air around her pulsed. She looked down. The wide silver band of her watch caught the bright light. Red. Blood.

Her palm was covered in blood. Rain began to fall, fat, large drops crying from the heavens like tears, splattering in her palm, washing the crimson stains away.

"Mommy, hurry. Hurry. Run!" Hannah's voice.

Jesslyn looked around. The darkness was impenetrable, but alive. She skidded and slid down the hill. The more she tried to hurry, the slower she went. The coppery smell of blood surrounded her. Fog caught her heels, held her when she tried to flee.

"Please," she begged, pulling, hurrying, terrified.

She heard a growl, low and feral. The sound children fear from under their beds. The sound of monsters.

Moving, Jesslyn finally managed to reach the Jeep. Slowly, so slowly as though the fog swirling at her feet held her in its clutches.

She hopped into the Jeep as lightning flashed. Thunder crashed around her, shook the air, and ripped it apart.

In the Jeep. Safe in the Jeep. Jesslyn was shaking. Terror tore at her as fiercely as the monster stalking her. Then she heard the noise. Right behind her.

"MOMMY!"

The blackness swirled around her. Pulled her in different directions. Grays, bright whites, deep crimson reds. Cold. It was so cold.

She couldn't see. Noises. Humming. Something or someone was humming a familiar tune. White against her eyes. Then the reverberation of thunder tumbled down the mountainsides.

The choppy sound of lapping water filtered through. Cold, she was so cold.

Movement. Floating. Sinking. Why couldn't she see? Where was she? Where was Hannah?

"Mommy. Wake up. Wake up. You have to hurry. Hurry. Time's running out."

The cold got worse. It froze half of her. Where was she? Jesslyn focused on what was around her.

A boat? No a dashboard, but water was everywhere. Rising. Quickly rising.

Like a lover's hand, the water caressed her face. She couldn't breathe. Couldn't breathe. Her lungs burned.

Freezing. It was so damn cold she couldn't feel her feet, or her hands.

Lightning flashed above her, far, far above her. Swirling around. Why couldn't she breathe?

Underwater.

"Mommy hurry, hurry. There's not much time. Harder. Don't give up."

Too far. It was too far. Something pulled at her.

Then the cold murky water gushed unmercifully into her lungs.

* * * *

A choking sound woke him. He sat up. Jesslyn.

She moaned and pushed against the air. Strange gurgling sounds came from her throat as she thrashed about in the tangled covers. Just as he reached down to take her arms, she sat up gasping for breath.

"No!" she all but screamed out, trying to throw him off.

"Easy, honey. Easy." Aiden wrapped her in his arms. "Come on, now. Come back."

Her chest moved in hard fast pants. She was freezing and trembling.

Cold fingers curled against his bare chest. He rubbed his hands up and down her back trying to calm her down.

"Jessie. Jessie, it's okay. You're okay. You're safe, here with me. Come on, talk to me. What did you dream?" he whispered against the top of her tousled hair.

She clung onto him as though he were her lifeline. The trembling was so bad he wondered if her bones would snap.

"I couldn't breathe." She panted against his chest, her breath warm. "The surface was so far away. I knew I couldn't make it. The water was so cold, so cold." Her jagged whisper was so soft, Aiden strained to hear. "I didn't get away from him. The fog wouldn't let me get away."

Fog? Water? "Wouldn't let you get away from whom?" he asked her.

"The monster. The killer. He was there and I couldn't get away. Behind me. Then the lake. I couldn't get to the top. The water just came gushing in. I couldn't breathe. Couldn't breathe. Hannah kept telling me to hurry." She shuddered against him, tightening back up almost into a ball in his lap.

"Shhh. Shhh. You're safe. It was just a dream." He rocked her, tried to comfort her even as her words sent a chill down his spine. No wonder the dream scared the hell out of her.

Aiden continued to rub her back. When the trembling finally calmed to occasional shudders, he pulled her back and looked into her haunted eyes.

"Hey," he said, cupping her face in his palms. "I'm not about to let anything happen to you. It wasn't real."

"But, I've dreamt it before." Her brows furrowed in thought. "Three times now, or maybe four. It's hard to remember. I've never dreamt about the drowning part though." Her face was pale, and her hands, where they came up to grab his wrists, were still chilled.

"A nightmare, that's all. It wasn't real." He stared into her eyes, willed her to believe him.

"But it seemed so real, Aiden. I could smell the burnt smell that charges the air behind the lightning. Her blood, that metallic scent of her blood when she fell out of her white car. And I could feel him. I swear I could feel him right there beside me." Terror flashed in her eyes and a shudder wracked her body. "And lilies, I could smell those damn lilies." He pulled her back to him.

"With everything that's been going on, it's no wonder you'd have a nightmare." Aiden knew what he said was true, but he had a funny anxious feeling in the pit of his stomach. "Forget about it. Okay?" He pulled back and gave her his no-nonsense look.

"That's easier said than done." She tried to smile.

"Well," he said, more cockily than he felt, "Let's see what I can do to ease your mind. Shall we?" He leaned, rested his forehead against hers

He caught the glimmer of a twinkle in her dark eyes, the beginning of her one-sided grin as he closed the remaining distance between them and kissed her. Her lips were warm and soft beneath his.

Aiden lay back down and settled her in the crook of his shoulder, his hands always caressing her.

"Did I ever tell you about the time my twin brothers switched places—which they were known to do a lot. But this time it backfired and they still got away with it?"

Aiden rambled on. After a while Jessie relaxed against him, her breathing evened out.

He'd keep watch over her.

Her hair was soft as he brushed it off her forehead, leaning down to kiss the smooth skin. She was so perfect. He hadn't lied to her. He would protect her and keep her safe. If she'd let him, he'd do it for the rest of his days.

Or would he? There was a thought. What exactly was between them? Was he ready to define it? Was she? And if they were, then what?

Aiden had no idea. He liked being with her, he worried about her, and he loved to see her smile.

Yeah, he would protect her, with his life if he had to.

After all, that was the Kinncaid motto: *This I'll defend.*

And for Jesslyn, he'd defend her against her own dreams, the demons that haunted and plagued her—for now. Maybe one day he could do more.

Her words still chilled him. Killers and storms, lakes and blood. What did it all mean?

It didn't matter.

He kissed her hair and settled her more comfortably against him.

Tomorrow they would talk more about her dreams.

Tomorrow.

Chapter Twelve

This morning was just full of revelations. He'd heard, of course. Who hadn't?

What was he to do?

The harlots were never meant to be found. He ran a hand through his hair in frustration.

Never to be found. SHE had never been found. Others had never been found.

That was how it was supposed to be. Destiny saw to that, had seen to that so many times before. Why now? Why were the whores turning up now, to haunt him from their graves? What was so different?

He could all but hear his father's disdainful voice, dripping with disappointment at this last turn of events. That cold, calm, instructing voice that often masked the rage that could strike unawares. He'd learned to read that calm, to anticipate its facade. It had been the only way to survive. The loud voice of the past screamed in his head.

"No good, you'll never amount to anything."

"You must guard against harlots. God will protect you as long as you're doing His will . . ."

"Adultery is a sin . . ."

"Marriage a holy sacrament . . ."

The words and phrases careened in his mind, jumbled and sharp scattered fragments of his past, mixing with the present.

He wished he could pace. He needed to pace. But stillness led to calming, and he had to be calm. People noticed strange behavior. He swallowed a laugh. Pacing up and down the sidewalk or around the tables would be strange.

He closed his eyes, took a deep breath to alleviate the worry skittering through his nerves.

Perhaps this was a test, a new test, more challenging, to dedicate his faith.

Yes, that had to be it.

Would they find the others? Were they meant to? There was a question.

He wasn't stupid. The times they lived in made it hard for one such as him to evade forever.

Worry crept upon him, drowning out the voices around him, roaring in his head. His fingers drummed out the rhythm of his favorite symphony on his leg.

Forensic science could find out all sorts of things. Had he been careful enough? What would they find on the bodies? Two. They only had two. He'd been careful.

Always the gloves, the coat, the knife. What else was there?

No fingerprints. He left no mementos except what he took.

The harlots had all deserved death, but no one else was likely to see it that way. Silently, he prayed.

The prayer rolled familiarly through his mind. Calmed him as the words tumbled forth.

A horn blared from the street.

He reached up and fingered the pendant under his shirt.

Courage.

He would need courage to continue and continue he must.

For now his question about her *had been answered. It was too much to leave to chance. If none of the others had ever been connected . . . But they had.*

The hunger furled in him, coiling tighter, waiting until it could spring. Until the monster could strike.

The roaring subsided.

The beast rested.

The haze clouding his vision receded. Life focused before him. People walked along the sidewalks, talked about the day, drank coffee, ate pastries. Horns blared and cars hummed and whined on the street.

Two women directly in front of him bustled along, laughing and shifting shopping bags as they made their way around the iron tables and through the side gate to the sidewalk.

Did they not see? Blind, they were all blind.

He would have to take more care next time. He picked up his coffee, sat up at the table, and uncrossed his ankles. He needed a plan to get rid of the innocent. There was simply no hope for it. She couldn't be allowed to stop his mission.

"Can I get you anything else?"

He looked up and this one smiled.

The look in her eyes told him what she was thinking, what she was wanting.

He cocked his head and returned her grin. *"I was thinking of some company,"* he answered her.

Her pink tongue darted out and licked her lips.

Whores, they were all whores.

"I can't now."

He thought for a moment. Was it too soon?

Her expression was one of hope and daring.

"How about tonight?" he asked. "Can you get away tonight?"

She looked around. "I don't know. My roommate wondered the last time I stayed and talked to you. I was supposed to have gotten home sooner."

And she should have. Not flirting with him as she had been.

"Well, you only live once."

She grinned again, her gaze running down him. "Are you certain you can get away?"

"Not a problem."

He must make certain she was never found. Ravines were no longer an option, too many hikers. They had worked so well before, but apparently he'd have to change.

There were caves and cliffs that were off limits. Lakes.

"Where?" she asked quietly.

Lakes. He smiled up at her. "How about a romantic evening up at Emerald?"

She worried her lower lip. Finally, she nodded. "Okay, I'll meet you up there about seven or so."

"Fine." He watched as she nodded, blew him a kiss and walked away.

A lake.

Perhaps God would align the heavens so he could kill two birds with one stone. Two birds with one stone. He chuckled at the thought. He'd never done two in one night before.

The possibilities were endless.

Endless.

* * * *

Jesslyn awoke. Her eyes were gritty. Damn, she'd forgotten to take out her contacts. But then again, with everything she and Aiden did, who the hell would have remembered contacts?

She turned her head. Aiden slept quietly beside her. In sleep, he was as intimidating and as handsome as he was awake, but in slumber there was a softness to the edge that surrounded him. Long black lashes lay spiky against his cheeks. Her fingers itched to trail down the strong, straight nose, to rub against the rough stubble darkening his jaw. Raven locks stood up from his head, disarrayed from her fingers running rampant through it.

On a contented sigh, she slipped from the bed.

Coffee. She needed coffee. In the living room, she pulled on Aiden's blue silk shirt. Shivering as the soft material slid over her skin, she buttoned up a few of the buttons. It looked like a hell of a party had gone on in here. One of her stockings draped over the lamp. Lord only knew where the other one was, or the rest of her clothing. She started to pick it up, but decided she'd get the coffee started first. After all, there were priorities in life. Coffee first, clean later.

Jesslyn fiddled in the kitchen, hunting up a breakfast of strawberries, bagels, and cream cheese. Her coffee was a bit on the strong side, but she didn't care. In a minute she'd wake Aiden.

Balancing the tray with the food, juice and coffees wasn't easy, but she was a talented soul. Halfway up the stairs a knock sounded at the door.

Well, hell.

Sighing, she carefully set the tray on the steps and hurried down to the door. She should probably put on some more clothes, but what was she supposed to do? Yell for them to hang on through the door?

The knock was harder this time.

To hell with it. She was showing a little thigh, but other than that, she was covered — sort of.

Jesslyn opened the door, and leaned against it.

An older couple stood on the threshold.

"I told you this wasn't the right house," a large man grumbled to a shorter woman.

"This is the address," the redheaded woman answered.

"Can I help you?" Jesslyn asked.

"Oh." They turned to her

Jesslyn cocked a brow and waited, crossing her arms over her chest. Better not to reveal too much.

"See, Kaitie lass, I told you this was the wrong damn house," the man said on a frustrated sigh. He was tall, taller than Aiden, and had the shoulders of a lumberjack. The shadows didn't allow for her to make out his definite features, but it was hard to miss his white hair, streaked with gray.

"We're sorry to disturb you so early. We're looking for a house," the woman replied. She had red hair and stood a bit taller than Jesslyn did.

"And whose house are y'all looking for?" she asked.

"Aiden Kinncaid's," the woman answered.

Who were these people?

"I doubt she knows who the hell it is, Kaitie, he's just renting it," the man growled.

"Jock, will you be quiet?"

Jock? Kaitie? As in Kaitlyn? Oh God.

"You're um — um. I didn't get your names."

It wouldn't be them. It could *not* be his parents.

"I'm sorry. I'm Kaitlyn Kinncaid and this brute with me is Jock."

Jesslyn closed her eyes, licked her lips and stepped back.

"This is the right house."

As they stepped into the entry, she didn't miss Jock's shocked gaze as it ran over her. "Well, if this is the house, then who the hell are you?"

That was a very good question. And her mind went utterly blank.

"Jock, we've woken the poor girl up. Leave her be," Mrs. Kinncaid said.

"Poor girl is about right." His gaze raked over her again. "My son isn't going to have to worry about prison is he?"

"Wh-what?" she stuttered.

"How old are you, Missy?" Jock asked, bushy white brows furrowing.

Jesslyn finally found her voice and her brains. "Almost a decade past eighteen, but thank you, Mr. Kinncaid. I'm Jesslyn Black. The owner of the house. I'll . . ." She backed towards the stairs. "I'll just go get Aiden. Please, make yourselves at home. It was nice to meet you."

At the stairs she stepped over the tray and kept going up to her room.

His parents. Oh, God. And she was only wearing his damn shirt. She'd met his parents practically naked.

Slipping quietly into the room, she ran and pounced on the bed.

Aiden bolted, but she sat astride him.

"Why in the hell didn't you tell me your parents were coming today?" she said right in his face.

His glower did not deter her.

"Or better yet, why not tell me they were coming this morning? I might have put on something other than this."

His gaze ran over her.

Aiden's heart slammed against his chest at being jarred awake. Blinking the sleep away, he noticed Jessie looked delectable wearing nothing but his shirt. His heartbeat would never be the same after her waking him up by bouncing him awake, but that was okay too, he liked where she landed.

"What are you talking about? I thought you said you weren't a morning person?" He wrapped his arms around her and pulled her down for a kiss, but she planted her hands on his chest and pushed back.

"Will you pay attention?"

He looked at her. She was clearly upset about something.

She leaned down and her cascading hair tickled his face. "Your parents are downstairs sitting in the living room." She sat straight up, her hair sliding over the silk shoulders of his shirt. "Oh my God. They're in the living room! Great. Contact me for a tour of Black's Whorehouse."

What was with her? His parents? Here? Whorehouse? "Will you calm down? I knew they were coming yes, just not today. They must have changed their minds and come early."

She wiggled against him and the sheet didn't do much to separate her warmth from his groin. Aiden jerked her down across his chest.

"What's wrong with them being in the living room?" he yawned.

Her brow quirked. "You haven't seen the living room this morning." She stacked her hands atop his chest and rested her chin on them. "Do you happen to remember what we did downstairs last night?"

How in the world could he not remember? Like he'd ever forget Jesslyn in garters and hose.

"How bad is it?" he ventured.

As red as her face was, the answer was obvious, but he wanted to know what to expect.

"Well, let's just say, they won't have to use their imaginations to figure out what went on downstairs. There's a stocking thrown across a damn lamp!" Her voice rose on the end, mortification clear even to his tired self. Aiden couldn't hold his chuckle in. To have seen the look on his father's face.

"Yes, I remember what we did. It's the same thing we're fixing to do right now." Aiden rolled and pinned her beneath him.

"Will you stop and think for five seconds?" she asked him.

He kissed the side of her mouth, his hands slipping beneath his silky shirt she wore. "I am. One."

"I'm serious." She wriggled.

"Two." He licked her earlobe and she shivered against him.

"Aiden."

"Three." Her neck was as sweet and tangy as he remembered. He loved the taste of her.

Her sigh filled the air, but she was softening under him.

Aiden propped on his elbows. "What is the problem? You met my parents, so what?"

Her brown eyes rounded. "Practically naked. This was all I had on. Your dad looked at me like I was a gold-digging Jezebel."

A laugh threatened out, but he managed to halt it. She was actually worried about what his parents thought of her? This was different coming from her.

"Did you not want to meet them?" he asked, fishing, hoping. "I had planned for us to have a nice sit-down dinner to get acquainted."

Her eyes rolled. "Yes, I would love to meet your parents. Or rather, I would have loved to have made a better first impression with a bit more clothing."

Her look told him she thought he was stupid.

"Does it matter to you what they think?"

She opened her mouth, then smartly shut it. Her eyes held his before skirting away. Shrugging, she answered him. "I don't . . . That is . . . Ah, hell."

Aiden chuckled. He loved to rile her. "Jessie girl, Jessie girl. You walked right into that one."

Her lips were soft under his as he kissed her. "Don't worry so much," he whispered.

"That's easy for you to say. The living room needs picking up and I'm not about to traipse back down there to get my garters. Your dad —"

"I'll take care of Dad. And I'll go get your dress, but not just yet." He kissed her hard, letting his hands roam over her warm body. "Right now, not my father, nor the living room, is foremost in my mind."

There was that one-sided grin he loved. "And what is?" she asked, licking her lips.

He claimed her mouth again, showing her who, rather than what, was occupying his thoughts.

* * * *

Kaitlyn looked around the living room and tried not to laugh aloud. Her son was busy, and with a blushing girl, no less.

Jesslyn Black. Kaitlyn knew of Ms. Black, she talked to her son several times since he'd been here. For the first time in months she could hear a smile in Aiden's voice.

Maybe he'd finally found her.

"Would you just look at this?" Jock muttered.

Kaitlyn chuckled. "Jock dear, our son is thirty-five years old. Surely you didn't think a son of yours would still be an unwed virgin at that age, did you?"

He turned a glare on her, which didn't faze her in the least.

"What in the world will Brice think?" he asked.

She shook her head. How many times had she told the man the wedding was really off and not just postponed as Brice had told everyone? Of course part of the blame lay in Aiden's field, as he had yet to tell Jock the whole story.

"Jock, I've told you and told you—Brice and Aiden are through. Through. It's over between them. Leave him alone to find his own happiness."

Her husband grabbed a black stocking off a lamp and flicked it in the air. It slithered down like a satin snake. "This is his happiness? What is he thinking? The girl simply knows his name and went after him."

That was enough. "Jock Kinncaid, you listen to me." She had his attention now. He propped his hands on his hips, his eyes shooting arrows, but she continued. "Aiden is a grown man who will choose his own path, not one you mapped out for him. Brice is a self-centered, coldhearted bitch. To put it bluntly. And I'm damn glad she's not going to be marrying our son. You were always blinded by her. Do not do anything to rock this boat."

His sigh was strong enough to fell a tree. "Kaitie lass."

"Don't you 'Kaitie lass' me. When they get downstairs, you be nice and polite, or it will go badly for you." She turned on her heel. "I'm going to find some coffee."

* * * *

Aiden hurried downstairs in jeans and a pullover. Jessie was pacing upstairs, still worried about his parents. She mumbled something about yoga.

When she was really flustered she couldn't even come up with a good line.

And speaking of his parents, where were they? He looked in the living room. Where the hell was Jessie's dress? There, draped over an armchair. Okay, dress. Stockings? What about her shoes?

Damn. Aiden turned around.

"There's a hose on the end table, dear."

Aiden jumped a foot and spun to face his mother. She was holding a coffee cup and grinning her one dimpled smile, her eyes, green as Ireland, sparkling with suppressed laughter.

"Uh—Um." What the hell did he say to that? "Thanks, Mom."

Her laugh tinkled on the air. "Don't mention it. Your father probably would have looked for the rest, but I was tired of listening to him, so I dragged him to the kitchen."

"Where the hell is the boy? You think he could at least come downstairs and greet us." His father stopped as he came up to stand behind his wife. "There you are."

Aiden tried to think of a delicate and easy way to get back upstairs.

"Hi," he tried. "I had no idea you'd changed your plans and decided to come today instead of tomorrow."

His father shrugged. "We have to run everything by you?"

"No."

Aiden walked to his mother and hugged her. "I'm glad you're here." He hugged his father. "What time did you fly out this morning?" He checked his watch. It wasn't even nine.

"Early," his mother said.

Something black near the fireplace caught his attention. Garter belt. Hell. Sighing, he hurried across the room and snatched it up. He had no idea where her shoes were or anything else and he wasn't about to stay down here and look for them.

"A garter belt?" Jock asked as Aiden passed him. Aiden could only smile. "What kind of a woman wears garters and hose and — and . . . ?"

On the way up the stairs, he heard his mother say, "I never heard you complain about them before."

"Kaitie lass, that's different."

Aiden shook his head. That was too much information in his opinion. He opened the door.

"Jessie? Here's your dress and a hose and your garter belt. I couldn't find the rest of it and I didn't want to stay around to look."

She crossed her arms over her chest, her bare toes tapping. "What's the matter, Aiden? What's the big deal?" Her eyes rounded. "Embarrassed?"

"I am not," he tried in his most affronted voice.

She strolled to him, the silk of his shirt pulling and sliding over her scantily clad body. "Hmm." One of her fingers trailed over his ear as she reached up on tiptoes. "Your ears are red." Her chuckle danced between them. "How cute."

Cute? Aiden sighed and tossed her stuff on the bed.

"I'll be downstairs." He patted her bottom and turned to the door.

"I'll be down in minute. I really need to get some writing done and then I'm heading to The Dime. It's Saturday and we'll be open for lunch."

"Hmm. You wouldn't be running away now, would you?"

Her shocked expression tried to match her voice, but he saw through the lie. "No. I just have things to do and I'm certain your parents would like to spend some quality time with you." Jessie wiggled out of his shirt and it slithered to the floor. "Guess it's time I move to the cottage."

Aiden's breath caught. He watched as she pulled open a dresser drawer, rummaging through it. Her lines were slightly curved, more toned than anything. He loved the way her back curved, barely dipping at the base before the flair of her perfectly rounded ass. "God, you're beautiful."

Her brown eyes locked with his over her shoulder before she turned around. A small smile played on her mouth. "Man, give a guy some sex and he turns to mush."

Aiden narrowed his eyes and strode to her. He kissed her, walked, until he pushed her back on the bed. "Sex? Is that all it was to you?" Then her words registered. "And you're not moving to the damn cottage."

Her catlike smile grew. "Great sex?"

Aiden leaned down and kissed, pressed his groin into her naked one. Even through his jeans, he could feel her heat and dampness.

"Wonderful sex?"

And kissed her some more, ravaging her mouth, his fingers caressing her body. She arched her neck and he kissed his way down the pale column.

"Mind-altering sex?"

He pulled back. "I was thinking more along the lines of lovemaking, but mind-altering sex will work. Glad to know I was that good. I feel like a god."

Her hands fisted in his hair and she jerked him down for another kiss.

"Puh-leeze. A god? How about a compromise?" she asked.

Aiden shook his head. "No, a god. No compromise."

"I meant mind-altering lovemaking." Her laugh was throaty and sexy.

He rocked against her, grinned at her sharp intake of breath. Rocked against her again. "A god who can perform mind-alerting lovemaking." Whispering against her lips, he said, "I like that. I like that a lot."

Chapter Thirteen

Jesslyn came down the stairs, her boots thumping on the wood. She'd put on her boots and jeans, but left Aiden's shirt on. It was stupid, yes, but she didn't want to take it off just yet. If he asked, she'd just say she hadn't had a chance to do her laundry.

Voices from the kitchen made her want to sneak off to her office at the back of the house. Or maybe the cottage. The office at The Dime. Yeah, she needed to look over the books again. Or maybe . . .

"Jesslyn, come here." Aiden's demand carried out the doorway and to where she stood on the bottom step.

Come here? Like what? Coffee, she just needed some coffee.

At the kitchen doorway, she stopped and bowed. In a raspy voice, she strangled out. "Yes, master. I hurried at your summons."

He rolled his eyes. "Mom, Dad, the smart-ass in my shirt is Jesslyn Black. She owns the house. Jessie, this is Kaitlyn and Jock."

Aiden stood leaning against the counter, his arms folded across his chest, his face set. He was not happy.

His mother giggled and walked over, offering her hand. "It's nice to meet you again. Sorry about the way we just popped in."

Jesslyn waved it off. "Don't worry about it. Aiden's renting the place."

"You have a beautiful home." Kaitlyn was one of those women who looked like she stepped out of Nordstrom. Perfectly put together, not a wrinkle in sight and a smile in place. Her curly red hair danced just above her shoulders, her green eyes danced with laughter.

Yeah, this was *real* funny.

"You sleep with all your renters?" Jock asked.

"Jock Kinncaid!" She whirled to face the man at the table.

"Dad," Aiden warned, the word sharp as a blade.

Jesslyn strolled over to the coffeemaker. "Just the ones that need knocking down a few pegs."

Aiden glared at her, and she gave him an unamused full-teeth grin as she dumped sugar in the black brew.

"Jock, behave," Kaitlyn said.

"It was a legitimate question, Kaitie."

Jesslyn shook her head and turned. The breath froze in her lungs.

Three long-stemmed white lilies, their blooms open as if on a scream, lay on the counter by the sink.

She stared at them. Memories flashed. Maddy. Lilies. The man in black. A long-bladed knife.

"Jessie?"

She jerked back from the hand he reached out to her, her cup shattering to the floor.

"Is this some kind of freaking joke?" she bit out, surprised to see her hands were shaking.

"Is what a joke?" he asked, part confusion, part aggravation.

She pointed to the lilies. "Those."

He looked from her to the flowers. "No, I wanted to know where you got them."

"I told him they were on the deck when we got here. I thought maybe they were forgotten out there, what with you and he and everything . . ." Kaitlyn cleared her throat.

This was not happening. Why now? Burglar her ass. She knew, *knew* the man was more than that. Lilies.

"Damn it." She kicked a big chunk of coffee cup out of the way and grabbed up the cordless, her trembling fingers fumbling on the rubber buttons.

"Jesslyn." Aiden had straightened from the counter and stood in front of her.

"Did you get them?" she asked, looking up at him.

"No," he said, calmly, though his eyes were anything but.

Shit. "I wish to God it had been you."

The phone rang on the other end. T.J. answered. "What?"

"Hello to you, too."

"Jesslyn, this is *really* not a good time."

"Too damn bad. I've got something to tell you and — "

"Chief is on the way to see you, Jess," T.J. interrupted.

"What? Why?" Jesslyn ripped her eyes from the pure blooms and stalked across the kitchen to the doorway then whirled around and paced back.

She could hear the shuffle of sounds through the phone in the background, other voices.

"Tinks?"

Her friend sighed. "First off, the coroner is releasing Maddy's body today. We need to be at the funeral home at noon to make arrangements."

The words were ice on an already chilling morning. The slap back into reality was never a pleasant one, was it? Funeral homes. God she hated those places.

"Today?" she asked.

"Yeah, I was going to call you in a bit, I've been really busy." To someone on her end, T.J. said, "Don't do that, you idiot. Bag it." Then back to her. "I know you don't like to plan these things and whatnot, and if you can't make it . . ."

Jesslyn sighed, rubbing the back of her neck where a headache was already building. "No, I'll be there. Hell, maybe I should open my own. I'm starting to know the business forwards and backwards."

For a minute T.J. didn't say anything. "Thanks. Tim and I are going to be there. But I don't know anything about any of it. I've never been . . . I don't know . . . Shit, I cannot think about Maddy right now. Jesslyn, I've got to go. I'm sorry."

"Wait. Why is the chief coming?"

"What? Hell." More shuffling. The background noises were gone when T.J. got back on. "We found another one."

She knew, but still she asked, "Another one?"

"I shouldn't be telling you this. We haven't even released a formal statement, but some campers found a body in a ravine up Ohio Creek Road. Chief thinks it's another one."

"Another one? Like Maddy?" And then she remembered what she read. "Like Lotten?"

Silence, then, "Yeah."

Jesslyn closed her eyes. "Jesus. You're sure?"

"Sure? Jess, the woman's been out here for months. God only knows, but Chief called in the state boys."

"And he's heading over here to see if I know anything new."

"You could be a witness."

A witness. "That's me the loose end. Did Lotten have red hair? Did this one?" She didn't know why she asked, but she did.

"Why do you ask?"

"I don't know. I don't think I fit, Tinks. Otherwise why didn't he finish it the other night when he had the damn chance? He had the knife, I saw it in the car lights. Hell, he was right there, I was right there. What, it might have taken him a few more seconds to kill me. So why didn't he?"

She paced around the kitchen into the entrance, ignoring the fact that Aiden's eyes bore into her.

"I don't know and I really don't want to think about it, Jesslyn." T.J. said, clearly tired.

"I'd rather not either, but things change."

"What do you mean?"

She stopped in the doorway of the kitchen and looked past Aiden to the countertop and the flowers. "There were lilies on my porch this morning."

"Damn it."

"Yeah."

"The chief should be there soon. I don't believe this. Maybe you shouldn't meet Tim and me. We can—"

"The hell I won't. I'll be there, Tinks. Noon." A flash out the window caught her attention and she saw Garrison drive up. "Chief's here. I should go."

"Jesslyn?"

"What?"

"Be careful. I love you."

Jesslyn smiled. "You be careful. And you too. I'll see you at noon."

With that she hung up and started for the door.

"Jesslyn."

She turned at the sound of Aiden's voice. Cool steel.

"What?"

"What is going on?"

"Oh, just your average murder in the mountain day. Dead bodies turning up and it seems the man sent me flowers."

"Excuse me?" He strode to her. "Do you care to explain without the sarcasm?"

Her doorbell rang and a knock reverberated through the house.

"That's Garrison. I'll explain later." She turned and opened the door, and wondered exactly how she could explain what she didn't understand herself.

* * * *

Late that evening, Jesslyn parked her truck at the curb and looked at The Mountain Bean — the local coffee shop. She was tired.

Aiden was pissed at her for not leaning on him more. He would be. The man needed to comfort and protect. And she didn't know how to take that.

Closing her eyes, she willed away other thoughts that kept intruding. That morning Garrison had taken her to The Dime to walk her through everything she and Maddy did that night. Aiden had wanted to go, but she'd talked him out of it. Barely. If it hadn't been for his parents, she wouldn't have had an excuse. As it was, she was glad he wasn't here because she was about to leave to meet Tim and T.J.

The morning had *not* been easy. At The Dime she'd gone through Maddy's slot in the back with the chief. The employees each had a slot thanks to a stack of milk crates creating cubbies for everyone to put their stuff during working hours. In Maddy's cubby, pictures decorated the inside — Maddy and Kirk, Maddy and Tim, and of Maddy, T.J. and Jesslyn behind the bar. Why hadn't anyone cleaned it out? Jesslyn had only managed to untape the picture of the three of them before the reality of the situation hit her like a rock slide. Before she was buried under the tidal wave of grief, she hurried back to the office and attempted to look through other things, letting Garrison look through the rest of Maddy's slot. Anything to keep her mind from dwelling on Maddy.

But it wasn't easy when Garrison's next stop with her had been Maddy's house. Jesslyn had come damn close to breaking there, but she'd held it together. Barely.

Instead she lost it later at the funeral home. Guess everyone had a breaking point.

Sighing, she cut the engine and climbed out, walking into the coffee shop. She needed to let Sally and David Hewett know about the arrangements. The coffeehouse was open from seven until seven. Usually Sally worked the evening shift, but tonight both were here.

And so was Tammy.

"Hey, Jesslyn!"

"Hey, Tammy," she slid into a table by the bar.

"Want what you usually get?"

The dreadlocked girl, into new age mysticism, smiled. Crystals, in various colors, shapes and sizes hung in her hair, around her neck and in her ears. Tammy glanced around, then plopped in the chair opposite Jesslyn. Her head cocked to the side, purple and red crystals and beads tinkling. "Your aura's troubled. Not surprising, all things considered."

"No secrets in small towns."

"Maybe some Chai tea instead?"

Jesslyn didn't think of herself as a close-minded person, really. But she generally ignored most of what Tammy told her. Yet, the girl's words struck a note in her.

Shaking her head, Jesslyn said, "I just had a really shitty day. So if my aura is dented or something, that would be why. And you know how I feel about that tea of yours. I need caffeine. Lots and lots of caffeine."

Tammy's lips twitched.

Sally Hewett walked over. "Hey, Jesslyn. Has it been decided yet when the funeral will be?"

Like a bucket of ice water, the question shocked her back to why she was here. People wanted to know. Everyone liked Maddy.

"Yeah, it's day after tomorrow. Ten o'clock at the Wheeler Funeral Home in Gunnison."

David Hewett came up to stand behind his wife. Jesslyn had worked here when she first moved to this town. Probably why she was so hooked on coffee.

"You need anything, anything at all, Jess, you give us a call," David said, wrapping his long arms around his wife and keeping his eyes on Jesslyn.

She nodded. "I will. Thanks, guys."

Sally gave her a quick hug and David patted her on the shoulder. "It's a shame."

Conversation flowed around her. There were tourists, she saw, clustered around tables. Not too many regulars this time of day. Most of the ones she knew and who knew Maddy were the morning crowd.

"Will you guys let others know?" she asked.

Sally nodded. David said, "Sure."

When Tammy plopped a to-go cup in front of her, she stood, tossing bills down on the table. "Thanks, Tammy."

Tammy cocked her head. "I heard you have a new man in your life. Got a glimpse of that long cool drink of water. Damn, you're lucky."

In spite of it all, Jesslyn smiled. "As I said, no secrets."

"You need some meditative time, Jesslyn. Here." Tammy took off a necklace that had a black stone at the end. "Wear this. It wards off negative vibes."

"And evil spirits?" she joked, but didn't smile. Tammy held it aloft until Jesslyn wrapped her fingers around it and held it in her hand.

"If you like. Take a bit to clear your head, think, get things back in perspective." She walked behind Jesslyn and said, "Here, let me put it on you."

Jesslyn set her cup down, held the necklace up and let Tammy put it on her. "You make this?" she asked.

"Would I give you something I hadn't made? The business is really starting to take off. Lots of people want jewelry that has a purpose, you know, that means something." The necklace latched and Tammy stepped back around. "I try to incorporate ancient meanings and usage of metals and stones."

For lack of anything better, she said, "Cool."

"So wear this. There's darkness near you and this will help clear things up. And like I said, some good meditative time would do you wonders."

"Yeah," Jesslyn said. "I was thinking of driving the Emerald Schofield loop, to clear my head. Maybe it'll polish my aura. I've got some things to figure out. But I need the Jeep."

"And it's starting to get dark," Tammy said.

"So it is. I should get going."

"Be careful, Jess."

She nodded and walked out the door and collided right into Kirk Roberts, her triple café mocha all over him.

"Damn it to hell and back! Can't you even watch where the hell you're going?" he asked.

Jesslyn was not in the mood to put up with him. She tried to step around him, but he followed her.

"How dare you," he bit out, his fists at his side.

Swallowing, she stepped back. "Move, Kirk."

"You didn't even ask if there was something I wanted done. I wish it had been you that night."

Chills danced up her spine. And she tried to shake them off. "What do you mean?"

"Lots easier for me if you'd died too."

Jesslyn looked over her shoulder. The door to the coffee shop and all the windows were open. Tammy and Sally stood at one, looking out, listening.

"Would it?" she asked. "Maybe you should mention that to Garrison."

"Fuck you."

Riding on too much emotion, Jesslyn shoved around him, but he caught her arm. Jesslyn looked at it. "Is that the best you can come up with? Guess your nose is feeling better?"

"You're a coldhearted bitch. I swear you have ice in your veins. God only knows why Maddy was friends with you."

Jesslyn ripped her arm free of his and stalked to her pickup. Inside, she revved the diesel engine to life and watched as Kirk just stood there staring at her.

Asshole.

Her tires squealed on the asphalt as she pulled onto the street, almost hitting a pedestrian.

"Sorry!" she yelled out the window.

It was getting late and it was raining. Already, it was after six. What a damn day and she had no idea how the hell it was going to end. At the funeral home, she'd flipped. Completely wigged. Her breakdown was shattering her control little by little. The lilies, the tour of Maddy's stuff, the questions, and questions, forcing herself to remember it all. And the damn funeral home. God she hated those places.

This morning, she'd awakened smiling, thinking the future might hold something for her.

But now? Now she wasn't so certain she could face it all again if everything went wrong. If at some point she lost it all, had it ripped away from her. More than once she'd thought that perhaps she'd rushed things with Aiden. Now she knew she did. He was just a guy here on vacation and she was a convenient . . . Nothing she came up with set well with her. Strangely, part of her really wanted something with Aiden. She'd forgotten what it was like to be able to talk to someone about anything or nothing.

This was a day from hell.

Tim had called twice, once to make certain she was all right after she practically broke down and ran out of the funeral home earlier, and the other time on the excuse to remind her to put the checks in the bank. Jesslyn turned her phone off when it rang and she recognized her home number on the caller ID panel. Aiden.

She hadn't been ready to talk to him. Not then. Not really now. But she had nowhere to go right now, except to work, and Tim told her not to come in. Maybe she would anyway.

Kirk's words still rang in her ears.

It was no secret around town Kirk was being questioned by the police regularly. The more she thought about it, the more she wondered. Was Kirk the killer? Had he killed Maddy?

There were no answers. The only sound in her pickup was the CD she had blaring. Her wipers shoved the misty rain off the windshield. Before she realized it, her truck sat in front of her two-story log and rock home. The lights from the inside crystallized the clear windows through the foggy, wet weather.

Might as well get this over with. Putting it off wasn't making it any easier. She took a deep breath. Was halting things with Aiden the right thing to do? She'd planned to tell him later, but later, smater, it wouldn't matter. No, tonight. Be done with it. It had to be the right thing to do. Jesslyn wasn't certain she could handle anything else. They'd had a good time while it lasted, right? No big deal. She'd just stop the relationship before it really started. Before she got too attached and he left. Or worse they got really attached and God forbid something happen to him. She couldn't deal with that. Not that.

At the door, she took another deep breath, blew it out, then quietly opened her side door. This was why she didn't even have a pet. No cat, no dog, not even a damn fish. Pets you got attached to and then they died. And Aiden she'd get more than attached to. Thunder boomed along the mountainsides, the storm brewing, promising its arrival.

"There you are, Jesslyn. Aiden's been worried about you," Mrs. Kinncaid said, standing in the entrance of the kitchen, noting her arrival. "You're wet, dear, and it's rather cold outside."

Jesslyn turned and shrugged. "I'm okay, Mrs. Kinncaid."

The woman waved a hand. "Please, call me Kaitlyn."

"All right, Kaitlyn." Jesslyn shoved her hands in the pockets of her jeans and walked towards the woman. "Aiden's in the living room?"

"Well, if it's off then why in the hell is Brice telling everyone the wedding is only postponed?" Jock's voice boomed from the living room. The older man stood glowering at his son.

Jesslyn waited in the doorway beside Kaitlyn. Aiden stood, hands fisted on his hips. "Dad—"

"Don't you 'Dad' me. Are you engaged to her or not? Kinncaids keep their word. If you told Brice you'd marry her, then you'll marry her."

Aiden took a deep breath. "I will choose my own life and my own wife, thank you very much."

"Who? This Jesslyn woman? She's after your money."

Jesslyn cleared her throat. "Actually, Mr. Kinncaid, your son can keep every last penny. I don't want a dime of his money. I have my own."

Aiden turned and spotted her. "Jesslyn."

She'd come home intending to end it. She wasn't ready for this. He was dressed in jeans and a dark ribbed crew neck that molded his perfect torso. What if she lost him and had to go through all that pain again. The funerals, the heartache. No, she'd end it. Jesslyn opened her mouth.

"Are you still engaged to Brice?" She blinked. That hadn't been what she'd planned to ask him. What if he was? Anger shimmered in her blood.

Aiden only looked at her hard, his gaze narrowing.

Jesslyn took two steps into the room. "Well?"

His glare didn't answer her question. "How in the hell can you ask me that?" Neither did his words.

"It's a legitimate question from what your father just said and from what I overheard. Someone doesn't know what's going on, either your father or me. And the man is your father." The more she thought about it, the madder she became. She walked up to him, and before he knew what was happening, she hooked her foot around his ankle and jerked. He fell back onto the couch. Jesslyn leaned down into his face. "Are you still engaged to her?"

His eyes mirrored his disbelief. "No. No. No. What kind of man do you think I am?"

She sighed. Aiden's eyes studied her. "Would it matter to you if I was?"

She leapt back. "Now who's asking dumb questions? I will be no one's other woman."

Amusement shifted in his eyes, but so did anger. "And I never thought you would be." He shook his head and stood. "I cannot believe you thought— After all we've—"

Jesslyn backed up. This was going all wrong. What was with her? She'd planned to come in and tell him this was going too fast. And here she was pissed because he might have done something that would end it. Isn't that what she wanted? Was to end their new relationship?

"Whatever. I don't care," she muttered. "Doesn't matter anymore. Easier this way." This was going all wrong.

She needed to think. Jesslyn rubbed her forehead. At his sigh, she looked up.

"Are you okay?" he asked, starting towards her, but she backed up yet again.

"I'm fine. Why?"

"Tim called."

Jesslyn looked away and licked her lips. Of course, Tim had called. Tears pricked the backs of her eyes.

"I'm fine," she repeated. At his raised brow she added, "I'm fine. I just need to—"

"Well, pardon me, Missy, but you don't look fine. You look like a wind could blow you over. You're a bit pale." Jock commented the last bit softer than the other words.

"Dad." Aiden's patience was clearly growing short.

Jesslyn only saw concern on his face. The tears threatening choked her.

"You want to talk about it?" he asked.

Jesslyn looked away, but still his gaze stayed on her. She could feel it. She knew every time he tried to read her.

"No, not really." She wanted to be by herself, figure out how she felt about things, didn't she? By herself she didn't have to worry about losing someone, anyone else in her life. It was why she'd been alone this long. Or one of the reasons.

"Jessie." The way he drew her name out made her feel like crying all that much more. All she had to do was walk to him. He'd put his arms around her and let her cry on his shoulder.

And she would have done that, if things hadn't shaken her up this afternoon at the funeral home. It was that young couple who had been in making arrangements for their child.

The feeling of loss that plagued her all afternoon roared to life, but she tried her best to ignore it. This was nice, had been wonderful with Aiden. But if she ended it now, then it couldn't hurt her more later.

"Jessie, look at me," Aiden said, stepping towards her, but she backed up.

No, she couldn't lean. If he touched her . . .

She shook her head no, but her mouth opened up on its own. "I'm fine, really. I am. I just need—need to go write. Think."

His eyes narrowed in their study of her.

Jesslyn couldn't look away and the words pressed up, blurted out. "You know, most of the time I understand death. I do. It's simply part of life. Maddy's not the first friend I've lost, but the rest were distant, you know? Jerrod lost his younger cousin in an auto accident." She shrugged. "That same fate ripped my whole world away. Death can be understood, even expected, but it can shred your soul, too. The sad thing is that if I sat down and put pen to paper, I'd bet my next contract I've been to more funerals than to weddings."

She looked at him then. "What in the hell does that say about me?" She sniffed and walked to the window.

Rain dripped off the eve of the house, the water dull in the fading light.

Now Maddy. "You know, everyone was so anxious or scared that I'd have a breakdown or something when Mama died." She licked her lips and wiped a tear away. "But I didn't. I helped Daddy with all the arrangements, all the phone calls, all the everything that no one realizes such a situation entails."

She turned back to Aiden. "This isn't what I wanted to say, and I'm getting off subject." She put her hands out. "Look, I just need some time by myself. Need to sort things out." She felt like her line to level ground was starting to fray. Maybe it was all the time she spent with Aiden that was making her forget things. Maybe it was the reminder of everything today.

"You're tired," Aiden said. "Why don't we get something to eat?"

"I'm not hungry." And yes she was tired. Jesslyn was tired of death, sick of its wake throwing her about. Why couldn't life be simple?

Why was all this—this emotion swirling around her now? Her throat closed up. She swallowed hard, trying to fight the battle she'd won all day against, but Aiden was right, she was tired and battered. It wouldn't be long before her emotions broke and she hit bottom.

"I can still smell her blood on my hands. And today at her house, I swear I could smell those damn lilies. I hate lilies." She rubbed her forehead.

Aiden walked to her and she didn't pull away as his long fingers smoothed along her hair, her neck. "You need to eat, or I'll be feeding you some bready carbs again."

She tried for a smile. "I'm—I'm fine."

Aiden bent his knees, his hands on her shoulders, and stared at her in that intense way of his, straight, unblinking, the corners of his eyes slightly creasing. Paradoxically, it was unnerving, yet comforting.

"Your 'fine' rings hollow, but I'll leave it for now. I know if I pushed, you'd only push back and that would only put more distance between us than what you're already throwing up. I'm a patient man, Jessie, I told you that last night, and I didn't lie. But, I also know when to press an issue."

Right now, she wished she were the person she had been last night. The woman who was tired of living alone. But today brought too many painful memories back and she had been flooded with bittersweet images of her lost family, of her mother, of Maddy. Jesslyn knew the pain that could result if she came out of her shell. It was sometimes lonely here, in her world, but it was also safe. She only had herself to depend on, to comfort, and didn't have to worry about that other person being taken away from her because the other person was herself.

He leaned over and pressed a kiss on her cheek.

"I thought I was ready for this," she whispered. "But—but—I don't think . . ."

The muscles in his face grew taut. "Don't."

She opened her mouth to try to explain, but nothing came out. Jesslyn shook her head. Why did she get in these moods? She just wanted to be left alone. Go into her office, turn off the lights, turn on some music and write.

Who was she kidding? She just needed to get to her office before she completely fell apart in front of Aiden. She didn't want to be bothered. She didn't want to talk. Didn't want to think.

"I need to get some—some writing done. And . . ." Again her eyes pricked with tears.

"You're shutting me out." He tried to pull her to him, but she shrugged him off, and stepped out of his hold.

"Aiden, sometimes, I just want to be alone. That's—that's all." *And my friend's dead, and I never got to say good-bye. And I should be used to death, but I'm not. And I'm terrified that I need you, but I do. And . . . And . . . And.*

"Well, that's too damn bad, isn't it? We rarely get what we want." His eyes bore into hers, daring her to challenge him.

She opened her mouth, anger the first thing surging to the front, but decided that would only take more energy. She was tired and her heart hurt.

"Whatever," she said. "I thought you said you were a patient man." Tears clogged her throat. She *had* to get out of here.

Aiden reached over and grabbed her hand. "I did too, but I'm finding with you, my norm is a bit off. I. Am. Here." Each of his words precisely spaced, his tone brooked no argument. "Talk to me, damn it. I've been worried about you since Tim called and that was well over an hour ago. I learned at the hotel today that another body was found. Nice of you and Chief to keep that little bit to yourselves. Where the hell have you been anyway? And why wouldn't you answer your phone?"

Jesslyn took a deep breath, tried to pull hard on her emotions, but it wasn't working. Anger warred with grief, heartache with hope.

"I was driving around. Is that okay with you? I needed to think." She was *not* going to take this out on him. She closed her eyes. Silence stretched between them and his warm sigh whispered on her face. Finally, she asked, "What did Tim tell you?"

Aiden studied her for a minute. "That you were all making arrangements for Maddy's funeral when you suddenly jumped up and left. He was worried about you." His mouth thinned at the corners. "You could have called me. I would have gone with you."

She nodded. "I know. I knew that. And I did think about it, but I didn't." She shrugged, the battle with her tears lost.

Jesslyn stepped back away from him, the trickle of tears over her cheeks warm.

Aiden hated to see her crying, to see her this vulnerable. He wanted to pull her into his arms and tell her it would be okay. But she was so distant, so far from him that she didn't think she needed his comfort. And to be honest, he thought this show of emotion would be good for her. In fact, he thought it was about damn time she broke. She'd been holding it all in.

He watched as she rocked from her heels to the balls of her feet.

"You know, I went in so damn cocky. I figure I've been through this so many times I'm a pro, right? My heart's hardened." She swiped at her cheeks. "I mean, do you want a coffin that's metal and seals? Or a wooden one? Vault or not? How would you like the programs printed? Anything special to mention inside? God, there is so much to do for a funeral. And I was fine. I was fine." Her shaking hands raked through her hair.

"What happened?" he quietly asked her.

Her head shook, her damp hair falling over her shoulders. A muscle jumped in her jaw as she moved it back in forth, probably in an attempt to control her emotions. Her jerky movements, tensed looks told him the slightest touch would shatter her.

"There was—there was this woman in the restroom. She was crying and I asked her if she was all right, if she needed anything." Her arms were wrapped tight around her middle and the tears fell in earnest. "I'd read in the paper a couple of days ago about a hit and run just outside of Gunnison, a little boy on his bike. It was his mother. He passed away yesterday."

Her chin was trembling. Aiden couldn't stand it, he started to go to her, but again she backed away from him.

"Aiden, I couldn't breathe, I just couldn't. I looked at this woman and I knew what she was going through, what she still has to go through and I just lost it." Her head shook back and forth, her eyes black pools of agony. "There's this horrible pain that you can't help your babies, that you didn't—you can't kiss it better, you can't rock it or sing a song and make it better. That you didn't protect them somehow. It's so big, so black, so consuming, it just swallows you whole and you just don't know what to do. And I could see that, Aiden, I could see all that in her eyes because I've seen it in mine for the last three years." Tears streamed down her face. "I left and drove around."

Aiden crossed his arms over his chest. His parents were still in the room, they'd gotten caught in the middle of this. He didn't care about them. He was worried about the woman in front of him, trying so valiantly to shield herself from him.

"Did you know, I thought of all these things to tell you on why this wouldn't work between us. I thought of your parents, the financial difference—though honestly that seems archaic, our jobs. Everything so that I wouldn't have to admit that I'm scared. I am so scared." She shook her head. "I can't survive it again." She stopped, looked at his dad then back at him. "You promise me you're not still engaged to Brice?"

The pain in her eyes was so clear it stole his breath. "I promise, Jessie. Dad's just hopeful. He doesn't know what you do."

She nodded. "I could say I don't believe you and throw a fit and kick you out or something. Or I could just move over the garage until you leave."

"You could try." She might think she could end this between them, but he'd be damned if he let her.

"I shouldn't care either way, but I'm glad you didn't lie to me. I'd have to kick your ass if you did."

She was a foot shorter than he was and weighed a hell of a lot less. But he didn't laugh, in fact, he didn't find any of this amusing at all.

Her face crumpled. "I'm tired of planning funerals, Aiden." Her shoulders shook.

To hell with this. He gathered her to him and held her while she cried. About time. Carefully, he maneuvered them over to a chair and sat in it, with her across his lap. "It'll be okay, Jessie. Let it out, just let it out."

He watched as his parents quietly left the room.

For a moment she leaned into him, let him give her the comfort he offered. Her tears soaked into the shoulder of his shirt.

Her sobs shook her small frame until he worried she'd make herself sick. He felt so damn helpless.

"Jessie, Jessie," he muttered against her hair, rocking her.

Moments and minutes passed until she finally quieted.

Suddenly, she pushed against him. "I've got work to do."

Aiden sighed, but kept his arms locked around her. "No, you don't. You need to rest and eat." He didn't want to go through another ulcer-no-ulcer argument.

"I've got to go to The Dime, and I need to think." She put as much space between them as his arms would allow. "I need to think."

"About what?" he ventured.

"You. Me. Us. Life."

He mulled over her words. "You're pushing me away."

"I don't mean to."

"Yes, you do." And that hurt more than he would have thought, understanding or not. "You have me. You're not alone anymore."

"I have to be," she whispered.

Aiden didn't know what to do. What if he pressed it and pushed her completely away? "No you don't. I'm here. Let me . . ."

"I don't . . . No. Don't you see? I can't." She jerked back and his hold broke. Jessie started to get off his lap, but he grabbed her arm and didn't let go. Finally, she sat again. "I can't." Her voice was breaking. "I can't need you. What if I lost you?" Her dark eyes shimmered with emotion, the lashes spiky.

He tried once more. "What about last night? Living a little? Tired of being lonely? Tired of the fear?"

She shook her head. "That's easy for you to say." Her voice cracked. "You don't have any idea what it's like to lose *everything*. Everything that matters! You don't know what real silence is because you've never had your house filled with laughter and giggles. Or sleeping on the floor because you can't stand to sleep alone in a giant bed. Or not even being able to open a damn box of crayons because of the memories."

Her words slid her pain through him.

She swiped at her tears. "I depended on someone once with everything in me, with all that I had. I gave everything and everything was so . . . so . . ." Her lips trembled. "Perfect. It was perfect. When it's ripped away . . . When it's . . ." She stopped, squeezed her eyes shut, and took a deep breath. "I had to learn to be on my own. I had to, or I never would have been able to pick up the pieces. And even when I did find the strength to put the pieces of me back together, I'm still jagged because the pieces will never fit perfectly again. I don't know if I can depend on anyone again." Her brown eyes, black with shimmering emotion, pierced him. "I just don't know, Aiden. Part of me wants . . ."

Aiden cupped her face and kissed her trembling lips. He tasted the salt from her tears. He broke their kiss, but kept his forehead against hers. "Wants what?"

Her eyes looked down at his mouth. "You. Part of me wants to hold on to you with everything in me. But, I'm so scared and part of me hates myself for that alone."

Aiden released a breath he hadn't even known he held. "Then I won't let you let go. You can push, but I'll still be here."

She pulled her lip between her teeth. "I don't know what to do, Aiden." Her sigh warmed his lips. "I really need to go. I need to be alone to think, to put this all in perspective. I'm just messed up right now."

At least she didn't shut him completely out. In fact, he'd waited her out and found out what happened.

"I can't believe you came home thinking you could end it. Did you honestly think I'd buy that?"

"I hadn't planned to tell you at all today, but Kirk pissed me off and before I realized it, my plan went out the window."

He noticed when she didn't get bogged down in thoughts, she turned to him. But what she said clicked.

"Kirk?"

"Yeah."

"And what did Mr. Roberts do?" he calmly asked. Jessie was his and the idea of that creep bothering her angered him.

"Nothing. We just got into it because no one told him about the arrangements." She shrugged. "Honestly, can't blame him for being upset if he honestly had feelings for her, ya know? I was already in a mood and didn't want to put up with his shit. But . . ."

"What did he say?"

"Just that it would have been easier if I'd died that night. Maybe he is the killer."

"He said what?"

Her head shook against his. "He was just swiping in anger. Kirk's a coward."

"Cowards can bite."

"I need to go." She leaned forward and touched her lips to his.

Aiden closed his eyes as she slid off his lap.

"I'll call you later, okay?"

He stood up. "Where are you going?"

"I don't know. For a drive, then to The Dime." Her brow furrowed. "I'll call you later."

"Will your cop be following you?"

"What cop?"

That answered his question. "I just figured with the lilies and all that someone would be watching you again." They damn well better be.

She shrugged. "No one's said anything. I figure they're all really busy trying to find the guy, what with the remains being found this morning and all. This isn't a huge police department with men to spare."

He sighed. "What time are you done? I'll come by and make sure you get home okay." He brushed his finger down her cheek.

She nodded, surprising him. "Okay, I'll give you a call before I leave. Can I take your Jeep?"

He looked out the window. "It's raining."

Her sigh and eye roll told him what she thought of that. "You think, Sherlock? And, actually, it's more a mist. If you tell me no, I'll just jump-start my own." She tugged keys out of her jean pocket. He noticed she still wore his blue silk shirt, tucked into her waist. Something about that made him smile. She was gorgeous, pale, eyes red rimmed and puffy and wearing his silk shirt.

"All right. But put on the jacket that's shoved in the side pocket," he told her, walking her to the door. He wished she'd stay. Something told him to keep her here. "You could call Tim and just stay."

She shook her head, tossed him her keys and grabbed his out of the bowl on the side table. "I'm sure Tim would agree, but that's too bad. You should tell your dad the truth, by the way. And the point is space away from you to think. And since you're in my house, then I'll think elsewhere."

Hurrying to him, she stood up on her toes, and he leaned down to kiss her.

"What's to think about?" he asked.

Jessie patted his cheek, tears in her eyes again. At the door, she stopped. "To figure out if I really love you or not. And if I do, what I'm going to do about it."

Before he could react to her words, he heard the Jeep start.

Aiden ran to the door, jerking it open, but he was too late to say the words back to her. Slapping his palm against the door frame, he turned around to see his father shaking his head.

Well, damn.

Chapter Fourteen

He sat staring through the trees. It was almost time. She should be here soon.

Anticipation raced through his system, made him feel excited, expectant. The monster was hungry and would soon be fed. Soon . . .

Rain softly pattered, dripped off the boughs of the spruce and furs, to absorb into the wet needled ground. Sounds weren't heard here. The forest swallowed them into its sleeping silence.

She'd agreed to meet him here and he knew then she was another harlot. She became HER!

Thunder rumbled down the canyon and the wind picked up. It would be dark before long, and darkness he needed.

And even better, the other one, the innocent might come. Perhaps the heavens would align, God might guide her to him.

His motorcycle was hidden up the road behind the trees. He'd thought about pretending he was broken down when she finally got here. Let her try to help him before he struck. But, that idea was quickly discarded. The chance was still high someone could come along. He didn't want anything drawing attention, and a single motorcycle by the lake might be noticed by someone passing on the road above.

He looked up studying the road far above. No cars passed, no lights shone. The other side of the lake was empty. No campers here today. It was a sign, an omen to bless his cause. The path had been cleared.

The minutes ticked by. Rain fell harder, ran off his hood, dripped beneath the edge. The darkness grew.

If all went well, he'd be done and back on the road in no time. If she would just get here. Where was she? They'd decided on seven. It was after that now.

Everything was perfect, but he couldn't tarry. He needed to get back. The Gothic Road would be quickest, but he might have to cut across Washington Gulch. A backup plan was always needed.

To be prepared was to be successful. His father taught him that.

Finally, the glow of headlights rounded the bend in the road. Then, they crested the small rise and started down to the lake.

He smiled.

Chapter Fifteen

Jesslyn pulled over to the side of the road. Where was she going? She had no idea. The rain was really only a light drizzle and it wasn't quite dark yet. Maybe the storm would blow over. Jesslyn got out, and realized she was past the police department on Gothic Road. She could go in and talk to T.J., but being alone sounded better. Or she could go up to Emerald Lake and just chill. She'd been up there plenty of times, rain or shine, dark or light.

Please let the coat be in here. After digging around in the back of the Jeep, she found one in the side zipper pocket. The navy nylon shell was top of the line and huge, Aiden's obviously. His scent wafted up to her as her body heat began to warm the inside of the jacket.

She turned her head up to the sky, the sharp cold drops of rain slicing down to mix with her tears. God, she couldn't believe she'd practically told the man she loved him. His shocked expression was etched in her memory. She didn't want to think about her foolish but truthful outburst. Wearily, Jesslyn climbed back into the Jeep. She shook her head as she pulled back onto the road, the tires sluicing through the wet muddy ground, the windshield wipers popping.

She'd told him she loved him for God's sake. If that wasn't pathetic, she didn't know what was. What happened to her control? First she'd all but ripped into him for possibly lying to her, then she'd fallen apart in front of him, and then she ended it with an "I love you —I think."

Hell.

She needed to call Tim. Unclipping her phone, she dialed his number and explained that she'd be at The Dime within the hour.

"You okay?" Tim asked her.

"Yeah," she sighed, maneuvering around a group of chug holes.

"T.J. and I were worried." His voice faded in and out. Jesslyn pulled over at the first spot she could. The ground ended feet away, the East River Valley a dark abyss below.

"Jesslyn? What's wrong?"

"Nothing, everything. Look, I'll be in later. I just need to clear my head, okay?"

"Where are you? Where's Aiden?"

She chuckled. "At home, I think. I left him rather shocked."

"What does that mean? Never mind."

A headache throbbed behind her eyes and in her temples. Her heart felt bruised and tattered. "I'm fine. I'll see you in a bit."

The rain dripped off the bikini top of the Jeep, made dull thumping sounds as it hit the vinyl backseat.

"Jesslyn, I can hear you crying. Go to The Dime, or go to my house. You don't need to be by yourself." His voice gave her little room for argument.

"Tim, I'm fine. I just need a little time." Why was it that simple thing seemed beyond the comprehension of men?

"I'd like to know what Aiden was thinking to let you leave," he muttered.

"What?"

"Nothing. Where are you?" he asked.

"Driving. I just needed to get out. I need to think."

"In this weather? Get back here, would you? It's insane to be out in this."

Her sanity was already questionable at the moment. "I'll be back, don't worry."

Seconds stretched. Jesslyn could picture Tim running his hand through his hair, slicking his mustache down. Finally, he said, "Call me, or I'll call you. Just be careful."

The wet smell of rain and soft scent of aspens and flowers rose in a cacophony of fragrances around her.

"I will. Bye." Jesslyn flipped the phone shut and sat staring at the rain glistening on the windshield before the wipers arched the wetness away.

She put the Jeep in gear and drove on, thinking about the past couple of weeks with Aiden, how wonderful it had been and if she really wanted to end it. Jesslyn tapped the steering wheel.

Okay, to be honest, she didn't really *want* to end things with Aiden.

But she was scared to move forward, or to keep moving forward. How pathetic to realize she let go of love because she was a coward. Not that she knew if he loved her, but he *might*. And she knew he cared.

Gothic came into view and she slowed at the stop sign. The little cottages were discernible in the dark by the square lighted windows. She wasn't ready to go back. She'd turn around at Emerald Lake. Maybe it'd stop raining and she could get out, clear her head in the fresh air.

What did she want to do with her life? Live it in fear? No. She liked being with Aiden. And if she were honest, it was nice to lean on him earlier, for someone to tell her everything would be okay, even if she knew those words were hollow.

Jesslyn's headlights cut through the mists as she rounded the canyon curve before Emerald Lake. The cold wind blew down the ravine, wrapped in and through the Jeep, chilled her in its wake. Lightning flashed behind the mountain to the left, lit the sky and reflected off the misty water. She turned onto the access road, sloping down to the water's edge as thunder rumbled.

The tires sucked at the dark black mud as she drove around to the far side of the lake. Maybe she'd hike to her spot, think for a few minutes before heading back. It was almost dark, but there was still enough light.

The Jeep bounced through potholes, her beams of light jumped haphazardly through the darkness. Finally, on the other side, she pulled to a stop where she and Aiden had parked the day she brought him here.

Climbing out of the Jeep, she grabbed her phone in case someone called, and shoved it in the large coat pocket. In her earlier attempt to find a jacket, she'd seen a red metal flashlight, one of those long heavy kinds. In the back floorboard she found it, mashed the rubber button and watched the bright beam of light reflect off the water. It was so quiet here. The scent of pine mixed with scents of flowers and the lake to create that sweet, almost-citrus fragrance. It was barely raining here. At the water's edge, Jesslyn kicked a pebble into the choppy water lapping at the shore. Soft mists rose from the waves.

Aiden. Her and Aiden. She'd told him she'd loved him. Damn. Why? Was she imagining it all? No, there was something between her and Aiden. Now that her emotions were calming, some part of her knew it wasn't all on her side. Aiden worried about her, cared about her, and though he didn't say the words back to her, Jesslyn suspected he might love her too. She hoped he did anyway.

And that would matter because?

She loved him. She loved Aiden. She was totally, completely and madly in love with him.

So where did that leave her?

Holding him or pushing him away? Jesslyn's heart whispered: *hold him tight, don't ever throw love away.* And once she listened to that deepest part of her soul that had been guarded and frozen for so long, she heard, and knew the truth.

Not like the arrogant man would let her push him away in any case. No, Aiden would wait her out. Somehow, he'd managed to get by all the walls she'd built up. Grin by grin, laugh by laugh and kiss by kiss, he'd crumbled her fortress.

The wind picked up, pulling at her hair, tangling it around her neck and face. Jesslyn grabbed at the errant strands and tried to shove them behind her ears. If she was hiking up the knoll, she'd better hurry. The flashlight bobbed along the ground as she walked.

Something nagged at the back of Jesslyn's mind as she started for the corner of lake where her trail began. Her skin prickled and she stopped, listened.

* * * *

She came. He smiled, watching her.

When the headlights had cut around the bend and started down to the lake, he'd cursed and wondered who it was. It could have been anyone. He'd quickly shoved the whore into the car, deciding he'd have to wait until whomever it was left. He hoped they left. Then, he could finish what he'd started.

There had been no place to really go, as the ground back to his bike was at least two hundred yards of open space. The only cover was the ten-foot-tall hedge of bushes growing wild by the edge of the lake. The shrubs sporadically dotted the shore. Luckily the car was behind the next copse. He hid in the last one, closest to the newcomer. There was no way anyone would see him nestled in between the pale green leaves.

The whore was dead, as dead as she was supposed to be. A giggle threatened. He needed to dispose of her now, but that would be easily solved once the new arrival departed on her way.

He'd thought it might be lovers come for a quick tryst. But then he'd seen her get out.

She walked with her left hand in the pocket of a coat too big for her, while the other carried a flashlight. He saw her clearly in the beams of her headlights as she walked to the edge of the lake.

The wind grabbed her hair, wrapped it around her face, her neck. He'd always liked her hair, that soft color between blonde and brown. She shook her head, turned and walked towards him. He held his breath. What if she found him? He couldn't let that happen. Not again.

His question had been answered.

But how to end it? She wasn't a whore. Not like the others. Hers had to be different. Didn't it? He didn't want to hurt her. He knew she wasn't a whore, but she couldn't know either. He knew that now.

The fruity scent of her shampoo, the light airy perfume she wore wafted on the air behind her. He'd always liked her scent. Found it intriguing.

Now where was she going? Then, she stopped, turned almost back towards him. Her head rose as though scenting danger, as though recognizing him.

If the little lady only knew. If she went much further she'd find the damn car. Maybe she wouldn't notice, wouldn't look too closely.

But if she did . . .

Well, as the saying went, curiosity killed the cat. Killed the cat. Killed the cat . . .

And after all, she had to die anyway.

* * * *

Jesslyn strained to hear any sound, but nothing came back to her. With a shrug, she went on.

Kind of creepy out here at night. Come to think of it, she'd never before ventured out here after dark. It was probably spectacular on a clear evening, the starlit sky or a full moon reflecting on the calm serene waters. Now though, the scene reminded her of her nightmares. Fog lifted off the water. Her steps slowed as those images from sleep intruded.

Paranoia could be a healthy thing. Jesslyn forced herself to hurry on. She'd run away enough tonight, she wasn't about to leave until she had things sorted out. Her nerves were just frazzled. Death and lilies. Killers and funerals. And Aiden.

Tammy was right. Meditation would be nice.

Jesslyn rounded another bunch of the cloying sweet-smelling bushes and the circle of light shone off the wet mud at her feet.

Rain started to fall again, quicker and harder. The light patter on the water became a drumming. Lightning flashed, blinding her in its brightness. She stopped in her tracks. To hell with this. There was determined to prove something to herself and then there was just stupidity. Thunder crashed, echoed off the mountainsides around her.

A chill raced down her spine. *Thunder, lightning, fog. Hannah's voice from her dream, "He's watching you."*

Rain pelted her head, Jesslyn spun around, circling the flashlight out in an attempt to see into the night. A murderer. Out alone at night. Stop it! No one had followed her, she'd checked. The night absorbed her light.

She should go. Go now. Again, she turned around, and saw it.

How could she have missed it? The front of the car was only a few feet away. If she'd walked on, with her head down, she'd have run into the damn thing. Her flashlight came up, shown into the windshield and the driver's window.

The wind picked up, howled and moaned around her. Jesslyn stood frozen, her beam of light catching the dark, smeared handprint on the window. One step towards the car. Lightning flashed and with it stark realization.

White car. Oh, God. Thunder ripped the air. She noticed the water trickling down the glass didn't disturb the grotesque warning. Inside, the handprint was inside. One more step. Her light caught the fiery strands of red hair slumped over in the seat. Crystals from the dreadlocks caught and held her light.

Tammy!

The flashlight fell from her hand. Nightmares collided with reality. Sweet Jesus!

Jesslyn bent to her knees in the mud, grabbing for the flashlight, only to have it slip from her trembling fingers before she tightened it in her fist.

Whether on the wind or from the memory of her mind, Hannah's voice carried the warning, *"Hurry, Mommy. Hurry!"*

She jumped to her feet, slipped and slid in the mud. Tore off towards the Jeep. Oh, God. Oh, God. She was out here all alone. No one knew where she was.

The pocket of her coat banged against her thigh. With barely a pause in her run, her fingers closed around the phone. Awkwardly, she yanked it from her pocket. Flipped it opened.

Please let it work. She dialed nine-one-one. The call went through. *Thank you, God.* She heard the ring through the ear piece.

Not, now. Please don't screw up on me now.

It rang again. Did she dial right? Did it matter who was on the other end? Who the hell had she called?

Jesslyn saw the Jeep as she barreled around the last group of bushes. Rain plastered the hair to her head. The mud jerked her feet out from under her as she rounded the back. A muffled voice sounded through the phone before she dropped it. Frantically, she searched for it.

There under the tire. Damn it! She jumped into the driver's seat, still clutching the phone.

"Hello?"

"Nine-one-one dispatch, what's the emergency?"

"Hello? Please, help me. I'm at Emerald Lake! He's here . . ." No keys.

"Ma'am, who's there? Are you in danger?"

Where the hell were her keys? She'd left them here. Right here in the ignition.

"Shit. My keys. My keys are gone. Oh, God. Oh, God." She held the phone between her ear and shoulder, patted the sides of her wet jeans, the pockets of her coat.

"Ma'am, calm down. Who's there with you?" a voice asked.

"I don't know who the hell he is. But she's, oh God, she's dead. Please, help me."

Jesslyn leaned down to search the floorboard.

"Looking for these?"

She jerked up, screamed at the coated figure jingling her life line. The phone dropped to her lap. For a second, she couldn't move.

He lunged for her.

Jesslyn clutched the phone in one hand, the flashlight in the other and dove across the seats, falling out the passenger's door. She was up and running even as he climbed out.

The flashlight was heavy. She could use it for a weapon if she had to. Mud sucked at her feet.

Her heart raced. She pounded along the shore of the lake. Wind pushed against her, slowing her down. The storm swirled and let loose its fury around her.

Redial. She needed to redial. If she could put enough distance between them. She dared a glance back over her shoulder.

She never saw the branch lying across the ground, the large log it was attached to.

Her foot caught and she went flying. Her face hit the ground, her fingers squeezed the oozy mud between them. Where was the phone? The flashlight?

Jesslyn hurried to get up. His footfalls thundering closer.

She made it to her knees before he was on her, knocking her flat again.

"No!" she screamed. Kicking out with her foot, Jesslyn twisted and clawed at her assailant.

Her short nails scraped down the leather of his long coat. His hood obscured his face.

She fought, punched and kicked. She tried to use her defensive training. But he was strong. She futilely screamed at the top of her lungs in a vain hope someone might hear her over the thunder. His hands grabbed at her waist, and he tossed her onto her back. Then, he was over her. Jesslyn shoved her hand up, tried to hit his larynx, but her wet hands slicked off. Again she tried, but only managed to push against his hardened jaw. If she could just reach his damn eyes!

The beam of her flashlight absorbed into the black duster he wore. Jesslyn strained back towards the metal weapon. Her fingers inching over the wet, slick mud. She stopped.

"Ma'am?" she heard come from the phone.

Something pressed against her neck, cold and hard. Oh, God.

"Please," she whimpered. She didn't dare move, not even to lower her own hand from his face.

"Bitch. You're no different than the rest of them, are you?" His voice grated out. "I ought to cut your throat for that."

"Ma'am!" again from her phone.

The man reached over and grabbed it, clicking it shut before he tossed it away.

Please, someone help her.

He changed his hold on the knife, his hand passing hers on the ground as he grabbed for the flashlight.

Lightning shot the sky, illuminated the grim reaper above her. Thunder tore through the air, vibrated the ground.

The steely blade of the knife pressed against the soft skin of her throat. A cold sting bit as the skin broke.

She was going to die. Aiden. She'd never get to see Aiden again. The knife lessened its pressure. With no warning, he brought the flashlight up over him. In that split second, the light fell on his face.

Jesslyn recognized death before light exploded behind her eyes and darkness swept her away.

* * * *

His whole body trembled. What the hell had happened? When he'd realized she was on the phone, he'd panicked. Even now someone could be coming. Breaking speeding records to get here. The fact he didn't know how much time he had ate at him.

Hurry. Hurry. Hurry.

He hadn't expected her to run. She'd fought back. Little cat went for his face, his throat. Few fought back. But, the terror in her eyes had been the same as all the others. Terror was the same for all of them. The anger burning in her darkened eyes was a surprise.

He didn't know if he wanted to be sick at the thought of what he'd just done and whom he'd done it to. Yet, the excitement was there. The knowledge of what he could do was a praise to him.

He looked down at her, still now. So still. Blood trickled in a line across her neck, the water running the crimson stain on both sides of the smooth pale column. His leather-clad fingers trailed down her perfectly arched neck, now turned to the side, smearing a red trail.

Blood flowed from the left side of her head, ran in rivulets down the side of her face, into her hair.

He smoothed the wet tangled hair back from her cheek, bent and placed a kiss on her mouth.

"Pretty, pretty." The beast stirred in pleasure. She moaned.

He had work to do. Hurry, hurry. The woman had made him angry at first, when she'd fought him like a tigress, but then, he had to admire her determination. In afterthought, he was glad he hadn't stabbed her like the whores, or cut her neck, like he started to. No, hitting her on the head would suffice. Now, she'd just go to sleep and never wake up. Sort of peaceful, wasn't it? Like Sleeping Beauty without the waking kiss. He ran a finger across her cheek.

"Pretty, pretty, Jesslyn." Just one more taste. He leaned down and kissed her.

Rain poured down in sheets from the warring heavens. He stood, heard her keys jangle in his pocket. What a lucky idea that had been. He'd seen her stop by the car. Backtracking to the Jeep, he'd beaten her there, removed the keys from her ignition.

He'd keep them. The keys would be a nice memento. Though a piece of her hair would be nice too. Sort of like the rest, but not. He bent down, humming Berlioz as he cut a strand of her hair before picking her up.

In less than five minutes, he had her strapped into the passenger seat of the little white compact car. The whore was between them, partially slumped over.

Hurry. Hurry. Hurry. They might be coming.

He drove the car up the hill a ways, positioned it just right. He didn't want it veering off now, did he? He put it in park and left the parking lights on to see what he was doing. The rope came out of his pocket. Preparation was a virtue in his mission.

He tried not to think of her sitting in the passenger seat. A slight movement made him study her. After staring at her, he figured it didn't matter. In a few minutes, she'd be as dead as the whore. And his problems would be over.

When the steering wheel was secured, and the harlot strapped into the driver's seat, a smile lit his face. Perhaps, he would toast the life of the innocent. He did feel bad about having to kill her, but one must do what one must do. Didn't one? For the barest of moments indecision crept upon him, but he quickly brushed it off.

Finally. He grabbed the heavy flashlight out of his pocket and secured it to the accelerator with the extra rope. Last, he pulled the crushed lilies from inside his coat pocket and tossed them into the car. Rain still pelted off his coat as he shut the car door. Through the open window, he flicked the car into gear before jumping back out of the way. The car careened down the slope and hit the water. He stood on the hillside, watched the car slowly sink into the deep lake. The water churned and roiled in the wake of its grave.

Damn! He'd forgotten the parking lights! Hell. The monster roared. A muscle bunched in his clenched jaw. It was too late now. On a curse, he ran in the rain to his motorcycle hidden in the forest. Someone would be here soon, better take escape B.

On the road high above the lake, he pressed his lips to the tips of his fingers, and blew a kiss to Jesslyn.

* * * *

Cold, it was so cold. Someone moaned. The gush of water roared in her ears, lapped at her consciousness.

Pain stabbed through her head, sharp, piercing. Blackness pulled at her, begged her to give in to the sweet oblivion.

A groan, and she tilted forwards.

Jesslyn opened her eyes, slowly, carefully.

Where was she? It was so damn cold. She tried to lift her hand, but it moved slowly as if through water. Through water . . .

Everything was blurry, unfocused, but she felt water all around her. Dizzily, she made out a dashboard in the darkness. What was happening? Where was she?

Jesslyn moaned at the pain in her head, her dripping hand came away sticky. The dark liquid evident on the ends of her fingers.

Blood. She was bleeding.

Then, reality set in. She was in a car. Water gushed in through the driver's window. The woman slumped against the harness holding her in the seat as the car dipped down and sideways at an angle. She reached out to shake the woman. Red, dreadlocked hair fell to the side when the head lolled, and familiar eyes stared blankly.

Oh, God. Tammy. Oh, God. Jesslyn sat frozen, unable to link what she was seeing with what was happening.

"Tammy?" She reached out and touched the girl.

Have to get out. Have to get out. Something was holding her in. Seat belt. Seat belt.

Her fingers, numb from the icy water, fumbled with the release button. The water rose. Now it was at her chest. The cold seeped into her, around her, froze her in fear.

Finally, she managed to push the little square and the seat belt gave. She fell forwards, deeper into the water, almost under the dash.

Hurry. She had to hurry. What was she doing with Tammy in a sinking car? Did it matter? She had to get out, had to get them out.

Reaching over she unbuckled Tammy's belt, but the girl didn't move.

The dull glow from the dash lights made her remember the battery was obviously still working. The window. She had to get out. Or the door. What had her dad always said about a sinking vehicle? Wait till the water level was high enough she could open the door? Wait till it filled? She couldn't remember and it hardly mattered.

Her numb fingers ran along her door. Searching, searching.

The water rose, and the car dipped nose-down. In the murky depths, Jesslyn saw nothing past the windshield.

She could have cried when her fingers found the indentions of buttons. Water rose, and she gasped a mouth full of air before it closed over her head, pressing the first indention. The muffled clunk echoed eerily in the water. The doors. Hurry, hurry.

Cold so cold. Another button. The window gave and started to roll down. She reached out and grabbed Tammy's hand, pulling her up. The window made it almost to the bottom of the slot before everything went black. The window stopped.

Darkness closed around her. No. No. If it wasn't for the icy water she'd have thought she was unconscious. Sinking, the car was sinking, further and further down. They were going to die.

Jesslyn wiggled through the opening. She gripped and jerked on Tammy's wrist. The girl was heavy. Currents pulled at her, tried to clutch her in a watery trap. No. No. Please.

The car groaned and water sucked her down. Tammy's hand pulled in hers. The girl was still in the car. Jesslyn held tight, but the car groaned again and the hand jerked in hers. The water pulled until Tammy's hand slipped away. Jesslyn only held a bracelet. No!

For a single moment she wondered what to do. She reached out, frantically. Nothing. Nothing but water.

She had to breathe. She swam upwards. Upwards . . .

Lightning flashed in a muted rippled world above her. Harder, she had to swim faster.

Her lungs burned. With one final kick, her head broke the surface. The gasp of precious air, the sputtering cough that followed was lost in the rage of thunder.

She pulled air into her bursting lungs. The world started to gray around the edges. She couldn't discern the roar of blood in her head from the pouring rain. Where was she?

A flash lit the shore, the heavens deluged. She was tired, so tired.

Tammy. Oh, God. She couldn't just leave her there. But it was too far down. And the girl's eyes. She was dead. Some part of her knew that, but . . .

The pain in her head beat in a pulsating stab. Jesslyn tread the cold water and tried to get her bearings, but the world kept tipping, tried to slip away from her. Nausea swirled hot and fast in her stomach.

The chattering clink of her teeth kept her centered on what she was doing. She had to get out of the water. Get help. It was freezing. Her fingers were numb and her legs felt clunky.

Gritting her teeth she started to swim, hoping to get to the shore before the pain in her head beat her consciousness. Before the water claimed her in death.

Death . . .

Tammy . . .

Something else . . .

What was she doing here? She thought she was at Emerald, but couldn't remember . . . remember . . .

Minutes passed. Another flash of lightning showed her she was almost at the shore. Jesslyn thought she was swimming to it, when she'd been swimming along it. It seemed an eternity passed as she clumsily tried to fight her way through the churning water. Her feet finally touched the silted bottom, tried to sink before she tiredly pulled them from the weighted ooze.

On her hands and knees, she gasped her way out of the cold lake. The icy wind chilled her even more. She was tired, so tired.

Then something stirred in her mind, and fear crept in her soul. Danger. Away. She had to get away. From?

Evil.

Jesslyn staggered to her feet, weaved in the heavy rain. Without thought to where she was going, she stumbled on.

Away . . . Had to get away . . .

Up. She crawled up. The rocks nicking the flesh on her fingers didn't register.

Icy cold pervaded her bones to the point she thought she'd shatter. Finally, she made it to level ground.

Wind howled around her, a taunting lullaby. But the rain had lessened. Hadn't it? God, her head hurt. The sudden burst of blinding light had her swaying as the world dipped dizzily around her.

Exhaustion beckoned.

The huge log offered shelter from the merciless wind. Jesslyn fell to her knees, moaned at the stab of pain through her head, and scooted up against the underside of the mammoth fallen tree.

What was she doing here?

The question swirled in her graying mind.

Something screamed in the distance.

So . . . cold . . .

Her trembling jaw sliced white hot pain through her skull.

Need . . . to . . . get . . . warm.

She huddled in on herself. Pulling the jacket up around her head, she curled into the wet depths of the nylon.

Splinters of ice pricked her whole body, her skin, her bones, her very blood. Blood . . . The coppery sweet fragrance tickled her senses.

Warm. To be warm . . .

Rain pattered on the jacket covering her. Her breath raged in jagged pants.

The screaming grew louder. She huddled tighter into herself.

Aiden . . .

The gray storm pulling at her mind strengthened, grew to a smothering black void, pulled her into the abyss of unconsciousness.

Chapter Sixteen

Aiden sat at the kitchen table talking to his father. Rain poured off the eaves of the house, thunder boomed down the mountainsides. They'd called the hotel for some take-out, and since dinner, he couldn't shake the feeling something was wrong.

It was almost eight thirty. Why hadn't Jessie called yet?

"Are you serious about this girl?" his father asked him.

Was he serious about Jesslyn? He hadn't really thought about it until this evening, or rather he had, but not as much as he had since she left. Was he serious? Damn straight. She loved him, and the thought pulled a faint smile from him. Aiden shook his head, and looked into Jock's eyes, the same blue as his own. "Yes, Dad. I am. If she doesn't completely bolt, if she gives us a chance, I plan to marry her."

His father sighed and ran a hand through his gray hair. "You just met her. What? A week ago?"

Aiden shook his head. "It doesn't matter."

"Your mother kept telling me I needed to let go of the idea of Brice and just support your decision." His finger thumped the tabletop. "She was right."

This was new. Aiden found himself asking, what he couldn't before. "Why didn't you? Why didn't you support my decision, Dad? Wasn't it enough I didn't want to marry Brice?"

Jock looked at him, and Aiden suddenly realized how much his father had aged. When had it happened? Since the heart attack last year? Lines ran deeper in his father's face, and he noticed the large-than-life man didn't move with the ease he once had.

His father cleared his throat. "I don't know. I should have. But Eddie and I had always hoped our kids would get together." Edward Carlisle was Brice's father and a good friend of Jock's. "Will you tell me what happened?"

Aiden sighed. He'd never wanted to burden his father with the truth, knowing the value the man held with family.

"We were simply too different. Brice was only interested in the Kinncaid name following hers on a check."

His father scoffed and leveled a look at him that Aiden knew all to well. "It was last year, right before your heart attack. I was in Dublin, just came up from visiting Grammy. Brice surprised me at the hotel, she'd just come off a photo shoot in France." The thought of that night sent his blood boiling.

"We were both not in the best of moods, I'd had a long week, and had a bad meeting that afternoon. We got in this fight." Aiden leaned up on his elbows. "Hell, I don't even remember what started it." But he damn sure remembered how it ended. "She yelled that if I had my way, I'd have been holding my son a couple of months after the wedding."

He expelled a breath.

"What?" asked his father.

Aiden looked back into the eyes of the man that had raised him to hold the same morals and principles high that Jock did. "I asked her that same question. She had an abortion, Dad." The moment froze between them. Finally, Aiden said, "I called off the wedding because I could not, would *not* marry a woman who put her career above the life of our child. Am I antiquated? Yes. Do I put family, children above all else? Yes, but that's who I am. Brice was not of the same mind and I realized it too late."

His father simply stared at him. Seconds stretched. "You never knew?"

"No. Quinlan and I were doing a lot of business around that time, she was off on shoots and we didn't talk as much as we should have. I don't think she ever meant to tell me." In fact, he knew she didn't, because she'd denied it after he'd flown into a rage. But he had contacts, contacts that found the information he needed.

"I called off the wedding, flew over to London, and spent the worst few days of my life."

His father had gone pale. "My grandchild?"

Aiden didn't think that needed answering. Granted, the thought that Brice's child might not have been his did cross his mind. But it hardly mattered at this point. The final outcome would have been the same. Children weren't the only things he was antiquated about. He had this idea about fidelity too. Clearing his throat, he said, "Jessie loves kids. Her own died in a car accident with her husband. She has so much heart, so much emotion, she just shuts it off. I love her, Dad."

There he'd said it and nothing fell from above.

Taking another breath, he repeated. "I love Jessie. She's the woman I want to be my wife, the woman I want to have my kids."

A muscle bunched in his father's jaw. "Does your mother know?" Then he snorted and muttered, "What doesn't your mother know?"

Hell. "About Brice? Yeah, I told her sometime while you were in the hospital. She thought I was taking your attack too hard, and she pulled it all out of me."

"That's your mother." Blue eyes met his.

Aiden glanced once more at the clock as silence settled between them.

His father cleared his throat. "Why don't you call the girl?" he offered, standing. "I heard you tell her to call, and she was pretty upset." Jock patted his shoulder on the way out the door. Aiden watched as the man slowly made his way up the steps, his shoulders stooped, the muscles in his face pulled taut.

Aiden wished he'd never told him, but the man would have found out sooner or later.

Walking to the phone, Aiden dialed The Dime. Tim answered.

A few minutes later, Aiden hung up, his worry growing. The prickling on the back of his neck so strong he rubbed it. Where the hell was she? He looked out the large picture window in the kitchen. Rain still fell, the wind howled and lightning flickered across the dark sky.

Tim said he'd just gotten to The Dime about half an hour ago. Something about the dogs he bred out in the storm and he had to chase them down. Aiden hadn't listened or cared about that part.

He tried her digital again. It rang. Once. Twice. Three times. "We're sorry, the customer you have dialed has turned the unit off or is no longer in service," said a recorded voice.

Damn. Aiden slammed the phone down. Where would she have gone?

He paced, and then paced some more. At nine he called Tim back. Neither had heard from Jesslyn. Tim said he'd try T.J.

Feet sounded on the stairs and he looked up to see his parents descending.

"Aiden, dear, you'll wear a hole in the floor. What's wrong?" his mother asked, as she walked into the living room and sat on the couch.

Aiden held a cordless in his hand. Fifteen minutes since he'd called Tim, why hadn't the man called him back?

"Did Jesslyn make it to Tim's place all right?" his father asked.

Aiden only shook his head. "We can't find her." He ran a hand through his hair. "Something's wrong, I know it." Again he rubbed the back of his tingling neck.

Someone knocked on the door. *Please let it be her.* Aiden strode to the door, and jerked it open. On the porch stood T.J. and another uniformed officer. Barney. No Merrick.

His stomach knotted, and fear speared through him.

"Aiden?" T.J. asked.

He stepped back and motioned them in. "What is it? What's happened? Have you seen Jesslyn?"

Please, let her be all right.

T.J. licked her lips, and wiped at a tear running down her cheek.

Oh, God. Everything in him froze and for a moment he couldn't breathe.

"What is it? What? Just tell me." He shut the door and stood facing them.

T.J. took a deep breath. "We're looking for Jesslyn, Aiden."

Relief slid through him and he nodded. "Good. Great. I was about to call you. I can't find her and she was supposed to have called around . . ."

"Aiden."

His name stopped him.

T.J. looked at Merrick, who said, "Mr. Kinncaid, dispatch received a call from Ms. Black just after seven up at Emerald Lake. T.J. here thought you should know."

Seven? It was going on ten now.

He turned to her. "Why the hell didn't you call me? Or Tim?"

She shrugged. "Chief didn't want anyone else up there. But SAR, search and rescue, needs more volunteers. With the rains, the temperature dropped and . . ." She took a deep breath. "We need volunteers."

Her face crumpled, but she shook her head. "I wanted to call you both. And I have to ask you this. Chief doesn't know you all that well, and he doesn't think you have anything to do with this, but where were you around seven, Aiden?"

He couldn't believe this. He didn't have time for this.

"My son," Jock said, coming up behind him, "was with us, picking up take-out at our hotel. You can check with the management of Highland Hotel, if that will satisfy you."

Aiden looked hard at T.J. "Then we came back here and ate. She was supposed to have called me. Jesslyn left here about six forty-five."

T.J. looked at the man with her. "Go on, Merrick. I'll wait for Tim."

The other man nodded, darted a quick glance to Aiden and left.

Why were they just standing here?

"Come on. Let's go," he said. He had no idea what was going on, but he was damn well going to find out. "Jesslyn left her pickup and . . ."

T.J. shook her head. "No, her truck will never make it up there in this weather. Tim's on his way. We can ride in his SUV."

At that moment, the door opened and Tim stood on the threshold, rain running off his hair.

Aiden turned to his parents.

"We're going with you," Jock said.

Aiden shook his head. "You're blood pressure and —"

"Don't talk back to your father," his mother said, grabbing coats. "Come on."

Aiden hurried to the SUV and climbed in the front. He turned in the seat to T.J. "Talk."

Her sigh was trembling and watery. She sat in the back with his parents. "Dispatch received a call from Jesslyn. Someone was dead, a 'she.'" She took a deep breath. "Jess was panicky and saying he was there. We heard a voice in the background when she was looking for her keys. We think she fled, and . . ."

Her silence stretched.

"And?" Aiden asked. By God, if anything happened to her . . . If anyone had dared to harm his Jessie.

"It was awful," she whispered brokenly.

Kaitlyn Kinncaid did what Aiden knew she did best, she comforted. "It's all right, dear, just get through it."

Again T.J. took a deep breath. "He chased her and they fought." She stopped, but added, "That's all I know."

Aiden knew she was leaving something out, but he didn't know how to press her into telling him everything. He had a feeling she wasn't supposed to have told him what she did. It didn't matter, he'd find out everything he wanted to know.

Aiden sat back, his heart pounding fear and rage through him. "Can't we go a little faster?"

He knew it. He'd known something was wrong. Dammit! Why did he let her go?

Please, please, let her be okay.

He couldn't stand to think of anything happening to her. The thought of losing her . . . NO!

Her words earlier haunted him. *"You don't have any idea what it's like to lose everything."* He hoped to God he'd never find out. Jesslyn was his everything, he couldn't lose her. He just couldn't.

Aiden felt like he couldn't breathe.

"I can't . . ." he muttered. She had to be all right. She had to. Aiden couldn't think about anything else. Didn't dare contemplate the meaning behind T.J.'s tears or what she might have heard on the dispatch tape. She'd fought with the man. Oh, God.

Tim glanced at him. "It'll be okay."

"I love her, Tim," he said quietly. "I can't lose her." Aiden looked away from his friend's knowing face and stared out the window, the world a chaotic blur beyond.

* * * *

They crested the hill and took the access road down to the lake. He couldn't believe the sight before him.

Red and blue lights flashed through the misty weather. A uniformed officer stopped them and Tim apparently recognized the guy. T.J., being in the backseat, told the man to let them through.

Aiden could see two spotlights on boats out on the water. Fog floated above the lake, a low wispy cloud like the steam from a witch's cauldron.

"They're dragging the lake," T.J. said from the backseat.

Aiden felt like he'd been sucker-punched. This was not happening. Vehicles were parked haphazardly on the far shore. Flashlights bobbed in the darkness through the little valley he and Jesslyn had walked through.

The SUV hit potholes and bounced, but never slowed down. Tim had barely pulled to a stop before Aiden tossed the door open and all but tore out of the car.

"Aiden! Wait!" T.J. hollered behind him.

Several people stood near the water's edge. A part in the crowd allowed him to see divers in wetsuits kneeling by a black bag.

A body bag.

His world fell out from under him. Aiden didn't remember running. He shoved his way through the people, their voices and hands lost in a blur of terror.

God! Rage roared through him. "No!"

Someone grabbed him hard.

"It's not her, Mr. Kinncaid. It's not Jesslyn." The arms that held him were like manacles, and still he fought against them.

"Mr. Kinncaid!"

All Aiden saw was the black bag, a grotesque slap into reality.

He finally stilled when he realized he wasn't getting out of the stranglehold someone had on him.

"Mr. Kinncaid, if you don't calm down, I will remove you from these premises. Calm down and listen," the voice said.

Aiden could only nod.

The arms around him loosened and he jerked away. His eyes still zeroed in on the bag.

"It's not Jesslyn."

It's not Jesslyn. Not Jesslyn. Oh, God. He closed his eyes.

Finally, he looked up and into the whisky-colored eyes of Derrick Garrison, the Chief of Police.

"It's not her," the man told him.

Aiden's throat was so tight he couldn't get a word out. He just stared at Garrison. The Chief of Police was dressed in jeans, muddy hiking boots, a dark hooded rain parka, and a Colorado Rockies baseball cap.

"I don't like civilians at crime scenes," the chief continued. "And family and close friends, I ban. However, if you can follow orders like anyone else, I figure we can use another pair of eyes and legs in the search. There's a lot of ground to cover."

Aiden nodded. The man took his arm and steered him away from the body bag and through the crowd to stand by a police-marked Explorer.

"I need to ask you some questions," Garrison said.

Aiden cleared his throat. "Fine. What do you want to know?"

"Do you know what Jesslyn Black was doing up here during a storm at seven tonight?"

A glance at his watch told him it was ten o'clock. Three hours. Damn it.

"Yeah, I do," Aiden answered. "She was upset about several things and wanted some time to think."

Why the hell hadn't he just kept her at the house?

"What was she upset about?"

Aiden gave him a brief rundown.

"That's your Jeep?" Garrison pointed to the black vehicle with his pen.

Aiden turned his gaze back to Garrison. "You know it is. Can we cut the crap? Where is Jesslyn? Have you found anything?"

Who was in the body bag?

Jesslyn's name carried on the chilled, wet air as people yelled it out.

Garrison ran his tongue around his teeth. "We've found a car at the bottom of the lake, and a murder victim. We're looking for Jesslyn."

A motor from the boat cut through the air, and drew his gaze to the darkened water. "You're still dragging the lake, why?" Aiden asked.

The Chief of Police sighed. "I'm covering all my bases, Kinncaid."

Christ, this was not happening. It was *not*.

T.J. came up then with Tim and another man. Introductions were made and flashlights were passed around.

"We'll be looking at the south side," T.J. said.

Garrison leveled a look at him, which Aiden only quirked a brow to and crossed his arms.

"I'd guess the temp's in the forties," Garrison said. "Hypothermia is an issue especially if Jesslyn got wet. If you find her—" His gaze sharpened on Aiden. "Do not, and I repeat, do *not* move her until SAR gets there. They are trained professionals."

Aiden nodded again. He turned around and followed T.J. and Tim. His parents stood off to the side and he made his way over to them. They wrapped him in a hug.

"You okay?" his mother asked.

"No." He looked to his father. "We're going to be searching. It's more of a hike. Please stay here, or around here. I don't want to find out you had another attack because you were traipsing around at this altitude."

His father's eyes flashed, but his mother only said. "We'll be fine, Aiden. Go, do what you have to. Don't worry about us."

With that, he turned and jogged to catch up with Tim and T.J. The air was wet, heavy with the piney sweet scent Aiden remembered. It wasn't raining, just windy and cold.

The red and blue lights swirled in the air, reflected in muted tones off the clouded lake. SUVs with MCBPD painted on the side, an ambulance, sheriff's cars, and other civilian vehicles. Sirens were silenced, but rotating lights bounced off the mountainsides and lake. Dogs barked and Jesslyn's name carried on the wind.

This had to be a horrible, terrible nightmare . . .

Nightmare . . . Oh, God. The memory of Jessie's words just that morning startled through his mind. A dead woman, the monster, the water drowning her. He looked at the lake. How could such a place of beauty become such a living hell? Aiden begged and pleaded with God that they find her. She had to be unharmed. She had to.

The reality of the situation slammed into him, almost bought him to his knees. Fear slithered through his system. It would do her no good if he fell apart here. And he'd come damn close when he'd seen that black bag.

A muscle bunched in his jaw. His hand tightened around the flashlight he held.

"*Jessssllyyyynn. Jeeesssslllyynnn.*" Her name bounced and carried on the air as it was called out from various locations.

Aiden looked at T.J. "Where do we start?" he asked as he caught up with her and Tim.

T.J. pointed towards the far side of the lake he and Jessie had hiked to the day she'd brought him up here. A strange feeling tingled his nerves.

Aiden didn't say a word, just followed along. He called out for Jesslyn, hoped for an answer, prayed for an answer, but the name only echoed back eerily on the wind, tore around him, through him, could have broken him.

* * * *

An hour later and still nothing, or almost nothing. The temperature had dropped. Tim saw T.J.'s breath puff in the cold damp air. Aiden's nerves were stretched, Tim could tell. The man said little, hardly acknowledging anyone. He just studied the ground, the beam of light, and called Jesslyn's name.

Aiden was in front of them, heading back down the path towards the knoll. At first, their group had headed through the dense vegetation, but left that for the other teams and started where the land sloped up. They'd covered hundreds of yards in the forest. There was a knoll below them that overlooked the lake and all the busy activity below in the valley. Colored lights swirled even though the engines couldn't be heard up here. Beams of flashlights bounced and jumped throughout the countryside.

Finally, Tim could stand it no more. He stopped and looked at T.J. He had his suspicions but asked anyway, "Teege, why are we up here? What are the chances the guy brought Jesslyn all the way up here? The dog found her phone down by the lake."

Their search had been on for less than ten minutes when a dog had let loose a bark. That it had only been Jesslyn's phone was both a hope and a disappointment. The search continued. His stomach turned as he saw they still dragged the lake. It was a deep lake.

T.J. stopped. The lights from below cast Aiden as a black silhouette with a flashlight in the darkness. Finally, T.J. turned to him. His light, though pointed to the ground, let him see her face clearly. Tears glistened in her eyes and she swallowed.

"I didn't want Aiden to see . . . I saw Maddy." The watery drops trickled in shiny paths down her flawless cheeks. "You're right. I figured this was the last place he'd bring her. I want to be down there." She pointed with her flashlight to the valley below. "But I couldn't let him see that. Aiden loves her so much. You can see it every time he looks at her. And Jesslyn's crazy about him. They just need a chance," her voice broke, and Tim gave into the urge and pulled her into his embrace.

She was so incredibly tiny. Jesslyn was small, but T.J. was fairy-like, slight and fragile. He kissed the top of her damp head.

"I couldn't let him see that, Tim. I couldn't. Not if . . . not if . . ." She started crying against his chest.

"Shh, baby. It'll be okay. It will." Emotions swirled within him. Oh, Jesslyn . . .

T.J. leaned back, viciously swiped at her cheeks. "I don't have time for this and neither do you. She's our friend, and she needs our help, not our damn tears. Come on." She pulled his hand and they started down the mountainside towards Aiden.

* * * *

Aiden heard them approach. He stood a few feet away from the giant fallen tree. "She brought me up here the first day we were together," he told them, remembering everything about that day. How they'd hiked up the other side, closest to the lake. Her laughter, the sun shining in her hair. "This is one of her favorite spots."

Tim stood quietly beside him, his beam of light gazing the ground, looking, searching. "Aiden, don't do this to yourself."

Aiden walked to the log. He sighed, bent his head, the flashlight weighed in his hand.

Why hadn't they found anything yet? Anger clawed through him and he reared back to hurl the flashlight over the damn hill. He stopped. That wouldn't do a damn bit of good. Guilt punched at him. If he'd only made her stay. If he'd told her he loved her, ran after her quicker. The possibilities were endless.

The bottom line was that he'd failed her. T.J. said she'd run, or fled from her attacker. He imagined her screams and pleas. The images echoed endlessly in his brain. Red haze cleared from his vision and he scanned the ground again. *Jesslyn* carried on the wind. Nothing. They'd found nothing but her blasted phone.

"I thought she'd be here. As crazy as that sounds I thought I'd find her here. Right here." He hit the smooth wet wood with the bottom of his fist, propped his foot on the ancient tree.

T.J. turned to him. "That's only natural, Aiden."

He shook his head, "No, you don't understand. It's not just wishful thinking or maybe it was. But since we started searching it was like something, or someone was pulling me here. Practically whispering at me. Right here." He scanned the area with his flashlight. The fallen log, a blackened ring from an old fire, gnarled trees, and water-laden flowers. No Jesslyn.

Please God. Please. Let me find her. I love her.

Aiden stood up on the log, started to hop down to the other side. Something flashed in the beam of his light. He almost fell off the grounded timber, stumbled and managed to land on his feet.

"Are you all right?" Tim asked him on the other side of the log.

He dropped the damn light.

"Fine," he muttered, picking up the flashlight and looking to see what had caught his attention.

His breath stilled at the jacket bunched and wedged beneath the giant log. He knew that jacket. It was his. Aiden shakily reached his hand out and the light caught again. Her ring winked at him. Her finger.

"She's here," he hoarsely whispered out. His hand paused, afraid to touch her, afraid not to.

"What?" Tim asked, hopping down beside him. "Sonofabitch."

Aiden took a deep breath, picked the edge of the coat up. The air whooshed out of his lungs. She looked so peaceful, like she was asleep. Huddled and curled into herself in a fetal position, covered in the clinging wet coat.

Aiden reached out and touched her right hand. Cold, she was so cold.

"Don't move her, Aiden," T.J. reminded him.

Jesslyn's hand hung lifelessly in his as he tried to find her pulse, his own heart hammering against his ribs. "Come on, Jessie girl. Come on, baby, help me out."

"Team to base. Team to base. We've got her! Over," T.J. said into the radio. The click of the button popped as she released it.

Aiden vaguely heard Garrison's voice over the pounding of blood in his ears. "Roger, Team. Location?"

"The knoll above the south edge of the lake." She waved her flashlight down to the cars below. Flicked it on and off.

"Gottchya. T.J., is she alive?"

Is she alive?

He couldn't find anything in her wrist. Oh, God. Please. Aiden moved his hand to Jesslyn's neck, and didn't so much as move her head. An eternity seemed to pass. "There." It was thready and slow. "I have a faint pulse," he told T.J., not caring if his voice was hoarse.

She relayed the message over the radio. All he wanted to do was pick Jessie up and hold her against him. But he remembered Garrison's warnings about moving hypothermic victims. Instead, he reached again and held her cold, limp hand.

He'd found her and by God, he wasn't about to lose her now.

She was so still, he couldn't even tell if she was breathing. Panic threatened to tear through his relief.

"I knew you were here, baby. Everything's going to be all right now. You're safe, Jessie. You're safe. I promise. No one is ever going to hurt you again." And though he was frightened beyond anything in his life, Aiden knew in some part of him that Jesslyn would be okay.

It took almost another hour before she was in the ambulance and on her way to Gunnison County Hospital. SAR had all but shoved Aiden out of the way. He didn't want to let her go, but he knew he couldn't help her now. Orders had been barked. Needles probed, instruments listened, and gauges read. They had finally thought it safe enough to move her onto a rescue board. The bright orange gurney obscenely lay on the ground as they gently and easily rolled her onto it.

Aiden remembered the rage that had choked him at the sight of her bloody bruised head, the cut at her smooth throat. She was pale, her mouth and fingertips blue from cold.

Jesslyn didn't respond to any stimulus. One of the medics had told Aiden to yell at her. And he had right in her face. He yelled for her to come back to him, that he loved her. Nothing had brought her eyes open, and that terrified him to the bottom of his soul. No one knew if the head wound, shock, or hypothermia kept Jesslyn unconscious. Finally, she'd been loaded in the ambulance.

Scenery flew by in an unseen blur. Aiden sat in the front seat of Tim's 4-Runner as they sped to Gunnison. T.J. was slumped in the backseat with his parents.

Aiden didn't know who had hurt Jesslyn, but he vowed, if it were the last thing he ever did, he'd hunt the bastard down and make the monster pay for what had been done. That thought led to another and then another. Did he remember to grab his phone? A lump in his pocket slid relief through him. Thank God. First chance he got, there was someone he needed to call.

The Kinncaid motto echoed through his mind, his father's voice and grandfather's before him. All the Kinncaid men said it on their wedding day to their brides, on the birth of their children: *This I'll defend.*

Aiden knew he'd failed at keeping Jesslyn safe and protected. Never again. Never again.

Chapter Seventeen

Aiden sat in the waiting room of the Gunnison County Hospital's ER. He'd alternated between pacing, standing and sitting. It had taken too damn long to get here. Why in the hell hadn't they flight lifted Jesslyn?

He checked the circular black and white clock hanging on the pale green wall. After midnight. Over an hour, and no one had told them a damn thing. Tim and T.J. sat in the corner on worn frayed chairs. His parents weren't here, but he knew they were around somewhere. His mother, using her career as a prominent surgeon in one of the nation's leading hospitals, finally found out that they were trying to stabilize Jesslyn.

Stabilize? Aiden leaned his head back against the wall. A dark-headed woman across the way moaned between sobs and incoherent Spanish babbling. She rocked in her chair and held a beaded rosary between her fingers. He stared at her, wondered what she was doing here, who she was praying for. Her crying and rambles grated on his nerves, but considering his own state he couldn't blame the woman for her obvious worry, hope and concern.

Garrison would occasionally stick his head in, then just as quickly leave. Garrison . . . He knew the town, the people. Doubt crept in where the Chief of Police was concerned. Aiden closed his eyes. Doubt.

Where the hell had Tim been before? Something about dogs? No, not Tim. Then there was Kirk. Or just some village citizen who simply got off on killing women.

Damn it.

He had to see Jesslyn. What was going on?

The creak of the chair beside him opened his eyes. His mother stared at him and Aiden's stomach dropped. He couldn't move, only stared back, willing her not to shatter his world.

"They've managed to stabilize her." She put her hand on Aiden's arm. "Her unconsciousness was not so much from hypothermia as from her head wound. They performed both a CAT scan and an MRI to determine the damage. We're waiting on the results. I told Dr.

Williams to let me tell you. I didn't think you'd yell at me, but would listen." His mother gave a small grin, but Aiden didn't return it.

"Is she going to be okay?" That was all he wanted to know, all he cared about.

She sighed. "I don't know, Aiden. Jesslyn still hasn't regained consciousness and they're worried about that. Dr. Williams called in a neurologist from Montrose, or Mongose or something like that."

"Montrose," Aiden told her.

He needed to make a phone call. A very important phone call. Standing, he patted her shoulder, walked past everyone and out into the cold night air. Around the side of the building, he paced down the sidewalk, debating. Ah, hell. Quickly, he punched the numbers he'd memorized from the last ambiguous postcard he'd received in the mail weeks ago. *Please, God. Let this one be the right number. Don't let Ian have changed it.* After the first ring was answered by silence, he gave a sequence of numbers. His voice was followed by a series of different decibels of beeps and whines. Finally, a computerized voice came on and he only said, "A.I."

No names was the rule. That and no one else in the family could know that he ever had contact of any kind with the black, disowned sheep of the family.

His thumb pressed END. Now what? Hopefully, it wouldn't be long. Aiden didn't want to be gone long. Hurry, up. Hurry, up.

His phone rang.

"Hello."

"What the hell is going on now? Can't the family stay out of trouble for more than a couple of months?"

Aiden sighed. Ian's voice soothed like nothing else had thus far. A quick glance around showed him he was alone.

"What?" Ian asked when Aiden didn't answer his brother. "Is it the same as before?"

The last time he'd made a call had been almost a year ago when their father had a heart attack.

"No. I just need your help."

A throaty chuckle answered him. "Well, that's good news. I was hoping it wasn't anything important."

His brother had a dry sense of humor. "I don't have time for this. I need to get back inside."

"Tell me," Ian said in his deep gravelly voice.

And Aiden did. Everything in a quick, condensed version.

"Well, this is interesting. Hell, I'm sorry. What do you want me to do?"

Aiden shook his head. Another ambulance, its siren blaring, turned the corner and pulled into the entryway of the ER.

"I don't know." A visage of Jessie's face flashed in his mind, bloody and deathly pale. "I want this bastard found." He bit out.

"And when he is?" Ian asked.

Truth or lies? Truth. "I want to kill him with my bare hands. Slowly."

"Well, if he's found, that can always be arranged." His brother cleared his throat. "Give me twenty-four hours to find something out. I'll call you tomorrow at this time."

"That's fine." Aiden somehow knew that Ian could find out things no one else could. Probably in unorthodox ways. Aiden didn't give a damn.

"Where are you again?" Ian's question pulled Aiden's thoughts back to the conversation.

"Colorado." He filled him in on the particular location.

"Hmm . . . They have a state level sort of FBI. Actually, it comes up that a certain Chief of Police has already requested their assistance in this case."

That was a surprise. And how had Ian found that out this damn quick?

"Dare I inquire how you know that?"

Another gravelly chuckle was his answer. "I have all sorts of toys."

"I'll just bet you do. Thanks."

"Don't mention it. Tomorrow."

"I owe you," Aiden told his brother over the phone.

"Well, perhaps one day you can repay. For your sake, we'll hope not." The smile in Ian's voice almost had Aiden returning it, but he couldn't.

The line went dead.

The sky overhead was still inky black with no sign of clearing off. A light mist started to fall again. On a curse, Aiden hurried back into the hospital. The doors whooshed closed behind him. His strides paced him down the line of chairs and back up. Finally, he sat down in the chair he'd vacated earlier.

He wearily ran his hands over his face and leaned forward. Elbows dug sharply into his knees as he rested his forehead on his clasped hands.

Thank God, he'd gotten hold of Ian.

The speckled beige linoleum glared back at him. The Hispanic woman started in on another Hail Mary. At least, he thought that's what it was.

"Aiden?" He lifted his head as his mother crouched before him, lacing her fingers to cup his knee.

"Mom, you and Dad should really head back, get some rest." It was almost one in the morning for God's sake.

She merely quirked a brow at him. "That, dear, is a stupid thing to say." Her gentle reprimand pulled a small smile from him. "I wanted you to know, the boys will be here in the morning, early, probably."

"The boys?"

"Your brothers. Your father called them during the search and told them to get their asses here, that you needed them."

He moved his hands to cover hers and sighed. "I wish he hadn't done that."

"Why? Kinncaids stick together, or have you forgotten?" His mother's eyes studied him, and she rubbed the back of his hand absently.

Aiden shook his head. "No, I haven't forgotten. How are they getting here so fast?"

She smiled. "Your father sent Rodger home with the jet this morning when we got here. Bray wanted to fly up to Maine or something." Her hand waved absently. "They were coming anyway in two days, they'll just be coming a little early."

"What do you mean Jessie hasn't woke up yet?" The deep resonating voice brought Aiden's head around, and he saw his father, his arms crossed over his massive chest, talking with Tim.

His mother said, "Do you honestly think he's going to go home? He's worried about you, about Jesslyn. For all his bluster, I think he actually likes her. I told him he needed to rest. With all the excitement today, it would be good for him to lie down."

Aiden smiled at the thought. "I see he listened."

His mother's dimple peeked out. "You know your father." Her voice lowered, her smile eased away. "He said he wasn't there for you when you needed him before, and he was damn well going to be here for you now. Please don't be too hard on him, Aiden, he's being hard enough on himself."

"For what?" Aiden asked.

"For not supporting you completely when you called off the wedding to Brice, for taking her word over that of his own son, explanation or no. His words not mine, by the way."

"And he wonders why he has high blood pressure? The man worries too damn much." A huge breath puffed out.

For a moment, neither spoke. His mother cleared her throat.

"Things have been hectic and we haven't really talked. Honey, do you know what happened? Do you want to talk about it?" she asked. "I know you found her and she's in serious condition. I know too from what the doctor has told me that someone inflicted her head wound with a long, dull instrument."

Aiden's stomach rolled at her words. His father walked towards them, and the chair squeaked when his father lowered his considerable build into it.

For a moment Aiden couldn't speak. In his mind he saw Jessie curled up, her lips blue, the blood staining her face and neck. His eyes never left his mother's. A muscle bunched in his jaw.

"She was so cold, Mom. So cold, I thought she was dead when I touched her and everything in me just stopped." He didn't see his mother, only saw Jessie, hurt and alone. He told her how he'd found Jessie, and where, amazed still he hadn't stepped on her. "He cut . . ." Aiden stopped, cleared his throat and shook his head. "He—the son of a bitch cut her across her throat, not deep, but it's there." Rage conquered the fear. "The bastard hit her with something, the whole side of her face was bloody." Aiden bit down.

"This I'll defend," he murmured. "Great damn job I did. They haven't even let me see her since they loaded her into the ambulance."

He needed to pace, but without toppling his mother over, he didn't know how to extricate himself. Aiden wanted to see Jesslyn and he wanted to see her now.

His father cleared his throat, coughed and cleared it again. Aiden felt his father's hand on his arm. He looked at him, saw the weariness in his father's eyes, the lines more haggard than he remembered. Jock's flaming blue eyes bore into him.

"Son, this is not your fault. I don't want to hear something that stupid again. I raised an intelligent man. One more intelligent than myself, it seems. Now quit beating yourself up and concentrate on Jesslyn."

Aiden really hated when his father used that don't-give-me-that tone of voice, usually because it was honest and made sense. Concentrate on Jessie? What the hell had he been doing?

Instead of the terse remark that immediately came to mind, Aiden found himself saying, "I can't lose her, Dad." Aiden shook his head. "I just can't lose her."

A squeeze of hand from his mother and a slap on the shoulder from his father. The entire evening seemed surreal.

"Mr. Kinncaid?"

"Yes?" came two male replies.

A short, balding man in blue scrubs gave a tired smile. "Travel in pairs, huh? Usually do in this place. I'm Dr. Williams."

Aiden, along with everyone else, stood. He stared at the doctor, waited to see what he was going to tell them.

"Why don't we all sit down?" The doctor gestured to the chairs.

"Why don't you just spit it out?" Aiden said. He'd had enough. "I want to see Jesslyn. Now."

The doctor merely raised a brow at him. "I understand your anxiety, Mr. Kinncaid. Let me say that Jesslyn is stable, all her readouts are well. We were initially concerned with her EKG." He waved a hand absently and clarified, "Her heart beat. Ms. Black's body core temperature was low enough that we were worried about several things. However, the transport went well, no real jostling before the blood started flowing good again. Actually, her body core temp, though low, wasn't as bad as we thought. Once on heated, moist oxygen—which, by the way, she's still on—her temp rose and some of the worries decreased. We're also giving her warm IV fluids. Her temperature is almost back to normal. So, as far as the hypothermia goes, we're pretty much out of the woods on that one." The diminutive man rubbed the back of his head.

"When can I talk to her, Doctor?" Aiden glanced to see who'd asked the question, Chief Garrison.

"You won't be, Chief." The doctor's tone brooked no argument. "Right now our biggest concern is the head wound. Ms. Black suffered from a concussion, slight swelling and a little hemorrhaging. The bleeding stopped a while ago, the swelling is going down. However, all that said, she still hasn't woken up. The longer she's unconscious, the more likely . . ." He trailed off, frowned as three high notes whistled from the beeper clipped to his drawstring pants. Looking down, he punched a button.

"The more likely what?" Aiden bit out, almost at the end of his patience.

"Oh, sorry. Well, in cases like this there is often memory loss either of the accident itself or of events prior to. Between the head wound, shock, and hypothermia, I wouldn't be surprised if when Ms. Black wakes up, she's fuzzy or blank about certain things."

Aiden sighed, relief slowly starting to trickle through him.

The doctor wasn't finished. "Having said that, I think you should also be aware that it's possible Ms. Black could slip into a coma. I don't think it's likely, but it is possible."

Aiden's heart dropped. No, she was not going to slip into a coma. He'd be damned if she would.

He crossed his arms, chewed on the inside of his cheek. "When is the neurologist getting here?"

Dr. Williams checked his watch and shrugged. "Should be anytime now. He was flying in the chopper, not driving. They flight lifted another patient earlier in the evening to St. Mary's so he's catching a ride back."

"I want to see her now."

The doctor looked at him with a raised brow. "Are you family?"

Aiden silently played through the consequences of decking the little know-it-all. He stared at the doctor. "I will be."

The doctor nodded, smiled. "Figured it was something like that. Come on back with me."

* * * *

The room was quiet save for the soft almost silent bleep of the heart monitor. The shuffle of feet beyond the wide door, muffled voices, and the clatter of rolling carts intruded periodically. The small but sprawling hospital was more modern than he had at first credited it being.

Aiden stood, staring out the window. Dawn was breaking, the sky turning a brighter blue, the pink and lavender bottomed clouds a contrast to the covering slate gray otherwise. More rain dripped off the eve. He rubbed his hand through his hair again, looked back at the bed.

Jessie still hadn't woken up. She looked so small and frail in the big hospital bed, her face pale against the purple bruise peeking out from under the edge of the bandage on her head. Her glorious hair lay lackluster on the white pillow, some of the strands still matted with mud and blood. IVs dripped into her arm, hung from metal-curled loops on a stand by the bed, and the transparent tubes glistened with slow-moving liquid. Blankets were tightly tucked up under her chin, covering her from neck to toes. The fogged oxygen mask still sat over her nose and mouth.

Anxiety and worry crawled through him. Aiden couldn't sit, or stand still, and the room was too small to pace. He'd rubbed her hand through the blankets, not wanting her to get the slightest chill. There had been whispered pleas, furious demands and silent prayers. And still she lay as quietly as when he'd walked into the room hours ago following Dr. Williams.

The neurologist had not added much past what Dr. Williams had imparted. They were all waiting on Jesslyn to open her eyes. No one knew exactly when that would be, but the sooner the better. Nurses came and went. They took her blood pressure, read the little square box on the IV stand, turned dials, and punched buttons.

Aiden sat in the chair he'd pulled up by the bed. Tim had finally taken his parents home, but Mom sent some of his and Jessie's things in a duffel bag. The jeans, tee and sweatshirt, were clean and dry. He was exhausted.

His brothers should be arriving soon. Mom told him Gavin planned to come directly to the hospital—always the doctor. They'd also gotten hold of Mr. Victor Black, Jesslyn's father. He was going to be on the first flight that landed here in Gunnison at eight this morning.

Aiden leaned his forehead on the blanket, knew her hand was right against his head. For the hundredth time he sent a prayer up, and hoped it was heard.

Chapter Eighteen

The world was white all around her. She'd been so very, very cold before. Jesslyn couldn't remember why, but the cold was deep within her, almost buried her beneath its claiming fingers.

She looked around, trying to figure out where she was. The air was bright, so bright she squinted. A soft breeze carried the heady scents of flowers.

The rock Jesslyn sat on was a large slab of limestone. A butterfly flitted by her arm, a bright yellow gossamer flutter. She looked up, tried to follow it in the enveloping light.

"It's about time you joined me."

Jesslyn jerked her head around. There beside her sat Jerrod, his wavy blond hair ruffled in the wind. The light shot off the golden tresses like glinting topaz. His light eyes, forever lost in that color where the blue sky met the grassy horizon, danced in merriment.

"What are you doing here?" she asked him.

He shrugged, dressed in a flowing white shirt, white pants, and bare feet. The smile he gave her was so familiar she felt a tug of wistfulness for what might have been.

"Now there's no point in that," he told her, reading her thoughts.

She always forgot how Jerrod simply knew what she was thinking in this dream world.

"What is, is," he said. "And what can be, can." His leg swung back and forth from the height of the rock.

Jesslyn glared at him. In this realm their thoughts could fly, be spoken or not, and still be read. The fact Jerrod did the whole telepathic thing very well aggravated her and earned a hearty chuckle from him.

"You're still the same Jesslyn. So impatient. Always thirsting for knowledge so you can understand everything. Many things simply cannot be understood, just accepted." He pulled his other leg up and draped his arm on it.

"I hate when you do that. Can't you at least allow me the illusion of keeping secrets from you?" She leaned back onto her palms flattened against the cool stone.

His warm smile settled over her. "There are no secrets here."

"Where is here?" She looked out, saw only white, pristine and untouched except by the occasional butterflies.

"In between," he answered.

"In between what?" She loved seeing him in dreams, but the riddles drove her nuts.

"Everything." Jerrod shrugged. "Sleep and awake, cold and heat, light and dark, life and death."

Her mind couldn't comprehend all that.

A tingle of apprehension skittered in her stomach.

He stared at her for a moment. His eyes almost jeweled in their sparkle. Peace and contentment spread through her. He swept his arm aside. Before them, the white wall parted, and she saw darkness. Reds and blues flashed through the night, rain fell and the distant rumble of thunder echoed.

A chill ran up her spine and she looked at Jerrod. "What is this?"

"An answer to your question. A window, if you will."

She saw people surrounding something on the ground, heard a familiar voice. Aiden.

Aiden's voice carried to her, full of relief and something she couldn't name. "I knew you were here, baby. Everything's going to be all right now. You're safe, Jesslyn. You're safe. I promise. No one is ever going to hurt you again."

That was her on the ground, she realized with shock. Aiden held her hand.

The window started to fade at the edges, blend into the surrounding white.

"No, wait," she grabbed Jerrod's arm. "What happened? What's going on?"

"Right now, that isn't as important as what you want to do."

Again, Jesslyn looked back at the man she had loved with everything in her, the man part of her would always love.

His head lowered a fraction, his voice softened. "That's as it should be, Jesslyn. Love is eternal," he said as he read her thoughts.

Jerrod sighed, put his hand on hers. "It no longer matters what could have been, but what can be. You've passed through the darkest night and found the dawn again. Are you going to run from it? Let fear and memories keep you only in a world of limbo? Not quite day, but not yet night?"

Her brow furrowed as she realized what he said. "Do you like him?" she asked.

His slow straight smile. "Yes, I do. He's a good man. Honorable. Trustworthy, and it's killing him to see you like this." Jerrod pointed back to the window.

Aiden sat in a room with chairs, his head hung wearily on his hands, his arms draped over his knees. He seemed so lost.

Jesslyn glanced back at Jerrod. His bright eyes bore into hers and she felt he could see into her very soul.

"Not quite no, only He can see into souls."

She let out a huff. "Will you quit doing that?"

His eyes twinkled merrily, then sobered. "You must decide what you want. You asked God 'why,' for reasons, and for justification for so long. He left you for a reason, but now it is your choice."

"What do you mean my choice?"

He smiled a secret smile. "There are still rough times ahead, doubt it not. But there are wonderful surprises in store."

She thought for a moment. What he'd said was true. For years she'd wished she had died in the accident with her family, but no . . .

"Where are Hannah and Holden?" Usually they were all together.

"This isn't their time."

Jesslyn felt a sort of parting at Jerrod's words.

"This is good-bye, isn't it?" She knew it was, in some deep part of her.

"That is up to you. But since I know you're going back, then yeah, it is."

"But why?" She didn't like the thought of having to let him go again.

"It's not like that, Jesslyn. There really isn't 'good-bye.' Think of it as 'I'll see you one day.' I've always been here for you, a part of you. It's just taken you a while to realize that. But now that you have, you don't need me, at least not in the venue I've been visiting you in."

Jesslyn hated good-byes.

"I'll still drop in from time to time." He slung his arm around her shoulders. "Have to make certain Aiden treats you right," he said into her ear.

His words fell over her like a warm blanket.

She grinned up at him. "So Aiden and I will be together for a while?"

His smile answered her. "If you're not afraid to hold on tight to what is given to you."

Jesslyn sighed. Looking back towards the window, she saw herself lying in a hospital room. Aiden stood to the side.

"Why am I in the hospital?" she asked. Jerrod didn't answer her. Fear started to creep into this safe sanctuary.

"The monster," she whispered. Running from the monster . . . Fog clouded her memory. But the tingle of fear remained. "Who is the monster, Jerrod?"

His solemn look deepened the lines around his mouth. He shook his head. "I don't know. I can't see."

He knew everything.

"No, I don't," Jerrod answered her thought. "He knows everything and only Him. We see bits and glimpses of what He permits us or gifts us with. Only He can see both. We cannot get close to darkness."

"I don't understand." Jesslyn shook her head, tried to comprehend all he said.

"We here are light, and love, and goodness. The opposite of darkness, hatred and evil. Rarely can we get close. I was allowed to come to you now, but I do not know the answer to your question." For the first time his voice held that hint of impatience that it always had.

"Be careful, Jesslyn. The night isn't over for you yet. You must be strong and brave." All she could see were his eyes. "The darkness is very close to you. I tried to get to you earlier, but I couldn't get through."

"That's why Hannah and Holden aren't here, isn't it?" She waved a hand towards the window of the world. "This is too . . . dark for them?"

His smile brightened her spirit. "The little ones are treasured above all others. Though Hannah still has a mind of her own."

Jesslyn thought for a moment. "God is all-knowing. So why did He let Hannah warn me?"

"I don't question Him. Though perhaps for that very reason – to warn you. Now," he said as he gave her a hug, kissed her cheek. "It's time for you to head back. You can't stay here forever. Unless, of course, that is your wish."

She felt the gentle brush of his hand as it pushed her hair back. Jesslyn shook her head at him. It was peaceful here. So very peaceful. Yet, the thought of Aiden worried, of her father finding out what happened to her, swirled within her.

"I love you, Jesslyn. I always will," he whispered.

"I know. I love you too, Jerrod." She cupped her hand to his jaw, felt warmth flood through her like a soft golden light.

He smiled softly and nodded. "I know. Now go. Be careful."

Jerrod started to fade, the white darkened. Fear slithered through her nerves. His voice came through the graying light. "Look up."

The butterfly, a small dot of sunshine, flitted about. Up and down, around and around. Jesslyn focused on the little yellow wings. Happiness and hope.

Her vision narrowed and saw only the butterfly. Blackness swirled around her faster and faster. A vortex of darkness and fear pulled at her, sucked her down. Down. Down . . .

* * * *

Jesslyn fought against the void pulling at her. The darkness became tighter and fiercer the more she tried to fight it.

Then, through it, came his voice, soft and echoed as if he spoke in a tunnel. Pleading with her.

"Come back to me, Jessie girl. Come back. Please, open your eyes."

Aiden.

With supreme effort her eyelids barely rose, the darkness of her lashes obscured her view. Jesslyn tried again, forced her eyes to open all the way.

The world was blurry. She could make out shapes, colors, images, but everything melded together.

Her head hurt and she closed her eyes against the pain, hoped it would go away.

It didn't. She'd kill for some aspirin. What the hell? Did she get roaring drunk and pass out? Hadn't she heard Aiden? Where was he? A hundred trolls beat at the inside of her brain with picks and sledgehammers. Aspirin. Water.

A familiar scent tingled her nose. What was it? Where was she? A clatter rolled by somewhere. The beep of a machine intruded. Realization slammed into her. A hospital!

Jesslyn's eyes flew open. What the hell was she doing in a damn hospital? Had there been another accident?

Try as she might, she couldn't focus on a single thing. She was so tired. But she wouldn't give in to the beckoning exhaustion. When you went to sleep in hospitals you only awoke to horrible nightmares. Children dying. Funerals to plan.

She licked her lips, fought to control her breathing.

As panic started to grab her by the throat, she heard his whisper again. "Please wake up, baby. Please."

Something lolled on her hand. She tried to move it.

"Aiden?" Her whisper was lost behind her mask. Jesslyn took a deep breath and tried again, tried to focus on the black blob that could be his head.

"Aiden?" The blackness moved, swift and sharp. Glasses. She needed her glasses.

Then he was above her, leaning over her. She tried to lift her hand to remove the offensive mask. But her hand wouldn't move. She felt trapped.

"Oh, thank God. You're awake. Shh . . . Don't try to talk. Let me get the doctor." His voice sounded strained and excited. He pressed something, she heard it click.

Then a voice from behind and above her. "Yes?"

"She's awake."

Jesslyn was too tired to care. If Aiden were here, things were fine. Everything was fine. But what had happened? She muttered her question to him.

He leaned close to her. "Shh. Jessie. Everything's okay. You're safe."

Safe? Safe from what, she drowsily wondered.

"Well, I see you're right, Mr. Kinncaid," came the same voice she'd heard behind her, now across the room.

Intercom, the fuzzy thought floated to her.

"You've had us all worried, Ms. Black, though none more so than Mr. Kinncaid here."

Jesslyn listened to the woman's voice, chattery and chirpy, and it grated against the pounding in her head. Something vised on her arm, making the tips of her fingers tingle. The hiss of air and slow loosened grip told her—blood pressure. Why wouldn't her mind work?

"BP's good. Though your heart rate jumped a little bit ago. Now we know why. Normal. Perfectly normal." Someone quickly patted her right hand. The nurse, the pat wasn't Aiden's style.

"Glasses," she managed out.

"Oh, yeah. Sorry 'bout that. Tim and T.J. went by and picked up some of your things. I know I saw a little blue case." Aiden's voice changed as he moved about the room. Ruffled noises came from her left. She tried to turn her head, but stopped as pain shot through her skull. A gasping moan escaped before she could stop.

Something clattered on the floor, followed by Aiden's muffled, "Hell."

"Don't worry, Mr. K. She just tried to move her head. I know it hurts, honey. I'd give you something for it, but the doctors want to see you first. So hang in there, all right? Dr. Williams and Van Berger should be here pretty quick. I'll just go page them now." The woman pulled the covers even tighter and Jesslyn felt smothered.

"Please, don't. Could you loosen them a little? I don't like feeling trapped," she whispered.

Another quick pat. "Don't you worry, dear. I'll be back in a moment." Jesslyn heard her leave the room.

Then Aiden was at her side. Gently her glasses were put on, the bows easily slid along the tops of her ears. The world came into focus.

She breathed a sigh of relief. Though things were still a little fuzzy. Not necessarily out of focus, just . . . different. Again she tried to move, but couldn't. Tears threatened. She hated, hated to feel helpless and trapped.

"Hold still," Aiden told her, leaning down close enough that she could have counted the dark whiskers stubbling his cheek had she been so inclined, which she was not. She just wanted the damn covers off.

"Please," she said.

"What? What do you need?" His face was so earnest, so concerned, a surprised smile pulled at her lips.

"To move," she mumbled.

"Oh," and still he didn't smile. Thankfully, he loosened the covers enough that she could move her hands up and out from under the stifling confines.

"Thank you." Her hand was immediately clasped in both of his. Aiden sat partially on her bed.

His face looked weary, exhausted, and hopeful all at once. His eyes—how she loved his eyes—burned into her, and comforted her like nothing else could. The faint smell of his aftershave tickled her nose as his hand tightened on hers.

The dark head shook back and forth. He opened his mouth as if to speak and closed it again. She didn't miss the tick of muscle in his jaw. Jesslyn wanted to run her fingers down his proud straight nose. When she looked back up into his eyes she was surprised at the sheen she saw in them.

What had happened? The more she tried to think on, to try and figure it out, the more obscure and muggy things became.

Remember . . .

She remembered planning Maddy's funeral, getting in a fight with Kirk, crying and arguing with Aiden. Telling him that she loved him.

Driving . . .

Rain. It had been raining, hadn't it? Heartache . . . pain . . . crying . . .

Jesslyn closed her eyes, tried to think, to concentrate, but pain iced her brain.

Water. And hope . . . Hope . . .

Her eyes opened, looked into intense shimmering cobalt depths. With her free hand, she reached up, and shakily pulled the mask down to her chin.

"I figured out something," she whispered and saw him stiffen, the harsh features becoming grim as his lips thinned. The tears didn't fall even when his eyes narrowed.

Before he could say anything, and she could tell he was getting himself ready to, she plowed on. "I do really love you."

He shook his head, opened his mouth, but once again she beat him to it. "Just thought you ought to know."

Like she hoped, that earned her a smile, though ever so small it was.

Jesslyn closed her eyes. She was so tired. God her head hurt.

"You remember what happened?" he asked, wariness evident in his voice.

She thought some more, but nothing cleared, nothing congealed. Aiden — love. Rain — peace. Water — fear.

She sighed, tried to shake her head, and was quickly reminded why she should stay still. "Not really. I went to the lake. I remember that . . ." Walking along the shore, then . . . Nothing.

"That's okay, just rest. Rest," he urged her, his thumb rubbing circles on the back of her hand, down her wrist.

Jesslyn opened her eyes and looked at him perched on the edge of her bed. He was so big, sometimes his size surprised her. She'd never asked him exactly how tall he was, but she would guess a couple of inches over six feet. The hypnotic motion on the back of her hand and wrist was soothing.

Finally, she answered him, "I will, believe me. I sort of remember the discussion-crying-jag with you. I think—I think I drove in the rain. I don't know. Things are fuzzy. But I do remember knowing I loved you."

So tired . . . Jesslyn licked her lips, they were chapped. Exhaustion pulled at her.

She felt Aiden shift, and tightened her hold, though it was weak, on his hand.

Her eyes halfway opened. "Please. Please, don't leave me." Jesslyn hated the weakness in her voice, the fear that slithered through her. She needed him. "Stay with me. Promise me you'll stay."

He nodded, sat in the chair she heard scrape the floor as he pulled it closer to the head of the bed. "I promise."

She felt his warm lips on the back of her hand.

Jesslyn closed her eyes, tried to fight the exhaustion pulling at her, but couldn't. "You'll keep the monster away." He tensed. "I love you," she whispered.

"I love you, too." His voice was deep, strained. "God, I love you."

She heard him cough, mumbled something about defend, and then sleep stole over her.

Chapter Nineteen

July 4th

"Aiden, please?" she whined. Jesslyn hated to whine, but she'd do what she had to. She'd just gotten out of the tub and sat on the bed, dressed in leggings and a tunic, brushing her wet hair. Very, very carefully. Her head still hurt.

"No."

"Come on."

He propped his hands on his hips and stood by the edge of the bed staring down at her. "What part of no didn't you understand?"

Jesslyn rolled her eyes, and sat her brush on the nightstand. "I am fine."

"You just got home yesterday on the agreement you'd stay in bed." He leaned down until his face was right in hers. "And in bed you'll stay."

She changed tactics. "Well, I suppose that wouldn't be so bad if you stay with me." She reached up to grab his shirt and pull him to her, but he fisted his hand over hers and simply stared.

Apparently that tactic didn't work either. Damn. "But today's the parade. Please."

He only held her stare, didn't budge an inch. "No."

Jesslyn almost grinned. "Fine. Can I at least sit on the damn couch in the living room?"

His eyes slid closed, and his sigh wafted against her lips.

"Please?" she whispered. "I won't even walk if that worries you." She was edgy and tense and needed out of this damn bed.

The fact she was missing hours of her life was what wore on her. Not the fact she'd been attacked by a killer, though faceless images stalked her dreams. No, it was the fact she couldn't remember.

The doctors told her not to push it, to take it easy. It was not any less than they expected with the amount of shock to her system and her head injury. Jesslyn was to rest and not to worry about her memory loss. More than likely everything would come back when it was supposed to and not a moment sooner. Those were fine empty words. Not a single one of the doctors had to worry about missing time, or the possibility of remembering who a killer was before he struck again.

What she needed was to do what she felt she must. How was she supposed to remember a damn thing if no one would tell her anything? She'd finally worn Aiden down enough that she managed to get a scattered story out of him. No one wanted to talk about it, always hurriedly changed the subject. Their collective silence was not helping.

"Come on, it's a couch. I'll be reclining here, reclining there. The added benefit is I won't complain there," she tried again, cupping his cheek against her palm and leaning up to kiss the corner of his mouth.

His eyes opened and one brow arched.

"I'll let you carry me," she said.

He shook his head. "You need to rest," he calmly reasoned.

She had a feeling he wasn't as calm as he seemed. Aiden still thought she should be in the hospital. The neurologist wanted to run more tests. Not. Jesslyn was sick of being poked, probed, scanned, whatever else the medical personnel could conjure up. The only thing that kept her from tearing out of there had been Aiden's constant company and the visits from friends. So many people had come by to see her and wish her well. T.J. and Tim, David and Sally Hewett, all the Kinncaids, and even old Mr. Reeves. Daddy had come and stayed until late yesterday.

Aiden had hovered over her for the last two days, rarely leaving her side, and watched her constantly. She liked him being there, knowing he was there, but his hawk gaze missed little.

"Come on, you said, you liked carrying me. It makes you feel manly. Besides, I'll rest later. I'm hungry and I hate to eat in bed," she lied.

His loud sigh told her how frustrated he was.

"You're still not going to the parade," he said, gently lifting her against him.

Jesslyn wrapped her arms around his neck and settled her head on his shoulder. His aftershave, strong this morning, filled her senses. She could practically taste the spicy scent, leaning up a bit, she licked his neck. "Hmmm."

"Cut it out."

"No fun."

A muscle in his jaw started to tick.

At the doorway, she asked him, "Can you get me my laptop?"

He kept walking.

Oh well, she'd try for that later.

Once downstairs, the sounds of breakfast drifted from the kitchen, voices floating on the air. Aiden's entire family was here, having flown in Sunday. She hadn't really had a chance to say more than hi to any of them other than his parents.

Aiden set her down on the couch as though she were made of the finest china.

Jesslyn inwardly sighed. "Honestly, Aiden, you act as if I'll break if you move too quickly."

He didn't comment, but she saw the edge of his mouth tighten as he grabbed a throw off the back of the couch and tucked it around her. When it was to his perfection, he knelt down on his haunches beside her.

"You are a very bad patient," he told her.

"I hate to be sick. Hate to sit around in bed if I can move about. I was growing mold, for God's sake. And you're not a very agreeable nurse either."

He smoothed a finger down her cheek. "Hmm . . . You said you were hungry. What do you want?"

"What, no gruel?"

"Mom made pancakes," he said, ignoring her remark.

Her stomach growled and she smiled. "That sounds great."

He stood, walked to the doorway and stopped. "I still think you should be in bed."

"Pancakes?" She would have jumped off the couch and gotten them herself, but figured he'd fall over.

He shook his head and left.

Jesslyn leaned her head back against the cushions and waited. She hoped he remembered she liked orange juice and not milk. Yawning, she cuddled down into the blanket and reached for the remote. Glancing guiltily at the doorway, she cut on the television and flipped it to a news channel.

"What the hell is she doing out of bed?" Mr. Kinncaid boomed from the kitchen.

She strained to hear the voices and answers, but they were mumbled and lost in the clang and clatter of dishes. Her own father probably would have said the same thing. He flew back to Idaho late yesterday. It had been great seeing him, though she felt bad for worrying him so much, and Victor Black had been worried for her. But as the days passed in the hospital and she'd gotten better, though she still couldn't remember a damn thing, he'd relaxed. And he and the Kinncaids had gotten along pretty well, at least, as far as she could tell. When he'd left yesterday, her dad had only said, "I'm glad you're okay. It's great to see you smiling again, Jess. Aiden's a good guy."

That thought still made her smile. Her dad liked Aiden. Now whether Aiden's dad liked her was still questionable in her mind.

"Okay," Aiden's voice made her jump. "Here are the pancakes complete with Mom's special apple walnut compote."

Jesslyn scooted up as he set the tray on her lap. Pancakes, fruit and orange juice. She smiled and looked up at Aiden, who sat at the other end of the couch. "Thank you."

"You're welcome. Are you sure you're okay? You're not too tired being down here, are you?" His gaze ran over her face.

"I'm fine, Aiden. Quit worrying." She picked up the juice and took a long swallow.

"Missy, you should be in bed," Mr. Kinncaid said.

Carefully, she sat the juice down and looked up at the man. "But then I'd miss sparring with you, Mr. K."

His finger waggled at her. "You eat everything on that plate. You're skinny and pale enough. You look like you could fade away into the cushions of the couch." Turning to his son, he ordered, "Aiden, make sure she eats."

"Yes, Dad. It's a constant battle between us."

Kaitlyn walked up to stand beside Jock and said, "Jock, dear, leave them alone."

"Yeah, Dad," said a newcomer in the room. "Your bark is enough to give her a headache." This was one of the twins. Gavin Kinncaid, the doctor, she'd spoken to him in the hospital. The other one was Brayden, who had the little girl. Both favored their father in the rough, blunted features, though the coloring of eyes and hair were the same as Aiden's. Jesslyn figured they all inherited the jet-black hair and cobalt eyes from Jock.

"How are you feeling this morning?" Gavin asked, reaching out to take her pulse.

Jesslyn jerked her hand back. "Excuse me, you're not *my* doctor."

He flashed her a smile. "I'm everyone's doctor."

The charming, witty ob-gyn.

"I'll just bet you are," Jesslyn answered.

His grin grew. "I figure if I take your pulse and tell them all you're fine, they'd listen to me as a doctor. Aiden might back off enough so that you could eat and Dad would quit grumbling and biting."

Jesslyn sighed and held her arm out. His fingers were cool against her wrist.

After several seconds, Gavin turned to everyone. "Her heart rate is a bit elevated." He reached his hand out to her forehead, and she pulled back, but he followed. "Yep, and she's kinda warm. Might have a low-grade fever."

"I knew it!" Aiden all but leapt off the couch. He started to take the tray.

"See," Jock said. "I told you she should be in bed."

Gavin started laughing, and Jesslyn was clamping her hands on the tray that Aiden tried to take away.

"I'm joking," Gavin admitted.

Aiden whirled on him. "That's not fucking funny! She could have died!"

Gavin backed up and negligently sat in the chair, his palms up. "Sorry, thought I'd liven things up."

Jock muttered something in the doorway.

"Gavin, dear," Kaitlyn said. "I don't think you want to press your brother right now. I wouldn't feel the need to interfere if he knocked your teeth down your throat."

Jesslyn couldn't help it, she laughed. This family was unlike any she'd ever met.

Gavin pointed to her. "See, she's laughing."

Aiden was still glaring at his brother.

"She's fine, Aiden. Everything is normal." Gavin's serious face must have convinced Aiden because he only shook his head and sat again on the couch.

Jesslyn started eating. Finally, she looked up to the Kinncaids still in the doorway. Jock leaned on the door frame and held Kaitlyn in his arms.

"Mrs. K? These are the very best pancakes ever." In fact, she could probably eat few more.

"Why, thank you, dear. And it's Kaitlyn. I'm glad to see you eating. You look good this morning."

Jesslyn smiled. "Thank you." She looked to Aiden, who sat watching her every move. "See, I told you I felt fine."

"You're still not going to the parade," he told her.

"Well, of course she's not," Jock said. "And speaking of which, we should get going."

They ought to be warned. "Make sure you sit in a dry zone," she said.

"A dry zone?" Gavin asked.

Definitely warned. "This isn't your average Fourth of July parade with brass bands and pompoms. The only real band I've ever seen is a German polka band that comes in from somewhere. Most of the floats are trailers with equipment on them. The fire trucks are a big hit and I always love the library's float."

She settled back into the corner of the couch. "In certain areas the fire trucks open up their hoses and spray the water above the crowd, getting the said people wet; thus, wet zones. Make sure you sit in a dry zone."

"And that's the biggest thing?" Jock asked, obviously trying to figure out the dynamics of the community.

"Um, actually no," Jesslyn said, popping a bite into her mouth.

Aiden squeezed her knee. "And?"

"Everyone waits for the Rocky Mountain Biological Laboratory to come dancing through," she told them, smiling at Aiden.

It was great to see Jessie smiling again.

That one-sided grin peeked out at him, Aiden leaned over and kissed her. "Why do people wait to see some science group?"

Her grin grew and he caught the twinkle in her eye. "Because, they tie wild cabbage leaves together and prance down the street. Some don't bother with clothing underneath." Jessie shrugged and took another bite of his mother's pancakes. He was glad to see her eating again.

"Oh my," his mother said.

"Cool, naked women. Something different for me," Gavin quipped.

Jessie turned to Aiden's brother. "You're a smart-ass, Gavin."

"I'm so glad someone's noticed," he answered back

"Are there naked men?" Kaitlyn asked.

Jessie's eyebrows shot straight up and Aiden swiveled on the couch to look back at his mother.

"Kaitie!" his father said.

Jessie chuckled. "Sadly, there have been known to be. Of course, if you watch the cowboys that come down the street, some of those young buckaroos give a new meaning to bare back." She clasped her hand to her chest and sighed. "What some of them can do to a pair of chaps."

"Chaps is the right word in my opinion," Gavin said ruefully.

"Really?" his mother drew out.

"Kaitlyn Kinncaid, that's enough. I won't have my wife ogling other naked men."

Jessie laughed her full throaty laugh that made him want to kiss her.

"How young?" Aiden asked her, nudging her knee.

"Any cowgirls?" Gavin inquired at the same time.

"Missy, are you joking?" his father wanted to know.

She finished off her juice. "I don't know, Gavin. Watch and see," she answered his brother.

"A naked cowgirl, there's a fantasy." Gavin nodded and rubbed his hands together.

"Gavin, please, a mother's ears shouldn't hear these things." Kaitlyn shook her head and smiled.

"Missy, I asked you a question," Jock reminded Jessie, while patting the air down next to his wife.

"No, I'm not joking. Some of the locals seem to strip at any opportunity. The ski patrol and mountain workers used to wait till the end of the season and . . ." Jessie lowered her voice. "Ski down the mountain stark naked."

"My, God. We're in Sodom and Gomorrah," his father replied.

Again her laughter rang out. "It's not that bad. Some around here are just a little more . . . liberated than others."

"Maybe we should just stay here," Jock said.

"You wouldn't be missing much if you did," she agreed.

What?

"I though you wanted to go to the parade?" Aiden asked her.

Jessie licked syrup off the edge of her mouth, her tongue darting out. Aiden shifted on the couch at his reaction to that simple action.

"Well, I figured if I asked for something big, like the parade, the living room and breakfast wouldn't seem so drastic."

She'd manipulated him and he'd fallen for it.

Damn it, this was her health they were talking about. Aiden opened his mouth to say something, pointing his finger at her, but nothing came to mind.

"That's the way, Jesslyn," his mother said. "Men bully, and women think. You go, girl."

Aiden didn't really care for her input here. You go, girl? Where had his mother learned that?

"I'm ready for the parade!" Six-year-old Victoria Kinncaid barreled into the living room. Her father, Brayden, followed behind her. "Hi, Jesslyn. Are you feeling better today? I'm going to the parade. I want to get a balloon."

Jessie smiled softly at his niece. "I'm feeling much better. Thank you, Victoria."

The little girl stood by the couch. "Oh, call me Tori. Everyone does. Unless I'm in trouble, then it's Victoria Reily Kinncaid."

Jessie's grin grew. "All right, Miss Victoria Reily Kinncaid, I will call you Tori. Try to talk your daddy into sitting up close to the curb so you can catch the candy the parade people toss."

Tori nodded. "I will."

Everyone shuffled out. Aiden watched them all go. His mother leaned over and kissed Jessie on the cheek and his father told him to make sure she rested. Gavin winked at her as Bray and Tori made their way out the door. Quinlan didn't have time for the parade. He was going to the hotel. Christian, or Chris, Bills was the last out of the house, carrying Tori's backpack.

When the door shut and the house silenced, he turned back to Jessie.

"How does Chris fit in with your family again?" she asked.

"Well, she's been with our family for six, no seven years. I think." Hell, he couldn't remember. "Christian showed up at my parents' house one weekend when Tori was just a baby. Hired her as the nanny. She's helped Bray raise Tori, and been with the family ever since. She's part of the family. As far as we're concerned, she's our sister, and Tori thinks of her as a mom."

Jessie yawned and sighed.

Aiden reached over and moved the tray. "You tired, Miss Devious?"

Her grin warmed him.

She nodded. Carefully, he picked her up and cradled her next to him. Her fruity shampoo tickled his nose as he carried her up the stairs.

He sat on the bed with her, leaned them back and settled her under the covers. "Do you need anything?"

"Can we turn on the TV?"

He kissed the top of her head and reached for the remote. "You aren't balking at being back in bed?"

"I got to eat breakfast downstairs, didn't I?"

She had. Aiden wanted to keep her in bed until she was back to her old self. She was still too damn pale and the side of her face and head was still molted with different shades of purples, blues and greens. He hadn't asked her this morning, but he wondered if she remembered anything about the attack.

"Besides, I figure if I go along easily, you might let me watch the fireworks tonight downstairs, out on the porch." She yawned again.

"You can see the valley from the balcony right out there." He pointed towards the doors that led out to their private deck. He'd ask her if she remembered anything later. Tomorrow they were supposed to go to the police station to talk to Garrison and a couple of people from CBI.

"Yeah, the balcony would work too."

"Go to sleep."

"If I do, I won't sleep tonight," she said.

Aiden rubbed her shoulder and inwardly sighed. He was worried about her, but he was glad she was home with him. The hospital had her tense and uptight the whole time, and knowing what he did from her and what her father had told him, it was no wonder she couldn't relax there. Too many bad memories on top of a horrifying situation.

Some bastard had tried to kill her, and damn near succeeded. Aiden couldn't get past that. He looked down at her and noticed she was already asleep. A smile caught him off guard. She thought she was so strong, and she was, but sometimes she needed someone to take care of her, whether she admitted it or not.

Garrison called daily. The couple of times Jessie had talked to him, she'd become so upset, Aiden had put a stop to it. Or he tried. Woman was damned stubborn. Now, they were going tomorrow to the station. When he told her they could meet here at the house, she'd replied she didn't want this brought into her home.

Tammy's mother had also called. Aiden didn't know what was said, and Jessie hadn't told him, but she hadn't talked for over an hour after that phone conversation.

Ian called every night at the same time. He was currently cross-checking missing persons and other unsolved murders in other states. Apparently it was taking longer to find this guy than anyone cared for.

It didn't matter how long it took. Aiden would find out who the bastard was who dared to touch what was his.

Chapter Twenty

Damn. Damn. And damn again. Stupid. So pointlessly stupid. If he'd only finished the job. He paced his confines, thought about what to do. Berlioz blared through his speakers. The dissonant notes filled the air as the bells bonged.

The fact Jesslyn was still alive beat at him like a time bomb.

Tick. Tick. Tick.

He wanted to laugh at the whole situation. *What were the chances? Not that it mattered.* She was alive, and she was a threat. Still. He stopped, his brow furrowed.

He'd gone to see her in the hospital. Several times in fact. A few she knew about, others she didn't.

But she was never alone! It would have been so easy at first, but someone was always with her, Kinncaid, or one of his brothers, her father, Kinncaid's father, even his damn mother, then the doctor and nurses. Hell, the woman always had what might as well have amounted to a bodyguard.

No, the hospital was out of the question. Though it would have been perfect. No one would have questioned it much. She'd been so small, frail, weak. It could have been over before she or anyone else had even realized what had happened. Something in her IV, a pillow over her head. Or he could just mark her as he did the others. It didn't matter now.

A sign of the cross. Four perfect points, right over their betraying hearts. To remind them. To remind them of God's will. To try and give them redemption in that last moment. Everyone knew that the way to redemption was through the cross. Through the cross. Through the cross.

Jesslyn might not be *her*, but she still had to die. There was simply no other choice. He didn't like it. He didn't. The thought rolled his stomach, but failure was not an option. He shook his head and raked his hands through his hair. Not an option. God told him what he must do, the stars told him what he must do. Everything told him, screamed it in his mind. It didn't matter what he wanted.

In that moment like a visage from the depths of his memory, he saw his mother laughing. Her head thrown back in joyous laugher before she ruffled his hair.

Those had been good times. Times before *her*.

He fisted his hands against the side of his head. Then he remembered his father with her *long red hair slung over his arm as he carried her limp body out into the night.*

He remembered the fights, the screams and yells. He remembered finding his mother in the bathtub.

The sound of his father's prevaricating voice, the voice the congregation followed, listened to, prayed with and for, filled his mind. That same voice, lashing out at him, demanding more. Always more, always better. He could never stray. Never stray. Not like his father. They'd made him betray his vows with their wicked, evil ways and their black hearts.

Tick. Tick. Tick.

He shook his head, fought off the battles of the past, focused on the present, the possibilities of the future. Slowly, he lowered his hands. Apparently, Jesslyn didn't remember, or that was the rumor going around.

But the mind was a funny thing. The simple fact that she could . . .

He had seen the recognition in her eyes just as he had crushed the flashlight into the side of her head.

Yes, she had to die. Had to die. Had to die. And soon.

He chewed on his lip. There was a way, there always was. He'd simply watch her, and strike when she least expected it.

Tick. Tick. Tick.

Chapter Twenty-one

Jesslyn sat in the sparse office of the Police Chief. Aiden stood behind her, with his hands on her shoulders, a constant comfort and reassurance. Behind the desk sat Chief Garrison. Lounging against the wall beside Garrison was CBI Agent Steve Litton. By the window was Litton's partner, Agent Cynthia Jones. The faces of all present were tense and serious.

"Jesslyn, this isn't an interrogation," Garrison said again.

"Well, it feels like it. I've told you, I don't remember." They had been here for at least an hour.

Derrick Garrison had come by the hospital once, the house twice, and finally yesterday, she agreed to coming here. Aiden didn't like it —he was so protective he was driving her nuts. He was caring, tender, loving, and so incredibly quiet as though a loud noise would hurt her. She'd had enough.

Jesslyn didn't know what Aiden was so worried about. Okay, so maybe she did. She'd taken, as he had told her, at least ten years off his life.

"Ms. Black, did you hear me?" Agent Litton asked.

With a shake of her head, Jesslyn sighed. "Sorry, no I didn't." The man was of medium height, much shorter than Aiden, and in fact shorter than his partner, Agent Jones, who was a tall woman. Dark sandy hair matched the tawny color of his sharp eyes. His features were normal, nothing to notice or draw attention. Jesslyn figured that was a plus in his line of work.

His smile was one of patience, yet one of understanding all the same. "The Colorado Bureau of Investigation is helping in this crime. Chief Garrison called us in to assist with the investigation. We realize it must be difficult for you not to know what happened, and yet we're pounding you with questions. The fact is, any information you could give us would be greatly appreciated."

Jesslyn met his stare, silence stretched between them. "And what is it you think I've been doing? Knitting?" She regretted her snapped comment. "Look, I realize this is your job and must, at times like this, be incredibly frustrating, or it would be to me. In any case, I will do what I can to help, though I don't know what I can do." Jesslyn sighed. A headache throbbed behind her eyes, not that she'd ever gotten rid of the thing since she'd awakened in the hospital.

Agent Jones walked to the desk and sat on the front corner facing Jesslyn. Jones had to have Vikings in her family lineage. The woman was six feet tall in flat, practical shoes. Silvery blond hair weaved in a French braid and her sky blue eyes sat perfectly above broad cheek bones. Where Litton was your average Joe, Jones was a breathtaking goddess. Though her aura appeared icy, reserved and distant, she was the more approachable of the two.

"Why don't you tell us what you can remember? Anything at all. Maybe that would help." Her voice was crystalline, soft for such a large woman.

"Yes, I'll do that. Aiden, sit down, please. You're making me edgy." She patted his hand on her shoulder.

He walked to her side and sat back down in the chair he'd vacated earlier. He leaned back and reached towards her with his hand. She grasped it. The look in his eyes was anything but calm. She gave him a small smile, squeezing his hand to reassure him.

Jesslyn took a deep breath, then let it out. "I remember bits, more feelings and emotions than any actual events." The unknown ate at her. She was a control freak. Always liked to know what was going on, when it happened, how it happened, why. Not a single one of those questions was answerable.

Tentatively she said, "Sometimes, like an immediate flash, a thought or feeling shoots through my mind. But most are like smoke. The harder I try, the more elusive the images become."

Everything she'd found on the cyberspace gateway of knowledge said basically the same thing. There were no guarantees of when or if lost memories would return. Many people simply remembered, others had something trigger the locked box of their minds and yet others had never regained access to lost hours, weeks, years . . . The stories had been endless and had made her eyes cross. She knew she shouldn't complain, at least she remembered something, and for that small amount of knowledge she was thankful. And she was alive.

"I remember fear. That's always there," she whispered. Aiden's hand on hers tightened. "I remember rain and lightning, thunder and storms."

She narrowed her eyes, not seeing the occupants in the room, just a fog-filled area of her mind, where upon occasion, the mists would part and allow her a quick glimpse of what lay beyond.

"I remember being cold. So very, very cold, like ice water flowed instead of blood." She shivered. Ever since the attack, she couldn't get warm. Aiden's thumb absently rubbed to and fro on the back of her hand.

"Maybe the tape will help," Garrison said. Out of the corner of her eye she saw Aiden's head turn sharply.

"Tape?" she asked, looking from one to the other.

"What tape?" Aiden asked.

Garrison cleared his throat and laced his fingers together on top of his desk, leaning up on his elbows. "You know your phone was found. Do you remember having your phone?"

Her phone? What did that have to do . . . "Are you telling me you have the dispatch tape of my call?" That made sense. Of course they did.

"Yes." Garrison's brow furrowed. "You called nine-one-one."

If there was a tape, maybe it would jar her memory.

Garrison started to say something, and Aiden's hand tightened on hers. Jones spoke, "Do you want to listen to it?"

Jesslyn thought for a minute, then shrugged. "I don't know. I mean what's . . ."

"I don't know if that is the wisest course," Aiden bit out.

She turned to him, then back to the three law officials.

"It might help, right? What did I say on it?" she asked them.

Then the mists parted, sucked her back. Fear exploded as she remembered running, praying for her phone not to screw up as she tried to dial nine-one-one. Slick mud pulled at her feet.

Thunder echoed in her mind, as she tried to grab the wet fender. Hurry. Have to hurry. She's dead. Dead . . . Dead . . .

Jesslyn felt Aiden's hand on hers, as she tried to catch her breath. Even as she tried to hold on to the terrifying image, it faded.

A chill prickled the skin on her arms. She blinked and brought everyone back into focus.

"What?" Aiden quietly asked. Jesslyn could see the anger simmering in the blue flames of his eyes, and she knew it wasn't at her, but for her.

She took a breath. "Nothing much really. I remember dialing my phone, and running back to the Jeep. I know I was afraid the phone had screwed up. It was raining—yeah, it was. I slipped in the mud as I rounded the back fender." Jesslyn thought for a minute more. "I remember thinking she was dead." Once again she tried, closed her eyes, and concentrated on what she had just seen. "Yeah, I remember thinking she's dead." She opened her eyes, blew out a breath and shook her head. "That's all. That's—that's it."

Damn it, this was so frustrating. Why couldn't she remember?

"It's all right. That was good. Really good," Jones said in her calm voice. Her expression turned thoughtful, then, finally she continued. "You know, I agree with Chief Garrison. I think the tape might help, but it's your choice."

Jesslyn looked at Aiden. A muscle bunched in his jaw, and he was entirely too still. He reminded Jesslyn of a wild cat of prey getting ready to spring.

"Fine," she agreed. "Let's get this done."

Litton walked out the office.

Cobalt eyes narrowed at her beneath black brows. "You don't have to do this. The neurosurgeon said not to push yourself too hard and—"

"Yes, Aiden, I do have to do this. For myself. For Tammy. For Maddy. I can't stand the not knowing," she admitted to him. It was the first time she'd said as much about her memory lapse bothering her. "And I'll stop if it gets to be too much."

His sigh was one of resignation. Litton came back in with a mini-recorder, which he set on the desk.

Jesslyn stared at it and looked over at Aiden. He ground his back teeth, his strong jaw moving back and forth.

"Are you sure about this?" he asked, his eyes narrowing. His hand on hers tightened almost painfully. The muscle in his jaw quirked. His eyes burned into hers. "I don't want you going through this again."

She tilted her head to him. "I'll be okay. You're here."

Yeah, Aiden thought, he was here for all the damn good it was doing. Aiden raked a hand through his hair. He wanted to take her home and get her the hell out of here and away from all this.

Jessie took a deep breath and nodded to Garrison. Her voice filled the room.

"Hello?"

"Nine-one-one dispatch, what's the emergency?"

"Hello? Please, help me. I'm at Emerald Lake! He's here . . ."

"Ma'am, who's there? Are you in danger?"

Aiden's heart took a deep breath and he gripped the armrest.

Shambling sounds as though the phone was jostled.

"Shit. My keys. My keys are gone. Oh, God. Oh, God." Her panicked words chilled him. He stared at the recorder that shot arrows into his soul.

"Ma'am, calm down. Who's there with you?" the dispatcher's voice asked.

"I don't know who the hell he is. But she's, oh God, she's dead. Please, help me."

"Looking for these?" A new voice said from the background. Aiden fisted his hand as Jessie's scream tore through him and around the room.

Shuffling noises muffled in silence.

Then panting, puffing as though someone were running. Thunder crackled through the small office, the rhythmic pound of something. Feet?

"Ma'am?"

She was running—trying to get away. Aiden's blood froze at what he was hearing.

Someone gasped. *Thunk.* The silence stretched.

"No!" she screamed.

A black cloud roiled and built within him. Her terror bit at him.

More scuffles and scampering sounds filled the air.

Another piercing cry shot through him. Oh. My. God.

"Ma'am?" the dispatcher tried.

"Please," Jessie whimpered.

At the terrified sound, something in him roared.

"Bitch. You're no different than the rest of them, are you?" A low graveled voice grated out. *"I ought to cut your throat for that."*

"Ma'am! Ma'am!" the dispatcher yelled.

Silence.

"Jesus Christ," Aiden muttered. He looked at Jessie. She was white as a sheet and he didn't know who held whose hand tighter.

He bit down, felt the muscle in his jaw bunch. Jessie's eyes were closed and her fisted hand was white knuckled. This had been a bad idea. A very bad idea.

"Jessie?"

She shook her head.

The words jumbled through her mind as though trying to find their place in a scattered puzzle. Bouncing and jarring against what she knew and what she didn't.

"Looking for these?" The voice tugged at her, made her blood freeze in her veins. Her own scream seemed to plead with her.

Jesslyn sat frozen in place while the short message played out.

" . . . I ought to cut your throat for that."

Cut your throat . . . Cut your throat . . .

It was so damn close! Jesslyn felt like screaming. She started to tremble, and she stiffened to try and keep under control.

"Again," she said, barely a whisper, but commanded all the same.

"Jesslyn," Aiden said, his voice barely containing the fury she felt coming from him.

She ignored him, but squeezed his hand even tighter than she already was.

This time, she was prepared. Jesslyn closed her eyes, let the words fall where they would, concentrated on the noises, the sounds. Slowly, images, forms and shapes drew together.

Lightning flashed all around. The thunder ripped the air apart.

Hurry. Had to hurry. Coming, the monster's coming.

Jesslyn's chest tightened, her breath came quicker.

Scuffling noises.

" . . . throat for that."

Her hand flew to her neck. Fingered the small scabbed slice across the column. Death above. Flashlight. Cold. The knife was so cold, stinging where it cut.

Just as quickly the vision was gone.

Her hand trembled in Aiden's.

"What did you mean, death above?" Jones asked.

Only then did she realize she'd spoken out loud.

She took a deep breath, tried to calm her jittering nerves. She thought about the question, what she had seen. "Like – um . . ." She swallowed, attempting to ease the dryness of her throat. "Pictures of the Grim Reaper. A dark hooded figure above me."

"Above you? As in taller than you?" Jones continued in smooth even tones.

Jesslyn shook her head. "No, I-I don't think so." She thought about what she'd seen. "No, I-I was on the ground. On my back and he was . . . He was over me."

A shudder racked her body, even as she tried to hold it in.

"Anything else?" Jones's foot moved slowly back and forth.

The headache was full blown now. Jesslyn pinched the bridge of her nose, tried to come up with something that would help. Finally, she shook her head.

"No, I'm sorry. There's really nothing else. Scattered thoughts about hurrying, that feeling that someone is coming right behind you. But that's it." She knew bitterness crept into her voice at the end.

"Any features? Anything about him you remember?"

Jesslyn shook her head.

"What about his voice? Any accents?"

"American." She grinned ruefully, but thought. "It wasn't Southern, or Texan, no thick Bronx or New Jersey." She shrugged. "You heard the tape. He just sounded . . . normal."

Jones leaned forward and patted Jesslyn on the shoulder. "You did really well. I've worked cases before where there was head trauma and the victim never remembers. The fact that you are already is a good sign. Just be patient."

Victim. Jesslyn hated to be victim.

"One more question, Ms. Black. Do you remember being in the car?" Litton asked.

Jesslyn sighed. Car? "What car?"

They all looked at Aiden, then back to her.

"It was in the paper," Jones added.

She shook her head. "I haven't been interested in the paper."

Garrison cleared his throat. "We found Tammy's car at the bottom of the lake. You were holding a bracelet, presumably one of hers, as it was similar to the ones she was wearing."

Jesslyn thought for a minute, the pain in her head tensing her neck muscles. Nothing. "I don't know." She shook her head. "I'm sorry, I don't know," she sighed.

"I think that's enough for today, Ms. Black. If you feel up to it, can we talk again tomorrow? A bit of time might jar something else." Jones was obviously the spokeswoman of the two agents.

Jesslyn nodded. "Sure, that's fine. What time?"

"Same as today?"

She looked at Aiden. He merely raised his brows and shrugged. "Up to you."

Once again, she nodded to the law enforcement officials in the room and got up. Aiden pulled her to him and kissed the top of her head.

Garrison spoke, "Jess, we can do this at the house if you'd feel more comfortable."

Aiden shook his head and pinned the chief with what could only be construed as a glare. "No. We'll be here." Without another word to anyone, he steered her out of the police station and to her pickup.

After Jesslyn was settled, he went around to get in the driver's door. She leaned her pounding head back against the seat and prayed the nausea would ease back. God her head hurt.

The driver's door opened and Aiden slid behind the wheel.

He studied Jessie. She looked so pale and small. He'd wanted nothing more than to pack her up and get her the hell out of here. As long as he lived, Aiden would never remember that night or what she'd gone through without terror stabbing his heart.

His Jessie, so brave, so strong, and so frightened. Aiden hadn't protected her from the monsters, couldn't even keep her safe during sleep. She awoke every night in terror and there wasn't a damn thing he could do about it. Nor could he take away her terror. Proud Jessie tried to hide that from him, but he knew, saw the fear in her, noticed she never stepped foot out of the house by herself. Not that he'd let her. Normally, she would balk at that, and she hadn't muttered a single word.

This was killing him. He wanted to *do* something.

Aiden lifted a hand and slid his fingers beneath her hair to her neck. He traced the pulse from her jaw to her collarbone with his thumb. The damn tape and her whispered memories filled him with rage. Just a little deeper and the bastard would have . . . That didn't matter. Nothing mattered now, but Jesslyn.

He swallowed the fury, or tried to. "You okay?"

She opened her eyes and turned her head on the seat. He drifted his thumb along her jaw to the corner of her mouth.

She gave him a small smile. "Yeah, I'm okay. It's just frustrating and infuriating that I can't remember. I'm so close. It's like when a song's been stuck in your head, just a chorus or a few lines, and then when you want to remember it, you can't, but you know you should. Does that make sense?" Her brow wrinkled.

"Yes. I'm with Jones, just be patient. Don't push it." She was pale and he could see the pain of a headache in her eyes. "And I think you pushed it too much today already."

Damn it. He never should have agreed on them coming today, regardless of who the hell she wanted to help. He hated to see her this vulnerable. Rage and fury roared within him, pounding in his veins, demanding to be released. He wanted to hit something, and hit it hard.

He closed his eyes and took a deep breath. The red haze receded. Opening his eyes, he saw she was staring into space. For the longest time she didn't say anything, yet he knew her well enough to know by the look in her tired eyes that she was building up to it. Jessie had been so quiet lately.

She cleared her throat. He didn't take his hand away from her neck, just kept up the light caress.

"I'm sorry," she said.

"What?" he asked. What the hell was this? "What are you apologizing for?"

"For not staying that night with you and working it out. For worrying you. For doubting for a minute what we had. For thinking you might have lied to me about the Brice thing."

"You can be so stupid sometimes," he whispered.

Her eyes narrowed on his and he knew she was thinking about denying it, but then the lie cleared and she murmured so softly he had to lean close to hear her. "I had planned to end it that night with you, which you already know, but when I heard your father thought you were engaged, something in me just got mad. Something else

230

just cracked because I thought you'd lied to me. That I could have been the other woman. And, you're right, I'm stupid sometimes."

This was a surprise. "Ah, Jessie." Aiden shook his head, even as he caught a teardrop falling from her eye. "There's nothing to forgive. In the scheme of everything, Brice and your reaction to my nonexistent engagement isn't important. You love me. I love you. And we'll figure the rest out."

A small smile played at the corner of her mouth. "Yeah, I do love you. So much, it frightens me."

"Tell me about it."

She pulled the same corner of her mouth in, nibbled on it. "I just wish I could remember everything else about that night so I could get on with my life."

"Patience." Though he was about out of his.

"Aiden, I'm tired of waiting." She shifted in her seat. "I want this over. I swear if you had your way I'd still be in bed." Her tired voice was laced with exasperation.

Aiden gave her what he hoped was a wicked grin that masked his anger and said, "That, Jessie girl, is the best idea I've heard all day."

Her one-sided grin peeked out and he saw his need answered in her eyes. His dropped to her mouth and he watched as she licked her lips.

"I think when we get back, you need to take a nap," he whispered, and gently pulled her towards him. They met over the console. Her lips were sweet and giving. The kiss, soft and gentle, made him wish they were at home and not sitting in the police department parking lot. Aiden reluctantly pulled away.

Jesslyn's eyelids half covered her dark eyes. They rose as her gaze met his. "I was thinking more along the lines of a bath."

This time when their smiling mouths met, it was a kiss driven from need, from want, from hunger. He nibbled on her lower lip, licked the inside of her mouth slowly, grazed his finger around her ear.

Her breath shuddered into his mouth. "I've missed you," she whispered.

Finally, he pulled back, the blood roaring in his veins. "We'll have to see what we can do about that." Aiden turned the key, backed the truck around, and headed home with thoughts of making love to Jesslyn keeping him occupied and his rage leashed.

* * * *

The room was hazy with the late afternoon light slanting through the wooden blinds.

Aiden sat back in the chair, Jessie straddling him, her knees wedged between his hips and the chair.

He ran one hand slowly up her naked torso. Some bruises mottled across her chest and torso. He leaned up and kissed one, then the next. He licked the undersides of her breasts and she moaned, spearing her fingers through his hair.

Soft music played from a stereo in the bathroom. They'd had their bath and he'd given in to her when she'd gotten out, dripping wet and sat on the counter beckoning him. He'd made her come, pulsing against his mouth before slipping inside her. He could still taste her essence mixing with the flowery musk, purple bubble bath she'd used.

He licked his way to wind around her nipples before pulling them into his mouth, scraping them lightly with his teeth before suckling her hard. Her moan reached into him and grabbed hold. Her skin was moist and warm against his mouth, the chair's leather cool against his back. The contrast spiked the need in him even more.

She rose up on her knees, then slid slowly back down on him. He closed his eyes, letting her ride him. Up and down, slowly, torturously.

Aiden leaned back and watched her. They were both silent, only watching, the sounds of their breaths mixed between them.

Her lashes fluttered down as he reached up and rolled her nipples, then pulled them between his fingers.

She arched her neck and he ran his hand up her, cupped her face, then skimmed his hand down the toned lines of her.

Her pace increased, but he stood, pulling her legs from between him and chair before sitting down again.

Aiden hooked her knees over his arms and watched her eyes widen, watched passion shift in the dark depths as she realized how vulnerable she was. He ran his hands up and down her back, then caressed her buttocks.

"Am I hurting you?" he whispered, watching her as he shifted deeper. She was so small he could feel her womb against him.

Her eyes clouded and she licked her lips, shaking her head.

He grazed one finger between the globes of her backside and smiled as she shuddered against him, clenching tight around him.

Aiden held her hips, moved her on him as he wanted, reveled in the fact she was his and trusted him enough to give him the control.

Grinning wickedly, she bent back, reached behind her and fondled him.

Aiden sucked in his breath and shifted her again. "My way."

She pouted, then gasped again as he reached between them and flicked his finger over that one little spot that would send her spinning.

He kept the pace slow and controlled until she begged him. Pressing deep inside her, he also pressed her clitoris against his finger and shaft, watched her as she threw her head back and shattered in his arms. Aiden pumped once more and emptied himself into her, dropping his head to her shoulder and feeling her heart against his lips as she leaned forward.

He wondered if he'd ever get enough of her.

Chapter Twenty-two

Sometime in the early hours before dawn, Jesslyn awoke. Terror choked her. Sharp images flashed in her mind, then broke off, cloaked in darkness. But the fear remained, jagged edged fear that iced her veins and made tears sting in her eyes.

Calm down. She had to calm down. Concentrate.

Jesslyn had been through this mantra endless times. Think about the oxygen bringing peace to her, while the carbon dioxide expelled the tensions. In. Out. Deep. Again.

When she'd battled the terror back enough to think clearly, she remembered where she was.

Aiden? She reached over, and warmth touched her fingertips.

She was so cold. The feelings of the dream lingered, but try as she might she couldn't conjure up a memory of what the nightmare had been about. Something nagged at the back of her mind. Water. Blood. Then nothing.

The fear swirled around her, pulled at her mind. Chills raced up her spine. Jesslyn tried to hold the shudder in. She didn't want to awaken Aiden, but it was pointless. The cold seeped deep into her, settled in her very soul.

Why couldn't she remember? Sleep pulled at her, even as the darkness pushed her to stay awake. The terror reduced her to a child, afraid of the monsters hiding in the shadows. Awake one could guard; asleep, one was open to attack.

Aiden's arm, wrapped around her waist, pulled her back against his solid warmth. The heat radiated out of him, across her, through her, dispelling some of the cold, banishing the panic back to anxiety.

Jesslyn worried her bottom lip, tried to force herself to relax.

"What's wrong?" Aiden's gruff whisper tickled her ear. He tried to clear his throat.

She didn't want to bother him, maybe she could pretend to be asleep. His arm tightened. "Nothing."

"You're cold." Aiden leaned up on his elbow, tried to turn her over, but she wouldn't let him.

"I'm fine. Sorry I woke you."

Aiden put his finger under her chin, forced her face to turn to his. In the silvery light of the moon, he studied her. Those eyes, heavy with sleep, were still intense. A frown marred between his onyx eyebrows, dark stubble dusted his jaw.

"What?" he demanded.

"I just had a dream, that's all. Nothing big." She sincerely hoped she didn't look pale and gaunt as she usually did after a journey through her nightmares. Aiden would hound her endlessly then.

"Bad?" His eyes mirrored his concern.

Guess she looked like she felt. "I don't know, I don't really remember."

His confusion was evident in the pull of his brow, the narrowing of his gaze.

"I mean, I just get flashes. Nothing really. It's just the feeling won't go away." Jesslyn scooted back onto her side, and after several stretched moments, Aiden lay again beside her. His arm an anchor around her, his breath and heat warming her.

This was nice. In her exhausted state, her mind wouldn't complete her thoughts logically. She was getting lost and confused. Just wanted to sleep.

But, slumber was not always safe. The wary were brought down, devoured in fear. Strong became weak. Adults became children. The hardened cried.

Jesslyn sometimes loathed sleep.

After a few minutes, she thought Aiden was asleep when he asked, "Feeling? What feeling?"

She tried to shrug.

"Jessie." He drew her name out, more of a demand than a request.

"I don't know what the dream was of. But it was bad. I wish I remembered what happened in it."

"Why?" he asked, puzzlement clear in his voice.

"Because I think it was important." His warmth was calming. Reassuring. Safe.

A few more minutes passed. Their breathing filled the silence. The wind, whipping through the window, hummed and cooled the air around them. The heady perfume of damp grass and dew-heavy flowers lingered in the air.

"You should try to sleep, Jessie girl." Aiden's deep voice was a comfort.

Drowsiness tugged at her. He wasn't the only one worn out.

Just as sleep started to descend, a flash, crystalline in its clarity. A bloody handprint on a window. Swimming in a churning crimson lake with bodies floating around her. Lightning ripped the sky in two.

Jesslyn turned, burrowed into the security Aiden offered. His arms held her to him. The strong, steady beat of his heart soothed in its rhythm. Slowly, peace settled into her, vanquishing the image. Aiden kissed her forehead and rubbed her back up and down.

"You're safe, you know."

"I know." Was that her voice?

His hands continued to soothe, to calm. Finally, she started to ease. For him, she evened her breathing, forced her muscles lax. What was wrong with her? Why did she have to be tormented like this? It was humiliating to be brought this low, to be this vulnerable. In minutes, Aiden's movements slowed. His breathing leveled and she dared a look at him.

When she knew he was asleep, she carefully slipped from the bed. Grabbing a sweatshirt from the chair, she pulled it on over her pajamas, then grabbed a pair of socks and quietly slipped out the door.

In the living room, Jesslyn stared out at the darkened predawn morning, at the engulfing blackness beyond the window. She rubbed her arms, tried to dispel the chill. She didn't even feel like sitting in the little window seat, or going to the office.

The tension and anger in Aiden had been evident to her all week. The fear something might have changed between them haunted her beneath the terror. For the first time in a long time, Jesslyn needed someone, and she was scared she was losing the only person she wanted. Not that she'd ever tell Aiden that. He'd roll his eyes and tell her she was being stupid.

For the last week, he'd been gentle, kind and caring, so attentive, she'd wanted to yell at him. His touches were fewer than before the attack, and maybe even more hesitant, as though careful not to startle her. Jesslyn had decided she was going to have to seduce him if she had to, but thankfully, something had changed all that this afternoon.

Their love had pushed the fear back, kept it at bay. Aiden could do that when she let him. She sighed. Beautiful. Life with Aiden was beautiful. Or it could be.

Besides the fear stalking her, was sorrow too. She'd missed Maddy's funeral because she was in the damn hospital and no one would let her go. T.J. and Tim had threatened to tie her to the bed and Aiden said he would have helped them.

There was simply no way she could go to Tammy's. She felt horribly ashamed for that. Cowardice was never something she liked to admit to, but a coward she was. Jesslyn just wasn't ready to see Tammy's mother, or go to the ceremony.

Death, fear, funerals, sorrow. Hell, at this rate she'd be locked in a padded room in no time.

She rubbed her face and turned from the window. The house was silent except for the hum of the alarm system, the ceiling fans. Why had she never noticed that before? Quiet sounds. Her edginess had honed her senses to the point she was jumpy. She headed towards the kitchen through the darkened living room.

A noise had her stopping, straining to hear. Nothing—stupid, she was being stupid. Another thing she hated. Fear. Since the lake, Jesslyn was afraid of everything, though she'd never admit it to anyone. The thought of sleep frightened her, startling noises made her jump, the thought of something happening to Aiden, or again to her, intruded on her carefully illusioned peace. It was almost as though she was waiting for something to reach out of the darkness and grab her.

Calm down. Think of something mundane. Mundane . . .

Tea, she'd make some tea. Not any of that herbal and flavored kind Kaitlyn had stocked up on, but some nice strong tea like her Nana used to make. Shaking her head, she continued into the kitchen, quietly picked up the kettle and started to fill it with water. She was not about to start losing her mind. Every little noise made her leap out of her skin. With a sigh, Jesslyn tried to relieve some of the tension that always shrouded around her.

The soft pale light from the stove cast a yellowed glow over the kitchen. As water gushed into the pot, she stared out the window. She'd always loved the nights, the peace and stillness they offered, the stars. Before, she might have picked such a night as this to take her tea and sit out on the porch in the old rocker, to let the quiet stillness settle her. But now, the idea of going out there terrified her. Anyone could be out there, watching, waiting . . .

A fog clouded her eyes. She heard the lap of water. Felt eyes on the back of her neck. A circle of light. White car.

Water poured over her hand as it ran down the side of the kettle, pulling her back from the flash in her mind's eye. Jesslyn tried to concentrate as the image faded. She fought to hold on to it, but it slipped past her. Damn. If only she could . . .

"What are you doing up?"

She whirled. The kettle dropped to the hard wood floor with a resounding clank. Water soaked her feet, the hem of her flannel pants. Her heart beat faster and faster. She couldn't catch a breath.

"Missy? Hey, honey, I'm sorry. I didn't mean to frighten you. Calm down."

As if through a tunnel, Jesslyn saw the massive form of Jock Kinncaid walking towards her, felt the wetness on the floor, heard him talking, but couldn't make out the words.

Jock's deep voice, like the rumble of a thundering waterfall, pulled her back. Back, back, until she stood staring at him, blinking to clear the image, the terror, from her mind.

"Missy, why don't you sit down? You're as white as the moon." He held a large hand out to her.

Jesslyn couldn't figure out what to do. Then clarity returned and a deep cleansing sigh drooped her rigid shoulders.

A fool. The man probably thought she was a fool. The water still gushed into the empty sink. Jock reached around her and turned the faucet off, never making a move to touch her.

Jesslyn saw concern in his blue depths. She shook her head, pushed a strand of hair back from her face, and tucked it behind her ear. What to say to him? Her teeth scraped over her bottom lip. The habit of nibbling on it when she was nervous had made it sore lately. She tried for a small smile.

"I don't know who jumped more, me when you startled me, or you when I dropped the kettle." Jesslyn wondered why the entire household wasn't up and investigating the noise. She saw his hand drop back to his side.

Her socks were soaked, as were the hem of her pajamas. She noticed Jock's socks were standing in the puddle as well, and like her, the bottom of his blue striped p.j.'s were absorbing the moisture.

Jock didn't return her smile, just studied her in that intense way his son often did. In no time, the two of them working in silence completed the task of cleaning up the mess. They tossed the gobs of wet white towels in the trash and stood staring at each other.

Jesslyn started to feel self-conscious. She'd go back to bed if she could sleep, but she knew full well that wasn't going to happen.

"Little early, isn't it?" Jock asked, as he refilled the kettle with hot water and sat it on the stove. "Why don't you sit down?" Like Aiden, Jock had a way of making questions sound like demands. "You're still a bit pale." He leaned back against the counter, crossed his arms over his wide chest.

Jesslyn started for the table. She was tired, but tired and sleepy were two vastly different things.

"On second thought," he said, "why don't you go change your socks. You're leaving wet footprints." His large finger pointed behind her. The faint glow from over the stove shone on small wet prints across the wood. "Wet socks aren't good, they let you get cold. And you, Jesslyn, do not need to get cold."

Without a word to him, she left the kitchen, crept down the hall and back into the bedroom. Aiden slept on his side, facing the door. The covers tucked beneath his arms. As quietly as possible, she got out a clean, dry pair of socks and slipped them on after tossing the soggy ones into the bathroom. The bottoms of her p.j.'s clung to her legs. On a sigh, she slipped those off and pulled on a pair of sweatpants.

Once back in the kitchen she sat at the table, saw two mugs sitting on the counter, but no Jock. Maybe he went back to bed. When the kettle whistled, she got up and moved it to the back burner. She didn't want a mug of tea, but figured Jock might, so she poured one of the mugs full and watched the tea bag in it bounce to the top. Chamomile. The scent wafted strong from the rising steam. Jesslyn opened the cabinet to the right of the stove and dug around until she found her box of loose leaf tea. She dumped a couple of tablespoons into the kettle and set the lid back on it.

Someone cleared their throat and she turned to see Jock standing a ways away.

"That isn't going to relax you. You're supposed to drink herbal stuff." His finger bobbed in the general direction of the mugs.

"Yeah, well." Jesslyn picked his mug up and carried it to the table. "I don't really want herbal stuff right now. So, I'll wait about fifteen minutes and drink a nice big glass of strong, iced sweet tea. But here." She gave him a smile and said, "Your herbal stuff." She set the mug down at the head of the table and plopped down in the next chair. "It's called chamomile by the way. Sometimes it smells really good, and other times, the smell completely turns me off. This is one of those other times."

Jesslyn pulled her right leg up and propped her chin on top. She watched Jock as he walked to the table and lowered his large frame into the wooden chair.

He dunked the tea bag for a minute. "You okay?" he asked into the awkward silence between them.

Did he actually care? Yes, she knew he did, but she was tired, and the animosity that still lingered between them was wearing on her.

She nodded. "Yeah. I'm fine."

His eyebrow rose in a perfect imitation of his son's. "Forgive me if I don't believe you."

A small chuckle surprised her. "I will be."

Finally, he dropped the tea bag back into the mug. His blue eyes bore into hers. "Another nightmare?"

The fact the whole house knew of her dreams was hardly a surprise after she'd awakened everyone screaming on her first night home. She dropped her gaze, jerked her shoulder and nodded.

"We listened to the dispatch tape today," she told him. Her chin moving against the back of her hand as she spoke. The slide of the mug between Jock's palms hushed along the tabletop. "Did Aiden tell you?"

He ran his tongue around his teeth. "Yeah, he might have mentioned it while you napped this afternoon."

"What did he say?"

Jock shook his head. "Let's just say, I've never seen the boy that mad, and leave it at that."

What did that mean?

"Did you remember anything else?" he asked.

For such a large man, his deep voice could be very soothing, at least when he wasn't barking at her, but she didn't have the energy to get into that right now. Aiden's voice had that baritone quality, but Jock's was complete bass.

"A little, not much of any help though." For the life of her, Jesslyn didn't know why, but she sat there and told this man, who had made no secret of disliking her, everything about the memories. "I'm sorry." She lifted her head, waved her hand. "I don't know why I went into all that."

Jock studied the cooling mug. Jesslyn noted the little paper square still dangled from the floating tea bag. Apparently, Jock didn't want that herbal stuff after all.

"I owe you an apology."

Her eyes jerked to meet his. Surely she'd misunderstood him. "Excuse me? For what?"

He shifted his large frame as he sighed. "For my attitude towards you." A large scarred finger reached up and scratched at the side of his salt-and-pepper hair. "I know I didn't take to you at first. Truth be known, I wanted Aiden to marry someone else."

Warmth spread through her at his words, even if she was a bit shocked. Jesslyn couldn't help but grin, she knew this man rarely apologized. Reaching over, she patted his hand.

"Don't worry about it. Aiden told me you'd adjust," she joked. "Besides, it's not like we have any plans to marry." Did they?

Jock harrumphed. "Be that as it may, Aiden had the right of it. I should have supported him when he called off the wedding. Left him alone to find his own way. You'd've thought I'd've learned," he muttered, his blue eyes piercing her. "And he did, in you. Aiden loves you. I hope you know that."

She was taken aback a bit by the power she saw radiating in those cobalt depths. "Yes, I do. He told me in the hospital and every day since."

Jock shook his head. "I honestly don't know what that boy would have done if something had happened to you."

"Jock," she said, raising her brows, "something did happen to me, and Aiden is slowly coming around." Jesslyn tried to be lighthearted.

"That's not what I meant. If you'd . . . After what Aiden told us today . . ." He quickly cut himself off, cleared his throat, and looked down at the mug he still held. "I'm glad you're in Aiden's life, and if he's smart, he'll make you part of this family."

For some absurd reason, Jesslyn felt like crying. Instead she smiled. "Your life will never be the same."

"I was afraid of that."

"Thank you, Jock."

He nodded. "When is that real tea going to be ready?"

Jesslyn smiled, the bonding time was over. She squeezed his hand before she got up. "It'll only take a minute."

As she stood, she looked over to the wall by the light switch. For the first time, she noticed the hole in the wall, the fractured sheet rock.

"What happened there?" she asked as she made the tea.

"Oh, nothing. Aiden just mentioned the dispatch tape," Jock evaded.

Jesslyn turned and cocked a brow. "I knew he was still pissed when we got home."

Jock snorted. "Hell, can you blame him? I have a feeling, Missy, that boy is going to be — as you put it — pissed for a good long time."

Jesslyn sighed and shook her head. "He's still not getting the deposit back."

Aiden was Aiden.

* * * *

Aiden quietly stood in the shadow beyond the doorway. Emotion clamped his jaw. He'd awakened and found the bed empty beside him. The fear that had crawled over him made him almost frantic to find Jesslyn, to find her in a cozy chat with his father was surprising.

Pissed? That was putting it mildly. He would have ripped the damn phone off the wall and thrown it through the window this afternoon, if his mother hadn't stopped him. Aiden rubbed his hands over his face. If they could just put this all behind them. God after this he needed a real vacation.

Aiden talked to Ian again tonight. No real information there, but Ian did say that what he found, he'd feed through the "proper channels." Proper channels being the CBI. Of course, it was a silent agreement between the two that if Ian found out who this murderer was, he'd tell Aiden first. As to what he'd do with that information was still unclear to him.

Jesslyn's laughter pulled him back to the moment at hand. The corners of his mouth pulled into a smile as another sigh of relief escaped him. Jock Kinncaid apologized to few people, the fact Aiden had heard him do so twice in the last week was almost more than he could believe.

With a shake of his head, he turned around and headed back to the bedroom.

Part of the family? Damn straight.

Chapter Twenty-three

The night was still and quiet around him. The shadows swallowed him. If only the moon were not full and bright.

Ah well, one did what one must.

The house was dark. He'd waited and waited.

It probably had a security alarm. He played with the idea of getting past it, how, he didn't know.

But then again, he hadn't come to get past it. He would just watch again.

The house beside hers had someone in it watching her. Cops. Thought they were so damn smart, but he'd been here before and no one saw him.

Last night, he'd seen her standing in the kitchen staring out into the darkness. He'd known it was her, he saw her profile.

The ground cushioned his footfalls as he made his way to the house. He slipped the knife from his belt. Better to be prepared than sorry. Who knew? Maybe she'd step outside for some fresh air. The tall full trees out front hid him from view as he slipped through the night. Once on the shadowed porch it would be easy.

Pretty, pretty Jesslyn was causing all sorts of problems.

* * * *

Jesslyn sat in the window seat. Again sleep eluded her. Monsters and blood stalked her dreams. She was tired of waking Aiden up, he did need his rest too. Of course if he found out she was up and sitting here alone in the dark again, he'd be pissed, but he'd get over it.

She looked over at the monitor on her desktop. The scene she'd just typed was tripe. She could see it, feel it, all but taste the kiss the characters shared. But, it was no use. The words were stilted at best, complete crap at worst. Sighing, she looked away and leaned her head against the window. Maybe she should try writing it again in the morning.

Her eyes watered on her yawn and she settled more against the cool pane of glass and closed her eyes.

She just needed to think. Tomorrow, she'd get the old pen and tablet out and plot the damn scene by hand. Sometimes that really helped.

And then . . .

She was sleepy, so sleepy. No way was she going to sleep.

Her eyes slid shut and her mind drifted, and drifted. She saw friends and relatives, people she loved.

It was a party, outside.

Laughter rang on the air mixing with yells and chatter. Someone called her name and she turned to look. Streamers and banners waved in the breeze, bright and colorful. A great gust of wind blew, tree limbs bowing and shaking until the streamers, like airborne snakes, slithered unattached in the wind.

The warm air changed and grew cooler.

The wind carried moans.

She looked around and noticed the people were all pale. Maddy stood in front, a hand outstretched. Tammy stood beside Maddy offering a bracelet. Other women were in a group behind them. All of them had red hair. Pleading, begging.

For what she didn't know.

"Wake up," they whispered. "Wake up."

The whispers grew to the sound of a hundred wings beating the air.

What were they trying to tell her?

Maddy shook her head. "Wake up, Jess. Now!"

Her eyes snapped open and in the window a face stared back at her, squashed against the glass. Red eyes glowed with a feral light, as the moon glinted off the knife the monster held. The smell of lilies permeated the air.

She screamed.

Jesslyn's breath caught as her eyes shot open. She didn't move. Not a single muscle. She was afraid to.

Was she dreaming still? Awake?

Breathe. Breathe.

The glass of the window was cool against her forehead. Blinking, she looked out to the darkness beyond. No one, nothing.

Nothing.

Just another dumb nightmare.

But she didn't move. Something told her to stay still.

Her eyes narrowed as she studied the colorless, moonlit landscape.

The hair rose on her arms.

A creak, faintly echoed.

Was that outside?

She was going nuts.

Be still. Be very still.

The moon shone on the boards of the porch, slanted and silvery.

Another creak, this time closer. And definitely outside.

Carefully, she turned her head, to look more out the window.

Maybe it was just the swing.

Creak.

Or the rocker.

Her office was at the end of the house, behind the living room. If someone were coming, they'd have to walk down the entire side porch.

Creak.

Or . . .

A shadow fell across the slatted boards. A long shadow of a man. Something was held in his hand.

She couldn't breathe.

He came into view, a black silhouette in the night. Whatever was in his hand, he propped on the railing.

A knife. Images flashed in her brain. Storms and thunder, a man and a knife.

A knife that cut flesh.

She took a deep breath and watched as he dragged the knife down the top of the railing.

Move. Move.

Quietly, she slid from the window seat and backed away.

What to do? What did she do?

Carefully, she backed through the office, never taking her eyes off where she'd been.

A shadow fell over the window.

Jesslyn froze, then dropped soundlessly to the floor.

The man squatted down and peered inside.

Shaking started deep within her, and terror roared to life.

He stared in, looking from side to side. She stared out, at him, trying to recognize his shadowed features.

Who was he?

Straightening, he moved on down the porch.

Her breath huffed out and nausea rolled her stomach.

Quietly, she stood, and found her legs shook. Keeping her eyes on the window, she backed towards the doorway, hit an alarm panel she'd had installed in here. Just as she pushed the button, arms wrapped around her from behind and she screamed, pulling away.

"Hey! Jessie, it's me," Aiden said.

Aiden.

"He was here." The alarm pad beeped and beeped again.

He looked at her, then whirled around and raced for the back door.

"Aiden!"

Feet pounded overhead. She hurried after Aiden. The other man had a damn knife. What was Aiden thinking?

At the back door she stopped. "Aiden?"

"Get back inside, damn it."

Lights from the house down the lane came on and she could see people running across the lawn towards her house.

Aiden's curses echoed through the night.

The killer was gone. She knew it. Rubbing her arms, the cold settled within her again.

* * * *

Aiden watched as the police walked the perimeter of the house.

Her house.

Damn it. Rage pumped through him still.

It was three a.m. and everyone was up. Jessie had told her story so many times even he knew it by heart. Yet he still sensed she was leaving something out. He turned from the doorway and walked back into the living room. Jessie sat on the couch talking to Litton, Jones, Garrison and T.J.

He sat on the back of the couch and put his hands on her shoulders. The muscles beneath his hands were tight and tensed. She probably had a headache.

"Well, the good news is we may have a print from this guy's shoe," Garrison offered.

Aiden had hoped she'd dreamed the whole thing, that it had been like a sleepwalking nightmare or something. But, the first thing the police asked about was the porch light. No, no one in the family had broken it that day or any other.

The jagged groove, etched in the top of the railing, was an all too familiar reminder of how close this bastard was.

Again.

Aiden decided it was time to move his family to the hotel.

He rubbed Jessie's shoulders. From now on, he'd tie her to him at night, damn it.

"The bad news," agent Litton continued, "is he knows who you are and where you are, but we'd already figured that. And somehow managed to get past the security next door."

Which was a remedy Aiden would fix tomorrow morning. He'd already made the phone call. "Tell me, please," he asked, trying to keep his voice calm. "How the hell is it, the man got by the notice of the professionals?"

The law enforcement officials only looked at him.

Jones said, "From now on, there will be a patrol car parked outside of the house."

Aiden nodded. "Fine, but just so you know, tomorrow there will be someone from our security firm guarding Jesslyn."

Jones smiled at him. "Just let him talk to us so that things don't get confusing."

Aiden conceded that point, and ignored the fact that Jessie was trying to turn around to glare at him.

He'd already made a phone call this evening. Ian was worried about this guy feeling pressured and making, albeit dumb, risky moves. Risky moves could still take Jessie away from him. So, Ian said someone would be there in the morning to keep an eye on things. Aiden had asked if it would be him, but Ian, apologizing, said no, though he'd love to help out, he'd only be able to send someone.

The man's name was John and he'd be here around eight.

"You know, Jess," T.J. said, then looked to him. "You could always go away for a while."

That was a damn good idea. He'd already thought of that, just wondered how to broach the subject with her.

"No."

"But . . ."

Jessie looked at her friend. "And if he killed someone else while I was away, because I wasn't here?"

Aiden's sigh mixed with T.J.'s.

"No," Jessie said again. "I won't run away. I'm not hiding so he can find someone else to murder. I don't like the fact he watches me, or knows me, or whatever, but at least he's not out killing some other redheaded woman. I'm just a loose end he wants to take care of."

He tightened his hands on her shoulders. She leaned her head back. "I'm not going," she told him. "Hire your Doberman, just don't expect me to pack up and leave."

"How long would it take you to forgive me if I just drugged you and put you on my plane?"

Her brow cocked and she only said, "You *don't* want to find out."

The discussion continued and it was another half hour before the house was left to just the Kinncaids. The only addition was the lone policeman sitting in the marked Explorer outside.

Aiden pulled Jessie to her feet and led her upstairs.

In the shower, he leaned down and kissed her neck. "Just think, Jessie. Sandy beaches, crystal waters, just you and me."

"I'd get burned."

"There's sunscreen."

"No," she said, turning in his arms, her hands sudsy with lather smoothed over his chest.

"Europe? Let's go to Ireland. Grammy would love to meet you."

When she smiled, he knew she was wavering.

"Scotland?"

Her wet body slid against his.

"I have a castle."

"That's what they all say. What about your gala thing at the hotel?"

The grand opening was tomorrow night. Actually, they'd been accepting guests and reservations for the last two weeks. But every last detail was finished today, or rather yesterday.

"Okay, we wait till after the party. Everyone is leaving Sunday anyway and heading back to Maryland. We'll just leave with them." He wiped water away from her face as he kissed her on the mouth.

Her head shook. "I don't know."

At least she hadn't said no. He still had time to work on her.

"I'll persuade you," he promised.

Her grin warmed him. "You can try."

"I plan on doing more than try, Jessie girl."

Chapter Twenty-four

The phone ringing at eight in the morning jarred Jesslyn and momentarily quieted the boisterous group at the dining table. Aiden patted her shoulder as he passed to get to the phone in the kitchen.

"I think it's a good idea, Mom," Gavin said and forked another mouthful of Southwest scrambled eggs.

A discussion was going around about plans for this afternoon. Kaitlyn wanted to go shopping. Gavin and Jock were going with all the ladies.

Jesslyn didn't really want to go, but Aiden needed to go to the hotel with Quinlan and Brayden. The grand gala opening for the hotel was tomorrow night.

While they talked, Jesslyn looked at the man sitting at the counter. He was about five-ten, brown hair, gray eyes, and strong, don't-screw-with-me features. Her bodyguard. John. No last name, just John. John wore jeans, a pullover stretched tight across all those well-honed muscles, and a shoulder holster, with the attached gun. The personified guard dog. She'd use him as a model for some mean-assed hero in one of her books.

Jesslyn still didn't know what the hell she was supposed to do with him, he'd only been here for fifteen minutes and she didn't know what to think. Was she supposed to talk to him?

"Great, then it's settled." Kaitlyn turned to Jesslyn. "Is there a place in town where we can get some games to play tonight?"

"Games?" Jesslyn asked.

"Yeah," Gavin volunteered. "Games, interactive board games."

This was a foreign concept to her, but whatever. If she had learned anything in the last week, it was that the Kinncaids were a close-knit family who liked to do things together when they could.

Board games. Lord help her.

Jesslyn nodded. "Yeah, there's the bookstore and a toy shop. Both have games I think. Though what kind, I have no idea."

Quinlan pushed his chair back, wiped his mouth. "I'm sorry, Mother, I'll try to be back tonight for dinner, but there is the hotel . . ."

Kaitlyn merely shook her head at him as he leaned down and kissed her cheek before heading out.

"I swear that boy will never learn to relax," Brayden muttered.

"Jessie," Aiden called, leaning around the doorway, "phone."

Jesslyn walked to Aiden and grabbed the phone.

"Who is it?" she asked him as he walked back into the dining room without answering her.

"Hello?" she asked, still looking after Aiden, who settled in a chair.

"Jesslyn, this is Chief Garrison. I'm calling to let you know there's been an arrest this morning. Or rather earlier this morning."

The air caught in her lungs, held and then expelled on a smile.

"Really? Who? Can I ask that?" her words fell over each other.

Garrison laughed on the other end. "Yeah, and it's Kirk."

"Kirk? But how? Why?" Jesslyn was confused. "I thought he was out of town."

"Without going into detail, suffice it to say, his alibis didn't hold up."

Jesslyn tensed again. "Kirk."

"I can't go into anymore. I just wanted to let you know." He muffled the phone and Jesslyn heard him faintly speaking, but couldn't make out the words. She leaned against the door frame and grinned at Aiden, who was looking over his shoulder at her.

Garrison's voice said into her ear, "Jesslyn, I'm sorry, we're busy here. If you remember anything else, or think of something, call me. I've got to let you go."

This was too much. "Umm. Yeah. Okay. Thank you, Garrison. Does this mean it's over?"

There was a short silence. "Well on the way. Just hang in there."

"Thanks again." Jesslyn heard the click on the other end. Apparently the man wasn't big on good-byes. She looked at the phone, hit the OFF button, and stood for a moment, trying to take in the fact that the killer was with the police.

Jesslyn frowned, trying to picture Kirk as the one who attacked her, who killed the other women. It actually wasn't very hard. Maybe the women represented Maddy to him, or something. Maybe. And then again, maybe not. Why did this seem too simple? Too easy?

Jesslyn sat the phone back in its rechargeable cradle and walked back to the family. Aiden grabbed her hand and pulled her to him. A scan around the table showed her Quinlan wasn't the only departure. Christian and Tori were gone.

"The girls went to get ready to go into town," he told her. Jesslyn stood between his knees, her hands clasped in his.

Gavin spoke up, "Are you ladies ready? We need to find some fun games. Something we men can conquer." Black eyebrows wiggled above cobalt as a wicked grin crooked his mouth. "Something manly."

"If that were the case, we'd simply save our time and money. Especially where you're concerned, Gavin." She tapped her fingers against Aiden's palms.

"What did Garrison want?" Aiden interrupted.

Jesslyn looked back down into his eyes. She should be happy, shouldn't she? Then why wasn't she doing a jig, or at least feeling relieved? "He wanted me to know an arrest had been made."

Aiden tugged on her hands until she obliged him and sat on his leg, her toes on the floor between them.

"It was Kirk."

Aiden swore.

"Then it's over?" Kaitlyn asked.

Jesslyn shrugged and nodded. "Yeah, I guess so. Seems to be."

Aiden watched her for a minute, his eyes narrowed. "Then why are you still so tense?"

Would she ever hide anything from this man? "I don't know."

"It's probably just the excitement of it all, the stress from your memory problems, and everything else. I'm sure it'll all hit you sooner or later," Jock pronounced. He dwarfed the juice glass in his hand as he swallowed the orange liquid, then set the empty glass aside. "I wouldn't worry about it, Missy."

She smiled at the older man. "Thank you, Jock, I'm sure you're right. This'll take a bit to get used to." Jesslyn nibbled on her bottom lip. "I just wish I could remember."

Aiden's hand rubbed her back. "You will." His sigh brushed against the side of her face. "I, for one, am damn relieved." His eyes looked anything but. A protective fire of retribution flamed in the blue depths.

"You look it, too."

He merely quirked a brow at her.

Brayden shook his head. "That's Aiden. He'll drive Quin and me crazy all afternoon." Leveling a look at her, he said, "Make sure you have a phone with you. Aiden gave you a new one, right?"

Jesslyn rolled her eyes. They were all acting like protective brothers or something. Then again, what the hell did she know of protective brothers? She and Jackson communicated, but they could never be what one could even loosely term as close. "Yes, Brayden, Aiden gave me a new phone. And a guard. My heart just flutters at his romantic gifts."

Out of the corner of her eye she saw John Nolastname grin.

Brayden nodded. "Good, now make sure it's on. Are you ready to go shopping? Mom's got the day all planned. She'll probably run you ragged since you haven't been out much in the last week." Silence settled around the table as everyone looked at her.

She tried for flippant, no use in announcing she was a terrified coward. "Yeah, like Aiden would have let me take two steps out the door before he and his army descended."

"True." Aiden pulled her to him, kissed her on the temple. "Very, very true. In fact, I'm not ready to let you out of my sight yet. So, go do whatever it is that you and Mom need to do to get ready to go. Then you and Dad and Gavin and everyone else can go have fun while I go slave at the grindstone."

She knew the only reason he was still letting her go was because everyone else was going, or more to the point, John. Not that Gavin couldn't handle something, or probably Jock either, who was big. No one would mess with them. But it took one look at John and people probably moved. Be interesting to see if that happened today in town. The man looked like little kids would have nightmares about him. At one time, it would have riled her, the bodyguard, but damn it all, the fear was still there, and her relief at his presence couldn't be ignored. What happened to her?

Where was the kick-ass woman of a few weeks ago? Jesslyn laid her head on Aiden's shoulder. She was still there. Though she couldn't remember what happened at the lake, she knew if it weren't for her determination, she wouldn't be here, sitting on Aiden's lap.

Maybe the kick-ass woman found her a kick-ass guy. The thought made her almost giggle.

"What has you smiling?" Aiden asked her, pulling his head around to look at her.

"Nothing." Jesslyn kissed his cheek, hopped off his lap and looked at Kaitlyn. "It'll take me about ten minutes, you?"

Kaitlyn's dimple peeked out. "About the same."

* * * *

Jesslyn, Kaitlyn, and Christian walked down the sidewalk. They'd bought clothes, knickknacks, and games.

Jesslyn could already feel a tension headache building. Even though Garrison had called her with his news, she still felt vulnerable. She hoped the others didn't notice her nervousness.

"Thank God for tourists," Gavin muttered as he steered her around a group of people.

"True," she answered, glancing to see John stood just behind her, Tori skipped beside him. So much for giving kids nightmares.

"Oh, look!" Tori said. "There's a bookstore. Can we go in it?"

Everyone agreed.

"I want some coffee," Gavin said.

"As long as we stop and sit at a table to drink it." Jock herded Kaitlyn and Christian along with him.

The coffee shop. Jesslyn sighed and steeled herself. Tammy wouldn't be there, but she had to go in sooner or later.

Her head hurt bad enough, nausea rolled in her stomach. She rubbed her forehead. She just needed to get out more. Perhaps Jock was right and she just needed some time. That long Scottish vacation didn't sound so undoable at present. Jesslyn sighed and glanced at her watch. It wasn't noon yet, but she was ready to go home. Flowers grew out of little pots and barrels along the storefronts.

"Your friend that came by the hospital, he and his wife own the coffee shop, do they not?" Kaitlyn asked, pulling Jesslyn's attention back.

Jesslyn almost nodded before her headache spiked again. "Yes. David and Sally Hewett. Though I'm not that close with them, but yes, I do consider them my friends, sort of. Why?" They had reached the bookshop set back off the street in a renovated cottage.

"Oh, no reason. Just trying to remember everyone and where they go." Kaitlyn's shoulders shrugged. "You know, Jock dear, why don't we get a table at the coffee shop and Gavin and John can take the girls to the bookstore."

"Sounds like a plan to me," he agreed. "Then we can grab some lunch and get back to the house."

Jesslyn started to refuse. She wasn't hungry, but she'd tell them that later. She didn't want to go to the bookstore, she didn't want to eat, and she damn sure didn't want to go into the coffee shop. Fear crept up her spine.

This was stupid! Not to mention, she'd only make the situation worse if she gave in to her anxiety. It had taken every ounce of her will to convince herself and then Aiden that she was fine and could go to town. Now, here she was wanting to beg Gavin, or John, or someone to take her home.

Forcing a smile, she nodded. "That sounds good to me."

"What do you like?" Kaitlyn asked.

"Just tell . . ." Jesslyn stopped. Tammy. Just tell Tammy. She sighed and rubbed her forehead again. "A double Americano. I'd like a double Americano over ice."

Kaitlyn gave her a look, but Jock was holding the door open to the coffeehouse.

Tori and Christian had already gone into the bookstore.

"You okay?" Gavin asked her.

"Fine," she turned and pushed the door open.

"You're such a people person," he said.

"Yeah, I'm told that all the time."

"Are y'all all like that from Texas? Borderline rude?" he asked.

Jesslyn grinned. "I've told you. It's y'all. Run it all together like it's spelled Y-A-W-L. No pause. You pause, you sound like a Yankee."

Gavin chuckled.

"You know, I think you say things just so I'll talk and you can make fun of my accent." The man gave her hell about it.

"You've found me out."

Jesslyn walked away from him to browse the nonfiction section of the store. John stood next to the door, his hands held loosely in front of him, his jacket covering the gun, his dark shades firmly in place. Everyone in the store stared at him.

Five minutes later, she walked out, leaving Christian and Gavin telling Tori which books were the best. The woman behind the counter knew her and was just full of questions and comments on being the victim of a madman. The gossipy woman usually humored Jesslyn, not today. With each inquiry and remark, Jesslyn's nerves had grown from tensed to taut. Finally, she'd mumbled something about an appointment and had simply left, not even bothering to tell Ms. Gibsy bye. The fresh air soothed some, but not enough.

"All right, then?" John asked, his British accent evident.

She nodded and hurried next door and walked into the familiar dimly lit room. The chattering sounds of people talking cluttered the air, the chink of spoons on saucers or against the sides of pottery mugs, the hum and gurgle of the espresso maker, all these were a balm to Jesslyn's frazzled mood. Almost. It was the same, yet different. A familiar face was no longer behind the counter.

Something prickled along the back of her neck. She scanned the coffee shop, turned and scanned back along the street. Nothing seemed out of place, no one seemed strange. Everything was simply as it should be. Jesslyn rubbed the back of her neck, shook off the niggling warnings and doubt and scanned the crowd again.

"Don't do that again."

She jumped and whirled.

Gavin stood glaring at her.

"Don't sneak up on me like that!" she hissed.

He shook his head and grabbed her elbow, trying to lead her over to the table Jock occupied. Jesslyn jerked her arm back and said, "Gavin, go sit down. I need a minute. That's all."

His glare didn't lessen, but he complied. God, these Kinncaids were from another time altogether, weren't they? They gave protectiveness a whole new meaning.

"You're a bit tense, why?" John asked.

She shrugged. "Something's just not right. I know they arrested Kirk, but . . ."

He tilted his head and pulled his shades off. Dark gray eyes the color of slate regarded her. "I always follow my instincts." Those eyes scanned the crowd. "Stay close to me."

She frowned and turned, walking over to the Kinncaids. She could feel John directly behind her. Kaitlyn sat at the end of the bar next to Mr. Reeves, talking to him and David. David Hewett was tall and lanky. He had always reminded Jesslyn of a scarecrow. He didn't have natural grace like Aiden, or an authoritative attitude like Tim. David was simply David. He was usually quiet spoken and friendly. She vaguely remembered talking to him in the hospital, but it was all such a blur. They hadn't really talked in about three weeks. Since Maddy died.

"There's the woman herself," David smiled as she walked up to the group.

"Hi, David. How are you?" Jesslyn leaned over and gave old Reeves a hug.

"Fine and you?" David asked.

"Miss Jessie, you are looking lovely today," Hap Reeves told her.

"Why thank you, Mr. Reeves." The elder's comment made her smile. Lovely wasn't how she'd describe her jeans and T-shirt, but his remark made her happy all the same. "Have you met Kaitlyn Kinncaid?" she asked him.

"Oh yes. I met your man's mama at the hospital, Miss Jessie. Nice family." He picked up his smoldering cigarette. The white stick, clasped between his fingers, wiggled as he pointed to Kaitlyn.

"Thank you, Mr. Reeves," Kaitlyn told him.

David set an order of drinks on the counter. Jesslyn's medium Americano was piled high enough with chocolate-drizzled whipped cream that David set the lid on the counter by the cup.

Kaitlyn passed out the drinks to Jock and Gavin. As she followed her son to the table, she stopped and said, "You're going to be wired all day."

Jesslyn raised her brows. "That's the point." She picked up the cup and gingerly licked around the edge of it, catching the extra white topping.

David leaned onto the bar. His black eyes questioning. "How are you doing, Jess? You remember anything about what happened up at the lake? I must say it is a relief to have that man off the streets. You did know Kirk Robertson was arrested, didn't you?"

The lightened mood was swiftly ripped away. Not that it ever really existed. Jesslyn inwardly sighed and stepped back. "Just bits and pieces. I talked to Chief Garrison and some people from CBI yesterday. I may have to talk to them again."

"Well, you just take it easy, Miss Jessie," Reeves warned her. "You'll remember what happened up there at the lake, don't you worry."

Jesslyn nodded, and wished more than ever she had begged off after all and was sitting at home. Hell, she'd even go sit quietly in a corner of Aiden's office if she could get out of here.

"Place just isn't the same without Tammy," Reeves muttered, taking a drag from his cigarette.

She sat her coffee on the counter before she dropped it. The thought of drinking it no longer appealed to her.

David looked at her apologetically.

Through the window, Jesslyn saw Tim across the street. Without a word to either man at the counter or to the Kinncaids at the table, she dashed out the door and hollered for Tim. He spun around, saw her and she hurried across the street as a dark sedan stopped for her. Yet even as she crossed towards him, her skin tingled along her neck as though unseen eyes stalked her. Jesslyn looked around as she reached Tim's side.

"I didn't expect to see you here." Tim gave her a hug, pulled back. "How you doing?" His gaze looked over her shoulder. "Who's that?"

Without looking she knew. "John Nolastname. Aiden hired him."

"For?"

"He's my bodyguard. Got a gun and everything."

"Only you could find the humor in this. How are you?" he asked.

"Fine," she absently answered, and scanned the street and sidewalk again. Nothing pulled at her. Just her damn nerves. The coffeehouse probably hadn't been a good idea, but at least it was over. Jesslyn shook off her wayward fears, and looked up at Tim. What was with him? Tim normally didn't hug.

"What has you in such good spirits?" she asked as she saw his gray eyes narrow on the multicolor bruise on the side of her head. His mouth firmed. "Tim. I'm fine, quit frowning."

His gaze returned to hers. "I heard they arrested Kirk. I could have knocked his teeth down his throat last night when the sonofabitch showed up at The Dime."

"Kirk was at The Dime? What did he want? What did he do?"

Tim was clearly agitated. The scrunch of his nose made his mustache twitch. "Are you here alone? With the bodyguard?"

Jesslyn quirked a brow. "No, I came shopping with Kaitlyn, Christian and Tori. Gavin and Jock tagged along. So, what did Kirk do?"

He shoved his hands in his pockets and shrugged. "Started in on how you were any form and variation of a loose and amoral woman. He made some nasty comments and then stated he wished you had done him a favor and died up at Emerald. Or maybe you got jealous of both Maddy and Tammy and . . ." His gray eyes hardened. "Never mind. I shut him up and threw him out."

Jesslyn sighed and grinned. "My knight. Aiden is going to be pissed. He so wanted to have a go at Kirk. The fact he didn't, especially if he learns what the jerk said last night, is going to drive him nuts." Jesslyn leaned up and pulled his face down to hers, kissed his whiskered cheek. "Thanks, Tim. You need to shave." She ran her hand over the rough skin as she dropped back down to the flat of her feet.

Tim straightened and his eyes twinkled. "T.J. doesn't complain."

Jesslyn shook her head, she was glad those two were together. Two of her dearest friends. "I'm glad she's with you and not Chief Tight Ass."

"Chief Tight Ass?"

She returned his smile. "Yeah, Garrison. I thought those two would get together, and you two just sorta happened. I'm glad. Are y'all coming to the party tomorrow night?"

His rueful look made his mustache crooked. "Yeah, we'll be there. I won't be able to stay long. But I was planning on dropping in and grabbing a bite before heading back to The Dime." Jesslyn started to say more, but Tim hurried on, "Here comes Mrs. K. and the entourage."

She turned and saw Kaitlyn making her way across the street as the others filed out of the coffee shop.

"Hello, Tim dear. Come on, where's my hug and kiss? I know Jesslyn got one." Her impish grin made her look younger.

Tim smiled, grabbed her up in a bear hug and kissed her cheek. "Your boys treating you right? If not, I'll come take care of them for you," he offered as he pulled away from Kaitlyn.

Kaitlyn laid her hand on his cheek. "You always were a darling boy."

"You're the only one that thinks so, Mrs. K., I assure you." Tim let Kaitlyn go, crossed his arms over his chest.

Kaitlyn shook her head at him, "No, I'm not. Now, we're going to go grab some lunch. Care to join us?"

"No, but thank you."

Kaitlyn headed towards the rest of her family. Jesslyn didn't feel like eating. In fact, she was sick to her stomach. Her headache grew.

"You want me to take you home?" Tim asked her, concern clear in his voice. "You don't look so good."

"Geez, you sure know how to make a girl feel good."

"I will," Gavin said, coming up behind them. "I already told Mom and Dad to go on to the restaurant. You okay?" he asked her. "I'll take you home if you want, or we can catch up with the others."

She wanted Aiden. "Home. Take me home, please," she whispered.

Chapter Twenty-five

The kitchen was alive with activity. Everyone was helping with dinner. A giant fiesta. In Aiden's opinion, there would be more food than any of them could eat.

The women were drinking margaritas Jesslyn made and he and his brothers were downing beer. The fajitas were grilling and Jessie was teaching Gavin how to make *pico de gallo*. Whatever the hell that was.

"Ah, damn, my eyes burn," Gavin complained, wiping them with the backs of his hands.

"I told you not to rub them until you'd washed your hands. Jalapeños will do that," Jessie said.

"Is that an I-told-you-so?" Gavin asked.

"Quit whining," he told his brother.

"Well for God's sake, son, she did warn you. Lord forbid any of my children do so great a task as heed advice," Jock said.

Aiden leveled a look at his father.

"When is all this food going to be ready?" Tori asked. "I'm ready to play games again."

"Later, honey," Bray told his daughter.

"I like that acting game," Jock admitted.

"You just want to try to beat us," his mother said, snatching a chip from the bowl and dipping it in hot sauce. "You'll lose again."

"Kaitie lass."

Aiden laughed. The game was fun. Classical music played low on speakers. Some various classic CD his mother had put on.

The plans for the party tomorrow night were in place, an arrest had been made, a well-equipped body guard watched over things just in case, and he'd heard Jessie's laugh more today than he had since he met her. All in all it was a wonderful day.

He walked up and nuzzled the side of Jessie's neck. "What are you cutting up?"

"The tomatoes. Want one?"

"Sure." When she popped the cut fruit into his mouth, he held her hand and sucked the juice off her finger.

"You are bad," she whispered.

"You know it." He kissed her quick on the lips, then popped her with the towel he was holding.

Her look told him he would pay for it later.

"Why am I cutting up all this again?" Gavin asked.

"Because I said to," Jessie answered.

"Children, children," his mothered waved at them.

Another symphony started on the stereo. Berlioz. Aiden sat at the table and dipped a chip in the *chili con queso*. He'd never really cared for this piece of music, it was heavy, dark. Jessie's laugh pulled his attention back to her as she dumped her pile of tomatoes into the bowl with Gavin's jalapeños and the onion he was cutting.

"It's for making fun of your twang, isn't it?" his brother tried.

"I have a twang?" Jessie drawled.

Aiden sighed. Those two were worse than a brother and sister constantly picking on each other. He was amazed they were still sharing the same chopping board.

Enharmonic notes of music filled and swirled in the air.

The two kept up their bantering. She walked to the sink and tossed over her shoulder, "And here I thought it was my good looks and sunny personality."

"Sunny?" Gavin waved his knife in her direction. "You aren't sunny. Good looks I'll give you, but not sunny. I'd even stretch it and say you were pretty."

"That coming from you could either be an insult or a compliment," she sassed, her hand on her hip.

Again Gavin waved his knife absently. The movement made Aiden nervous. He noticed John, standing in the corner, straighten.

His brother rolled his eyes. "Compliment, Jess. Pretty, pretty Jesslyn."

Jessie looked at Gavin, head cocked to the side and a look of confusion on her face. The music slowed. Bells began to chime. Her eyes were riveted to the knife Gavin held. The blood drained from her face.

"Pretty, pretty Jesslyn," she whispered.

"Jessie?" he asked and sat up straight. Deep full notes reverberated through the air.

Gavin started towards her, but she jerked back, her own knife clattering to the floor.

The kitchen stilled in silence.

She opened her mouth, as if to speak. Aiden could see her trembling from here. He stood and reached her in three strides.

"Don't," Gavin whispered. "Let her see it."

Aiden didn't know what the hell she saw, but it was bad. Her hands shook. Her chest pitched up and down in short quick pants. She was terrified, utterly and completely terrified. Then, her breath hitched. Her mouth moved, but no air came in or out.

To hell with this.

Aiden grabbed her face between his palms. "Jessie. Jessie. Look at me. Look at me." And still she didn't breathe. Her skin was pale as death. "Jesslyn. Breathe, damn it. Breathe."

Aiden's voice drifted to her as if down a tunnel.

The knife caught the light. Pretty, pretty Jesslyn. Water, water. She wasn't going to make it. It was too far to the top. Death. Cold. Water. So cold. Blood. Darkness. A brush on her face. Pretty, pretty Jesslyn. A whisper soft kiss. Humming. Someone humming this song. Dark thoughts swirled on the music as they did within her.

"Breathe!" Aiden shouted in her face. And the jumbled thoughts and feelings fell into place.

Jesslyn blinked, gasped for precious air as her head broke the surface of her watered memory.

The shaking started deep within her, worked its way out.

Aiden started to pick her up, but she struggled out of his hold and raced to the sink. Pretty, pretty Jesslyn. A whisper of a kiss. God.

Her stomach heaved. And heaved.

Oh, God. Tammy. Oh, sweet Jesus, forgive her for leaving her there. Down there. Tears stung her eyes.

Someone gave her some water.

She couldn't stop trembling. Aiden's arms wrapped around her and cradled her against him. His words, soft against her ear, were lost in the tide of dark images and feelings.

But the meaning behind them came through loud and clear. She curled into the warmth and comfort of his protective arms.

Someone tucked a blanket around her. They sat down, and Aiden held her still. This was safe. Right here, nothing could hurt her. No icy dark grave, no monsters, no fear. So many images and forms collided together and then slid so seamlessly into place. All but one. The monster had no face.

Tammy in the car. Oh, God. Oh, God. A sob grabbed her, and she burrowed deeper into Aiden's strength. She could handle this, she could. Yes. Breathe. In. Out. In. Out.

Jesslyn shoved past what she had seen, what she knew had been more than a close call, and tried to go back even further. She remembered the rain, the storm. Running from the monster was there, though blurred and jagged. His darkened silhouette above her was imprinted on her mind both awake and asleep. Had she seen him? Jesslyn couldn't remember. She did remember the pain in her head. The whispered words against her lips, a stolen soft kiss.

Her stomach rolled again.

Keep on. Think. Fit it all together.

The sinking car, Tammy, and the water. The terror and realization that someone tried to kill her sank home. For the first time, it no longer seemed like it happened to someone else. Now the bruise on the side of her head took on a new meaning. The fact she was held against Aiden was such a blessing.

Her mind kept coming back to Death, poised above her. Who was it? Jesslyn closed her eyes, tried to concentrate, to pull the edges of the pieces together. It was important, so important. Remember. But the harder she tried, the more futile it became. Dammit, she was so close. If only . . .

She heard the words, tea and shock. Then, Aiden said something about hospital and her head came up.

Jesslyn licked her lips. "No—no, I'm o-okay. I-I'll b-be okay."

"The hell you are." His blue eyes burned in anger and fear.

Rage roared through him. Uselessness and helplessness were not feelings Aiden particularly liked. Just like the other day in the damn police station when she'd had a flashback. "The hell you are. You're white as a damn ghost. You're cold and trembling."

"She's probably in shock." Gavin picked up Jesslyn's hand, his fingers at her wrist. She tried to jerk it away. Aiden almost told her to be still but saw Gavin give her a narrowed look as his brother held firm, checking his watch.

"I'm fine," Jesslyn repeated.

Her dark eyes were ebony pools of pain, tears glistened on the precipice of her lashes. A shudder racked though her. Aiden tightened his arms and tried to give her some of his warmth.

"Your pulse is a little rapid, but the hyperventilation could have caused that. Follow my finger." Aiden watched as her mouth twitched and opened to undoubtedly sass something back.

"Where's it supposed to go?" Her voice was soft, amused.

Gavin ignored her and held his finger aloft. Aiden watched as her eyes followed his brother's finger.

"Well, you're more alert now than you were a few minutes ago. You're still a bit cold and rather on the pale side." To him, Gavin said, "Keep the blanket on her. She needs warm liquids. Or some sort of sweet drink would work too."

"She needs some of that smelly herbal stuff tea," this from his father who stood by the fireplace glaring at them.

Jesslyn chuckled softly. The sound was so unexpected they all looked at her. "Chamomile. I told you the nasty stuff is called chamomile." Her head shook back and forth. "I really don't like it."

Aiden started to tell her . . .

"Well, Missy, that's just too damn bad." His father's finger pointed at her, waggled in what they all knew as one of his no-nonsense actions. "You'll drink what we give you."

The fact he and his father thought alike was not lost on him.

"Scare us like that," Jock continued to mumble.

Jesslyn's shoulders rose and fell as she released a sigh. Aiden snuggled her closer to him and she laid her head on his shoulder.

"I am fine. I'm sorry for blitzing out on y'all."

Aiden rolled his eyes. Jock just stared at her. Aiden had no idea where the others were, probably still in the kitchen staying out of the way.

Gavin shook his head. "Man, that's the last time I give a girl a compliment," he said, standing.

She stiffened in his arms.

"What?" he asked her.

"He said that to me. I couldn't see him, he'd already hit my head and things were really fuzzy. But—but he said that," her words were warm against his neck.

"What did he say?" he asked.

"P-pretty, pretty Jesslyn." Her sigh was ragged.

He took a deep breath through his nose. Another sigh tickled and warmed the skin on his neck. Silence stretched, then stretched some more. He wondered if she'd say anything else.

"It was so cold, so incredibly cold," she whispered. Aiden froze, as did everyone else.

"And so very dark."

Aiden didn't know if he should say something else, move her back to see her face, or just hold her. He decided on the latter. She was opening up and he wasn't about to stop her.

The click of his mother's heels, followed by Brayden's low voice, came from the kitchen. Out of the corner of his eye, he saw Gavin shush them with a pat of his hand on empty air.

"But I can't see him. I try and try but it won't come. My head hurt so bad. It took me a while to realize what was happening." Her voice faded.

"He hummed that song that was on a minute ago. I remember someone humming that part where the bells chime." Her breath heated the side of his neck. She tensed against him. Aiden didn't move, afraid to close the portal she'd opened.

Her fingers fidgeted in the weave of the blanket. He saw the material bunch as she fisted her hands. "The cold woke me up. I didn't know where I was and it was so damn cold. I couldn't feel my toes, and my fingers were fumbly. I could hear water, lapping, gushing."

Aiden wanted to stop this, shield her from it, but was impotent to do so.

"I thought maybe I was in a boat, then I focused and made out the dashboard."

She'd been in the car. The car they'd pulled from the bottom of the damn lake. Christ. Chills lightninged through him.

"I realized I was in water up to my waist, and it was rising. Tammy. Tammy was in the driver's seat, slumped against the harness of her seat belt. The water—the water rose so fast. I could see—I could see her blood cloud in the water. Her eyes. I'll never forget her eyes." Jesslyn's low voice flattened as though she were speaking of nothing more than the weather.

She'd been in the car. Aiden couldn't get past that.

"I finally realized the car was sinking. It took me forever to get the seat belt unlatched and when I did, I fell against the dashboard. The water was so murky, I couldn't see past the windshield." Her fist beat a slow steady movement on her thigh.

Her breaths started to shorten, to hitch. He could feel the rapid rise and fall of her chest against him. This time he did pull back, looking into her haunted eyes. "He can't hurt you. Nothing will ever hurt you again. You're safe now. Come on, out with the rest. It'll help." He knew she needed to voice the rest, though what she said chilled his blood.

Her eyes locked on his, but he knew they didn't see him. No, they reflected something else, another time, a horrifying place.

"I got one gulp of air, before—before the water closed over. I tried to find the door handle and managed to get the window mostly down before the battery went dead and the blackness closed in. It was so dark. I didn't want to die there, not down there. It kept trying to pull me back into the car. The surface." Something in her eyes flickered. "The lightning lit the entire roof of the lake. Or surface or whatever. It was almost beautiful, but so deadly. I didn't think I would make it, so far away. But I did. I remember swimming, but it was so cold and I was clumsy. I don't remember making it to the shore, or up to the knoll. I just—I just remember swimming in that icy water, trying not to drown."

God Almighty. Aiden pulled her to him, held her tight, pressed his face into her silken strands of hair.

Rage burned through him. At the bastard who did this, at himself for not protecting her. He opened his mouth to tell her, but clamped down as emotion flooded him, and he squeezed his eyes shut. He'd known he could have lost her. That gravelly voice on the tape stalked his dreams, his thoughts. The memory of fear for Jesslyn, the elation and anger when they'd found her. The unknown that had plagued them all since the beginning. All that collided through him. She could have died. He could have lost her forever.

The fruity scent of her shampoo calmed him as Aiden breathed deep. He'd been so close to losing her. So bloody damn close. He tightened his arms, trying to hold her as tightly as he possibly could. The thought of death so near her stopped his heart.

Her hair teased against his mouth. A shudder racked her body and he rocked her. "You're safe. You're safe. I promise," he whispered to her.

He opened his eyes to see his father looking at them as Jock followed the others from the kitchen.

Aiden felt her tears drop to his neck and wet his skin. Her voice stuttered out, "I—I—I just left her there, Aiden. I just left her. I tried to pull her through the window with me, but I couldn't hold on to her hand. She was stuck in the car and it kept sinking. Her bracelet came off. What if she was alive? What if . . . Oh, God."

He jerked her back, cupped her face in his hands, brushing the tears with his thumbs. "There was nothing, *nothing*, you could have done. Christ, woman, it's a miracle you even got out. Never, ever, say something so stupid again. None, and I repeat none of this is your fault." The urge to shake her threaded through him, but the tears trickled wet paths down her cheeks.

"He tried to kill me," her bottom lip quivered. "He killed my friends. Why?"

Aiden couldn't answer her. "I don't know, baby. I don't know."

He leaned up and kissed her gently, hoped to take away some of her fear, the feeling of violation.

His Jessie was all that was dear and precious to him. His treasure. His love.

Jesslyn looked into his eyes, burning like the hottest flames of hell. She pulled her bottom lip between her teeth, felt her teeth scrape the sensitive skin. With more patience than she realized she had, Jesslyn untangled her fingers from the folds of the green woven blanket. Her hands came up and framed Aiden's face.

"I love you."

A muscled bunched in his jaw. "I love you, too. When this is all over . . ." He shook his head. "Never mind. That can wait."

Jesslyn wondered what he'd been about to say, but her aching head didn't care.

"I'm glad you're here. I need you. I need you so much it scares me." Tears threatened again, but Jesslyn drew a deep breath, managing to check her emotions. "You make me feel safe and protected. With you I can be me and don't have to worry about who that is. It's just me, good or bad, strong or weak. And for some reason, you seem to like me."

His eyes widened and dark brows rose. "*Seem* to like you? Jessie, if I had lost you . . . The thought of how close it . . . I don't know . . ." His sigh brushed against her mouth.

She leaned forwards. "I know." She kissed him on his tightened lips.

Reality was a cloak she wished she could toss aside. "We need to call Garrison, huh?"

His arms were so tight around her. Black lashes shuttered his gaze as he blinked. Well-muscled shoulders shrugged.

"I suppose we do. They'll want to talk to you now." He lifted his hand, turned her wrist so he could read her watch. "And it's getting late and you need some rest after all this."

"Are you going to rest with me?" she asked, leaning against him again.

"Where else would I be?" He kissed the top of her head.

Then he leaned back against the cushions, craned his head back and hollered, "Someone bring me the phone, and something for Jesslyn to drink."

She smiled, relieved and comforted, as she watched his Adam's apple bob in his stretched neck. He was her strength, her source of courage, her guiding light.

Why couldn't she see the monster's face?

* * * *

The monster paced, a caged animal.

Tick. Tick. Tick.

Time was running out. No doubt about it.

She didn't remember, he saw that when he talked to her. So naive, so trusting. But memory would change all that.

He picked up his mug and swallowed a drink of the bitter brew.

The party was perfect. Perfect.

At the party. With the arrest, everyone would be relaxed. It wouldn't take much to get her alone. He'd have to wait until her guard dog was away. His fingers tapped against his thigh.

And alone it would end. It would end.

Once free of Jesslyn he'd take care of one last problem, and then . . . Well, the possibilities were once again open, weren't they? His mission would continue.

Chapter Twenty-six

Would this night ever end? He sipped champagne from the clear, crystal flute. The golden bubbles flat in his mouth. Beneath his lashes, he studied Jesslyn. She was so oblivious to the fate awaiting her. Whoever would have thought her destiny would be so intertwined with his?

His fingers tightened on the fragile stem. If only he could get her alone, but he had a plan for that, and if that didn't work, well . . . He'd come up with something else.

He always did. Always did.

God always showed him the way, in some form or fashion. Maybe the mission whispered in his ear when he saw her *awakening the beast, perhaps it was no more than the placement of the heavens. Whatever, unlike his father, he knew it didn't matter where the need came from. It just was, and the monster had to be appeased. Monster or Mission did it matter? No. He felt like hurling the glass across the room, but he couldn't do that. Didn't want to draw attention.*

Too bad Jesslyn had to die, she really was a beautiful woman, but some things simply had to be. Didn't they?

Yes, yes, of course they did. It hardly mattered who it was.

Needs must when the devil drives . . .

A sigh of resignation settled through him, even as he could all but feel the grains slipping through the hourglass.

The time was drawing near . . .

* * * *

The hair on the back of her neck tingled as a chill swept over her. Without dropping her smile, Jesslyn gazed over the crowd. Nothing was out of place. She knew almost everyone here. The Kinncaids, Mr. Reeves, who was sitting talking to Jock. David leaned against the wall, sipping his champagne and talking with Quinlan. Mark, the Realtor and his wife were there. Garrison stood to the side of them. He caught her eye and raised his flute towards her with a slight tilt of his head. Jesslyn smiled back at him.

Agents Litton and Jones made their way up to the Chief of Police, and the three started to talk. Jesslyn absently wondered when Tim and T.J. would get here. Again something niggled at the back of her mind, as though she were being watched. John stood off to one side, far enough to give her space, but there all the same.

Stupid, she was being stupid. Aiden's hand nestled protectively against the small of her back, reassuring, anchoring her worries, even as he spoke to a man she didn't know. Some sort of sales rep from Arizona.

Tori's laughter mingled with her grandmother's as it flowed across the room.

Jesslyn pulled on the sleeve of her long, white poplin shirt. She should have worn more comfortable shoes. But the little black zip boots went with her black, flat-front pants. She'd wanted to look nice, yet didn't want to seem flashy. Jesslyn decided on simple. The tight black pants went well with the oversized white button down, and she'd always liked the French cuffs. Aiden had given her a present as they drove up to the hotel.

A smile pulled at her mouth as she fingered the black pearl necklace. It was on a long silver chain, an ebony tear. She'd swept her hair up into a black clip so that curls crowned the top of her head. Sort of reminiscent of their date.

Aiden had told her she looked classy, and chic. Whatever. But the compliment made her smile all the same.

Again chills pricked along her skin. It was just her nerves. The last two days had been a roller coaster of emotions for her. First, she remembered most of what happened at Emerald and then she had to go through it over and over and over with Garrison and his cohorts. They'd talked to her again today. She'd had to hurry to get ready and had been so anxious she hadn't even wanted to leave the house, but now she was glad she had.

The party was wonderful. One of the ballrooms or meeting rooms or whatever it was held the private affair. The name was actually *The Gothic Room*. Trays piled high in every color of the rainbow held an assortment of foods for anyone who was hungry. There was everything from shrimp to canapés, tortes, sandwich makings, fruits, grilled fish, roasted vegetables. The list was endless.

The chatterbox Aiden had been talking business with for the last ten minutes had departed. Thank God. Jesslyn saw the loud man over by Jock—they ought to keep each other occupied for a while.

She looked back at Aiden, who wore a blue silk shirt, the same color as his eyes, tucked into black slacks. The soft material of the button down draped over his well-muscled shoulders, outlined his chest. But those details were hidden by his black jacket. Jesslyn thought about what she wanted to do to Aiden when they got out of here and back home.

"You keep looking at me like that and we're going to have to leave early," he told her, leaning down and whispering in her ear. His warm breath made her shiver and smile. "And think how disappointed everyone would be."

"Ah," she answered, slipping a finger under the seam of his shirt between two buttons. "But you own this hotel. Surely there's an empty room somewhere."

His eyes darkened, narrowed.

At that moment, Mark and his wife came up with their new baby. Aiden talked to the baby and made cooing sounds. He laughed when the little guy reached up and grasped his finger.

The moment imprinted on Jesslyn's mind and her heart squeezed.

Jesslyn sighed. There was still something she hadn't told Aiden, but she would. She needed to go back to Texas, put closure to things, and see what kind of future she and Aiden could have.

"What?" His brows furrowed as they studied her. Mark and his new family were walking away.

She compressed her lips, shook her head and smiled. "Nothing. Just thinking."

"About what?"

"Perfection."

A black brow winged upwards. "That sounds deep."

"Are you going to keep her attached to your hip all night?" T.J. interrupted chirpily. "I swear, where one of you is, the other is sure to follow. If neither of you will wilt, I'd like to borrow Jess for a minute." T.J. latched on to her arm and all but dragged her away.

Jesslyn turned back and shrugged towards Aiden as T.J. pulled her out of the room and into the lobby. John followed, but she motioned him back and he stopped at the doorway.

"What is with you?" she asked as soon as T.J. slowed down and sat on a covered bench against a wall. A large palmed plant hid them from view, yet allowed them to see across the lobby.

T.J. took a deep breath, then another. Her hands wrung on her lap. Jesslyn noticed she wore a short blue dress, the color of arctic ice, perfectly matching her eyes.

"Will you just spit it out?" Jesslyn sat down next to her.

T.J.'s eyes rounded, even as she pulled her dainty brows down. "I'm late," she wailed in a furious whisper.

"Well, of course you are. The party started an hour ago. It's not that big a . . ." Jesslyn trailed off. "Oh. Oh!"

"Yeah. Oh!" T.J. nibbled on her thumbnail.

"How late?" Jesslyn asked. Could just be nerves.

"Like about two weeks."

Jesslyn rolled her eyes. "God, I thought it was serious. About two weeks? That's not late, that's off a few days." Hell, Jesslyn had never been regular. There had been months she hadn't started. Stress was an interesting thing in life.

"But late is late," T.J. said, clearly exasperated.

Jesslyn reached out and patted T.J.'s hand. "You know, it's not like you have no stress in your life. The last few weeks have been hell on you."

T.J. took a deep breath. "Jesslyn, I'm on the pill. I'm never late. Ne-ver." She stressed the last, drawing it out.

Jesslyn released a sigh. "Okay, okay. Let's not borrow trouble until you know. That won't help." What to do?

"I bought a pregnancy test." T.J. whispered, latching on to Jesslyn's hand.

"And?"

T.J. shrugged. "I couldn't do it alone."

Jesslyn laughed. "Honey, there are any number of things I would do for you and with you. That isn't one of them. Some things you have to do yourself."

T.J. punched her shoulder. "Smart-ass. That's not what I meant. I brought it with me and thought I could take it and maybe you'd wait with me." She ground to a halt. Her pale eyes all but screaming "please."

Jesslyn rolled her eyes and stood up, pulled T.J. up with her. "Come on then, let's get this over with. I swear the things I do for those I love." A bubble of excitement spread through her.

She turned as she opened the door to the nearest ladies' room and scanned under the stalls. Good, it was empty.

"Okay, get on with it." Jesslyn all but shoved T.J. towards the nearest wooden three-quarter door. She leaned against the main door and threw the lock. No use in being interrupted.

"So," she said in the echoing confines of the tiled and mirrored room, "does Tim know? It is Tim's, isn't it?" Jesslyn crossed her arms, the French cuffs bending where they caught in the folds of her elbows.

"Well, yes," T.J. answered behind the door. "I'm not a slut for God's sake."

"I didn't think you were. I just haven't really talked to you in a couple of weeks, since everything happened. I didn't know if you'd ever gotten with Garrison before you and Tim sorta hooked up." Jesslyn crossed her ankles, saw the toe of her boot was scuffed.

"Garrison? Now you call him Garrison? What happened to Chief Tight Ass?" T.J.'s voice echoed back.

"We sorta became friends, I guess. And you're ignoring the question. Have you told Tim?"

The stall door opened and T.J. walked to the counter, where she gently laid the little white and purple stick, face up, then washed her hands. Her sharp eyes cut to look at Jesslyn, "No."

Oh, this was just lovely. Though Jesslyn was glad she'd been the first to know. She scratched her neck. "Tim's going to be pissed you didn't tell him."

"Well, first off, there might not be anything to tell and second, I don't know what he'll think. How he'll react." The rip of the paper towel filled the air before T.J. dried her hands off.

Jesslyn saw the pain and wariness in her friend's eyes. "Do you love him?"

T.J.'s pixie face twisted, and moisture glistened in her eyes as she nodded. "Yeah, but we've never talked about the future or families or anything like that. And it's not like I've told him I love him."

Several moments passed in silence.

"So what are you going to do if you are pregnant?" Jesslyn sidled over to the counter as T.J. moved away to sit on the little couch. T.J. leaned her head back, the short black locks a curled cap around her crown. She looked like a lost little elf. Jesslyn heard her sigh and glanced down at the test.

"I guess I'll have to ask him to marry me. My family will just love that. They already hate I'm a cop, the fact I may be pregnant out of wedlock and could marry a bartender will send them right over the edge." T.J. started laughing.

Jesslyn patiently waited. Finally, the dark head lifted and pale blue eyes questioned.

"You ready?" she asked her friend.

One deep breath and a nod later, T.J. said, "Yeah, as ready as I'll ever be."

Jesslyn looked at the oval window, saw two pink lines, though one was almost nonexistent, but it was faintly there all the same. Looking back at T.J., she grinned.

"Well, Tinks, fairy dust is powerful stuff. You better get down on your knee."

T.J. paled, then smiled gently, smiled more until the grin lit her entire face.

"I'm pregnant! I'm going to have a baby!" In seconds she was off the couch, grabbed Jesslyn in a tight hug. "Oh, my God." T.J. leaned back.

Jesslyn pushed a wayward dark curl off her friend's small forehead. "I'm so happy for you." And she was, though a small prick of pain echoed in her heart. She ignored it and hugged her friend again. "Congratulations!"

T.J. pulled away, wiping under her eyes. "I've got to go find Tim."

Before T.J. flew out the door, Jesslyn caught her.

"Do you want your little wand of proof?" She pointed to the counter.

"Oh, yeah." T.J. picked it up, wrapped it in a white paper towel and dropped it in her tiny purse. She grabbed Jesslyn's hand and squeezed. "Thanks, Jess."

And with that she swirled out the door. Jesslyn shook her head, waited a few minutes and then followed.

* * * *

He saw her walk out the bathroom door smiling. He sat on the bench, and just as she turned towards him, he hung his head. The champagne flute carelessly clasped in his hands, dangling between his knees.

The bodyguard was busy inside with the rest of the Kinncaids, talking to Aiden. Who knew how much time they had?

"What is this?" her voice carried over him, through him. Stirred the beast. "The trouble bench?" Jesslyn heaved a sigh and walked over to him before plopping down beside him on the leather covered seat.

"You know it can't be that bad," she quipped and pushed his shoulder.

His head came up. Could she see what was to come in his eyes?

"Hey, are you okay? What's wrong?" she asked, concern written on her features. Worry in her dark eyes.

Eyes. Her eyes. They'd haunted him, plagued him for the last week.

He shook his head, looked away from her, then back. "Nothing. No, everything."

His shoulders slumped. "I don't know who to talk to. I don't know what to do. Everything is falling apart." His head bumped as he leaned back against the wall. To himself, he smiled. This might just be easier than he thought.

Jesslyn looked towards the restaurant. And he could all but see how she was thinking that perhaps she should get back.

Too late for that, my dear.

It was always like that, as though they knew before what he had in store for them. No, he couldn't let her go back. No, he had to keep her here. Maybe she sensed the danger on some level.

Jesslyn looked back to him and a soft smile played on her mouth. "I guess I might as well make it two for two. When friends are in need . . ." He had no idea what she was talking about. He needed to get her out of here.

"Do you want to talk about it?" she tried tentatively.

He studied her, gave her what he hoped was a pitiful look and shrugged. "Might as well. Maybe you can help me, Jess." A sigh wafted from his lips. "But not here. Could we go outside or something?"

He saw the refusal swirl within the dark of her eyes. Her head shook back and forth. "Not outside. But maybe one of the conference rooms? There's a fireplace in one and like normal, I'm freezing. Come on. There's a cozy one just down the hall."

Hell. It needed to be outside. Away from everyone, away from it all. A conference room? That would be in some other part of the hotel. He'd planned to take her away from here, to finish it tonight. He started to refuse her while thinking about how to continue with his plan, but something stayed him. If the area was private it could work, and if it was all he could get, that's what he'd take — for now. Besides, he could always get her away later. After their private meeting. It would still work. Finally, he nodded, shrugged and got up.

Jesslyn did likewise and walked across the lobby towards the front desk.

"Ms. Black," the attendant said.

"Is the small conference room open?" she asked.

The blonde Barbie nodded. Damn it. He wanted no one to see them.

"Great, we're gonna pop in there for a few minutes. If Mr. Kinncaid comes looking for me, tell him I'll be right back." She grinned and led him down a dimly lit hallway. The sound of the party fading a bit as they went around a corner and then another.

A roar from the beast within him. Ahhh . . . Soon . . . All would be as it should be soon. Her smell drifted behind her. It brought back pleasant memories.

No, those didn't matter. He had to do this. Had to. No choice.

The thick carpet runners absorbed the sound of their footsteps. Finally, the hallway ended.

It would be finished. He smiled and started humming his favorite symphony. The notes whirled within his mind. A balm, an enticement.

Jesslyn stopped dead in her tracks. Slowly she turned. Her head was shaking back and forth. Her lips formed the words, "No, no." But no sound came out.

He saw the recognition in her eyes. The moment she must have remembered completely the power he had, the great things he was capable of. Slowly, he nodded.

The monster smiled.

* * * *

Aiden made his way around the room. Where the hell was she? The back of his neck tingled. He was being paranoid. They were in public, surrounded by plenty of people, in his hotel for God's sake.

He checked his watch again. She'd been gone for almost twenty minutes.

John came up to him. "Bathrooms are clear and so is the lobby. Doorman didn't see her leave. The receptionist is busy on the phone."

"What are you so anxious about?" Gavin asked, coming to stand by him.

"Have you seen Jesslyn?" Again he scanned the room. The girls were still at their table, though now Bray and Quin sat with them, as did his mother. Jock was talking to some men. T.J. was nowhere in sight and neither was Jesslyn. Where had the chief gone? And the agents? They hadn't even said hello. Something was up, he could feel it.

"No, I haven't. Relax, Aiden, everything is fine," Gavin slapped him on the back, and he ignored it.

"Something's wrong."

His brother's sigh filled the air. "You're overreacting. Calm down."

John said, "I don't believe in coincidences."

Neither did Aiden. "Where did you see her last?"

John scanned the room and walked towards the doors. "Going into the restroom with her friend."

T.J. walked through the door, looked around and headed for them. Aiden met her halfway. "Where's Jesslyn?" he barked without preamble.

T.J. looked distracted, and shook her head. "I don't know. I left her a few minutes ago in the bathroom. Have you seen Tim?"

Aiden shook his head and latched on to T.J.'s arm. He could hear Gavin mutter something about manners. He didn't care.

"Will you please slow down? God, how does Jesslyn put up with you?" She yanked her arm from his grasp. "What is your problem?"

Aiden stopped in the lobby and looked into her eyes.

"Stephens!" They both turned. Chief Garrison hurried towards them, behind him were Litton and Jones.

"What? What's happened?" T.J. asked her boss.

"They didn't match," Garrison said, coming to stop a few feet away.

What didn't match? Aiden wondered what the hell they were talking about.

"The samples? You're sure?" T.J. asked, clearly alarmed.

Jones spoke up, looked at Aiden, then back at T.J. "Yeah, Denver just called. Forensics are back. The samples from the Jeep and Maddy are identical. Kirk isn't our guy."

"What?" Aiden asked.

"Damn it," John muttered.

"Hair samples," Garrison answered. "They don't match. We arrested the wrong man."

The tingle on the back of his neck started to burn. The last time he'd felt it . . .

"Where the hell is Jesslyn?"

Chapter Twenty-seven

"David?" Jesslyn shook her head. No. It had to be a mistake. It had to. Slowly she took a step back. His dark eyes were no longer familiar. Images and memories jagged and blackened before, solidified into the entire remembrance of one horrific night.

He stood frozen, looking at her in that odd detached way, a chilling smile on his lips.

"But, but . . . You're my friend. What about Sally? The kids?" This had to be a horrible dream. The man was married with a family.

His dark eyes cast down and he raked a hand through his blonde hair. "Sally is just like all the rest." His low, calm voice all but sighed. He was so *normal*, as though they were discussing nothing more than the rainfall. "She went snooping." He tsked. "Shouldn't snoop. She and the kids are in the basement."

Terror clouded her mind, her thoughts, petrified her, until he looked at her again. His sheepish grin was one she'd come to know and trust.

She took another step backwards. If she could just get inside the conference room, maybe she could get away. The door was a few feet behind her. There was no way she could get around him.

Keep him talking.

"Why, David? Why? This isn't right. You know this isn't right," she tried.

His head swiftly came up, and the predatory gleam in his eyes made her breath catch.

Stupid! So damn stupid. She was alone with him and no one knew where she was. *See what ya get for ditching your bodyguard?*

Her gaze quickly glanced down the hallway, then down the hallways both right and left. No one. No help there.

"Because it was my destiny. My father taught me that. God told both of us that it was my path. Then when I questioned it, I also found the answer in the heavens, in the stars. Yes, this is my mission." His face was that of a stranger, twisted in some emotion she had no name for. "They were whores, all of them. Every last one of them. There's no need to feel bad for them. Every one of them got what they deserved."

282

My God, how many were there?

He stared at her with flat, shark eyes. "Jezebels. He told me that. Father taught me that." David's thin shoulders lifted in a negligent shrug. But his voice was razor sharp. "They betrayed, turned the heads of married men. They tempted righteous men from their vows! Marriage is holy. Sacred!" His voice sounded as if repeating a long remembered rule. "To be revered and respected." His lip curled back from his teeth. "And they only defiled it. God wanted them punished, and the heavens agreed."

"God?" God told him to kill women? The man was demented, and she was here, alone with him. *Think! Think! Keep him talking, about anything.*

"But you go to church, David, here in town. God doesn't tell us to kill each other. Or do you just ignore the services? Aren't you into astrology?" Keep him talking. Just keep talking. Another small step back. Her heel brushed up against the door. She leaned back, even as he raged at her.

"I've tried to find a balance between everything. God made the heavens." His voice was so calm, a teacher explaining an answer to a student. "If the stars give the signs, so does God."

There was something she never heard before. She didn't know what to say, decided to simply remain silent.

"They were all just like her. *Her!*" he suddenly yelled. Spittle flew from his mouth. His fists bunched at his sides

So far, David hadn't moved. He just stood there, waving his hands, calmly explaining one minute and losing his temper the next. It was like a switch going on and off. It was terrifying.

Aiden! Jesslyn licked her lips. The elongated handle bit into her back. "Who? Who do they become?"

A demonic laugh erupted from his chest. "Her! She ruined our family. The harlot broke our family. She tried to steal my father away from us, away from his calling. She dared to fracture what God put together. He couldn't allow that, could he?" His voice softened at the end. A confused little boy asking for help, trapped in the mind of a lunatic.

He was stark raving mad. Jesslyn slowly moved her shoulder in a shrug. What the hell did she say?

David shook his head, the dim lights reflected off his tawny locks. "No, of course he couldn't. I don't think he meant to kill her. She came by our house that night. When we got home we heard them yelling and fighting. Mother was very upset. Very upset." His soft voice reasoned, then rose. His hands came up, clenched the empty air.

"But that woman, that *whore* didn't listen." Menace dripped from his tongue as it leapt from his eyes.

Jesslyn moved a hand behind her, grasped the handle.

David's chest rose and fell as he sighed, a wry smirk on his lips. "He had to kill her, he simply had no choice. That's what he told Mother and me. God told him to kill her to save our family. I saw Father carry her out into the night. Her harlot's hair trailing like a condemning banner behind her."

Oh my God. Jesslyn's hand shook as she tightened her hold on the cool metal.

"But still it wasn't enough. I came home from school one day and found my mother dead in the bathtub, her wrists dripping blood. That slut stole my mother from me!" he shouted.

Then he shrugged. "I decided then and there I would rid the world of all of them. Those single women, trying their wiles on married men, tempting them from family and home. I prayed about it for years. My father hated her too for ruining everything." He sighed. "God wanted me to do this, to begin this mission. I redeem them. I gave them the cross."

What the hell was he talking about? She wasn't about to ask.

David reached behind him. Silver flashed in the light. Jesslyn's eyes locked to the knife. She knew what it felt like, pressed against soft flesh. The cold. The sting.

He took a step towards her. She jerked on the handle, could have cried when the door opened as she stumbled into the room. She shoved against the door to close it even as David rammed into the other side, shoving her back a step.

"Please, please, please." Her hands shook as she tried to get the door closed. His weight pushed the door open further. Jesslyn's eyes frantically searched the dimly lit room. Something. Something. The long conference table only held a glass bowl on its gleaming center. Chairs flanked a roaring fireplace. The fireplace!

"Jesslyn," his calm voice said, "don't do this. You'll only make me angry. I'll make it quick, I promise."

"Fuck you." Jesslyn jumped away from the door and sprinted across the room to the fireplace. She grabbed the poker and whirled.

David slowly got up off the floor. He kicked the door shut, reached up and flicked the lock.

Please, please, help me, she prayed. David smiled and started towards her.

Her hands shook on the iron weapon. It was heavy. She'd only get one chance. One chance.

* * * *

"Mr. Kinncaid, sir." The blonde desk clerk waved at him.

Aiden ignored her, turned his gaze back to T.J. "When did you see Jesslyn?"

He had to find her.

"In the bathroom, it was only about five or ten minutes ago or so." Her eyes looked around the room and he saw relief trickle through the pale depths. He quickly looked over his shoulder. Tim walked towards them.

"What's going on?" Tim asked

"We're looking for Jesslyn," Aiden told his friend.

Chief Garrison held up his hand. "I'm sure she's around somewhere. Let's not panic."

"Search the hotel," Litton advised.

Aiden nodded. "I'll have her paged."

He hurried to the front desk. "Page Ms. Jesslyn Black for me. Now." His palm slapped on the cool marble top.

"But Mr. Kinncaid . . ." she started.

"Now," he repeated.

Her small jaw firmed. "She went to a conference room. She said to tell you she'd be back in a few minutes. Another gentleman was with her. That was about—"

Aiden didn't wait for her to finish. "Which way did they go?"

"That way," she said, pointing.

His stride lengthened until he was running down the hallway to the smaller conference rooms on the east side of the hotel. He rounded the corner and shoved open a door.

The room was empty.

"Kinncaid, wait," John said.

Wait hell. Aiden pointed down both hallways. "Check the rooms."

He hurried to the next room. Hurry. He had to hurry. He'd promised to keep her safe. His hands shook.

He heard footfalls down the hall behind him.

The door stood closed. Aiden grabbed the handle. Locked.

He slapped his pockets. Where the hell was his key?

"Jesslyn!" He beat on the door. "Jesslyn!"

* * * *

David's head whirled at the shout, at the pounding, shaking the door.

Jesslyn took her chance at his distraction. One step. She planted her feet and swung the poker with all her might.

His arm shot up, blocked her blow from crashing into his head. He grabbed the poker and tried to wrestle it from her. "You bitch. I should have killed you when I had the chance."

Anger flamed through her, for herself, for all the innocent victims he'd claimed. For Maddy. For Tammy.

"Better a bitch than a soulless monster who believes he's doing God's will," she furiously said between her teeth. "You're pathetic. And evil." She spat in his face.

David roared, let go of the poker and struck her across the face. Pain sang up her knees as she hit the floor.

"It is my righteous duty to protect!" David screamed. He ripped the poker from her hands, the end tearing across her palm. David flung it aside. The poker landed by the door.

"Jesslyn!" She heard Aiden yell before something pinged against the metal doorknob.

Jesslyn tried to crawl back towards the door. Towards the poker. David whirled. The knife hung in his hand.

She kicked at his knee and he screamed.

"Jesslyn!" Aiden yelled. Something kicked the door, and she tried to get to her feet. David grabbed her hair, shoving her down, even as she tried to fight him off, to twist away. She fell back. His strong thighs locked against her torso as he straddled her. He gasped as she brought her knees up hard against his back, his hold only tightened.

"It's too bad you couldn't mind your own business, but you're like the rest, aren't you?" This man she didn't know—had never known. His eyes burned with a black and unholy fire. His chest heaved up and down.

Jesslyn fisted her hands and rammed them up against his sternum. David grunted.

More splinters from the door. With one hand he tried to hold her still.

"It's time to meet the rest in hell." He raised the knife above his head, even as she tried to twist to the side.

"Aiden!" she screamed.

A whoosh through the air followed by a string of pinging gunshots jerked her.

Blood poured over her. The coppery smell filled her nose, the metallic flavor coated the back of her throat.

David's flat eyes went blank. The knife fell from his hands as his arms dropped to the side.

Jesslyn couldn't move. A trickle of blood ran down from the hole in the center of his forehead, two in his chest, the poker a grotesque stake through the center of him.

Her breath broken and jagged panted out. David started to fall forwards.

Hands gripped her under her arms and jerked her up and back from the grisly scene.

Aiden clasped Jessie to him. Sweet Mother of God. Tremors shook them both as he buried her head against his shoulder.

"It's okay. You're okay. You're okay." Her chest rose and fell, quick and hurried, matching his. He could feel their hearts racing.

Jessie pulled back. She was covered in blood. Streaks of red marred her pale face and her white shirt was crimson. God had he been too late? His hands hurried over her, ripped her shirt apart to see her flat smooth belly, her chest untouched by the knife. It was a good thing they were sitting on the floor, or his knees would have given out. Her faint one-sided grin took him by surprise. "I'm glad you made it."

From somewhere deep inside him, laughter rumbled out. He framed her long heart-shaped face that had become so dear to him. When he'd fallen through the door and seen David Hewett poised above her, he hadn't even thought, just picked up the poker and lanced it through the air. Aiden didn't realize John had shot the bastard until he started to get up and saw the man lower his gun.

"I swear I am never, never, *never* letting you out of my sight, woman." He leaned forward and kissed her with all the emotions raging within him, and felt them answered in the return of love between their lips and tongues.

The kiss broke. "That's fine with me," she whispered against his mouth.

Garrison laid a hand on his shoulder, jerked his head towards the door. "Get her out of here. We'll be by later to get her statement."

Aiden nodded and helped Jesslyn to her feet. He leaned down and swept her up in his arms.

"I am perfectly capable of walking, you know." Her arms twined around his neck and her fingers raked the ends of his hair.

"I know, but you're not." Without a backward glance, Aiden carried her through the door and out into the hallway. There he took the private exit and let the fresh air soothe them both.

* * * *

The shower felt good. It washed away the blood, the fears, and the horror. Jesslyn's arms wrapped around his neck, her muscular legs around his waist, as he drove into her.

So hot, so right. Her back arched against the tiles. He leaned forwards and kissed the smooth column of her neck, arched her more and pulled her breast into his mouth, her moan driving him on.

She was his, and she was alive. The need to confirm their love, their breath, their beating hearts raged through him.

Her moan bounced off the walls. He loved the sounds she made in the back of her throat when they made love.

Jesslyn speared her fingers through his hair, jerking his head to hers and kissed him with all the happiness, joy and love she could.

Her teeth bit at his lips, pressed against his. She raked her nails across his shoulders and smiled when he squeezed her hips even tighter.

He was driving her wild. Water sluiced over them, carried the terror of the past few weeks away down the drain. Her tongue countered his, danced to the age-old tune of love. Her body tightened, coiled.

Aiden pumped into her, deeper and deeper still. "Jessie . . ."

She shattered. He pulsed within her.

He felt like his self had just been ripped from him, given to another.

Somehow, without too much trouble, he got them out of the shower and into the bed.

The sheets were cool and dampened where their wet bodies melded. She was beautiful. Her small, toned and pale body glistened with moisture. She tasted sweet as nectar. Never before had he met a woman he needed as he did this one, like water to a thirsting man.

Aiden rose over her, claimed her mouth in a possessive kiss, even as he slowly claimed her body. First with his fingers, roaming, caressing, branding where he chose and she let him. Then he conquered her slowly with his mouth, bit by bit, inch by inch until she sobbed his name. The hunger and need in him roared through his veins, fought for urgency. But he held back.

Aiden stripped away every layer she had until all that was left was raw nerves. Their kisses and caresses were hurried, demanding, driven out of the need to reassure, to confirm. He was moving so torturously slow, and the contrast between their wants and Aiden's control was too much. Their hands clasped, fingers entwined and held fast.

He looked at her, his features hard, his eyes dark. "You're mine."

Slowly, he slid into her and she watched as his eyes slid closed and a muscle bunched in his jaw.

Aiden loved her slow and deep, his strokes measured and controlled until she couldn't stand it anymore. Treasured and cherished. Sobbing, Jesslyn spiraled towards the stars, towards the sun, towards life. Aiden thrust deep and she cried out, flying . . .

Aiden threw his head back, groaned his release as he gave his soul to her.

"I love you," he whispered in her ear.
"I love you, too."
Their hearts beat as one, melded, bonded, promised.

Epilogue

Aiden rubbed his hand over his wife's distended stomach. At eight and a half months pregnant, Jessie tired easily. Tomorrow they were scheduled for her cesarean section to meet their twins.

He smiled into the darkness and wrapped his arms around her. Things were perfect. It had taken them a long time to get here, but they were perfect.

After the nightmare in Colorado, he'd proposed to Jesslyn, only to have her reject him and leave for Texas, where she wouldn't talk with him for almost six weeks.

Longest damn six weeks of his life.

Then one day she called, in tears.

Idiot woman had needed to settle her past. He understood that. What he still didn't understand was why she'd never mentioned her chance of not having children before. She thought that would change his mind about their relationship.

It hadn't. God, he'd been so enraged at her shouldering all her worries alone. Again. He had of course called the airport and had been in Austin that night at her hotel learning everything. How she had been scared she couldn't have kids because she'd been pregnant in the accident and there had been scarring to her uterus. How she'd wanted to know for certain before she accepted his proposal.

He'd wanted to strangle her. Instead he'd listened to how she'd learned instead at her doctor's visit that she was pregnant with twins and extremely high-risk.

The months had worn on her. But she'd finally stopped worrying. Bed rest and no excitement.

No sex on their wedding night. No traveling and the list went on.

But he didn't care. He had the woman he loved safe in his arms and she was happy and finally at peace.

"I love you," she said, turning.

"I love you, too." He kissed her softly. "Go to sleep, tomorrow will be a big a day."

She laughed. "I know, but I'm not tired. I can't wait to hold our boys, Aiden."

He grinned down into her eyes and knew again how lucky he really was.

Read on for more of the Kinncaid family
in an excerpt from *Deadly Ties*!

Some bonds are love, and some bonds are deadly — Taylor Reese
is done with men, except for her son, Ryan, and Dr. Gavin Kinncaid
realizes Ms. Reese is the only woman he's ever wanted to strangle,
but fate and passion soon twist their feelings into something other
than antagonism, first into passion and then into a committed love
while someone plots to rip this new happy family apart.

from **Deadly Ties**

"What the hell happened?" Aiden asked.

"That woman ran off the road," Gavin said, pointing to his car, where he saw Taylor sat half in, half out of the open passenger door talking to one of the uniformed officers.

"That woman?" Aiden drawled, a grin hinting.

"Yeah, and the idiot then decided to wave down a car in the middle of the damn road." The more he thought about it, the madder he was getting again. At her.

"And may I ask what that woman's name is?" Aiden crossed his arms over his chest.

"Taylor. Taylor Reese. Contrary, incompetent, and annoying."

Gavin stood staring as the medic turned Ryan's arm one way, then lifted it higher, holding the shoulder. Another EMT moved the officer away and checked Taylor. He was turning Taylor's face one way, then the other.

"Interesting," Aiden drawled again.

Gavin ignored him and walked to the car.

"I don't know what happened. We were going about fifty, probably closer to forty-five because I'd just slowed down to a crawl to look at the map. Anyway, we took the curve and the next thing I knew, I couldn't control the car and it was just flying off the road," Taylor said.

He saw then the shadow darkening the left side of her face. Had she hit the steering wheel? The window? Why the hell hadn't he noticed it before?

"I thought you said you were fine," he barked, all but shoving the medic out of the way.

One eyebrow cocked.

He reached out, but she pulled back, her brown eyes dark in the low light, the freckles on her face standing out.

Taylor leaned away from his hand, awareness tingling through her at his nearness.

"I am fine," she told him, tired.

"You look it, too." His sarcasm was not lost on her.

She glanced at his left hand, and saw there was no ring.

"You're not married, are you?" she asked. "No wife could put up with your do-as-I-say attitude."

His eyes left the side of her face and zeroed in on hers. "What a subtle come-on."

Taylor snorted. "That wasn't a come-on. You are the most arrogant man I have ever had the misfortune to meet."

He tsked. "You've already told me that." He held up a finger. "Watch my finger."

"Is it going somewhere?" She huffed out a breath. The man was impossible. "The medic has already done that, thank you very much. I don't have a concussion or anything else, so just stop being all . . . all . . ."

"My finger."

She rolled her eyes and took a deep breath. This close to him, his scent, some expensive outdoor cologne and rain, wafted between them.

Deciding it took more energy to fight the man than give in on this, she watched as his long, blunt-tipped finger went one way then the other.

"Anything else, Doc?" she asked.

"Yeah, how did you get this?" His brows furrowed as his fingers grazed her cheek. She pulled away, startled at the shock his touch sent through her.

Taylor stared at him, saw the way the soft rain glistened on his dark hair in the lights of the other cars. His square jaw was shadowed with stubble, sprinkled with moisture. For some absurd reason she actually wanted to reach out and touch his cheek.

Which was stupid and just went to show that she must have hit her head, or Mr. Gibbons had scrambled her brains.

"What happened?" he asked quietly, his voice low and deep like beckoning thunder.

"N-nothing."

One brow cocked. "It looks like nothing."

His finger touched it, pressed.

"Ouch."

"What happened? Looks like someone punched you."

"Someone did," Ryan said, standing beside Gavin.

Both black brows rose, then immediately beetled on a frown.

"Who?" Gavin asked her.

Taylor rolled her eyes and glared at her son. "It's nothing."

"Who hit your mom?" Gavin asked, partially turning to Ryan.

"A man."

"What man?"

She was seriously going to have to talk to her son about loyalty. He liked new words, she'd have to teach him that one.

"Mr. Gibbons," she all but sighed out. "It was Mr. Gibbons."

Gavin turned back to her, his head cocked. "The father of the girl who died?"

"Yep," Ryan said. "Knocked her right out of the chair."

Gavin's eyes narrowed, the blue hardened, iced. "Out of your chair?" he asked quietly.

Taylor looked to her son. "How do you know that?"

"I heard you talking on the phone to Mrs. Jenkins before we left. You said, 'Well, yeah, when the man knocks you out of the chair, it tends to hurt.'" Her son's small shoulders shrugged.

"Look up eavesdropping when we find a dictionary," she said.

The two males, one who must be in his thirties and the other eight, were not related, but the angry expressions, fierce eyes and tense jaws were identical. She couldn't help it, she laughed.

"I'm fine, you two. Quit frowning." To her son, she said, "You know it sometimes happens with what I do."

His set expression didn't change. "That doesn't mean I can't get mad about it."

True.

"What were you doing with the man?" Gavin asked.

She sighed. "Is it really that important?"

"Humor me," he muttered, while his fingers pressed around her eye, felt her cheekbone.

Trying not to wince, let alone shove his hand away, she said, "It was a legal meeting. Social Services, lawyers. The cop was outside the door." She shrugged. "Man just moved really quick."

Gavin grunted.

What did that mean? Her stomach tensed when his fingertip grazed her hairline near her ear.

"Did you have this checked out? X-rayed?"

The man was a doctor. And a bossy one at that, even if he did smell good.

Taylor made to stand, but he didn't move.

"Did you?" he asked again.

She glared at him. "I. Am. Fine. It's only a bruise. They go away."

He pulled back a fraction and simply stared at her with such an intense expression, she shifted.

"What?" she asked.

"They go away?" He stood, shoved a hand through his damp hair.

What was with this guy? One minute he was snapping at her and the next he seemed upset because she had a bruise.

About the Author

Jaycee never really grew up—she still enjoys playing with imaginary people on a daily basis. Sometimes those people are nice, sometimes they're not, but in the end the girl gets the guy, so all is well. Jaycee earned her degree in Elementary Education from Eastern New Mexico University. She lives in Texas with her family, who puts up with her when her characters demand more of her time and appreciates her weirdness—or so they claim. There are also the cats and the corgis, who, in truth, rule the family. When she's not chained to her keyboard, she's doubling as a parent, a teacher, a maid, a chef, a chauffeur, a therapist, and promoting her education in human development while finishing her masters in plant elimination.

You can learn more about Jaycee by visiting her website at www.jayceeclark.com or emailing her at jaycee@jayceeclark.com. Her newsletter and blog subscriptions can be found on her website, along with links to follow her on Twitter, Facebook, and various other sites.

Printed in Great Britain
by Amazon.co.uk, Ltd.,
Marston Gate.